little men

little men

novellas and stories

GERALD SHAPIRO

Library of Congress Cataloging-in-Publication Data

Shapiro, Gerald, 1950–
Little Men : novellas and stories / Gerald Shapiro
p. cm.
ISBN 0-8142-0960-2 (cloth : alk. paper) — ISBN 0-8142-9039-6 (cd-rom)
1. United States — social life and customs — fiction. I. Title.
PS3569.H34115 L58 2004
813'.54—dc22

Paper (ISBN: 978-0-8142-5752-4)

2003025231

Cover design by Dan O'Dair.
Type set in Adobe Granjon.

To Judith Slater and Michael Pearce

contents

acknowledgments

I'd like to thank the English Department of the University of Nebraska-Lincoln for giving me a sabbatical leave during which I finished most of this book. A number of friends offered me encouragement as I wrote *Little Men:* Hal Dresner, Erin Flanagan, Tim Schaffert, Grace Bauer, Joel Deutsch, and, above all, Judith Slater, who patiently read this book through its many drafts and gave me the benefit of her wise counsel and her love.

I want to thank Steve Woodall and Dominic Riley for teaching me what I needed to know about the restoration of old books. Neil Shapiro told me war stories of the advertising business, and Dan Mountain reminisced with me about the Chateau Marmont as it was in the 1980s. Peter Riegert taught me everything I'd never imagined about the heart and soul of Leo Spivak. Thanks very much to all of them.

Jonathan Freeman and Laurence Goldstein of *The Michigan Quarterly Review* published an excerpt of "A Box of Ashes" in their special issue devoted to "Jewish in America," published in fall 2002. Stories from *Little Men* appeared in the following journals: "Bernard, the Mummy" in *The Gettysburg Review*, vol. 13, no. 3, and reprinted with the acknowledgment of the editors; "The Naming of Parts" in *Witness,* vol. 13, no. 2 (1999); and "Teeth" in *The Beloit Fiction Journal* (2003). Thanks to Peter Stitt, Peter Stine, and Clint McCown, editors of those fine journals, for their support of my work.

This book was first published in French under the title *Un schmok à*

Babylone. My heartfelt thanks to my agent in Paris, Michelle Lapautre; my translator, Michel Lederer; and most of all my editor, Francis Geffard, and his staff at Albin Michel in Paris for seeing the potential in this book when no American publisher would touch it. In the United States, thanks to Maria Massie and the rest of the folks at Witherspoon and Associates for all their efforts on my behalf, and to Erin McGraw and everyone at The Ohio State University Press for bringing the book to life in English—a language I've been told I speak like a native.

a box of ashes

Making love to his ex-wife Pauline on Friday nights was probably the most sophisticated thing Ira Mittelman had ever done in his life. It made him feel like he'd taken up permanent residence in an insouciant, world-weary French sex comedy. *"Oh, yes, but of course I'd love to get together, only I'm busy tonight. I'm meeting my ex-wife for dinner—we have a standing date. We're still screwing, you know—once a week. Don't tell our lawyers! The 'marriage' may be over, but that's just a bunch of legal nonsense. Two healthy, middle-aged consenting adults—eh?"* To tell the truth, the sex itself wasn't earth-shaking, but it wasn't any worse than it had been during the five years of their courtship or the ten years of their marriage, and given the fact that he and Pauline were nearly fifty now and had been having sex more or less forever, it wasn't at all bad. Anyway, the sex was secondary. It was the kissing—warm, breathy, tender kisses before, during, and after—that mattered to him, he'd come to realize with some surprise, more than the familiar routine of foreplay and penetration, more than the moaning, the coming, the soft, sleepy bliss of afterglow. In truth, Ira had found that it wasn't all that hard to get laid in San Francisco—even Manhattanized, its features smeared over by a thick, noxious mask of Silicon Valley money-culture, the city was still incurably romantic, one big Lovers' Lane—but getting kissed by somebody who knew how to do it . . . well, that was something else again.

For the past two years Ira and Pauline had gotten together for dinner almost every Friday evening around six-thirty, at Cacciatore di Spello, a trattoria at the fringe of North Beach. Every week they sat at an out-of-the-way table near the kitchen and had a couple of drinks, then ordered ravioli, veal, a salad, and a bottle of Chianti. After dinner, they saw a film if there was something good at one of their favorite theaters, or took in a play, a concert at Symphony Hall or the Opera House if one of them had happened onto some tickets. Afterward, even if it was midnight, they went to her small apartment in Presidio Heights, shared a snifter of cognac, and made love. One week they turned the lights off (her preference), the next week they left them on (his).

When he and Pauline kissed at the end of a Friday evening, cupped in the soft embrace of her sofa and warmed by cognac, Ira felt a flushed, poignant tightness in his chest, a wave of emotion stronger than anything else he felt all week. She felt something, too, he assumed, though they hadn't spoken about it, perhaps afraid that if they put any of this into words, it would evaporate into thin air, just as their marriage had.

Every Friday evening Pauline arrived at Cacciatore di Spello full of office gossip, her eyes brimming with benign mischief. She wrote advertising copy at Reinhold and Rosen, a small direct-mail agency in the Financial District, and there was always something amusing going on at the office. Soandso, she reported, formerly on Lithium, was now on Paxil. This one was sleeping with that one; those two, very cuddly last week, were this week on the outs. She always included an update on her boss, a crazy little guy in his fifties named Kenny, who was going through a protracted case of confused sexual identity—flamboyantly gay one month, sashaying back and forth through the office in a flaming kimono, one hand on his hip, the other flapping the air, and the next month straight again, chewing a cigar and screaming "Give me a woman with bullet tits! I want bullet tits!" at the top of his lungs. Then there was the business itself: rumors were constantly circulating—accounts were about to be lost, firings were imminent, other accounts might be coming their way. Pauline reported all of this merrily, imitating various office personalities, doing the voices, hamming it up while she and Ira stirred their cocktails.

Then it was his turn. But what was there to say? He worked alone in the quiet privacy of his apartment in Noe Valley, rarely seeing anyone except the occasional client, a museum curator, now and then a book collector or dealer stopping by to chat or get an estimate. Once a week he took his laundry to a Chinese place in the neighborhood, and if he was lucky, the proprietor, Mr. Wu, said something memorably witty, which Ira could then pass on during dinner on Friday night. Now and then there was something amusing on the bulletin board in the market on 24th Street where he bought his groceries, and here again he noted it (sometimes even jotting down a reminder to himself) and let loose with the tidbit once Pauline had finished with her rendition of that week's shenanigans at Reinhold and Rosen. His car, an aging Volvo, had been stolen right in front of his apartment building three times in the past sixteen months (all it took, apparently, was a screwdriver and a sixth-grade education to hot-wire the thing), and these episodes had provided Ira with some nice comic material; he'd done decent impersonations of the police officers assigned to his case, and had described the various indignities his poor car had been put through with each succeeding theft—the vomit, the stench of marijuana, the melted candy bars, the used condoms, and so on.

But for the most part he was silent during these evenings with Pauline. The fact was, he'd never been a great conversationalist, even when he was young and hip and in the know; and now that he was graying and sensed his faculties beginning to slip (his hearing was fading in one ear, and he couldn't read a menu without moving the thing first into and then away from his face), he'd noticed that he'd begun to turn in on himself, like a fist. He had friends in town, but he didn't kid himself—they weren't close friends.

Though he wouldn't have wanted Pauline to know this, Ira prepared for his dates with her all week long. He considered the possibilities every morning, skimming the *Chronicle*'s arts section while he sipped his coffee, taking note of promising films, concerts, and plays. Sometimes he called Pauline on Friday afternoon to list their options and ask her preferences, but more often he surprised her, which seemed more to her liking. Then came Friday evening at Cacciatore di Spello, the romantic high point of his week. It was a life. It was *his* life.

Which explained why, even though Ira knew he should drop everything, do his duty and take his father's ashes back to Missouri where the old man had wanted to be scattered, and even though his sister Ruthie had been needling him in weekly phone calls from Seattle to get on a plane and fulfill his obligation to their dad, the ashes still sat in a brown plastic cannister the size of a kleenex box, perched next to an old tennis racket on a shelf in the hallway closet of Ira's apartment. "I can't leave town right now," he'd told Ruthie repeatedly. "I have this *thing* going with Pauline, I know it sounds crazy, but I can't leave, not even for a few days. You don't understand what's at stake here. I skip a Friday, it could all come unraveled."

"Oh, I understand what's at stake," Ruthie told him. "You're porking your ex-wife and you think that's more important than doing your duty to your father, your father who loved you so much it was like a sickness."

Ira's father had made his wishes known very clearly during the last few years of his life, while he was wasting away in the guest room at Ruthie's house, driving her family crazy. On the back of his will, he'd scrawled, "Scatter my ashes at HaHaTonka—Ira knows the way." He wrote the same message on post-it notes, more than a dozen of them, and left them stuck on every piece of furniture in his sickroom. Whenever Ira called his dad to say hello and check on his condition, it was the primary subject of their conversation. The old man was obsessed by this idea—being scattered to the winds at dear old Camp HaHaTonka, the Boy Scout camp in the Ozarks where Ira had spent five idyllic boyhood summers. "You'll do it for me, this one last favor, Ira," the old man croaked. "You'll do it for me because you were a Boy Scout, you were an Eagle Scout, you know your duty. You of all people should know how to do a good deed."

And yes, yes, if it weren't for the standing date with Pauline every Friday night, of course Ira would have been happy to do it, too—happy to do his father's bidding, and happier still to get the goddamn ashes out of his apartment. Having his father's ashes stuck up there on the closet shelf was no day at the beach. He couldn't get over the strangeness of it. He asked himself the same question morning after morning: how could they fit a person's remains into something so small and nondescript? Over the past ten months he'd grown accustomed to looking at the cannister for a few minutes as he went through his regular morning routine: get up, stumble through some stretching exercises, shower, brew a pot of coffee, pay a visit to Dad, then sigh and shut the closet door. Ira had become an expert at this particular sigh, a plaintive one which began somewhere up in his nose and ended deep in his belly. This was what he got for being such a bad son, he told himself. There was no use in denying it: he hadn't been sufficiently attentive to his father those last years, as the old man, moldering in Ruthie's guest room, slowly tilted forward into death—he hadn't called often enough, hadn't written, hadn't flown up to sit at the old man's bedside, feeding him chipped ice and sips of orange juice. Well, everything was different now: here he was, dutifully saying hello every morning. *Hi, Dad, good morning, nice to see you. Sorry you're still in that goddamn box.*

It shouldn't have been possible to squeeze eighty-five years of somebody's life into such a forgettable little cannister. Wasn't something a bit bigger, perhaps even grander called for? Ira wasn't asking for anything elaborate—an epitaph from Keats etched on a marble urn would have been too much, obviously. But *something.* He remembered the array of containers on display in the family bereavement room at the crematorium back in Kansas City—a wall full of marble, onyx, pewter and brass, everything dignified, understated, substantial. Surely something from that wall would have done the trick. *Anything.* But *this?* This brown cube of industrial plastic? How could it all come down to *this?*

He'd come to imagine his father not reduced to ashes, but whole—somehow miniaturized like the guy in "The Incredible Shrinking Man," and very irate about it—stuffed into the plastic cannister in the closet, wearing his brown *Shabbos* suit, beating on the lid with his tiny fists. "He wants out," he told Ruthie whenever she called to berate him. "I swear to god, I think I can hear him in there. He's pissed off."

"Why do you tell me this stuff? You want to go crazy, Ira, so go crazy—but I can't get involved."

"I'm just telling you what's going on."

"I'll tell you what's going on. You're *shtupping* your ex-wife, which for your information is a crime in about fourteen states, though of course not in California, no—the only thing against the law in California is jaywalking. Listen, Ira, I don't know what to tell you. You say Dad wants out of that box? So take him back to Missouri, dump the ashes at Camp Whatchamacallit, get back on the plane—you could do it in two days, shazam, you're done—you haven't missed a single chance to hop in the sack."

"Ruthie, that's unfair."

"I'm sorry, Ira. You know perfectly well what Dad wanted you to do.

You've known about it all along, you haven't lifted a finger, so don't come crying to me. I don't have time for it." It was true—Ruthie barely had time to breathe. Two nights a week she drove meals to AIDS patients in Seattle's iffiest neighborhoods; her Mondays and Fridays were given over to volunteer work at the Home for the Jewish Aged; she had a husband, children, even a recent grandchild—a life so full of good works, so laden with duty and obligation that when she called Ira to discuss their father's remains, her voice at times took on a desperate, strangled tone, like someone caught in a trash compactor.

"I paid for the whole shebang," she'd told him repeatedly, "the cremation, the memorial service—I bought the flowers, the buffet. I didn't ask you for a nickel. The least you can do is deal with the ashes. You're the son!"

"I know I'm the son," Ira told her.

"Why didn't he want to be buried, like Mom? They could have been buried side by side back in Kansas City. What's wrong with that? It would have been nice that way. Anyway, Jews aren't supposed to be cremated, are they? It's against the law."

"Dad wasn't much of a Jew, Ruthie. You know that. He ate bacon on Yom Kippur."

"He was your father, you were his son, that's a special bond—and don't bring up the Yom Kippur bacon, I don't want to hear about it. This is Biblical, Ira—there's something in the Bible about it, I can't remember where. It's in the Torah. The son says Kaddish for the father. That's your job."

"I can't say Kaddish. I can't remember the words. I don't even own a *tallis.*"

"So don't say Kaddish! Who's asking you to do anything? But tell me, what's the point of sticking the ashes in a closet and worshiping them? What kind of craziness is that? He wasn't that great a father, you know. He loved you 'til the day he died—but let's not pretend. We're not talking about *Father Knows Best* here. The man had many failings."

No one was disputing that point, Ira told himself—though this morning, a Friday in mid-June, waking up with a stiff neck, the issue of his dead father's many failings seemed utterly irrelevant. He stood at the closet, coffee cup in hand, sighed his sigh, and listened to the phone ringing in the living room. Reluctantly he shut the door. *See you tomorrow, Dad.*

On the phone was Henry Cruikshank, a regular customer, a dealer in rare books. "Listen up, Ira: I've got a live one," Cruikshank told him in a breathless voice. "First edition of *Paradise Regained*–1671, the Starkey edition, the one with *Samson Agonistes* added on. I'm talking big bucks here, Ira. I snagged it at an auction last week—the big players weren't paying attention, they were all off at another table, drooling over a first edition of *The Song of Hiawatha,* if you can believe that," he cackled, "and so I picked it up for pennies. And now I've hooked a buyer, some geeky kid down in Los Gatos—one of those dot-com gazillionaires. Unbelievable luck. The bottom hasn't dropped out yet for this kid—he's still raking it in. We can really make some money on this one—but we have to move fast. Next week he'll probably be worth nothing."

"Congratulations, Henry. I'm impressed."

"Ira, wait a second, I'm not finished. The problem is, when I had this kid on the phone, I-I sort of misrepresented the condition of the book. A little. I just exaggerated it a little bit. I couldn't help myself."

Ira tssked into the phone.

"Get past the binding, open it up, it's gorgeous! Milton himself probably held this book! Think about it! He would have been blind by now, you know, so he's running his fingers over the pages, feeling the print! Oh, man. Now listen: my buyer, he's scheduled to come up to the city to take a look next Friday. That gives us a week."

"A week? I've got a couple of jobs ahead of you, Henry. I don't know if I can get to it."

"Aw, don't tell me that," said Cruikshank. "The book just needs a little refurbishing, that's all. It's a—listen, Ira, do me a favor, at least take a look at this thing. As a favor to a friend."

"So what's the problem?"

A long groan whistled through the receiver like wind. "The binding's a mess. It looks like some know-nothing butcher tried to rework it, maybe mid-nineteenth century. The bands are ruined. There's glue all over the place. The boards are probably ruined, too. I'm telling you, whoever did this was a criminal."

"And how much did you pay for it?" asked Ira.

"Two thousand," Cruikshank croaked, and in a rush of breath, added, "You don't have to tell me—I paid too much. I know, I know, I know."

"You always pay too much."

"Don't, Ira."

"No, listen to me. That's why you're in the fix you're in. You see something, you fall in love with it, you forget you're in business—and bam, you're writing a check. You're hopeless."

"I know, I know, I know. It's my failing. I love books. That's my problem. I should have gone into antique furniture. Tables and chairs don't push any of my buttons. Books drive me crazy, it's like an addiction. But enough about my problems, doctor. Listen, can you take a look at this thing right away, tell me what it needs? I'm desperate, Ira. You know as well as I do, in 'fine' condition, this thing's worth eight thousand."

"Eight thousand?"

"Okay, seventy-five hundred. A new binding, some gold leaf, a little decorative tooling here and there—I love the craftsmanship you bring to your work. And that's the truth. I'm not just buttering you up." Cruikshank paused. "Look, okay, seven thousand, maybe. But still—that's enough to keep my head above water another couple of months. That's all I'm asking. And I'll split it with you, by the way. No kidding."

"You don't have to do that, Henry. I don't want that. Just my usual fee, plus materials."

"No, I mean it, Ira. We go fifty-fifty on this one. Listen: this buyer I've got on the line—he's a kid. He's got money coming out his navel. If he doesn't give it to us, he'll be spending it all on penny candy. He'll be down at the mall, playing video games, trying to sneak into R-rated movies. Look at it that way."

Ira cradled the receiver against his jowl and wound the phone cord around his wrist. "Okay, okay—I'm not making any promises. A week isn't much time. But I'll take a look. Bring it by around eleven this morning."

"You're a prince."

Ira hung up and poured himself another cup of coffee. He had two hours before Cruikshank would be there. His neck was throbbing: too many hours at the workbench yesterday, carefully re-pasting the red and black morocco spine labels on a fine three-volume first edition of Walter Scott's *Ivanhoe,* then cleaning the spines with a light wash of hydrogen peroxide to get them ready for a new layer of gold leaf. The volumes showed their age—some mold spots here and there, a bit of marginal dampstaining—but obviously these books had been loved for a hundred and eighty years, nestled securely in their slipcases, nurtured and caressed. This morning if he concentrated he could get the gold leaf applied to the bindings before Cruikshank knocked on the door.

But this was Friday, and every Friday morning Ira found himself lost in anticipation of the upcoming evening with Pauline. He could call her now—she'd be at her desk already—just to see what she had to say. She already knew the ongoing saga of his father's ashes, of course—he'd told her and told her—but even if this was the fifteenth time he brought it up, Pauline wouldn't yell. She wouldn't tell him he had to drop everything and go back to Camp HaHaTonka. She'd listen to him patiently, sigh with him, tantalize him with a brief preview of the latest dope on crazy Kenny and all the other mayhem at Reinhold and Rosen. Maybe he'd ask her for advice about what to do that night after dinner—but then again, maybe not. He had his eye on a month-long Buñel retrospective, in progress at the Vogue, the neighborhood cinema near Pauline's apartment; tonight they were showing *That Obscure Object of Desire,* which Ira imagined would provide a nice segue into the rest of the evening.

But calling Pauline would mean that he'd have nothing more to look forward to until that evening—so Ira reluctantly put off the phone call, and went back to his workshop. At least there was the three-volume edition of *Ivanhoe* to occupy the time. It had been rebound in the 1850s, a good piece of work, though the headbands had deteriorated and mold had crept into the second volume, penetrating deep into the pages and leaving behind a mottled pattern of foxing that obscured some lines of the text. Last night, after a day spent at the work table, he'd left the volumes to dry in the press; the paste he'd used to re-attach the Morocco spine labels needed a good twelve hours to cure as it penetrated the fibers of the old leather. Carefully now, he opened the press and lifted the first volume's cover, noting the way the red and black Moroccan leather over the spine joint wrinkled. Everything was in order. Now all that was left was the gilding of the top and bottom quadrants of the spines, and *Ivanhoe* would be finished: not just good as new, but *better*—solid and strong enough to last another hundred and eighty years, maybe longer.

The gold leaf itself, which he kept in a small box in a cabinet, was so delicate that it weighed almost nothing. Ira lifted out the box, opened it, and set it aside. In a small saucepan he mixed a *glaire*—a compound of egg white, vinegar and milk—then he plugged in an ancient, grime-encrusted hotplate and heated the mixture in a saucepan. Using a boar's hair brush, he painted the warm *glaire* in a thin layer onto the top quadrant of the first volume's spine. Then with tweezers he lifted one small tissue of gold leaf from the box. This was the tricky part; the gold leaf was so thin that a shaky hand, a momentary tremor in his wrist could tear it so badly he'd have to start over again with another piece. Slowly, carefully, he transferred the gold leaf onto the spine's newly *glaired* surface, where it lay slightly bunched in the center of the quadrant.

He leaned down over the book, held his breath, steadied himself, pursed his lips, and then popped them gently, a soft "ppp." A soft current of air fanned out over the tissue of gold leaf, smoothing it out perfectly over the surface of the *glaire.* Ira gazed at it a moment, saw that it was going to be fine, then he turned his head away and let out a slow breath. He repeated the delicate process with the spine's bottom quadrant, first painting on a thin sheen of *glaire,* then lifting a tiny sheet of gold leaf onto the surface, then popping his lips—"ppp"—to fan the golden tissue out smoothly. He used one of his burnishing tools to finish the job, first rubbing the tool against the smooth prow of his forehead to pick up a bit of oil, then embossing both sections of gold leaf firmly into the leather, taking special care with the corners, and then finally he was done. Then he turned his attention the second volume, and then the third—and as he entered what he thought of as his "work-zone," his concentration drifted, and though he wanted desperately to avoid the subject, soon he was thinking of nothing but Camp HaHaTonka, and the miserable brown cannister containing his father's ashes.

Each summer for five years, from eleven to fifteen, Ira had spent three weeks at Camp HaHaTonka, sweltering in the miasmic Ozark humidity, fending off clouds of tiny stinging insects while he made a succession of lanyards, wallets, and other handy craft items, and learned invaluable bits of Scout Lore, like "A chain is only as strong as its weakest link," and "Avoid persons who are coughing or sneezing." It had been nearly thirty-five years since he'd worn the olive-green uniform of the Boy Scout of America—thirty-five years since he'd seen Camp HaHaTonka—but what did any of that matter? He couldn't help himself—just the thought of the place, and the Scout Law came into his head: "A scout is trustworthy, loyal, helpful, friendly, courteous, kind, obedient, cheerful, thrifty, brave, clean, and reverent." The words were still etched on his brain in boldface. This is ridiculous, he told himself. He could remember virtually nothing of his childhood—so why did he remember this load of gibberish?

Probably because when he was eleven, he'd still believed in the incantatory power of mottos and oaths, secret handshakes, the kind of wisdom that could be collected in handbooks. Ira believed in God and Country back then—in Honor and Duty, too, though he didn't know what either word actually meant. All he knew was that saying them, or just thinking about them, brought a rim of tears to his eyes.

Eventually he'd climbed all the way to Eagle, the highest rank you could attain. When he mentioned this now to acquaintances in the book business, they looked at him as if he must be pulling their leg. At first glance, Ira knew, he didn't seem to be made of Eagle Scout material, and it was true that he lacked the hardiness, the ingenuity, the seriousness of purpose and firmness of character generally associated with Eagle Scouts. He'd read somewhere that only four per cent of boys who entered the Boy Scouts stuck it out all the way up the ladder to the rank of Eagle. And no wonder. Each rank carried with it an increasingly difficult series of tasks to be completed, merit badges to be earned, good deeds to be done: digging a field latrine, swimming half a mile in full uniform, reading a *Hardy Boys* mystery to a blind boy, repainting a neighborhood playground, paying hospital visits to people you hardly knew, learning to cook breakfast for six over an open fire, demonstrating the ability to clean and dress a serious wound, following animal tracks for a mile through heavy underbrush. Being a Boy Scout at any rank was work, but becoming an Eagle Scout was more like a full-blown career. Naturally enough, only the geeks were willing to stick with it all the way—the slavish knot-tying bird-identifiers, the scab-kneed pyromaniacs able to start a fire in the pouring rain with two pieces of flint and an abandoned robin's nest, the plucky few who begged to be allowed to sleep outdoors in the snow, and then were up at dawn, singing "God Bless America" while they fried bacon and eggs for the rest of the troop—these freaks of nature, these idiot savants. And then there was Ira Mittelman, the Good Son, who did it all for his father.

Ira's dad, Bernard, who taught Driver's Ed at a local high school, was the tenement-born child of poverty-stricken immigrants, and had never had a chance to join the Scouts as a youth. "Who had time for Scouting?" he demanded in a frantic voice—the voice of someone about to crash head-on into a concrete abutment—whenever the subject came up. "Who had time for fun, period, when I was a kid? Who had the money for it? Camping trips? *Forget* about it. We slept in tents, all right—whenever the rent came due. Mealtime was cold cereal, hold the milk. The Boy Scouts? That was for kids one heckuva lot luckier than me." He usually launched into these speeches as he and Ira preened in the mirror, adjusting their Scout uniforms before a troop meeting. "Look at us, will you?" Bernard Mittelman demanded, and Ira obediently peered into the mirror, unsure of what he should be noticing. His father tugged at his official Boy Scout neckerchief, then sat down and began to pump his right foot spasmodically into the floor, a nervous brake-slamming tic left over from his grueling daily routine of riding around town in the company of student drivers. Ira's friends had asked him occasionally about his father's nervous foot, and Ira, at a loss for what to say, hinted at war-related injuries, then tried to change the subject.

Ira's sister Ruthie, seven years older, hadn't been forced to do anything but play the piano. Nobody made her put on a Girl Scout uniform and sell cookies door to door. Ira pointed out this disparity to his father on more than one occasion—usually when they were on a camping trip, trying to figure out how to read a compass in pitch darkness, or pouring calamine lotion on each other to stop the itching from mosquito bites and poison ivy. "It isn't fair, Dad," he'd mutter. "Ruthie gets to stay home. She's at the movies right now, I bet. It's air-conditioned. She's eating buttered popcorn with her friends."

"Plenty of boys would give their eye-teeth to have the chance to be a Scout," his father would tell him, puffing furiously on a cigarette. "They'd line up for a chance to be here in the great outdoors with their dad. Plenty of kids would." Then he'd sit down on a nearby log and pump the dirt with his nervous foot while Ira hung his head, contemplating the depth of his ingratitude.

The thought of his father—just a fleeting mental glance at him—left Ira exhausted, filling him with remorse so leaden it threatened to plunge him right through the floor. He had not sufficiently loved his father. This simple fact outweighed everything else he'd done in his life; his accumulated good deeds, the years of kindness to strangers, the slowly accruing interest on all his accounts, season after season of dutiful motions, all of his best intentions put together were nothing compared to it.

And now this. Ruthie had been right all along—this business with the closet shrine was nonsense. What was the point of all that sighing? The fact was, it was too late to do anything for his father. The time to have been dutiful was while the old man was alive and *kvetching* at Ruthie's house in Seattle. Ira could have flown up there for a long weekend—he could have taken the old man to a Mariners' game, bought him a hot dog and a bag of peanuts. They could have gone up in the Space Needle and made jokes about the tourists. They might have become friends, at last, he and his dad—just a couple of guys out on the town together. Well, he'd blown his chance on that one. Now all he could do for the old man was open the closet door and say hi every morning.

If Ruthie'd been there to read his thoughts, she'd have had a fit. "So take the ashes back to HaHaTonka, then! What is it, Ira—do you *enjoy* making yourself feel like a jerk?"

No, he didn't enjoy it. And it wasn't just the standing date with Pauline that was holding him back, either. In fact, Pauline was just an excuse, and he knew it. The truth was, Ira was fundamentally opposed to such sentimental journeys—reunions, homecomings and the like—no matter what the nature of the errand. Revisiting the sacred sites of one's childhood—the very thought of it all brought phlegm to his throat. Everywhere he looked he saw American culture shamelessly chasing after its past. In a society afflicted with profound amnesia, cut off from any true understanding of its history, Top-40 radio stations excitedly announced "a nonstop hour of music from the '70's!" as if Tony Orlando and Dawn constituted something ancient and mysterious, like Etruscan ruins. On the J-Church streetcar a month ago he'd overheard a couple mourning in all sincerity the demise of an undistinguished chophouse, a tourist dump at the corner of Van Ness and Lombard: "I can't get over it. The place was there for ten years! Ten years! Now it's gone, overnight!"

It was his work, Ira reasoned, that had dimmed his view of what passed for the past these days. How could it not? Last week he'd slipped a damaged first edition of Dickens' *David Copperfield* out of its delicate tissue paper wrapping and held the fragile tome tenderly, inhaling the mysterious scent of must and mildew that arose from its mottled pages like incense. Not a reproduction, not a reprint—the first edition, with thirty-eight plates by Phiz, plus an errata leaf, Maclise's portrait of Dickens, his wife and his sister following the plate listing—even the blue printed wrappers were original! Right there, heavy in his own hands! Dickens himself might have held this edition, this very book. *That* was the past—no, *THE PAST,* the real article—not just a time, but a place, a world, worth spelling out in capital letters, worth yearning for, worth rescuing, worth restoring with all the care and expertise a craftsman could muster. Nowadays the past had been packaged, transformed into a hash of five-and-dime sentimentality, just another industry busily turning heartfelt human emotions into a bunch of interchangeable *tchotchkes.* The past—and in America that meant anything older than the fruit in your refrigerator—was just one more commodity to be bought and sold.

Ira had already missed his tenth, twentieth, twenty-fifth and thirtieth De Lesseps High School class reunions, and had no intention of attending the fortieth when that one rolled around. Despite a personal phone call pleading with him to attend, he'd also passed two years ago on a chance to get together with graduates of his Hebrew school at a testimonial dinner for dear old Mrs. Leibowitz, one of their beloved teachers who now lay at death's door. ("Aw, c'mon, Mitts," his old classmate Barry Sherman had cried over the phone, "it won't be the same without you!" No one had called him "Mitts" in years. He adored the name; it made him sound like a scrappy, devil-may-care kid you'd want to have on your side in a fight—which was just the kind of guy he'd never been.) No, none of these events had tempted him in the least. So why should a chance to revisit Camp HaHaTonka be any different? To hell with it. *Trustworthy, loyal, helpful, friendly*—no, he told himself, it was time at last to forget that stupid mantra. His father's ashes could stay in the hall closet, where they belonged.

Oh, but such a petulant, ungrateful train of thought was unworthy of an Eagle Scout, Ira knew. It was un-American, cowardly, self-indulgent—it violated any number of rules laid out in the Scout Handbook in large, boldfaced type. He should be ashamed of himself. But then again, who was he kidding? Despite his father's fond and fervent hopes—the pushing, the nudging, the pleading—the fact was that Ira had never been Eagle Scout material, not for a minute.

He'd tried to be a good Boy Scout—really, he had. *Boys' Life,* the official magazine of the Boy Scouts, came to his house every month, full of patriotic fervor, earnest how-to articles ("Make a holder for old copies of *Boys' Life* out of a cut-off box of Cheerios!"), and true-life adventure stories involving Boy Scout heroes, kids just like Ira, who rescued perfect strangers, preferably old folks or wheelchair-bound kids, from burning buildings or sinking rafts, then got big medals pinned on them by high-ranking officials. The back pages were strewn with ads that hawked useful weapons like BB guns, slingshots, and bullwhips ("Hand Made by Cherokee Indians!"). Every issue included a couple of full-page ads promoting sales schemes: you could join the Junior Sales Club of America, agreeing to sell boxes of occasional cards to friends, neighbors, and family members in exchange for great gifts. All you had to sell was sixty boxes of cards, and you could get a three-speed bike for free. "Most boys know sixty people—it's a cinch! Want a bugle? Sure you do! Just sell twelve boxes. How about a Marlin shotgun? It's a snap! Thirty-six boxes and she's yours!"

Boys' Life drove Ira crazy with desire. He felt like he was being ripped in half, from the inside out. On the one hand, he couldn't help himself: he begged his parents shamelessly for a bullwhip ("Aw, c'mon, just the 'Muleskinner,' model—it's only two dollars and fifty cents!"). He'd seen Lash LaRue on Saturday afternoon TV disarm a gunman at twenty feet using nothing but his bullwhip, and it seemed like a perfectly sensible weapon to have around the house. He longed to join the Junior Sales Club of America, because he really, truly wanted a three-speed bike, a set of Voit water skis, a Kodak movie camera, a bull horn, and a walkie-talkie set, and he knew he could have them all, too—just for selling two hundred boxes of cards. Sure he could.

But at the same time a dark, ironic voice in his head told him that he couldn't sell any occasional cards—that if he went around the neighborhood ringing doorbells, nobody would answer, and if anyone did, they'd slam the door in his face. He couldn't give them away, in fact. The voice in his head was chattering like a monkey by this time. If he ordered any occasional cards from the Junior Sales Club of America, he'd be stuck with them for the rest of his life. He'd still be sending them to people when he was ninety-five. The voice also told him that there was next to no chance that he could actually save anybody from a burning building or a sinking raft, not just because burning buildings and sinking rafts were hard to come by in everyday life, but because he was, to put it plainly, a coward.

Oh, sure, when the big day finally came, just after his fifteenth birthday, he walked across the stage and accepted his Eagle badge, executed the Scout handshake right and left, saluted everybody in sight, kissed his mother on the cheek like all the other boys—but Ira knew as he was doing it that he didn't deserve to be up there. He'd memorized everything, gone through all the motions, practiced his sheepshank, his sheet bend, his half hitch and his clove hitch until his little fingers were numb, but the whole shebang amounted to *bubkes.* He'd been a shitty Boy Scout. In fact, he hadn't even liked being a Boy Scout very much. Oh, sure, there'd been an occasional enjoyable moment here and there, usually when he was by himself in his tent at Camp HaHaTonka, weaving a lanyard or humming into his kazoo, just thinking about things. Most of the time, though, he'd found the Boy Scouts boring—and the parts that weren't boring were often sort of scary. Admittedly, it was pretty fascinating to read about emergency remedies for snake bites in the Boy Scout Handbook, but did everybody in Troop 144 really have to practice putting tourniquets on each other every week? He'd had practice tourniquets applied to every part of his body except his penis—and even the possibility of *that* had come up in casual Troop 144 banter. Over the course of five years in the Boy Scouts he'd suffered through poison oak, poison ivy, poison sumac, spider bites, and diarrhea. He'd gone camping in the rain and the snow; he'd sneezed his way through hay fever-ridden ten-mile hikes that left his feet a mass of blisters; he'd watched his thumbnail turn black and fall off after he'd accidentally smashed it with a rock; he tried not to complain, but that stuff *hurt,* dammit. Of all the gifts his father gave him that Ira didn't really want (Little League baseball, swimming lessons, boxing gloves, a chemistry set, a dyed-pink baby chicken) the Boy Scouts lasted longest, and loomed largest—and the guilt he felt about it all still rested in his heart like an anvil. *I'm sorry, Dad,* he said to himself almost every day. *You gave me what you wanted for yourself, and it was the wrong gift.*

■ ■ ■

Henry Cruikshank arrived twenty minutes early, catching him off guard, still lost in thought. Ira was so submerged in melancholy memories that when the knock came at the door, he looked around him uncertainly in a daze, half convinced for just a moment that his father had somehow gotten out of the container in the closet. Then the knock sounded again, and he scrambled to usher Cruikshank into his crowded workshop at the back of the apartment. Cruikshank was disheveled, as usual, with a two-day growth of beard flecked with bits of his breakfast. He was a tall, shambling man with haunted eyes, a collection of tics. Ira felt a deep kinship toward him, though he disapproved of nearly everything Cruikshank did.

"Hey, what happened?" Cruikshank asked him, casting a nervous glance around the workshop. The room was a mess.

"You're early," said Ira. "That's what happened." He propped the rolls of leather back into an oaken barrel in the far corner of the shop, then turned to the tangle of tools still littering the worktable: the small tub of wheat starch paste was open, as well as the can of rabbit-skin glue; he'd left the litho stone smack in the middle of everything after working on *Ivanhoe,* with the surface covered by the scraps of pared leather he'd scraped against it; around the stone lay a variety of calipers, the ballpeen hammer, several rollers, the narrow and wide scrapers, a chisel, the paste brush. The paste brush! Twenty-five dollars worth of boar bristle, and now he'd have to soak it in solvent overnight to get the paste out. There were a dozen curved embroidery needles scattered about, as well—the ones he used for sewing new bindings. If he'd been his own apprentice, he'd have fired himself for the sheer mess of it all.

With the clutter finally cleared away, Ira slipped Cruikshank's copy of *Paradise Regained* out of its casing and surveyed the damage. "Be careful, would you?" Cruikshank moaned. He leaned over Ira, sighing and clucking. The damage to the binding was extensive: the leather had deteriorated completely, taking all of the gold leaf lettering and the cords—the hemp supports girdling the spine—along with it. The spine had collapsed, and the joints, the seams where the front and back covers attached to it, were ripped from top to bottom. But still, it wasn't a total disaster. Cruikshank was right, for once: the book was potentially a magnificent find. The license leaf and title-page were a little stained, and the head-lines on pages 22, 26 and 27 were shaved—and naturally, given the age of the thing, the pages were brown and mottled with mold—but none of those problems posed a serious threat to the book's value. He might even be able to save the endpapers if he worked slowly and carefully.

Cruikshank paced back and forth in front of the work table, biting his lip, wringing his hands. "Can you do anything with it?" he asked at last. "I know it's in bad shape, but Jesus, I fell in love with it. I shouldn't have bought it. I know, I know. Not at that price, anyway."

"Yeah," Ira said softly, still staring at the binding.

"You know, just once you could tell me something just to comfort me. Would that be so terrible? Would it kill you? Listen to me, Ira. We could clean up on this thing. Five grand profit to split, and what would it take you? A couple of days? This buyer—the kid in Los Gatos—he doesn't even know anything about books. He's just buying up anything he can grab. He's into *stuff.* He tells me last month he went ga-ga over Fabergé eggs at Neiman Marcus. He bought three of them. Now it's books—he says he can hardly wait for next Friday, he's salivating for this Milton—he can't wait to see it."

Ira sighed and gently closed the book.

"Oh, no," Cruikshank said. "Don't do it, Ira."

"What. Don't do what."

"I can see it in your eyes. I know what you're thinking."

"No you don't."

"You're thinking it's too much profit. You're such a goddamn Boy Scout."

"Oh, don't say that. Please. I don't want to hear that kind of thing right now."

"I know the way you think. We've had this conversation fifteen times."

"Henry, look. I don't care what you charge the guy. Charge your client whatever you want, as far as I'm concerned. It's none of my business. Just don't tell me about it." Ira put an arm gently around Cruikshank's shoulder and led him toward the door. "I'll do the work. I'll get it done. I promise you I'll do the best I can with the restoration. You'll be happy."

"You always do your best, Ira. I knew I could count on you."

"But if you don't take off now, I won't be able to finish the job I've got scheduled before yours," Ira said, and opened the door.

"Right! Okay, then. Get back to work!" Cruikshank said. He

stepped out into the hall, then turned around. "Look at it this way," he said. "To this kid, five grand is what he gives the cleaning lady at Christmas. It's nothing. We deserve this, Ira, both of us. We've earned it."

"You deserve it, Henry," Ira said as he was shutting the door. "It's all yours. I haven't earned anything at all."

■ ■ ■

That night at Cacciatore di Spello, Pauline seemed shy and girlish; she patted her hair when she sat down at the table, which was something she'd never done before, and she smiled coyly when Ira kissed her on the cheek. Something was up, Ira knew. He'd told his story about Henry Cruikshank and the Los Gatos gazillionaire with the three Fabergé eggs, but Pauline didn't laugh—in fact she downed her martini in two gulps as she listened, and then she became fixated on her thumbnail, which she buffed with her napkin as Ira spun out the anecdote.

As usual, their table was at the back wall, away from the worst of the Friday evening crush. The red checkered tablecloth looked like it could have used a good scrubbing, and the candle stuck in the straw-bottomed, wax-encrusted Chianti bottle was little more than a stub—but that was part of the battered charm of the place. Bruno, their waiter, took away their empty glasses and brought the pasta course—a steaming platter of ravioli stuffed with chard and ricotta, topped with a light marinara sauce—and as the steam rose from the platter and Ira dipped his spoon to taste the marinara, Pauline finally came out with her news.

"You're what?" he asked, and turned his good ear toward her. He'd heard her, all right; this was a reflexive move, desperate, hopeful for the split second it took to turn his head. Then he caught a glimpse of her face, and he knew.

"I said . . . I'm getting married, Ira. He's a fellow from work. You don't know him."

"Oh, my god." He didn't want to do it, but he was unable to stop himself; he dropped the spoon into his ravioli and cupped his head in his hands.

"Look, we both knew this couldn't go on indefinitely."

He lifted his head from his hands. "We did?"

"Well, *I* did. It's been nice. But—"

"*Nice?*" The question came out louder than he'd intended it. "Okay, look," he said, now whispering, his head thrust toward her across the ravioli. "I'm sorry. I'm sorry. This is just taking me by surprise, is all." He paused, trying to catch his breath. "How long has this been going on? You and the guy, I mean."

"For a while. He's been pushing me to make a decision."

"Who is it? What's his name?"

"It's Kenny, Ira. Kenny, my boss. He's really a very nice guy."

"Kenny? Confused Kenny? One month he's—"

"He's really very sweet."

"You're kidding. He's crazy. He's a maniac. You tell me about him every Friday."

"Listen, Ira, I know how you must feel. I should have told you things were going along a certain way with Kenny and me. I should have done that. I know. Honestly, I wanted to tell you about this as it was developing—but if I had, what would you have said?"

"I would have said—I don't know." He threw up his hands. "How would I know that? I have no idea."

"Kenny's gone through some phases over the past couple of years, but he's settled down a lot lately," said Pauline. She broke off a piece of bread and shredded it into crumbs on her plate. "He's got grown children, by the way—a son and a daughter. Very nice. They both went to Stanford. I've met his ex-wife, too, for that matter. It turns out we go to the same place to have our hair done. She's a lovely person."

"Well, that's just great," Ira said bitterly, and blew out a sigh. "What about *us?* We had something going here, didn't we?"

"I don't know. I don't think so." Pauline sighed, shook her head, looked away briefly, then back at him.

"I'm not just talking about the sex, by the way. I'm talking about the companionship." He paused, reconsidering. "But okay, let's just—let's just talk about the sex, for starters."

"Oh, Ira, let's not. Please."

Ira shut his eyes, but instead of blackness, he saw what seemed to be blood red curtains floating thickly in the air. He opened his eyes. "You're just going to end this?" he said. "I can't believe it. We've been having such a good time together."

"We're divorced. We were married for ten years, it didn't work out, we got divorced, we got lonely, so we started going out again," she said in a toneless voice, as if reading it all off a cue card. "We were in a holding pattern."

He couldn't catch his breath; he felt as if something large and heavy had punched him in the chest. "You make it sound like it didn't mean a goddamn thing."

"All I'm saying is, we both knew we needed to be getting on with our lives. Didn't we?"

Getting on with his life? What was she talking about? This *was* his life. With his luck, he might keep living—breathing, eating, excreting waste—for another thirty, forty years. What was he going to do with all those Friday nights?

They sat listlessly, drinking the rest of their bottle of wine, staring at their ravioli until Bruno, their waiter, came to take it away. Around them, everyone at Cacciatore di Spello seemed suddenly to have come down with a terminal case of Friday night jollies. Tables erupted into gales of spontaneous laughter, the babble of conversation grew to an insufferable din, somberly clad diners were transported by fits of shrieking gaiety, waiters launched into impromptu arias as they carried trays of pasta; everybody was on the verge of peeing their pants. Bruno brought the scallopine, steam rising off the platter, and set it down gently between them. Ira stared at it as though waiting for the veal to speak to him. As for eating any of it—well, he might as well have contemplated eating his own arm, starting at the fingers. For her part, Pauline, too, seemed utterly lost. She rested her elbows on the table and held her wine glass in both hands just under her chin. She stared down into the glass thoughtfully, from time to time taking a sip. She didn't look remorseful; in fact she seemed to be struggling to keep a smile from spreading across her cheeks. Finally, when the veal had cooled completely and the marsala sauce had congealed into a brown pool of pudding, Bruno came back for the platter and took it away untouched, *tssk*ing audibly as he lifted it from the table. For a long while that evening—even after Pauline had risen from the table, kissed Ira lightly on the cheek, and made her way toward the door—Ira sat staring fixedly at the soiled red checkered tablecloth, as if some message for him might be hidden there among the stains and bread crumbs—something wise and pithy about how to survive in the wreckage of the world.

■ ■ ■

When Ira woke up on Saturday morning, he realized that he had to make some phone calls. In the night—perhaps in his sleep—he'd come to a decision. First he called the airline, which sold him a coach seat on the afternoon nonstop to Kansas City for an absurdly large amount of money. "I'm sorry, but family emergencies need to be confirmed by a doctor, preferably in writing," the reservations clerk explained, and Ira, too exhausted by grief to mount a counter-argument, simply gave over his Visa number and hung up the phone.

Then he called Ruthie, and thank god she wasn't home. "Something's come up here, and it looks like I'm free to take off for a while, after all," he said in a determinedly chipper voice when her answering machine beeped. "So you'll be pleased to know that I'm off to Camp HaHaTonka with Dad. The dutiful son at last. Is there a merit badge for ash-scattering? I bet there is. I guess I'll find out. Anyway, it's our final father-and-son picnic. I'll call you Sunday night, maybe Monday morning, whenever I get back to town."

And finally he had to call Cruikshank. "Henry," he said, "you're not going to like hearing this."

"Then don't tell me."

"Something's come up—I'm going to have to be out of town, just a couple of days."

"Oh, no. No, no, no," said Cruikshank quickly. "I'm hanging up now."

"Don't, Henry."

"You promised me."

"This is something I've got to take care of, something I've been putting off. A family matter," Ira said. "I'm leaving this afternoon, I'll be back on Monday. You won't even know I'm gone. Really, I'm not kidding. I'll start on that Milton the minute I'm back. Don't worry."

"Ira, this is an emergency. This kid is dangling, he's an impulse buyer, he can't dangle very long—he's not a good dangler." There were tears in Cruikshank's voice now.

Ira sighed, and his resolve wavered. Henry Cruikshank was his friend, and the poor jerk needed him. There was work to do here—the work Ira loved, the work that had saved him from despair more than once in the past. Restoring old books made him feel that he was somehow adding to the world, enriching it, saving something valuable from the inevitable decay that awaits all things, beautiful or humble. It was good, the work he did—it was, in fact, he saw now, perhaps the only good thing he'd ever done in his life, the only thing that lasted, the only thing that mattered.

But then he gazed around his living room and felt the air go out of his lungs, and once again suddenly everything seemed hopeless. He sat down, or rather collapsed, his legs giving way beneath him. If he'd had something sharp nearby, he might have stabbed himself in the heart with it. Pauline was gone, vanished, and with her everything else had vanished, too. His throat closed up. He couldn't imagine the future—he tried, he'd been trying to envision the future—tomorrow, the day after tomorrow, next week, next month—ever since he'd come home last night, and had been horrified to realize that he couldn't do it, couldn't imagine even the homeliest details, breakfast with tomorrow's Sunday *Chronicle,* a Giants game on afternoon TV. He stared at the bank of livingroom windows, which revealed a cool, breezeless morning that had nothing much to recommend it. June was half gone already, but as was often the case in San Francisco, summer still seemed months away, a distant rumor. The sky was gray, slack, a wall of cement—or so it seemed this Saturday morning to Ira, who was at the brink of fifty, staring at the fact that he was much nearer the end of things than the beginning.

"Ira. Ira. Hello? I'm drowning," Cruikshank said. "This deal doesn't come through for me, I might as well hang it up. I've got creditors, do you understand me? Save me, for crissake, will you?"

So was it truly necessary to get on a plane with that miserable little cannister of ashes and fly across country with it, back to his stupid Boy Scout camp, just to make up for the fact that he hadn't loved his father enough? Would any good deed ever really make up for that? At this late date, what was the point in trying?

"Ira, speak to me. C'mon. Hello. What's going on?"

But then Ira heard his father's tiny fists beating insistently against the lid of the cannister in the closet—tap, tap, tap—like the thump of a baby's heart—and before he realized what was coming out of his mouth, he heard himself say, "I'm sorry, Henry. I gotta do my duty. It's a father-son thing. My dad's dying wish. It's complicated, I can't go into it on the phone."

"Oh, Christ. I knew it. You're such a goddamn Boy Scout."

"I'll be back on Monday, safe and sound, I'll give you a call, it'll all be fine. You tell your Los Gatos kid—tell him for me—tell him dangling's good for his lower back."

■ ■ ■

The plane encountered turbulence flying east over the Rockies, and in the midst of it, as wide-eyed flight attendants were hustling up the aisles toward their seats and passengers around him were fretting out loud about wind shear, Ira worried that his father's ashes might be spilling in the overhead bin. He remembered all the dire warnings from past flights—"contents may have shifted during flight"—and imagined his father spilled out like so much gravel over someone's Panama hat or laptop computer. Across the aisle from him, a young woman bowed her head into her barf bag and gave back the miserable little snack the airline had recently fed her. Ira shut his eyes and leaned back into his headrest.

A moment later the turbulence eased, and he slid his headphones back in place. Ten channels to choose from—audio books, CNN news updates, plus lots of music. Channel four was titled "Dancin' the Night Away," and as Ira turned the volume up he realized he'd come in right in the middle of Gene Chandler, singing "Duke of Earl." He hadn't heard it in years. The song conjured up vivid memories of frigid rides in Mr. Sackett's '59 Impala on the way to Boy Scout Indian dancing lessons every Tuesday evening. He must have heard "Duke of Earl" hundreds of times back then, of course, but now it seemed to him the song existed only on the radio in Mr. Sackett's car. He couldn't help himself—Ira had Boy Scouts on the brain at the moment, thanks to his father's cockamamie dying wish.

Mr. Sackett had a good radio in his car, and he didn't mind leaving it tuned to WHB or KUDL, AM stations that played songs like "Duke of Earl." It was a long ride to Indian dancing lessons, all the way to Roebling High, on the remote northeast side of town. The dancing lessons consisted of a hundred half-naked boys from troops all over Kansas City, crowded into Roebling's dank, smelly gym, wearing Indian loin cloths and war bonnets painstakingly sewn by their mothers, learning to do what someone in the main office of the Boy Scouts of America had decided was Indian dancing. Very likely no Native Americans had been consulted. In fact, if someone had started yakking about "Native Americans" back in 1962, nobody would have known what they were talking about. Ira had never seen a real Indian at a Scouting function. Probably Indians weren't even allowed in the Boy Scouts, now that he thought about it. If one had shown up, he'd probably have been strung up in no time.

The dance steps he and the other boys had to learn were an elaborate hash of mincing circular movements, punctuated by occasional aimless lunges, forming a spastic serpentine pattern across the gym floor. As they danced, the boys were supposed to shout "hey-yah-hey-yah, hey-yah-hey-yah" at the top of their lungs. Ira asked everyone in Troop 144 what "hey-yah" was supposed to mean, and no one had a clue. Did it mean something in some Indian language? How could "hey-yah" mean anything at all? Decked out in the cotton-and-rayon Indian regalia his mother had made for him, his skin nothing but goose bumps in the underheated gym, making his way through the lurching conga line of dancers, chanting like a baboon, Ira had never felt less like an Indian in his life.

He gripped his headphones tighter to his head as "Dancin' the Night Away" segued from "Duke of Earl" to Smokey Robinson and the Miracles doing "You Really Got a Hold On Me." This was one of his favorites. Nobody wrote songs like this anymore. This one, too, seemed to exist only in the close, cramped environment of Mr. Sackett's Impala, during those rides to Roebling High School. Mr. Sackett was a gray-faced, harried chain smoker, nails bitten down to the quick, haunted by ghosts. He always turned up the volume when Herb Alpert's instrumental, "The Lonely Bull," came on the radio, which might have told Ira and the other boys something about him, had they been interested in thinking about him as something other than a nervous chauffeur. At stoplights, no matter what song was on the radio, everyone but Mr. Sackett would pile out of the car and race around it in a frenzied circle: "Chinese Fire Drill," the game was called, though no one had ever explained to Ira what was Chinese about it. When the light changed to green you had to leap back inside the car before it took off. Once Ira had been left behind, in the middle of a busy street in enemy territory, an unfamiliar neighborhood somewhere deep in Kansas City's east side. Mr. Sackett drove half a block before Ira saw the car pull over to the curb and stop, and then he ran through the intersection, cars braking and honking at him angrily, to get back in.

That kind of thing had happened to him often in Troop 144. The fact was, Ira didn't have any friends in the Scouts—not even, as it turned out, Larry Fontenot, whom he'd once considered his best friend for life. Larry Fontenot. Jesus, how long had it been since he'd spoken to Larry? He should have called him before he left San Francisco, told him he was coming to town. You could find just about anybody's phone number on the internet these days. It would have taken Ira only a minute or two to look Larry up—there were probably only a few Fontenots listed in Kansas City, and how many Lawrence Millard Fontenots could there be?

The thought occurred to him that Larry might be willing to go with him for a day-long jaunt down to Camp HaHaTonka. Ira wasn't at all sure how to get down there—it was someplace in the Ozarks, though he'd forgotten the name of the nearest town—but he had a feeling that Larry would remember the way. And it was the weekend, after all; Larry would likely be off work. Work? What did Ira know? They'd been out of touch for decades. Larry could be a neurosurgeon by this time, inserting cranial shunts all day Saturday. He could be living in Japan for all Ira knew. Well, he'd simply look him up in the phone book once he got to town. It was worth a try, anyway, and if he was still in Kansas City, a phone call wouldn't hurt, just to ask. It would be a chance to renew their—their what? Friendship? Well, that would be stretching it, at this point, Ira conceded—in fact he wasn't sure they'd ever really been friends—but still, they could try to reconnect after all these years, couldn't they? To recapture something that might never have been there in the first place? What could be better, Ira asked himself, than a couple of old Boy Scouts heading down to Scout Camp together to perform a Good Deed?

The whole reason Ira had joined Troop 144, instead of one of the two Jewish troops in Kansas City, was to hang out with Larry. They'd known each other since kindergarten, and had done everything together—built snow forts and tree houses, played Tom Sawyer and Huckleberry Finn, caught frogs and lightning bugs and garter snakes, trick-or-treated, camped out in each other's backyards. When they were seven they'd gone to see *Old Yeller* together one Saturday, and Larry hadn't said a word about the fact that Ira broke into hiccuping tears at the end. Oh, sure, it was convenient that Troop 144 met just a couple of blocks from Ira's house, whereas the few Jewish troops in town met at synagogues several miles from his neighborhood—but the truth was, in order to be in the Boy Scouts with Larry Fontenot, Ira would have joined a troop in Tierra del Fuego.

Larry told him he felt that way, too. "Oh, man, it's going to be great," he said. "We're going to have wild adventures together—just the two of us. Like brothers, you know?"

Brothers: the word had meant everything to Ira, who didn't have any. In all the Hardy Boys mysteries, Frank and Joe Hardy had each other. On Walt Disney's *Spin and Marty,* Spin had Marty, and Marty had Spin. Roy Rogers had Pat Brady *and* Gabby Hayes. Ira, on the other hand, had to make do with Ruthie. When he was a boy, just thinking about the word "brother" brought a lump to his throat. A brother meant somebody to talk to, somebody to share with. He didn't know what it was that he wanted to share, but whatever it was, he knew he didn't want to share it with Ruthie. He *couldn't* share it with her, even if he'd wanted to. Whenever he poked his head into her bedroom to say hello, Ruthie threw pennies at his head, five at a time, until he retreated to the safety of the hallway.

He remembered it all now, and the same longing he'd felt as a boy swept over him again. Dammit, he should have called Larry Fontenot before he left for the airport.

■ ■ ■

The evening air in Kansas City was balmy, so Ira rolled the window down on his rented Toyota and hung his arm out into the soft, fragrant breeze. He drove south into the city, past the old, defunct municipal airport, which now seemed just an oversized quonset hut surrounded by cracked, weedy parking lots. Traffic was heavy in the downtown area, and Ira, not quite sure of where he was going, swerved through three lanes of traffic to get off the freeway and onto the Southwest Trafficway. He didn't feel at home in Kansas City anymore—in fact he hardly recognized the place, though he'd spent the first eighteen years of his life here. Maybe if he'd come back for one of his high school reunions, or accepted his Hebrew school's invitation to fête lovable old Mrs. Leibowitz a couple of years ago, he might have maintained some sense of belonging here—but it was a late day for such regrets. In recent years he'd returned to

Kansas City only for funerals—first his mother's, then two years later, his father's—and each visit had left him convinced that in his absence, someone had shifted all the city's streets around. He'd spent hours driving in loopy circles, looking for familiar landmarks and finding nothing that rang a bell. Everything he recognized had been made over—glitzed up, polished, pumped full of sophistication, completely ruined. Where had all those new buildings come from? What had happened to the easy-going, dim-witted city of his youth?

The Southwest Trafficway took him to the Country Club Plaza, and from there he navigated through surprisingly familiar territory to Hartley, his old neighborhood. Hartley now sat in the geographical middle of Kansas City, though in Ira's boyhood the city limits were just a mile to the south of his house. A hundred years ago, before Kansas City annexed the area, Hartley had been a sleepy little town—Hartley, Missouri—and in the 1950's, when Ira was a boy, Hartley's old main street was still identifiable: a two-block row of down-at-the-heels two-story brick buildings housing a dusty, wooden-floored five-and-dime and two dilapidated auto parts stores which faced each other grimly across the street. The old wooden sidewalks, like refugees from a John Wayne movie, were still in place, raised a good two feet off the street.

This was not the Jewish part of town. It never had been, and never would be. Hartley's houses were mostly wood-frame bungalows built for working stiffs like Bernard Mittelman, returning veterans eligible for home loans on the G.I. Bill. They sprang up in the years just after World War II, block after block of them, hastily built, modest in size, their materials plain as sheetrock and linoleum. Unlike Kansas City's more affluent neighborhoods, there were no curbs on Ira's street; the pavement simply ran up to the ragged edge of grass-and-weed-choked easements. Hartley's sidewalks were cracked. The streets were full of potholes that the city never got around to filling.

In keeping with the look of the neighborhood, the Mittelmans' lawn was a piecemeal thing, lush in some spots, balding in others. The bald spots shifted around from one year to the next, as if on some sort of rotational schedule. Ira's father, for reasons Ira had never understood, refused to buy a lawn mower, renting one instead, year in, year out, every Saturday or Sunday during the lawn mowing season, even though it would have been much cheaper in the long run just to buy one. "I know it's stupid. I just don't want to be tied down," he explained whenever Ira asked.

"Tied down to what, Dad?" Ira asked one Sunday morning, the summer he turned nine.

"Don't ask so many questions," his father told him. "It's complicated. I don't want to get into it."

"But Dad . . ."

They were sitting on the front stoop together, eating bagels and cream cheese. His father said, "I don't want to talk about it," with a web of cream cheese at each corner of his mouth. The bag of bagels sat between them on the top step. They were eating on the stoop because they didn't want to wake up Ruthie and Ira's mother, who were still asleep inside. Sunday mornings were his mother's holidays—she slept late, and was glad to be waited on. Ira's dad made scrambled eggs with lox and onions, or matzoh brei, or laid out a platter of smoked whitefish and sable, garnished with sliced onions, tomatoes and cucumbers, and served her breakfast in bed with plenty of hot coffee and fresh-squeezed orange juice. As Ira and his father ate their bagels, their neighbors up and down the block were driving off to church. Ira thought of waving as the cars passed, but he decided it might be unseemly, a Jewish kid hanging out on Sunday morning eating bagels with his dad, waving to a parade of god-fearing folks on their way to the house of the Lord.

A mile west, in the neighborhoods on the other side of Holmes Road where much of Kansas City's new Jewish middle-class had moved after the war, larger houses were built in the 40s and early 50s, whole streets of them, tagged with poetic development names like Inisfree and Killarney. These houses were solid and substantial, stone-accented, with chimneys made of clinker brick, generously proportioned double garages and fake Tudor touches, miniature turrets punctured by tiny arched windows, pillared hemispherical porticoes with statues of grinning Negro jockies standing by. The lawns were manicured, divided one from the next by neatly sculpted boxwood hedges that looked like they'd been nurtured into maturity since the turn of the century.

Ira's Hebrew school bus dropped off children in these neighborhoods; he was among the last to get off, since Hartley was further east, and he was one of the only Jewish children who lived there. So he saw everything. As the bus rolled and stopped, rolled and stopped, he looked at his classmates' stately houses, one after another, and imagined what it might be like to live in one of them—what it might be like to roll around on one of those carefully tended, carpet-like lawns. Perhaps his father's foot would stop its frantic dance, and his voice would lose its terrified, about-to-crash-into-the-concrete-abutment quality. Maybe if they lived in a more Jewish part of town, his mother might relax a bit, too. She might even tone down her desperate insistence upon Jewish observance.

Sometimes it seemed to Ira that his mother was bent on making the whole world Jewish, one kid at a time. She encouraged him to have his neighborhood friends over on Saturday afternoons and talk to them about Judaism. "Just bring it up in casual conversation," she suggested. "If they start talking about Jesus, you come back with something about Moses."

"They never talk about Jesus, Mom. It never comes up. We don't talk about that stuff."

"You're so ashamed to be a Jew?" his mother asked him with a catch in her throat. "This is how we've raised you?"

So, Ira, unsure of how to proceed, dutifully invited Larry Fontenot up to his room one day in sixth grade, and spent half an hour trying to teach him how to say "schmuck." It wasn't what his mother had in mind, Ira knew, but he had to start somewhere, and "schmuck" seemed as good a place as any. Ira already had the pronunciation of "schmuck" down cold—it rolled off his tongue as naturally as "mazel tov" or "gezundheit"—just another word he'd absorbed during all those mournful services at the synagogue, he figured. Maybe being Jewish gave him a leg up on pronouncing Yiddish expressions. Whatever the reason, Larry couldn't get the hang of it. His rendition of "schmuck" came out sounding more like "smug."

"Say *sshh,*" Ira instructed him patiently.

"Sshh."

"Okay, now say *muck.*"

"Muck."

"Now, say "Sshh . . . muck."

"Sshh . . . muck."

"Now put 'em together fast! What've you got?"

"Smug."

At Chanukah his mother strung holiday decorations all over the house—giant dreidels made of construction paper, a glossy "Chappy

Chanukah!" banner she'd bought at the synagogue gift shop—and insisted that Ruthie and Ira invite some of their non-Jewish friends from the neighborhood over for a latke feast. "They should know," she explained. "They should see what we're like, that we're not so crazy. They think they *invented* the Bible—they invented *God.* They own the whole subject, lock, stock and barrel. Well, they didn't, and they don't. This is educational. They should know. It's important."

Now Ira was closing in on Hartley, cruising along on side streets, and he could hear his mother's voice above the rhythmic, rasping croak of insects—the sound of all the sultry Kansas City summer nights of his youth. When he pulled up in front of his old house, he stopped and cut the engine. Ira breathed slowly now, and sat still, just listening to the measured sound of his breath amid the noisy chant of the crickets. The house had always been white when his family had lived there, but the current owners, whoever they were, had painted it green. The cherry tree he'd played in as a small boy was missing from the front yard. The lawn seemed thicker than he remembered it, and the lilac bushes under the living room windows were lush. The front porch light was on.

He shook his head and tssked. This was precisely the kind of nostalgic nonsense for which he had no patience. But he couldn't help himself, now that he was here. And besides—he wasn't doing any of this for himself, he was doing it for his father, who rested on the seat beside him, comfortable in his cannister. "We're back home, Dad," Ira whispered.

He sat there for several minutes. It was very quiet. Nothing had changed. He inhaled deeply; was there any air precisely like this anywhere else in the world—the combination of lilac and roses and watered, freshly mown grass, the faintly sweet pungency of dogshit, of shellac drying somewhere not too far down the block, of gasoline and Windex and sweat and cinnamon? Ira leaned his head back and shut his eyes and breathed it all in.

In this front yard he'd learned to throw a baseball. He'd played in the mud at the edge of the street, building mud castles and tunnels on rainy afternoons. He and Ruthie built snowmen right there, in front of the picture window. He and Larry Fontenot had raced their model cars on this very driveway. Here he had helped his dad wash the family car on weekends, squirting him with the hose most of the time while his dad did most of the actual scrubbing.

God, it all looked so small.

After a few more minutes, Ira turned the key in the ignition and drove away from his old house slowly. He found it hard to press on the accelerator. He felt the accumulated weariness of the day—the night before, at Cacciatore di Spello, the past year, the last thirty years or more—closing in on him, like a pillowcase slipped over his head. His father's cannister bounced in the passenger seat as Ira drove over the familiar potholes of his old neighborhood. These were the same potholes that had been here forty years ago—he was sure of it. The city had never gotten around to fixing them; perhaps they'd achieved the protected status of historic monuments by now. He'd learned to drive on this street, with his father huddled miserably in the passenger seat, muttering clenched Driver's Ed advice and slamming his nervous foot into the floorboard. Not much had changed in thirty-four years: Ira was still driving, and his father was still in the passenger seat—though he was silent now, having been transformed by time into a box of ashes.

■ ■ ■

Ira stopped to use the payphone at Winstead's, a hamburger joint on Brush Creek Boulevard where he'd hung out back in his pimply high school days, slurping milk shakes and gazing mournfully at girls he was too much of a chicken to ask out. He flipped through the telephone book, hoping to find Larry Fontenot's number. And there it was. Lawrence Millard Fontenot. The one and only.

Ira's lips were dry. Should he call? The last time they'd gotten together, nearly thirty years ago, things had gone terribly. It was just after Ira's college graduation; the war in Vietnam was winding down, and a cousin's Orthodox wedding had brought him back to Kansas City for a long weekend. Ira and Larry had been out of touch since the old days in Troop 144, and Ira hadn't been sure they'd have anything to say to each other anymore. But he had something to ask Larry, a question he'd had on his mind for a long time. He called the Fontenot house, and when Larry's mother answered, he identified himself, and she said, "Oh. Sure. I remember you. How're your folks?"

"They're fine, Mrs. Fontenot."

"Well, that's a blessing. Hold on a sec." Then a minute later, Larry got on the line.

"Hey, man," he said in a low, breathy voice once he got on the line. "Long time no see. Get your butt out here, dude. We've got some talking to do."

Like most of the families Ira had known as a boy, the Fontenots had left Hartley by the early seventies, moving to the Missouri suburbs spreading south and east of the city. The city was changing—blacks and Hispanics were moving into formerly all-white neighborhoods, and the suburbs were filled to bursting with white families fleeing for their lives. Ira took Highway 71 out to Whispering Birch Estates, the vast, characterless Levittown knock-off where the Fontenots now lived. Their house, like all the others surrounding it, seemed to have been assembled off-site and lowered into place by helicopter. There were no birches, whispering or otherwise—in fact, except for weeds and a few stunted saplings, there wasn't any landscaping at all. The driveway was already cracking, and as Ira approached the Fontenots' house, he could have sworn the place was listing slightly to one side. Larry answered the door and led Ira back to his bedroom, a dimly-lit, windowless cell painted dark red. A poster on one wall was the only decoration. It showed a mushroom cloud and bore the slogan, "Kill 'Em All—Let God Sort 'Em Out!"

"That's some poster," Ira offered.

"No joking, man. They're coming. They're on their way. Are you ready?" Larry asked serenely. He lay back on his bed and rested his head against the wall.

"They are? Who they?" Ira asked.

"Oh, come on, read the papers, man. I don't have to spell it out for you."

"You don't?"

"They come out this way, I'll tell you one thing, this boy's gonna be ready," said Larry. He rolled over to the edge of the bed, reached an arm down, and pulled out a .22 rifle. "Doesn't look like much, I know. But it was a .22 that killed Bobby Kennedy good and dead. And this ain't all I've got, either. I got a .357 magnum, loaded, in that desk over there. That thing's a cannon. And look at this baby." Larry put the rifle back under the bed and whipped a long-bladed knife out of a sheath strapped to his ankle under his pants leg. The knife glittered in the dim light of the desk lamp. "Bingo," Larry said. "I'm good with it, too. They come out this way, they're going to get a nice surprise."

"Oh, okay. Well, look, that's swell," Ira said, and edged toward the door. "It looks pretty sharp."

"Oh, it's sharp, all right." Larry laughed, but he wasn't smiling. "It's real sharp."

"Hey, listen, I wanted to ask you something. It's been on my mind for a long time, and I thought maybe we could talk about it. That's sort of why I called you."

Larry shrugged. "Shoot," he said.

"Okay. You remember back when we joined Troop 144?"

"Yeah. Sure. How could I forget?" Larry's eyes narrowed. "What about it?"

"Why'd you dump me like that?" Ira asked.

Larry stared at him. His lips were moving faintly, but he wasn't saying anything.

"You know," Ira said. "You know what I mean. You got me to join the troop, and then once I was there, you turned your back on me. You know what I'm talking about."

Larry shook his head. "Like hell I do," he said. "That was a million years ago. You still thinking about that shit?"

"Yeah. I guess I am."

Maybe if Larry hadn't come on so strong about brotherhood back when they were eleven, Ira wouldn't have felt the sting of his betrayal so keenly. "Brothers for life, man," Larry'd told him. "We'll be like the two musketeers or something like that. Hey—we'll start a band. And then—or, no, wait, listen to this: we could win some kind of Scouting medal or something—they have these medals—and we'd get invited to the White House, and meet the President. I bet that'd be cool. Maybe he'd take us out on that yacht. Jackie'd be there, too, and we could, like, meet her, you know?" Larry gave Ira a significant, raised-eyebrows look, as if his plans for Jackie Kennedy involved more than simply shaking hands. Jackie Kennedy floated into Ira's imagination, wearing a one-piece swimsuit and a radiant smile. One of the straps was slipping off her shoulder. Did Jackie Kennedy have boobs? She didn't look like she did, but hey, who could be sure? Yeah—he and Larry were going to have to get started on winning that medal pretty soon now.

But once Ira had joined Troop 144 and paid his membership dues—once he'd coughed up most of his savings account for a uniform, hiking boots, a backpack, a sleeping bag, and an official Boy Scout canteen—

Larry Fontenot stopped talking about Jackie Kennedy, or being brothers, or winning medals. In fact, he stopped talking to Ira completely, hanging out instead with a group of other guys in the troop who were just as skinny and rambunctious as he was—guys who rolled their eyes and made little gagging sounds whenever Ira approached. He became one of the troop's two untouchables, the lowest of the low. Whenever the patrols had to split into partners—for tent assignments, or for merit badges that depended on teamwork—all the other boys in the Badger Patrol immediately paired off, and Ira inevitably got stuck with Rupert Mimieux, a chronic bed-wetter with a trembling lower lip. Rupert's only saving distinction—in fact the only thing that kept him from being lynched by the other boys in Troop 144—was his distant connection to the actress Yvette Mimieux, supposedly his fifth cousin twice removed.

Nobody called Ira "Mitts" in Troop 144. Instead, they made up a host of clever names for him: "Mittelberg," "Mittelstein," and so on. Sometimes they got right to the point and called him "Jewboy" under their breath, just to make sure he got the message. They'd say this in arch, ironic tones, as if there was something incredibly witty about calling a Jewish kid "Jewboy." Ira took it in silence for a few months, then he said, "Hey, knock it off, will you?"—which caused them all to groan in unison, roll their eyes, and say, "Oh, for crying out loud, take a joke, will you? Honestly. You people." Once in a while they'd ask him for spare change, and if he happened not to have any, they'd make a big fuss over it, muttering in dark tones, "Oh, yeah, that's right, Mittelstein, you folks are tight with a nickel, aren't you?" And whenever they got the chance—during Chinese Fire Drills on the way to Indian Dancing lessons, for instance—they ditched him.

Now, in Larry's dimly-lit claustrophobic bedroom, Ira asked, "You're sure you don't remember anything about dumping me, huh?"

"I'm telling you, it was a million years ago," Larry said, and put the glittering knife back in its ankle sheath.

"It hurt, Larry. That really made me feel like shit. Having to tent with Rupert Mimieux."

"Water over the dam, man. Ancient history."

Ira shrugged. "Well, okay. I just thought I'd check," he said, and glanced at his watch. "I know I just got here, but I've got to be going. It took a while to find this place, and I told my folks I'd be right back."

Larry didn't move from the bed. "You look different," he said.

"Yeah. Well, I guess so. You know." Ira was suddenly aware of his hair, which had grown big and bushy and explosive during his years in college.

"How long's it been since we got together, man?"

Ira pursed his lips, trying to remember. "A while," he said. When had they last seen each other? At the Eagle ceremony the month Ira turned fifteen? "Six years, maybe?"

"We really lost touch."

"Yeah."

"I guess you got through with college. That makes you a college graduate, yeah?"

Ira nodded. "That's what it says on the diploma, I suppose. What about you?"

Larry smirked. "I don't think so. Let me check." He paused. "Nope."

Ira looked around Larry's room and felt the walls closing in on him. "Look, my folks are probably wondering where I am," he said, edging still closer toward the door. "I told them I'd be right back. Hey, I'll keep in touch, okay?"

"Scout's honor?" Larry said. "Let's not lose each other again, man."

"You bet." Ira turned the doorknob. "So long."

As Ira stood in Winstead's sniffing the ambrosial odor of hamburgers frying on the ancient grill, all of that seemed to have happened to someone else, in another lifetime. Surely it was time to forgive and forget, to move on. They weren't boys anymore. They weren't even young men. Whatever had happened back then was over and done with. He dialed Larry's number and listened to the phone ringing on the other end. It rang six times, and he was about to hang up, feeling a mixture of disappointment and relief, when Larry answered, sounding as if he'd been awakened from a nap. "Fontenot residence," he muttered.

"Larry? It's Ira. Ira Mittelman."

"Ira?"

"Mittelman. Ira Mittelman. It's been a long time, Larry." Larry didn't say anything, so Ira went on. "I'm in Kansas City, if you can believe that. I should have called you sooner, but I didn't have your number. I was wondering if we might get together while I'm in town."

There was a moment of dead silence, and Ira, convinced the connection had gone bad, was about to snap the phone back into its perch when

Larry said, "Yeah. Sure. I don't have much on my social calendar these days. Come out to the house after you get settled in."

"Maybe we could meet someplace for a drink?" Ira asked. "I don't know where anything is in Kansas City anymore, but I could use a drink. You name the place."

"Well, I tell you, I'm sort of stuck here at the house. Why don't you come over for a little while, then maybe you can go out by yourself. But I want to see you," Larry said. "You got the address?"

"It's in the phone book. I'll find you."

After another long pause, Larry said, "Hey, don't laugh. Lemme ask you: you put on any weight?"

"Have I—well, yeah, I guess so," said Ira. What kind of a question was that? "A few pounds. I'll be fifty in a couple of months. I mean, we're the same age, right?"

"I just turned in May."

"Wow. It's been a long time since we've seen each other."

"I got fat," Larry said. "Just so you'll know."

Ira tried to imagine Larry Fontenot fat. It was impossible. As a boy Larry had been a daredevil, a freckled, scrawny scrap of a kid, the kind of boy who went through a can of band-aids every week, never looking before he leapt, climbing to the highest rung on the jungle gym and then hanging there, suspended upside down, screaming "Look at me!" and banging his fists on his chest like a monkey.

"Really? You got fat?" he asked.

"Yeah. You didn't?"

"I don't know. No, I guess not. I mean . . . I could take off a few pounds. You know."

"Well, I'm fat," said Larry.

"Okay. Fat. Well, that's really something," Ira said. "Hey, look, I'll see you in a little while."

After he'd checked into his room at a nearby Holiday Inn, Ira got back into the Toyota and headed for Larry Fontenot's house. He took the cannister containing his father's ashes with him, resting it carefully on the passenger seat. He considered putting the passenger-side seatbelt around it, then told himself that was going too far. "Hi, Dad," he said, and patted the cannister. "We're in Kansas City now. Camp HaHaTonka, here we come." The route to Larry's house took Ira past his old school,

DeLesseps High. The eighty-year-old building still looked like the high school Andy Hardy went to in the movies, red brick and limestone, massive, thick-walled, seemingly indestructible—though DeLesseps High had in fact been closed, locked and shuttered, for five years now, the victim of dropping enrollments city-wide. Once upon a time it had been the cream of Kansas City's high schools, a tony place utterly convinced of its own greatness, the nearest you could get to a public prep school—but those days were long gone. How could they have closed DeLesseps High? How could something this solid and prosperous have fallen apart? The question—just the phrase "fallen apart"—put Ira in mind of Pauline once again, and in an instant he was replaying once again the moment in Cacciatore di Spello when she told him she was through with him for good; he could smell the fragrant steam rising off that platter of ravioli, and for a breath it seemed to him that the steam had somehow entered his rental car, and was fogging up in the inside of the windshield.

Turning west at 63rd Street, he crossed State Line Road and drove through winding, tree-lined streets into the Kansas-side suburbs until he reached Larry's address, a small, dismal ranch house from the early 1950s with peeling turquoise paint. Ira rang the doorbell and waited on the cracked concrete stoop. Presently Larry Fontenot opened the door and stood there with a newspaper in his hand. He hadn't been kidding on the phone: he was fat. His stomach hung over his belt, quivering there like a giant water balloon. Ira stared at him, searching for Larry amid the slack flesh of this face.

"Larry?"

Larry pushed the screen door outward, and said, "Come on in."

From another room Ira could hear a high, frantic voice shouting, "Praise the Lord!"

"That's Belinda," Larry said. "My wife."

Ira stepped into the house, and immediately sniffed the warm odor of something rotten in the air, perhaps meat left out too long on a countertop, or something dead caught in a trap behind the stove. It was a thick, sickly sweet smell, and put him in mind of the girl across the aisle on the flight to Kansas City, the one with the barf bag. He thought for a moment that the best and easiest thing to do would be to excuse himself right now, get the hell out of there, before he vomited on Larry's shoes. But the moment passed, and he held out his hand for Larry to shake.

"Your wife," Ira said. "Gosh, I didn't even know you were married."

"No," Larry said after a pause. "That's right. I guess you didn't. It's been a long time. You came to see me once, after my folks had moved south. I remember that. Then we sort of fell out of touch, didn't we?" There was a note of accusation in his voice. "I've been married for twenty years. I got two kids. One of my kids just graduated from high school—my eldest, Larry Junior."

"Is that right. You must be very proud."

Belinda's voice came floating out to them again. "Praise the Lord!" she shouted.

"I didn't want to go into any of this on the phone when you called," Larry said. "It's hard to talk about. People get the wrong idea. Belinda's an invalid. She's real sick."

"My god, that's terrible."

"She's in bed, she can't move hardly, and she's in a lot of pain most of the time, so it's hard for me to get out much. She's suffering something awful, has been ever since it happened. I just stay with her, mostly. Do for her what I can."

"What happened? What is it?"

"You want to sit down?" Larry asked, and motioned toward a sofa strewn with trash. He swept an arm through the papers and clothing, making room for Ira to plop down on one end. Larry took the Barca lounger by the television set, and once he was seated, he leaned forward, his hands on his knees. "Belinda got hit in the head with a skillet," he said. "It's been two years ago now. Came out of nowhere. Hit her right smack on the head and she hasn't been the same since."

"My gosh. A skillet."

"Cast iron."

"Oh, that's awful."

"She can't walk, can't get out of bed, really. So of course she lost her job. She can't work, can't do a thing. I just got laid off the week before it happened, too. Isn't that something? Belinda'd been on her job almost six months—two days shy of it, in fact. At six months her health insurance was set to kick in, and we'd all have been on her policy, the whole family. That would have been something, all of us covered and able to go to the doctor. . . ."

"Two days? You mean they wouldn't just give her the two days?"

"We tried—we pleaded with them. They said if she could just come down to work and put in two days at her desk, even if she didn't really do anything, just sat there, they'd look the other way. So I got her bundled up, drove her down to her office—she was a secretary at this big-shot accountant's office downtown? I tried to get her to sit there at her desk, just so we could say she'd been to work, but she couldn't sit up, and anyway, she'd started to say stuff by then."

"Oh, yeah?"

"Real loud. After a couple hours . . . well, they up and asked us to leave."

"That's terrible."

"She can't help herself. It's the Lord's work, this happening to her. It was a miracle."

"Wow. Is that right?"

"I know you're skeptical. Most folks are. But I was there. And let me tell you: there wasn't a building around for that skillet to fall out of. Nothing. Where's a skillet, a cast iron skillet, going to come from? We were out in the park, walking around, looking at flowers. I'm not kidding you," Larry said. He hunched lower in his chair and looked up at Ira. "It came from heaven. Just fell out of the sky. Tell me that ain't some kind of miracle. It was God's hand that brained my dear Belinda with that skillet. It was a wake-up call."

"Praise the Lord!" Belinda shouted from the back room.

"My gosh. So . . . how do you live? How are you able to put food on the table?"

"Oh, the Lord provides. We're on the county now. Welfare," Larry said. "I used to think I'd be too proud to be on welfare, but that's all in the past. We get a tub of peanut butter, tub of lard, some flour, powdered milk, some bulk cheese from the county every two weeks. Now and then they throw in a little meat if they got any. Chicken backs, that kind of thing. I do a little janitor work down at the church, and they give us some food, too. Last week we got a case of canned creamed corn. It's charity, but I ain't too proud to take it. Man's got to eat. And I don't look like I've been missing any meals, do I?"

Ira sat silently. What was there to say?

"Sometimes it's just fried dough with peanut butter, but we eat something every day," Larry continued. "Problem is, see, I was one week shy of being eligible for my pension from the fire department when they laid me off because of my weight, so I don't have my pension, and plus on top of that I can't work much because I threw my back out."

"My god."

"And then on top of that I have to be here for Belinda, because she can't get out of bed without it hurting so much, so she does her business in the bed all the time, and then somebody's got to clean it up, and the kids are too busy with their schooling and all. So all's I can say is, thank God the Lord Jesus is smiling on us and helping us out, because without His love I don't know where we'd be."

Again Ira sat in stunned silence. For years he'd carried a stone of resentment in his heart toward this guy—Larry Fontenot, the jerk who led him into the Boy Scouts and then turned on him—but that was all gone now. What use was it to hold on to that anger in light of what the world had done to Larry? Ira glanced around the living room, taking in the standard dime store portraits of Jesus looking sad and mysterious and Swedish, the cheaply-framed needlepoint "God Bless This House," the odor of decay and desperation in the air. Who would have wished this life on anybody?

"We wouldn't be alive today without Pastor Moody's church. I can tell you that much. God's truth," Larry said. "Moody's Pentecostal Calvary Fellowship. It's like our second home."

"Pentecostal. Oh, sure," said Ira. "Isn't it kind of like . . . I don't know." He wasn't sure how to proceed. "Southern Baptists, something along that line?"

"Aw, no way," Larry said, and his lip curled into a sneer. "Southern Baptists! We don't have much use for those folks. They say a man can be born again without ever receiving the baptism of the Holy Ghost! They'd have a man believe that some *don't* speak in tongues, while others do!"

"Is that right," said Ira.

"'And they were *all* filled with the Holy Ghost, and began to speak in other tongues, as the Spirit gave them utterance'—that's what the good book tells us. Pastor Moody says we might be the only true church of Christ Jesus in the whole country. Like Pastor Moody says, 'Blessed are the people who know the joyful sound.'"

"That's really something," Ira said.

"Pastor Moody, he has a small business. Slug-a-Bug? He does pest control during the week, then on Wednesday nights and Sunday mornings we meet right there in his home, in the basement. He's been kind enough to let me clean up there, couple times a week, and then we don't have to put anything in the collection plate come Sunday. Pastor Moody's the one who showed us that all this happening to Belinda was really God's way of showing us the true path." Larry paused. "Well, look, I've been gabbing up a storm. I don't get too many chances to talk to anybody these days, what with Belinda and all. So . . . what's up with you? You married?"

"Was. I got divorced."

"That's a shame."

"Yeah. It's a shame, all right. We were together for fifteen years, all told. Married for ten. Actually we even sort of stayed together after the divorce for a while. You know."

"Ain't that something."

"I feel terrible about it. Like I failed at something important, you know?"

"You got any kids?"

"No. We talked about it a lot. We really did. But it never got beyond the talking stage."

"Is that a fact. My kids are the light of my life. Larry Junior's a musician—he plays the drums in a Christian group, they've gone all over this part of the country playing their music for folks far and wide." Larry stroked the bladder of flesh beneath his chin. "Faith Renee, she's fifteen now, she's interested in going into the ministry, she says she feels the hand of God patting her on her shoulder every day of her life. So we're mighty blessed. Where'd you say you're living?"

"San Francisco."

"California?"

"That's the one."

After a moment, Larry said, "That's where all the homos are." He gazed at Ira, his eyes cloaked with suspicion.

"Well, yeah," Ira said with a shrug. "There's a lot of them out there, all right."

"You're living right smack in Sodom and Gomorrah," Larry said.

"Oh, no, that's the suburbs, Marin County," said Ira, hoping to lighten the moment.

Larry nodded without smiling. "So tell me, what line of work you in, Ira?" he asked. "You don't mind my asking? You went to college, right? You must doing okay for yourself."

"Well, yeah, I'm doing okay. I have a small business, repairing old books. I used to make books—you know, handcrafted books, you see them at craft fairs, handmade paper and all of that. That was interesting, but then about ten years ago I sort of slid into repairing old ones instead, and I find that I enjoy it more. I feel like I'm really doing something. I take something that's falling apart and put it back together again. That's the part I like best."

"Old books. Is that right?"

"The materials I work with—well, they're just so beautiful. Books used to be works of art. Calfskin, gold leaf, fine paper . . . I don't have any helpers or anything, it's just me. It keeps me happy, and it pays the bills, but I'm not getting rich or anything."

"Hey, tell me: you ever work on a copy of the Good Book?"

Ira thought a moment. "Oh, the Bible, you mean? Sure, lots of them. I can't remember a specific one right off. Last year I did a beautiful old Koran, though—"

"Oh, yeah. Uh-huh," Larry said after a moment. "That's not the same thing, now, is it?"

"Full-paneled calf binding, gorgeous thing, three hundred and fifty years old, one of the earliest English translations, gilt-stamped spine, really a museum piece."

"Yep," Larry said, but his attention had drifted. "So anyway, what brings you back to Kansas City after all these many years?" he asked.

"Well, it's kind of a strange errand, really. I feel kind of like an idiot even bringing it up, but that's—that's really sort of why I called you." He paused, and Larry shifted his gut in the Barca lounger. "Uh, well—my dad died, see. About a year ago now, almost."

"Oh, that's just a shame," Larry said. "I remember your dad. He was a good man."

"I guess so," Ira said, though that wasn't really how he would have described his father. "Anyway, well, see . . . he was cremated."

"That's too bad. On judgment day your dad's going to be in a heckuva fix. How're you supposed to get up out of your grave and praise the Lord and walk with Jesus if you been burned to a crisp?"

"We don't believe in cremation, either. Jews, I mean."

"Oh, yeah. That's right. I forgot. You're Jewish."

He forgot? Oh, please, Ira thought. *Don't make me laugh.* "Anyway," Ira said, "I've had his ashes stored in my apartment for quite a while, and now I'm taking him back to Camp HaHaTonka."

"Is that a fact!"

"He wanted to be scattered there. His ashes, I mean. He wanted them scattered at the camp. He left a note. It was his last wish. He liked it there. The truth is, I think HaHaTonka was the only place in the whole world where my mom wasn't on his case about anything. He didn't have to do any chores around the house or go to the synagogue or take stuff to the dump or whatever else she wanted him to do. I think his favorite part was sitting up with the other dads around the campfire after lights-out. All of us were in our tents already, trying to sleep, and he could just sit out there by the campfire and smoke cigarettes and drink beer with the guys. My dad didn't have any friends. I don't know why, but he never had any. He was kind of a lonely guy, I guess. I don't think I ever realized how much he liked it at camp. I mean, I always knew he liked it, but you know."

"I ain't been back down to HaHaTonka in a long, long time," Larry said. "Larry Junior was in Scouts for a little while but we never had the money to send him down there. It takes money, you know. I don't know how my folks afforded it all those years. They did without so's I could go down there and have a few weeks of fun. Anyway, Larry Junior didn't take to Scouting much. I don't know why. He just didn't take to it." His voice was soft, full of longing.

Ira said, "So, anyway . . . I figured maybe we could drive down there together. If you could get some time off from what you're doing here. You know, for old times' sake." He hadn't been sure he would say this until the words were out of his mouth. Another voice in his head was telling him to flee, to get the hell out of there and leave Larry Fontenot, his bloated desperation, his bed-ridden wreck of a wife behind. These past few minutes in Larry's presence, listening to his tale of woe and soaking in the sickly-sweet smell of decay in this living room, Ira had felt a wave of sorrow lapping at him, threatening to wash him out to sea. How could someone his own age have come to such grief, such utter destitution? *A scout is trustworthy, loyal, helpful, friendly* . . . why was there nothing in that litany about pity? About empathy?

Larry sat back in the barca lounger. "Oh, that's a nice idea, Ira, but well, I don't know." His eyes narrowed. "It's awful hard for me to get away here. I got Belinda to take care of."

"Couldn't your children look after her for a day—day and a half, tops?"

"Nah. You can't ask kids to do that sort of thing for their mother. It wouldn't be right." Larry paused, and his face closed up a bit, like a purse being drawn shut. "You know. On account of the cleaning up and all. It wouldn't be right for them to see their mom like that."

"Well, how about this: maybe all three of us could go. We could take her with us."

Larry shook his head. "Oh, no. That'd be a real mistake, I think. Travel's awful hard on Belinda. We drive to church every Sunday in my van, and she just about goes through the roof from the pain of it all. I hit a pothole, she lets out a scream like you wouldn't believe. She says she feels like our Lord Jesus must have felt up on that cross."

"My gosh. That's horrible," Ira said, but then he plunged on. "See the thing is," he said, "I've got to do this. It's the last thing I'll ever be able to do for my father, and I've come all this way. I've got to do it. And I'm not sure I could find my way to HaHaTonka by myself. After all these years, all those back roads, I'd get lost, it's been so long. And I don't have much time, either. I have to get back to work, back in San Francisco, day after tomorrow. Things are going bananas back there." He thought for a moment that he'd have to tell Larry about Pauline, about their divorce and subsequent romance, about crazy Kenny and Cacciatore di Spello and the whole sad wreckage of his heart.

But no, he couldn't say any of that. He couldn't tell Larry about Pauline. What would Larry say? "All those summers we went down there, we were just on the bus and somebody else was driving," Ira went on, "and I never paid attention to anything. I was too busy singing 'Ninety-nine Bottles of Beer on the Wall.' I wouldn't have the first clue as to how to drive down there. I'm doing this for my dad. It's his dying wish, you know?"

Larry nodded, and gazed at Ira with an expression that might have been cunning in a thinner face. "I see your point," he said. "You're a good man, Ira, trying to do this for your dad and all."

What Ira wanted to say was, *No, listen to me—if I was a good man I wouldn't be here. I wouldn't have to do something like this. If I'd been a better son while my father was alive, I could have left that cannister in the closet next to the tennis racket. Better still, I could have tossed it into the garbage ten months ago, and gone about my business.*

"I'm tempted, I don't mind telling you. But I don't know, Ira."

"You think you could find your way down there?"

"It's been a while, but I got a good memory," Larry said. "I could get you down to HaHaTonka, that's for certain. But I don't know. . . ."

"I'd make it worth your while, Larry. This means a lot to me," Ira said. "Your time is worth something, and I'd be glad to pay you."

"Is that a fact."

"Say a hundred dollars for the day?"

"Well now, that's a real generous offer, Ira."

"That's on top of gas, and food, and lodging, too, if it comes to that." Ira paused. "And anything else that comes up. Incidentals, you know."

Larry made a show of considering this, thoughtfully stroking the fat where his chin once had been. After a moment he slapped his knees and stood up. "Tell you what. Why don't we talk this over with Belinda. You want to meet her?"

"Oh, gee. Do you think that would be too much of a strain on her?" asked Ira. He scratched his head. If it smelled this bad in the living room, how bad could it smell in her bedroom? He'd never had much of an appetite for hospital visits. He thought again of how he'd failed to spend much time with his father during the old man's slow-motion tumble into death. He'd had a hundred chances to fly up to Seattle to spend a weekend at his father's bedside. He could have whiled away hour after hour, dutifully giving him sips of orange juice or bits of crushed ice, listening to embittered recollections of Drivers Education fiascos, school board idiocy, various indignities his father had suffered at the hands of Jew-hating bastards. Now all those chances were gone, vanished.

"She'd love to see you. She knows all about you. We're blood brothers, ain't we?"

Ira couldn't remember. He and Larry had spent a lot of time talking about becoming blood brothers when they were kids, but he couldn't recall if they'd ever actually taken the plunge. It would have meant getting a razor blade and cutting each other someplace, on the arm or the finger or something like that, and then letting their blood mix together.

They'd seen it done on television, on Davy Crockett or The Lone Ranger or maybe Spin and Marty. It looked like it hurt, but that what was brotherhood was all about, wasn't it—suffering a little bit but going through it together?

"Yeah, sure, I guess so," he said, and obediently followed Larry through a narrow, trash-strewn hallway back to Belinda's bedroom. It was a small, airless room, and most of the space was taken up with her hospital bed. Belinda lay propped up, surrounded by pillows that cushioned her head. Her hair was short, a dark skullcap plastered to her moist forehead. Her eyes glittered, and her nostrils were black and wet. Belinda's nightgown was splattered with the remains of a meal, something that might have been strained carrots or sweet potatoes. The room smelled heavily of dust and baby food and diapers.

"Belinda, here's my old friend Ira. Ira Mittelman," Larry said. "He's the Jewish fella I told you all about. The one that called before."

Jewish fella? So what was all that crap a few minutes ago about *Oh, you're Jewish? I forgot?*

"He's my blood brother from way, way back. Remember me telling you about him? I told you all kinds of stuff."

"Praise the Lord," said Belinda. "Jews are our special brethren. We love the Jews. They are chosen among all the peoples of the earth."

"Well. Thanks. I certainly appreciate that. It's very kind of you," said Ira.

"Praise the Lord. His way is great," Belinda said. "The path is a narrow path but it is the only path to righteousness. Praise him." Her words came out in a tumble, like gravel pouring from a truckbed.

"Amen," Larry said, and quickly looked at Ira.

"Oh. Amen. You bet," said Ira.

"Ira's back in town on a special errand. He's on a mission."

"From God?" she asked, suddenly wide-eyed.

"More or less," Ira said. "I guess you could say that."

"Oh, praise him. Praise the Lord of Hosts," Belinda demanded.

This time Ira was ready. "Amen!" he said, pumping his voice full of fervor.

Larry stroked Belinda's damp forehead. "So I was wondering, honey, if maybe one of the women from church could look after you, just for tomorrow, while Ira and I go on this special mission from God?"

Belinda's face drew itself together into a wince. "For the hour is coming, in which all that are in the grave shall hear his voice! And shall come forth, they that have done good, unto the resurrection of life! And they that have done evil, unto the resurrection of damnation!"

"Amen," Ira said.

"That's a big Praise the Lord," said Larry. He fidgeted for a moment then moved to the foot of her bed. "So what do you think, honey? Could I take off, just for tomorrow? I'll have to miss Sunday church, but Pastor Moody'll understand. I'll be doing a good deed, going on a mission of mercy. And Ira here says he'll pay for everything, all our expenses, too. Plus something for my time. He's going to pay me a hundred dollars on top of expenses."

"This is a holy pilgrimage," she said with an air of finality.

"Well, yes. Something like that," Ira said. "I have to fulfill my father's last wish. I know it sounds sort of corny," he added, then stopped himself.

"Gives me the chance to be the Good Samaritan," Larry offered. "Yes, indeed."

"It's God's will that brought you to us," Belinda said, and then she fell into a fit of deep-voiced, phlegmy gibberish that started with something that sounded like "hubba-hubba" and went downhill from there, putting Ira in mind of all those moronic evenings of "hey-yah, hey-yah" he and the other boys were forced to endure, lurching around the Roebling High School gymnasium, half-naked. Belinda's arms and legs drummed the sheets in an ecstatic hokey-pokey dance. Spit covered her chin. After a moment the fit passed, her voice wound down and slowly died away, and Belinda sagged back against her pillows. "That was the spirit of God, the Holy Ghost, coming over me," she said proudly. "It just pours over me like honey."

"Belinda? Baby? Are you sure?" Larry asked. "It'll just be for one day."

"Jesus spoke to me," she replied. "He told me that you and your Jew friend here—"

"Ira," Larry prompted.

"You're to go on a long trip. This trip will be your trial. Jesus told me that. I heard his voice. He had the nicest voice. He sounded like Clint Black. He always does."

"Clint Black's her favorite country singer of all time," Larry said to Ira. "She's in love with Clint Black, but I don't mind."

"I don't think those thoughts," Belinda said. "You think I'm thinking those thoughts, but I'm not. You heareth the devil's voice, and you think it speaketh the truth." Her smile was beatific, revealing a row of small teeth the color of fieldmice. "He is everywhere, praise him."

"Amen," said Larry. "Praise the Lord. Now look here, Belinda." He cleared his throat. "Ira and me, we'll be taking off tomorrow morning first thing. I'm going to call Mrs. Dunhill from the church, okay? She'll come over and keep you company while I'm gone. Maybe Pastor Moody himself'll come by. You'll be in good hands, darling."

"The Lord'll be with me," Belinda said. "He'll be right here mopping my brow. And he'll be with you, too. Jesus is everywhere. You think you'll be driving, but he'll be the one behind the wheel. Jesus himself—he'll be driving every bit of the way."

"Amen," said Larry. "Praise the Lord. You just said a mouthful, Belinda darling."

Ira sensed that Larry and Belinda were staring at him, waiting—so he swallowed deeply and said, "Oh, yes. Yes indeed. Praise the Lord."

■ ■ ■

He awoke the next morning to the sound of church bells. For few moments he listened to them as he counted cracks in the plaster ceiling of his room at the Holiday Inn and pondered the day that lay before him. Then the telephone rang on his nightstand. It was Larry, saying he'd be by in fifteen minutes to pick him up. In the shower, Ira leaned against the tile and let the water pound him in the face. He wasn't certain, but he thought he might be crying. He'd had bad dreams, Pauline dreams, dreams in which he'd called her and listened to the phone ringing and somehow, by pressing the telephone hot and hard against his ear, he could hear through the receiver the sound of Kenny fucking her, crying "Give me a woman with bullet tits!"—then the rhythmic sighs of her pleasure that he knew so well, building to their familiar crescendo—and then somehow he found himself transported to Pauline's tiny apartment in Presidio Heights; he was sneaking up on the closed door of her bedroom, he was going to kill Kenny, that miserable mixed-up putz. Ira knew it was wrong, he knew that killing Kenny wasn't going to solve anything, but he was going to do it anyway, he couldn't stop himself—he was going to strangle him and throw the body out the window into the dumpster in the alley behind Pauline's building—but when he pushed the door open and flung himself into the bedroom, he saw Belinda, Larry's wife, tied up in the bed, legs akimbo, shitting a brown stream onto the sheets and screaming "Hubba-Hubba!" at the top of her lungs.

He stepped out of the shower and toweled off, pummeled by a wave of regret so strong it threatened to send him reeling back to his bed. He dressed slowly, his hands moving as if underwater. At the end of his visit to Larry and Belinda's house the previous evening, just as he was walking out the door, he should have pleaded longer and harder to use his rented Toyota for the drive to HaHaTonka. But Larry'd been so relentless in his insistence on using his own car, a rusted-out Plymouth minivan beater with a broken passenger-side window, that Ira had finally given in with a shrug. This morning the matter was clear to him: he ought to have put up more of a fight (his Toyota coupe had air conditioning, for one thing, and a good stereo—and all the windows rolled up, and stayed there). Oh, well, what the hell, he thought, waiting on the curb, holding the cannister of his father's ashes cradled in his arms. It wasn't worth raising a ruckus about the car. Besides, what did it matter? For that matter, why was he doing this, anyway? None of it made any sense. He'd stopped even trying to figure out what he was up to. The entire trip was foolishness—an escape from his life, but what kind of escape was it, when he dragged his life with him, slung over his shoulder like a leaden duffle bag?

When Larry's rusted-out van pulled up with a great squealing of brakes, Ira noticed the sticker on the back bumper: "*BAN GUNS! MAKE THE STREETS SAFE FOR A GOVERNMENT TAKEOVER!*" He sighed heavily. This was a bad idea. He got in and shut the passenger door, which caused the broken window to rattle in its wrapping of masking tape. "On the road again!" Larry sang. "Let's roll, brother!"

Once they'd left the city streets behind and the southern suburbs yielded to open fields, Ira relaxed into the passenger seat, clutching his father's ashes against his stomach. "This baby ain't been out of Kansas City in two years now," Larry said. "Just been going back and forth to church every Sunday, not much else to do. I get Belinda settled in the back there—" he pointed a thumb over his shoulder toward the rear of the van, where the back seat had been removed—"and we drive over to Pastor Moody's. She screams a lot, but she says she wants to go, so we go.

Anyway, this old van needs to get out on the road once in a while." Larry drove the car as if riding a rodeo bull—he hunched over the steering wheel and beat a syncopated tattoo on the sun-faded dashboard. Ira watched the countryside go by, and realized that rural Missouri was prettier than he'd remembered it. Hardwood forests grew up to the edges of the highway in lush stands of sugar maple, oak, shagbark hickory, ash, walnut, beech and birch and basswood. The terrain rolled, rising and falling gently. Everything was blooming. Wildflowers burst into color along the median strip in gay patches of red, blue, yellow and orange. Roadside signs advertised homemade honey and sugar cured hams and bacon, bentwood furniture, pottery, apple wine. This was a trip he'd made many times as a boy, but he'd never paid any attention to it. He'd always been focused on something else, something coming up, rather than the moment at hand. He'd been in a fog throughout his childhood, it seemed to him now. He hadn't known a goddamn thing about the world.

He glanced down at the cannister containing his father's ashes, resting now in his lap. What would his father say if he knew who was going along for the ride? Ira's dad always spoke kindly of Larry and the rest of the boys in Troop 144, even though he must have been aware of what Ira was going through in the Scouts. He'd have had to be blind to have missed it. Oddly enough, though, he never asked Ira anything about what was going on, and Ira, for his part, kept quiet about it, too. It was the one thing he wanted to tell his father, and the one thing he couldn't bring himself to say. He felt most tempted to bring it up when the two of them were preening in the mirror together before a troop meeting—just at those moments when his Dad was recalling his poverty-stricken, Scoutless boyhood, and saying proudly, "Look at the two of us, will you?" But week after week Ira held back. How could he have slipped it into the conversation at that point? He hoped his dad would mention something, maybe just ask him a question ("So, son, how're things going with you and the other guys in the troop?")—but no, not a chance; in fact Mr. Mittelman acted as if the boys of Troop 144 were about the best group of guys in the world. "These fellas—they're going to be your friends for life, Ira, mark my words. You camp out with guys, you backpack with them, you go through mud and rain and muck with them, you're friends for the long haul," he told him. Ira didn't want to be the one to disillusion his father. His dad seemed so disillusioned by life already. And besides, who would want to admit to his dad that he was the least popular guy in the troop? *I'm the lowest of the low, Dad. Your son, your only son—on camp-outs I'm paired off with a bed-wetter because nobody else will tent with me.* His father was already edgy enough; Ira imagined him falling into a great fit of foot-pounding anxiety at the news, eventually slamming a hole in the floor and perhaps breaking something important inside his foot at the same time.

There was also his mother to contend with. She was convinced that he was made of papier-maché, and wanted him at home where she could keep an eye on him and head off any possible injuries. Nothing would have pleased her more than to hear that he was miserable in the Scouts. It had all been his father's idea, from the very beginning, and his mother didn't miss any chances to bring up that fact. In the great war between his mother and father, Ira was the most hotly-contested piece of property, the Holy of Holies, the battlefield where they'd dug their deepest trenches. His mother wanted him to be studying for his Bar Mitzvah, which loomed in the not-too-distant future. She also wanted him to practice the violin and read good books instead of hanging out with non-Jewish kids she'd never met, learning God knows what. "Scout Lore," she'd sneer, and make a little hacking sound in the back of her throat as if a chicken bone were stuck there.

At night as a boy Ira could sit silently in his bedroom, frozen in place, and hear his parents arguing about him downstairs on a regular basis. "Tell me something: what good is it going to do him to learn how to lash two sticks together?" his mother would demand. "When is that going to come in handy?"

"You never know, Delores. That's the point," Mr. Mittelman would reply. "That's what the motto is all about: 'Be Prepared.' You learn to lash two sticks together so that if you ever have to do it, you'll be able to do it. You need to transport a wounded buddy out of a remote mountainous region—you lash some sticks together to form a makeshift stretcher, and you're on your way. It might be twenty years later—it might be *thirty* years later—but you'll remember, and you'll know how to do it. That's the Boy Scouts in a nutshell. Do you see my point?"

"No, I don't. What I see," his mother would continue, her voice rising into a rich contralto, "is a bunch of middle-aged men trying to be kids again, pushing their boys around, making them run around the woods in ridiculous costumes, whooping and hollering like wild Indians, eating Spam cold out of the can. Spam! Do you know what's in that?"

"I ate Spam during the war."

"Pig lips, that's what. I read about this in *McCall's*."

"Listen, G.I.s ate it all the time, it didn't kill anybody. I knew guys who'd eat it straight out of the can with their fingers."

"That's disgusting."

"If it was good enough for the guys in my outfit, it's good enough for Ira. A little Spam isn't going to hurt him. Trust me on this," his father said, in an authoritative tone that seemed to indicate that the conversation was over.

But his mother simply shifted her focus. "And what about his Bar Mitzvah?" she demanded. "Will he be ready? Do you think he's going to have the time to learn his *haftorah?* Are you kidding? How could he? When does he have the time to practice? Everybody else will be ready, all the other boys, but not Ira. We'll have to call up Rabbi Fish and say, 'Rabbi, Ira can't be Bar Mitzvah'd. He's a good boy, but he's been spending all his time with *goyim,* playing cowboys and Indians, lashing two sticks together, so he didn't learn his *haftorah.*' Then you'll be happy."

Before he joined Troop 144, Ira hadn't thought much about the fact that the troop met at a nearby church. He'd never spent any time in churches and didn't have an opinion of them one way or the other. But once he'd begun to go to troop meetings, he soon realized that the location, despite its close proximity to his house, was hardly what he would have called ideal. He was grateful for the fact that the meetings actually were in the church's basement assembly hall, rather than in the hushed, salvation-choked atmosphere of the sanctuary—but even in the assembly hall, he couldn't ignore the fact that this was, after all, a house of Christian worship. The assembly hall was low-ceilinged, dingy, and smelled faintly of mildew and vinegar, but he wouldn't have minded any of that. It was the large plaster crucifix hanging on one wall that got to him—a particularly gruesome piece of statuary, even for crucifixes. Jesus was nearly naked, covered by a flimsy loincloth that looked like it was going to fall off in about two seconds. He wore a crown of thorns the size of a sombrero, and the nails sticking from his wrists and ankles were as big as railroad spikes. To make matters worse, there were gobbets of blood splattered all over him—the poor schmuck was drenched in it. At random moments during Scout meetings, Ira would look up from what he was doing—practicing Indian sign language or morse code, honing the fine art of lanyard-weaving, or identifying animal tracks from a guidebook—and gaze at the blood-splattered, emaciated figure of Jesus on the cross, tormented, bug-eyed, writhing in agony. All Ira could think about was how much it looked like it hurt to be up there. Ouch—those spikes! He rubbed the hollow of his wrist and felt how sensitive it was. Who could have devised something this gory? Scoutmaster Cooney opened every meeting with a long-winded prayer which ended, "In Jesus' name, amen." The prayer was printed on mimeographed sheets which were handed around so everyone could join in. Ira recited the prayer along with the other boys, but when they came to that last line he just moved his lips silently, like a goldfish in a tank. One night he noticed several Scouts peering at him intently at the end of the prayer, trying to see if he was going to recite the last line along with the group. He met their gaze for a brief moment, smiled wanly, then looked down at his shoes.

▪ ▪ ▪

They'd fallen silent for half an hour when Larry asked, "Hey, you still in touch with Rupert Mimieux?"

"No. Rupert Mimieux? Of course not. Why?"

"I thought you two were friends! You and Rupe the Stupe."

Ira turned in his seat to stare at Larry's profile. "Why would you think that?" he asked. .

"Rupert's a big man in Kansas City nowadays. He's a celebrity. Mimieux Chevrolet!"

"We just tented together, Larry. We didn't even like each other. I haven't seen him since our last year at camp. I told you, I've been living in San Francisco. How would I know anything about Rupert Mimieux?"

"He's a celebrity—guy's on TV every night. 'Mimiuex Chevrolet! It's where the deals are!' Got so you can't watch TV without seeing old Rupe the Stupe's face five times an hour. 'Mimiuex Chevrolet! It's where the deals are!' Got it coming out my ears."

"I hardly knew him," Ira insisted. "I couldn't stand him, in fact. If I hadn't had to tent with him I wouldn't have given him the time of day."

"I thought you two were buddies."

"Nobody else would tent with me. You know that," Ira said.

"Oh, come on."

"It's okay. I'm not mad anymore. Honest. That's all ancient history, over and done with. But please—don't act like you don't remember."

Larry shifted nervously in the driver's seat. "I don't know what you're talking about."

Ira slumped in his seat. Just the mention of Rupert Mimieux and a whole wound-up ball of rotten memories came unraveling in front of him, starting with the terrible confusion he'd felt all those years ago concerning Yvettte Mimieux, who was supposedly Rupert's distant cousin.

There was a lot of speculation among the boys in Troop 144 about whether or not Yvette Mimieux was a real blonde; some boys said you could tell by the eyebrows that she was really a brunette, while another contingent held that the eyebrows had nothing to do with it, and you had to look at the pussy itself to get the real dope. Striking what he hoped was a thoughtful pose, Ira listened to these heated discussions from the edge of the circle. The other boys in the troop were just as inexperienced in sexual matters as he was, but they talked as though they'd been getting laid for years.

When he was a Boy Scout, Ira had never seen an actual picture of a fully naked girl. They were hard to come by back in those days. The sex pamphlets his parents had given him for his tenth birthday to explain "The Facts of Life" didn't have any photos, nude or otherwise, just a series of cutaway diagrams of men's and women's sexual organs that left him feeling insecure about the size of his penis. Just one nude photo of a girl would have been nice. He'd rummaged through Ruthie's underwear drawer, and had held up her bras and examined them, but that was about as close as he'd gotten. After much pleading on Ira's part, Larry had finally come over with a few of his father's wilted old issues of *Playboy,* but when he flipped them open in the privacy of Ira's bedroom, it turned out that the centerfold photographs had been taken through what looked like several layers of something—venetian blinds, candy bar wrappers, surgical gauze, it was hard to tell. Their poses were so coy, their limbs so artfully arranged that he couldn't get a good, solid peek at anything.

Ira tried to imagine Yvette Mimieux naked, and couldn't come up with much. She looked great in a bikini, though, and he could spend five minutes at a time driving himself crazy just thinking about her in one. He was so desperate to get a look at a naked woman that he spent twenty minutes at a time gazing at the photo of Venus di Milo in the World Book. He wasn't really all that attracted to her—not only because she was a statue, but because she didn't have any arms, and was therefore technically a cripple. She also had no pubic hair at all, nor did she have anyplace where it looked like pubic hair should have been. The truth was, until all the controversy about Yvette Mimieux's pubic hair arose in Troop 144, Ira hadn't been one hundred per cent sure in his own mind that girls really did have hair down there. He hoped they did—it seemed only fair that if guys did, then girls should, too—but somehow it seemed unlikely. He'd seen some paintings of nude women at the Nelson Art Museum, and none of them showed any pubic hair. These were very old paintings, though, and Ira figured that women could have changed over the last three hundred years. The whole issue of girls and pubic hair was very intriguing to him, but finally he told himself that it was like questions about God; you could talk about it all you wanted to—you could debate the issue this way and that from now until the end of time—but the bottom line was that nobody really knew the answer.

If he'd had a brother, things would have been completely different. An older brother—that would have been just the thing. If he'd had an older brother, he could have just asked a few questions. Every time he'd asked Ruthie anything about sex, she looked at him like he was some sort of pervert and punched him in the stomach; and so finally he stopped asking her anything at all, and instead retreated to the dark silence of his bedroom closet, where he sat perched on stacks of old *Life* and *Look* magazines and pondered the enigma of sex in solitude.

His first wet dream came as a frightening surprise. Sure, it felt good while it lasted, but it was also a lot messier than he'd expected, for one thing. It meant you had to wash your hands and your pajamas and probably your sheets, too. The sex pamphlets his parents had given him hadn't prepared him for any of this—but the Boy Scout Handbook reassured him (in its chapter on "personal health") that this sort of "nocturnal emission" was "perfectly natural and healthy and a sign that nature has taken care of the situation in its own manner." This was vaguely reassuring news, even though Ira didn't really understand what the Handbook meant by "the situation." It went on to say: "There are those boys who do not let nature have its own way with them but cause emissions themselves. This may do no physical harm to them, but may cause them to worry." These two sentences occupied Ira for an entire hour in his closet. He rolled them over and over again in his mind: "There are those boys who do not let nature have its way own way with them. . . ." Was he one of those boys? Was he the type not to let nature have its own way with him? And just what the hell did that mean? He wondered if Rupert Mimieux had wet dreams, along with peeing in his sleeping bag. Maybe wet dreams were related to bed-wetting. That thought caused the floor to open up beneath him, and sent him tumbling into a fresh new basement of despair. All that tenting with Rupert Mimieux had finally left its sticky mark on him.

The Boy Scout Handbook had nothing listed in the index under "sex." It went straight from "service projects" to "sheet bend," a complicated type of knot that Ira never got the hang of. Anyway, in the aftermath of his first wet dream, he suddenly found himself wary of the entire subject of sex, and even if there had been a page in the Handbook devoted to the subject, he'd have torn it out and flushed it down the toilet. He reconsidered the entire Yvette Mimieux situation: when it came right down to it, why was he supposed to care about Yvette Mimieux? She was undoubtedly a babe, as she had demonstrated so clearly in *Where the Boys Are* and *The Time Machine*. She was a movie star—but so what? And okay, so she was related to Rupert somehow. Big deal! Rupert had never talked to her, never written to her, never seen her in his life, didn't know where she lived, had no clue about her whatsoever. He hadn't even *seen The Time Machine!* It wasn't like he would have been able to arrange an all-night orgy with her for everybody in the troop, so they could say, "Hey, everybody—I did it with Yvette Mimieux." That would have been something, definitely—but it was out of the question. Forget about it. Not a chance. In fact, when a few of the wiry, suntanned, tow-headed guys in the troop (the same guys who made the gagging sounds whenever Ira approached them) suggested the idea of the orgy to Rupert, he asked them what the word "orgy" meant, and they took turns punching him. So instead of his Yvette Mimieux connection turning into a plus for Rupert—something that might have taken the edge off the bed-wetting and the sniveling—it ended up counting for shit.

Rupert's father made matters even worse. He had no business getting involved in Boy Scouts, because he was a soft-bellied, nervous, sweaty guy who commanded no respect from children, and had no leadership potential whatsoever. His idea of giving an order was to start pleading with the boys to do something: "Come on, fellas, get the flag out and unfold it, will you, please? Aw, come on." One of the things Ira held against Mr. Mimieux was that he'd forced his son to go through life named Rupert—which left the door open for the other boys in Troop 144 to call him "Stupert," "Rupe the Stupe," "Poopert," "Rupert the Dupert," and other clever names. Who would do that to a kid?

Ira got to know Rupert's father much better than he wanted to, because Mr. Mimieux hung around the tent a lot when they went on camping trips or to Camp HaHaTonka in the summer. "You and Rupert—you're a couple of crazy characters," Mr. Mimieux would say with limp bravado, punching Ira tentatively in the upper arm. "Oh, yeah, you two kids are something else. Oh, Nellie, look out for these two crazy guys." He'd go on weakly exploring this vein, trying to construct a wacky friendship between the two boys, as if they'd chosen to be tentmates and were having the time of their lives hanging out together. But in reality, they had little to say to one another, and Ira, for his part, resented terribly his having to tent with Rupert—resented the amonia smell of urine in the night, the muffled sobs, the constant mewling—resented most of all simply being lumped with Rupert, labeled as one of the two pariahs of the troop.

Until he realized the situation was hopeless, Ira spent a good deal of time and energy at troop meetings trying to re-align himself, to form other partnerships in the Badger Patrol, so that when it came time for camping trips and then Camp HaHaTonka, he could move out of Rupert's tent and bunk with somebody else in the patrol—but everyone he asked said, "Hey, Mittelberg, cool your jets. You and Stupert are a pair, pal. You're like Ozzie and Harriet. We don't know which one of you's Harriet yet." He even approached Larry Fontenot from time to time for a while, hoping for a reconciliation, but Larry just shook his head in a weary gesture of disbelief, as if Ira had suggested jumping off a cliff.

Every morning at Camp HaHaTonka Mr. Mimieux had to come to their tent and get Rupert's sleeping bag before breakfast, so he could air it out on a nearby tree limb. All the other kids hung around observing this routine, their silent faces clouded with a mixture of awe and disgust, as if they were watching charred bodies being pulled out of a car wreck. "Gosh, son, I sure wish you'd quit spilling orange juice in your bunk," Mr. Mimieux would announce in a loud voice, as if that was going to throw anyone off the scent. The boys taunted him as if he were someone their own age. "Hey, Mr. Mimieux," they'd call, "got a match?"

"No, sorry," he'd say, nervously patting his pockets.

"Your face and my ass!" they'd all yell, then they'd tear off into the woods to kill frogs. They never talked to the other fathers that way. Even Ira's father came in for more respect than Mr. Mimieux, if only because his nervous foot made him seem more capable of random violence. The other fathers kept away from Mr. Mimieux, as though they, too, were tempted to taunt him, and were trying to control the urge. The fathers of Troop 144 spent much of their time together smoking cigarettes and drinking, exchanging World War II stories in which they played gritty, hardboiled, unshaven roles in minor battles that Ira had never heard of.

Ira's first year at Camp HaHaTonka, it seemed to him that the fathers were having most of the fun. He was homesick—he'd never been away from home before—and so every night the first week he sat tearfully on the edge of his cot and wrote a poignant little postcard to his mother, along the lines of "I think I might be dying. I don't know what's wrong with me, I just don't feel good, and I'm getting worse. Come get me fast, before I'm dead. Your loving son, Ira." Each morning he'd mail the previous night's postcard, then he'd hang out by the entrance to the camp, waiting for his parents' car to come barreling along in a cloud of dust to rescue him. They never showed up.

By the end of three-week session, though, he had to admit he was glad they'd left him there. He'd come to enjoy his solitude, his freedom from the intense day-to-day grind of being a part of his family. And when the next summer rolled around, he found himself looking forward to HaHaTonka with genuine relish, despite the fact that by this time he'd already come to understand that Larry Fontenot had really and truly dumped him, and he'd be tenting with Rupert Mimieux for the rest of his life.

Camp HaHaTonka afforded more than just a chance to goof off for a few weeks in the summer. Ambitious boys could earn merit badges here—gobs of them, if they applied themselves. Merit badges were important, because you needed to pile them up in order to work your way up the ladder in Scouting. There were merit badge classes for sissies every day like basketry and leatherwork, and then there were the more all-American, testosterone-popping variety: canoeing, lifesaving, swimming, marksmanship, archery, fishing, pioneering and so on. You could learn how to walk like an Indian—pushing off with your toes for every step, coming down lightly on your heels, your toes pointed straight ahead, traveling lightly, keeping your chin up, swinging your arms loosely, gliding through the woods as if sneaking up on an encampment of enemy soldiers.

You could work on your Indian sign language, too. First everyone in Troop 144 learned the sign language for "go to hell" ("you-go-land-many-fire-smoke"), then they expanded their repertoire to tell each other get fucked, as well ("make-baby-you"). There were demonstrations of woodcarving, and small kits you could buy at the canteen that would allow you to carve your own neckerchief slide in the shape of a bear. There were supervised hikes where you could learn the tricks of the experts, like putting a pebble in your mouth to keep from getting thirsty. Camp HaHaTonka had everything.

For Ira, though, what was best about it was that his father couldn't stay at camp with him for the entire three weeks. During the summer Mr. Mittelman earned extra money by teaching Drivers Ed at local community colleges. In these classes his pupils were older than his usual tenth and eleventh grade high school students during the school year, but they weren't any more adept behind the wheel—in fact, since many of them had been out of school a while, these summer school students were more apt to mouth off, less willing to listen to advice. The result was that Mr. Mittelman was involved in a minor car wreck at least once a week. He'd drive down to Camp HaHaTonka for one weekend every summer during Troop 144's three-week stay at the camp, arriving on Friday afternoon, his eyes bloodshot, and his hands shaking so much he could barely light a cigarette. He'd join Ira's table in the chow hall and make a clown out of himself, using the tines of his fork to flip creamed chipped beef at other folks around the table, making manic jokes about saltpeter in the food, and carrying on like a teenager.

Then on Sunday afternoon he'd have to drive back to the city to get ready for another week of teaching. The moment of his departure was usually the occasion for a brief lecture. "You know how lucky you are, son?" he'd ask Ira.

"Yes."

"I don't think you do."

"I do, dad."

"You're out here in the great outdoors with these fantastic guys."

"I know."

"I don't think you do," his father would say with a sigh. Then he'd climb into his car and drive away—and as Ira watched his dad disappear into the dust of the gravel road, he felt free again, as if he'd just been pulled out of a lake full of glue. That feeling lasted a moment, until the guilt started nibbling away at his innards again, a sensation that made him imagine that some angry little carnivore that was trapped inside his stomach and was eating its way out.

If his dad had been around all the time, Ira would have had to show up early at every merit badge class and scurry around from morning until nightfall looking restless and driven. He would have had to demonstrate the fact that he was trustworthy, loyal, helpful, friendly, courteous, kind, obedient, cheerful, thrifty, brave, clean and reverent all goddamn day long. On his own, when the angry nibbling carnivore inside his stomach would let him, he could slack off a bit, working away at his merit badges at his own pace. Every day he got his assignments done and still gave himself plenty of time to just sit and think awhile. That was the best part of all—just sitting by himself and letting his mind wander. These weeks at HaHaTonka were the first chances he'd ever had to be free from the suffocating embrace of his family; it seemed to him that he'd been holding his breath for years, and now he could breathe again. The weather at camp was always hot and humid, the air thick with gnats during the daytime, choked with mosquitoes at night—perfect conditions for doing nothing. He could lie in his bunk daydreaming for hours on end, practicing his kazoo, working up a decent rendition of Little Eva's "Do the Locomotion." That was heaven.

"So you're telling me you and Rupert weren't friends, huh?" Larry asked.

Ira shook himself out of his memory—had it been a memory or a dream?—and opened his eyes. Here he was in Larry's van; it was today, a sunny day in the summer of his fiftieth year, and the past had never seemed so much with him as it was today. "No, we weren't," he said. He turned to gaze at Larry's profile again. "Listen. I have to ask you something. I'm not going to make it through the day without asking you this. It's been on my mind, I've been thinking about it for years. I wasn't going to get into any of this. I was going to leave it alone. But you brought up Rupert—you got me thinking about all of this, and I don't think I'm going to be able to leave it alone. I don't hold a grudge or anything. I'm serious about that. But I have to ask you, anyway. Why'd you dump me like that?"

"Dump you? Where?"

"When we were kids. I mean, we were just kids, I know that, and kids do things. But we were Boy Scouts. You know—trustworthy, loyal, helpful, friendly—all of that. The Eternal Brotherhood of Scouting. So why'd you turn on me like you did?"

Larry turned to give him an incredulous gaze. "You're still on that? After all these years?"

"Mittelberg. Mittelstein. Jewboy. All of that."

"That wasn't me, man. I never said any of that stuff."

"You heard it."

"I did not," Larry said, and slapped the steering wheel. "I never heard nothing. Listen—is this why you showed up now? After all these years? Don't you think I got anything better to do on a Sunday morning? This is why I'm driving you all the way down to HaHaTonka?"

"I'm just trying to get something straight in my head, that's all."

"This is why I left my poor dear wife Belinda with strangers, so's you can ask me all these stupid questions about stuff I can't even remember? I missed church, for this? You got some nerve." His voice rose higher now with every sentence. "What do you expect me to do? You want me to say I'm sorry? For something you say I did when I was eleven years old?"

"I'm just asking a simple question."

"What do you want from me!" Larry cried, and Ira heard the strangled tone of genuine desperation in his voice. "Get this straight," he went on. "I . . . don't . . . remember! It was a million years ago, like I told you when you asked me all this stuff before! Water over the dam! You can ask me all you want, and the answer's still going to be the same. And that's the end of that story. I ain't going to say I'm sorry. You want to know what I'm sorry about? I got a whole plate full of sorry, friend. I'm all full-up." Larry's face had turned an unsettling shade of purple. His sausage-like fingers curled around the steering wheel as if trying to strangle it. "Tell you what I should do," he said. "I should turn this van around right now. I should turn around go back up to Kansas City, let you sniff your own way down to HaHaTonka, see how you like it."

"You were my friend, Larry. I'm here because we were friends. You were the best friend I ever had when I was a kid."

"So that's what you do when you come and see your old best friend? You beat a dead horse, you drag out some nag that's been dead for thirty years and bang away at it?"

"We were blood brothers—or maybe we weren't blood brothers, I can't remember, but we were *going* to be blood brothers, we talked about it all the time. We were like brothers."

"That's not the way I remember it. The way I remember it, you were always acting like you were too good for me. That was you, through and through. Too good for anybody in Troop 144. Then you come over to my house that one time, way back when. You just got out of college, but you didn't look so smart. You looked like a bum, to tell you the truth, you know that? Your hair all over the place. If I hadn't known it was you, I might have shot you. You're lucky I didn't, now that I think of it."

"Larry, all I'm saying is, you got me into Troop 144. I wouldn't have joined if it wasn't for you. You know? That friendship meant a lot to me. We were brothers."

"For crying out loud, man, it was a million years ago."

"I could have joined a Jewish troop and saved myself a lot of grief."

"Well, so why didn't you, then?" Larry cried in a voice shaking with rage. Again his fat fingers choked the steering wheel, his knuckles turning white with the effort. "If everybody was treating you so bad, why'd you stay? Why'd you want to be someplace where nobody wanted you around? Huh? You ever thought of that?"

Ira sat back in his seat. Why *had* he stayed in Troop 144? Why hadn't he simply announced to his parents that he was quitting? *Mom, Dad, they hate me there, and I'm not going back*. It would have been simple. At least it seemed simple now. He could have joined one of the Jewish troops, made new friends—he could have quit altogether, and concentrated on something else, his violin lessons, or his religious studies. But if he'd done that, it would have shattered his father's fragile, taped-together heart. At least that was the way it seemed to Ira when he was a boy.

Ira's parents had always talked a lot about anti-Semitism, routinely launching into hair-raising tales about Jew-bashing over dinner, ticking off on their fingers the outrageous abuses Jews had suffered through history at the hands of Gentiles. "Thank God you've never had to go through any of this misery and suffering yourself," his mother would say in regular conversations after dinner, as he helped her dry the dishes. "Your forefathers, your grandparents—even your dad and I went through it so you wouldn't have to. We protected you from all of this. That's what we did for you. We took it, so you don't have to take it."

Ira's father was very proud of the finely-tuned anti-Semitism detector built right into his brain, a device capable of spotting Nazi sympathizers and potential collaborators up to three blocks away. Anything could trigger an alarm: if his shirts came back from the cleaners with too much starch, he muttered darkly about the anti-Semitic implications. They were everywhere, anti-Semites—the TV repairman was obviously a Jew-hating bastard, as was the guy who'd fixed their gutters the year before. All elected officials had it in for the Jews, with the possible exception of Jacob Javits and Abe Ribicoff. "You want to know about anti-Semitism? I'll tell you about anti-Semitism," his father said. "The first thing to remember is this: *goyim* talk a good game." His voice grew high and singsong. "God-so-loved-the-world-turn-the-other-cheek-amazing-grace-love-your-neighbor-blah-de-blah-blah. Oh, yeah. Bunch of bullshit, pardon my French. Let 'em have a chance, wait till the going gets tough, you'll see how much they love their goddamn neighbor—especially if their neighbor's some poor shnook named Goldstein."

Ira listened to these unnerving nightly accounts for years while chewing his pot roast and rearranging the carrots and peas on his plate into various geometric shapes, but nothing in his parents' spiels about anti-Semitism prepared him for the real item. He'd had no idea that being on the receiving end of Jew-bashing would make him feel so *ashamed.* He wasn't sure what he was ashamed of, but he knew what shame was when he felt it, and this was shame. He wanted to tell someone about it, but who was there to tell? Ruthie? If he opened up to her, she would tell him it was his own fault for joining a dumb organization like the Boy Scouts. Then she'd throw pennies at his head until he left her room.

But there it was, gnawing at him, at every troop meeting, on every overnight camping trip, every Scouting event. *Mittelstein. Mittelberg. Hey,*

Jewboy, got a dime? More than anything, he wanted to ignore the whole thing—to fit in, to get along, make the best of it. That's what the heroes of the short stories in *Boy's Life* magazine would do. Those boys had pluck. They were unsinkable. They whistled in the face of adversity, humming a merry tune as their mettle was being tested. If the world handed them a lemon, they didn't just make lemonade—they opened a lemonade stand, and used the proceeds to rescue a dog from the pound.

Oh, to have been the hero of a short story in *Boy's Life,* instead of Ira Mittelman.

▪ ▪ ▪

As they made the final turn toward Camp HaHaTonka, down a narrow macadam road so closed in by stands of oak and hickory that it felt as if they were hurtling through a tunnel, Ira asked, "So where do you think I ought to scatter the ashes?" They hadn't spoken for nearly at hour at this point, and Ira had to clear his throat to ask the question.

Larry sighed. "I don't know. I been thinking about that. How about we do like we used to do in the Sacred Tribe of Lo-Hoka? What'd they call it? A walkabout?"

"Oh! Yeah, sure. Go out in the woods and sit there for a while, commune with the spirits, all of that. Get in touch with our ancestors."

"Yeah. That's it. Remember that? Sacred Tribe of Lo-Hoka. That was something."

"Sure. Dad would like that."

Lo-Hoka was a bogus Indian tribe invented by the elders of the Kansas City Boy Scouts Council back in the 1930s. It was the hokum of the thing that Ira's father liked the most. He had a soft spot in his heart for mumbo-jumbo—and the Sacred Tribe of Lo-Hoka had mumbo-jumbo to spare. Membership in the tribe was open to both Scouts and their fathers. The fathers didn't actually have to do anything to join the tribe—they just had to think up an Indian name for themselves and hang around camp for a few days each summer, drinking beer and complaining about their wives. Bernard Mittelman's Lo-Hoka name was Falling Bear, which was given to him by the other fathers when he fell out of his bunk one night during an especially frantic spate of fender-bender nightmares. Like the Scouts as a whole, Lo-Hoka was codified and hierarchical—boys were inducted into the tribe as Braves during their second year at camp, and were thereafter entitled to paint one thunderbolt on their faces with war-paint during tribal festivities, and to wear one plastic eagle claw around their necks attached to a string of beads. As Braves, they were allowed to recite the Lo-Hoka Prayer to the Heavenly Father whenever the occasion called for it, and they could sing the Lo-Hoka Anthem, "Lo-Hoka Always Skyward"—but they could not take an Indian name yet, and under no circumstances could they peek into the Circle of Warriors around the campfire at Camp HaHaTonka, for in that Circle the secret ceremonies of the Sacred Tribe of Lo-Hoka were carried out, their specific nature known only to the Warriors of the Tribe, and to God.

Of course, if you worked hard at living your life by the Sacred Code of Lo-Hoka and were pure of heart and brave of spirit (which you demonstrated chiefly by showing up at Camp HaHaTonka for a third summer), you could ask to be put through the Great Trial of the Warriors, a three-day ordeal involving sleeping outside in the woods without a sleeping bag no matter what the weather, eating roots and berries (plus any snacks from the canteen that you could stuff into your jeans), making campfires without matches (unless you were smart enough to sneak a cigarette lighter along), and then finally drinking some vomitous crud out of a hollowed-out ram's horn while everyone in the Great Campfire Circle hooted and whooped and fell over themselves laughing. Once you were a Warrior, you could paint two thunderbolts on your face and wear two plastic eagle claws on your beaded necklace, and you could take an Indian name—one that came to you in a burst of spiritual inspiration during your time sleeping outside in the woods without your sleeping bag. Ira thought of Hawk Flies Low, because he was concentrating on a name for himself and saw what he thought might be a hawk flying low. Maybe it was a turkey vulture—in fact he realized that it probably was—but he wanted it to be a hawk. He was very pleased by this, but then his father fell into a pout and told him, "I thought you'd want to name yourself after me—Little Falling Bear—but I guess I was wrong." This was common practice; if your dad was already a Warrior, you took the diminutive version of his name. But Falling Bear was a joke of a name—his dad had fallen out of his bunk, after all, the laughing-stock of the fathers' bunkhouse. On the other hand, Ira didn't want to get anybody upset. He was doing all of this for his father, anyway. And besides, it didn't matter. He was so heartsick about losing Larry Fontenot's friendship, about tenting with Rupert Mimieux, about everything in Troop 144, that nothing really mattered much at all. So in the end he decided that he hadn't really been all that sure it was a hawk, anyway, and when he got to the big Lo-Hoka ceremony, he called himself Little Falling Bear.

"I still got my Warrior claws," Larry said. "I still put them on sometimes. Not very often. Just every once in a while. Belinda'll be asleep and the kids'll be out doing something, and I'll just put 'em on and sit there, watch some TV."

Suddenly they'd encountered a stream of traffic, swarms of cars that seemed to have appeared out of nowhere. "What's all of this? Are you sure this is the right road?" Ira asked.

"Sure. It's the road we always took to HaHaTonka, all right."

It was, indeed, the road to HaHaTonka. But far from the narrow, rutted country lane that Ira recalled, this had now widened into four lanes of blacktop—and as they neared the camp's entrance, the traffic increased even more. Ira recognized the route at last—remembered it, moment by moment, every sun-dappled leafy inch of it, every pothole. Each year as the busload of Troop 144 scouts rolled along this final section, he sang "We're Here Because We're Here," to the tune of "Auld Lang Syne" with everyone else in the troop. The only lyrics to "We're Here Because We're Here" were "we're here because we're here, because we're here, because we're here," but for some reason Ira had been quite moved by the song when he was in the Scouts. Perhaps he'd taken the words to mean something more profound than simply arriving at Camp HaHaTonka—he couldn't remember what could have been on his mind all those years ago. Now he hummed it under his breath.

Moments later, creeping along at ten miles an hour now, they made the final turn through the woods and drove up to the entrance to HaHaTonka. Ira felt his throat constricting. "We're here, Dad," he whispered to the cannister of ashes. "I did it. I brought you back. We're here because we're here." There was the old stone statue of the Indian scout standing at attention, his left hand raised in the Boy Scout greeting. The statue was inscribed with the legend, "A FRIEND" etched on its base. Ira had shot off a hundred inch-and-half firecrackers, one by one, right here, the Fourth of July, 1962. Right here, this very spot. It was his second year at camp. This was the epicenter of his boyhood.

This final approach to the camp had been gravel back in Ira's scouting days, but now it was paved in high-grade blacktop. One more turn to the right—and Larry slowly coasted to a stop. He and Ira didn't say anything. They simply stared in wide-eyed wonder.

Except for the statue of the Indian scout, Camp HaHaTonka had vanished. Where it had been, all Ira saw was a sea of automobiles, a parking lot so vast it seemed to go on forever. *"WELCOME TO THE SHEPHERD OF THE HILLS OUTLET MALL AND FAMILY FUN CENTER! SHEPHERD OF THE HILLS! COME JOIN THE FLOCK!"* proclaimed a gigantic marquee. In small letters near the bottom, the sign read, *"Former site of Camp HaHa-Tonka Boy Scout Reservation."*

Ira rolled down the passenger side window and stuck his head out to gaze at the vista. The Shepherd of the Hills Outlet Mall was as big as a college campus. He'd never seen anything like it in his life. There were two hundred stores, according to the sign—everything from Brooks Brothers to Nike to Corning Ware to Books for Life: a Christian Reading Warehouse—plus an eighteen-screen cinemaplex, an amusement park with a half-sized Olympic swimming pool, miniature golf, a shooting range, and a go-cart track, three motels, and an assortment of restaurants, barber shops, and beauty parlors, plus the Jim Nabors Ol' Fashioned Dinner Theater, currently staging a production of "The Music Man."

"Oh, shit," Ira groaned. "Oh, no. Shit, shit, shit. How could they just . . . ?"

"You know, come to think of it, I think I heard something about this," said Larry after a pause.

Ira fixed Larry with an incredulous stare. "You're kidding. You knew?"

"I didn't say that."

"You're telling me you knew it was gone?"

"I'm just saying, now that I think about it, I think maybe I read something in the *Star* about the Boy Scouts having some difficulties down here a few years ago."

"I can't believe it. We drove all the way down here, and . . ."

"It was in the newspaper. I just forgot about it, that's all. It was all that gay stuff—a bunch of queers took the Boy Scouts to court. Sued 'em for a couple million dollars. Said they were being discriminated against.

Can you believe that? Sued the Boy Scouts of America! The Boy Scouts! Took 'em to court and sued 'em like they're a bunch of criminals."

"Is that right?" Ira shut his eyes.

"Yeah, I remember it now. It's coming back to me," Larry said. "They had to sell off HaHaTonka to settle the lawsuit, pay the legal costs. That's it. Sold it to some real estate developer back East. Broke their hearts to do it, too. I remember it now. Doggone it. I just plain forgot, Ira. I'm sorry."

"Okay." Ira sagged back against the seat. He'd rolled his window down, but somehow the air inside the car was still hot and humid, rich with the odor he'd smelled in Belinda's bedroom. Suddenly he felt ill. He'd come all this way—and for what?

"I'm serious, Ira. I wouldn't have dragged you down here for nothing."

"I believe you."

"That court case got a lot of publicity. You didn't hear about it out there in San Francisco, huh?"

"News from Kansas City doesn't make it out to the West Coast very often. If my dad had still been living here, he'd have told me all about it—but he was already in Seattle, living with Ruthie. And anyway, none of that matters, Larry. It was probably in the news—I just missed it."

They sat in the car another minute, the silence building between them like a wall.

"I guess we might as well turn back," Larry said finally in a mournful voice. "Drove all this way for nothing." He let out a dramatic sigh. "Just my luck. I don't get out much. First time I've had a real vacation in two years. Ain't had time for a vacation. First day in two years I didn't have to change one of Belinda's diapers." He turned to Ira, shifting awkwardly behind the steering wheel. "You know what that's like, friend? Change a diaper on a full-grown woman?"

"No," Ira said.

"Puts the fear of God into you," said Larry. "Puts you right smack on your knees."

"I don't doubt it," Ira said, and he felt something cold inside of him starting to melt. How could he be angry at this poor guy? "Listen," he said. "We're here, we drove all the way down here. My dad wanted to come down here one last time. Well, he's here. I can't scatter his ashes at

HaHaTonka. But what the hell. I tried. I did what I could. Maybe we should just have some lunch, relax a little bit. We don't need to go back right this minute, do we? My flight's not 'til seven tonight. It won't take us more than an couple of hours to drive back to the city."

Larry sighed. "Oh, that's a big Praise the Lord," he said. "The church women are looking in on Belinda. Pastor Moody himself's looking in on her, I'd bet on it. She'll be doing just fine. And I'm hungry something awful. Let's eat."

As they were getting out of the car, Ira instinctively grabbed the container of his father's ashes. He considered stashing it out of sight under the passenger seat, but that didn't seem right; he wanted to hold the container, to keep it with him, to have it close by. The phrase *All this way for nothing* echoed inside his head. *Come on, Dad I'm sorry. I tried to do what you wanted me to do, but I let you down.*

"You going to take that thing along?" Larry asked, pointing at the cannister.

"Yeah."

"You don't want to just leave it in the van?"

"No. You've got a broken window, Larry. Anybody could just reach in."

Larry shrugged. "Whatever," he muttered, and hitched his pants a bit higher beneath his stomach. They walked across the parking lot, past the Wedgewood-Waterford store, past Ralph Lauren Polo, past Mikasa and Gap and Eddie Bauer and Ann Taylor and two dozen more outlets. Suddenly Larry stopped and pointed to the left. "There we go," he said. "Bingo. Just what the doctor ordered. Country Bub's Buffet."

"Good place, is it?"

"I ate at one of these once," Larry said. "Long time ago. You gotta see this."

Inside, Country Bub's was cavernous. The specialty of the house was chicken fried steak smothered in country cream gravy, but there were plenty of other choices as well: carved-to-order prime rib, roast turkey and ham, plus salisbury steak in mushroom sauce, deep-dish chicken pot pie, beef stew, fried catfish and shrimp and perch, whole racks of baby back ribs drenched in a glistening cloak of barbeque sauce. Tubs of ambrosia salad, three-bean salad, cucumbers and onions in vinegar, and sliced tomatoes with red onions filled the salad table. For dessert, diners could pick from a jumble of sugar-glazed pies and cakes, pans of Apple Brown Betty and peach crumble, mounds of fresh grapes and strawberries and blueberries, and a do-it-yourself banana split counter complete with several flavors of ice cream, real whipped cream and maraschino cherries.

"Oh," said Larry. "Ohhhh." It came out like a groan. "Look at that chicken fried steak."

The woman working the cash register eyed Larry warily. She was a small woman with a puckered face and a cloud of gray hair bound in a net. "You boys want the all-you-can-eat special?" she asked.

"You bet," said Ira, and watched her face fall.

"That'll be sixteen dollars for two adults," she said. She shook her head as Ira handed over the money, then after she'd rung up the sale, she gave him a plastic yellow "RESERVED" marker shaped like a highway pylon. "Leave this on your table 'til you're all done, then put it on the floor when you finish up, so they'll know to come bus your plates," she told him.

Larry picked out a booth near the chicken fried steak. Ira put the yellow "RESERVED" pylon on their table, and placed the canister containing his father's ashes gingerly on one of the red faux-leather seats. "I'll be right back," he whispered to the ashes.

Ira hadn't been gone more than a couple of minutes—just long enough to grab a plate of salad, a bowl of soup, a dinner roll, and a glass of iced tea—but when he got back to the booth, two small boys with hair the color of dishwater were touching the canister containing his father's ashes, poking it as if it might be alive. As he approached the booth one of them picked up the canister and shook it like a box of cracker jacks. Then they turned and saw Ira standing over them. "Okay," he said, trying to keep his voice steady. "Just put it down." They dropped it on the table and ran, shrieking and snickering. Ira shook his head, slid into the bench seat and put the canister next to him, where no one could reach it.

Listlessly he ate his salad, then his soup, though he didn't taste any of it. He might as well have been putting it all into someone else's mouth. Who could eat at a time like this? He felt the canister of ashes next to his right thigh. His father was in there. Here they were, together again at Camp HaHaTonka. He looked around the restaurant, trying to imagine where this spot would have been when HaHaTonka occupied these acres—when there were trees here, thousands of them, instead of pavement and brick and plaster. How close was he to the site of his old tent, the tent he'd shared with Rupert Mimieux? Where would the fathers' bunkhouse have been from here—the path to the canteen, the trading post, the latrine, the mess hall, the swimming pool?

Larry came back to the booth at last, carrying two plates piled high with chicken-fried steak, mashed potatoes, gravy, green beans, strawberry jello and ambrosia salad. He put the plates down, slid into the booth, closed his eyes, and folded his hands under his chin. "Dear Lord, thank you for this bounty, especially the chicken fried steak, which is a personal favorite of mine, and I ain't had it in a long, long time, and I didn't think I ever would again. And thanks for bringing Ira back here to me after lo these many years. In Jesus' name, amen." He opened his eyes then, surveyed the food before him, and set to it with great passion. He worked with knife and fork on the chicken-fried steak, using his fingers when he needed to speed the process along. A waitress brought plastic tumblers of ice water for both of them. In between gulps of food, Larry downed his water and slammed the empty tumbler on the table. Then he clambered out of the booth and headed back to the food tables.

Half an hour later, he was still going strong. He'd barreled through seconds, thirds, fourths, and fifths by this time. Ira watched as Larry waited impatiently at the chicken-fried steak table again, tapping his foot and eating biscuits off a tray as fresh-faced young women in hair nets refilled the vats of steak and poured in pitchers of country gravy. On his next trip to the food tables, the fried perch ran out just as Larry was approaching. When he returned to the booth again, his plate now piled with baby back ribs, shrimp and fried catfish, he was red-faced and sweating. "I wanted some of that perch," he said, and pushed a shrimp into his mouth. "There was some perch left on that platter. I saw it. They saw me coming and bam—off it goes. They just didn't want me to have any, simple as that."

"Why would they do that?"

"I don't know. They're just like that, I guess."

"Maybe they were just refilling the platter back in the kitchen. They do that, you know."

"They have it in for me, 'cause I'm big. You know what I mean. A place like this, they see me come through that door, it's lights out. I know a thing or two."

"Well, you're probably pretty full already, anyway, aren't you?"

"It says 'all you can eat,'" Larry said, and then he pounded a fist on the table. The salt and pepper shakers jumped. Even the napkins shimmied a little in their holder. "I ain't had all I can eat yet. My whole life I never had all I could eat—not even once. These days everybody's always saying something about my weight," he muttered. "But friend, I'll tell you something: they don't know how hungry a grown man can get."

"Okay. No problem. I was just asking. Just keep it up 'til you've had your fill."

Larry sucked a baby back rib into his mouth, and pulled it out again a moment later, the bone glistening. "Hey, here's an idea. When we're done here, let's ride some of them go-carts."

"Go-carts? Oh, no, Larry. I don't think so," said Ira. He'd never driven a go-cart in his life, and he wasn't in the mood to start now. They were on a long list of things that his mother had declared absolutely off limits—a litany of non-Jewish activities that would lead directly to financial ruin, blindness, facial disfigurement, severe and perhaps permanent hearing loss, paralysis, diarrhea, maybe even death. Ira glanced at his watch. It was a little past two o'clock. If they left pretty soon—if he could ever get Larry out of Country Bub's Buffet, that is—there'd be just enough time to make it back to Kansas City for his evening flight home.

"Oh, I get it," Larry said. "You think that kind of thing's just for low-class dopes like me, don't you." He pushed two fried shrimp into his mouth, tails and all.

"Aw, come on. Get off this. You've got me pegged as some sort of snob, and I'm not."

"You always thought you were better than me. From day one."

"Larry, that's ridiculous," Ira said.

"All I know is, I'm the one doing all the driving on this trip," Larry said. He mopped his face with his napkin. "I'm the one that drove you all the way down here. I'm your chauffeur."

"I would have been glad to drive. You know that. I rented a brand-new Toyota. It's sitting in the parking lot at the Holiday Inn right now."

"I never even asked you to take a turn behind the wheel."

"I offered! You said no!"

Larry leaned across the table. "Once we get back to Kansas City, I'm going right back into the diaper-changing business. You fly off back to

San Francisco, fix up your old books and such, your fancy job. You're single—you want to go out with a different woman every night of the week, that's what you do. We get back home, I go back to living off the county dole. You hear what I'm saying? Just for today, don't you think I'm entitled to a little fun?"

That was enough for Ira. And besides, at least the go-carts were somewhere else, he told himself—somewhere outside the cavernous confines of Country Bub's Buffet. "One time around the track," he said. "And then we're heading home."

■ ■ ■

There was a line for the go-carts, and except for Ira and Larry, it was made up entirely of feral pre-adolescent boys who spent their time in line punching each other in the stomach, making fart noises on their arms, and practicing a kind of fake laughter that sounded like "ack-ack-ack-ack!" At one point several of the boys used Larry as a kind of obstacle, racing around him in circles, thrusting their arms through his legs and pawing at each other wildly. Even at odd moments when they were standing still, a hum of energy came off them, like shimmering heat off a summertime blacktop. They must have been about ten or twelve, these boys, and Ira regarded them with a mixture of wonder and dismay. Had the boys he'd known in Troop 144 ever been this wild, this wiry, this hell-bent on violence? Yes. They had. He remembered.

"You're sure you want to keep your dad's ashes with you while we do this?" Larry asked. He shaded his eyes against the afternoon sun.

"I told you. I'm not taking my eyes off this thing." Ira hugged the canister closer to his chest. "I put it down for two seconds back at the restaurant and some kids started poking at it. Nobody watches their children anymore. The world's going to hell. If I'd been a minute slower getting back to the booth, they'd have started using it for a soccer ball. I'd have seen my dad scattered all over Country Bub's. He'd have ended up in the gravy, probably."

"Well, we could take it back to the van, you know. Hide it under the seat. It'd be safe there. No kidding."

"You've got a busted window, Larry. Any clod could reach in there and grab this thing, and then what? Sorry. Listen: in San Francisco I've had my car stolen three times in the past year. Nothing's safe anymore. I waited ten months to come here. Ten months. My dad wanted—he had one last wish, and I screwed it up, it's ruined, and I don't know what I'm going to do now, I don't know what I'm going to tell Ruthie—but I'm not letting this thing out of my sight. Call me neurotic, I don't care." What was he supposed to do? How could he explain to Larry what he was feeling? The day had been such a disappointment already. To have flown to Kansas City and driven all the way down here, only to find this. But it wasn't just the drive that was on his mind. Everything was gone. His high school was closed and shuttered. His house was occupied by strangers who'd painted it green. His summer camp had been turned into a parking lot, an outlet mall, an amusement park for morons. The canister in his hands was all he had left of his past: a box of ashes—the whole thing weighed no more than five pounds.

Finally the fleet of go-carts that had been running the course cruised into the holding area near the front of the line, and attendants helped the gaggle of young drivers out of their cars. The boys in line with Ira and Larry jostled each other, pushing and shoving to get the best angle for the front cars. Finally an attendant unhooked the chain at the front of the line and there was a mad dash for the go-carts.

Ira was pushed aside by a couple of the boys as he was about to clamber into a red go-cart near the back of the pack, but he managed to get into a black one just behind it. Larry had already claimed a yellow go-cart at the front of the bumper-to-bumper line-up, somehow beating the gang of boys to it and wedging himself into the seat. Ira couldn't understand how Larry had managed to squeeze into the thing at all. These go-carts were made for children, after all; Ira's knees were stuffed up against his chest, where the canister containing his father's ashes rested uneasily, and though his feet could, indeed, reach the accelerator and brake pedals, the position was hardly comfortable. With Larry's bulk, it was a wonder he could find the pedals, let alone operate them. And what about his bad back? Had it been miraculously cured by all that chicken-fried steak?

A pimply young man in a red T-shirt stepped out onto the track in front of the pack of go-carts. "Okay, everybody, listen up!" he barked. "Everybody wears a seatbelt, no exceptions! No ramming on the track! No contact on the track! Take it easy on the curves, stay in your lane! When I give you the yellow flag, pull in! No hot-dogging it, no showing off, and don't get out of your car on the track for any reason, no how! Any questions?"

Nobody had any—or if they did, they kept them to themselves. Larry twisted around in his seat and flashed Ira a maniacal grin—a smile that conjured up, if only for a moment, the impish boy Ira had been friends with so many years ago, the wiry little boy hanging upside down on the jungle gym, yelling "Look at me!" The pimply fellow in the red T-shirt removed the pylons blocking the lanes at the head of the pack of go-carts and stepped aside. And then they were off.

At first Ira's go-cart seemed sluggish, but that was because it took him a moment to figure out how much weight to put on the accelerator. The steering wheel was no bigger than a frizbee, and he had trouble adjusting to the quickness with which it steered the go-cart; one small quarter-turn of the wheel made the cart swerve violently. He quickly found himself at the back of the pack, and by the time he steered through the second of the big, sweeping "S" curves of the track, the first few go-carts from the front of the line were already on his tail. He could hear them right behind him, though without a rear-view mirror there was no way of knowing how close they were, or how many of them were there. He slowed down through the curve, then punched the accelerator at the start of the straightaway, but it was too late—two go-carts whizzed by him on the left, and then another one passed him on the right. One of Ira's disadvantages now was his height—the kids piloting the faster go-carts were small, and hunched over their steering wheels, they provided very little in the way of wind resistance. Ira stuck out of his go-cart like a stringbean, and the wind pounded at his face, pushing him backwards.

He felt like an idiot. Why was he doing this? He should have simply waited in the van while Larry drove his go-cart. He could have gotten a cup of coffee, called the airline to confirm his reservation on that night's flight from Kansas City to San Francisco—he could have done anything, in fact—anything but this. Vaguely, over the sound of his engine and the sounds of the other engines, he could hear spectators hooting and hollering at the cars going around the race track. He assumed they were laughing at him, at how ridiculous he must appear, a soon-to-be fifty-year-old man driving around the go-cart track with an odd-looking brown plastic canister wedged between his knees.

Larry Fontenot passed him on the next lap, laughing and screaming like a ten-year-old girl, pounding on his steering wheel as he crowded past Ira on the left. "Praise the Lord!" he cried over his shoulder. They were just entering the sharpest curve of the course, a hard, unbanked hairpin turn to the right, and as Larry went into it ahead of Ira, his go-cart jacknifed out of control, and in the blink of an eye he'd spun 360 degrees, and ended up stalled-out in the middle of the track, canted at an angle and taking up two lanes of traffic, facing Ira head-on. Ira had slowed considerably going into the turn, and seeing Larry ahead of him, blocking his lane now, as well as the lane to his right, Ira pumped his brake pedal frantically. A steady stream of go-carts whizzed past him on the left, buzzing in his ear like so many yellow jackets. If he'd tried to veer to the left, he would have clipped one or more of them—and if he kept barreling straight ahead or steered to the right, there was Larry, frozen now, staring at Ira with wide eyes.

Later, Ira would play this moment over and over again in his head, a loop of film that ran continuously, even when he begged himself to make it stop. He pumped the brake and pumped it again, and the go-cart slowed, but it didn't stop, there wasn't time to stop, and there was nowhere to go, nowhere to turn, nothing to do but drive head-on into the rubber-padded front of Larry's go-cart. The noise was muted, a dull thud muffled by the wind and the whine of engines going past on his left and the distant laughter of the crowd looking on.

And then the canister of his father's ashes, dislodged from its perch between his knees by the force of the impact, went tumbling out into the bright sunshine. Desperately Ira reached for it, but he was too slow. He watched the canister, silhouetted for a brief instant against the blue Missouri sky, before it came down in the middle of the track, rolled, and then disappeared beneath the wheels of one, two, three, four, five co-carts in swift succession. The first three hit it head on—thump, thump, thump—and sent it tumbling, bouncing across the blacktop and into the air again. The last two side-swiped it, having swerved in an effort to avoid it. By the time the last of them had plowed through, the canister was crushed and had spilled its contents, a few handfuls of what appeared to be gravel mixed with sand, in an arc across the track. Some of the sand was as fine as dust, rising softly in a small cloud for a moment before settling back to earth.

■ ■ ■

It was nearly midnight, San Francisco time, when Ira walked into his apartment. He'd missed the flight from Kansas City to Denver, taking a later one instead, which put him on the last available flight from Denver to San Francisco, a flight so empty that he'd had an entire row of seats to himself. But he hadn't slept—who could have slept at a time like that?—and now he felt exhausted, and very old. A veil of nighttime fog had rolled down from Twin Peaks into Noe Valley, as it did most nights during the summer, and when Ira opened the bank of windows over his sofa, the soft, salty scent of the ocean filled his darkened living room.

His answering machine told him there were three messages waiting to be played. First Henry Cruikshank, calling that morning. "Ira, it's Sunday, eight-thirty. I haven't been inside a church in thirty years, but I'm going today. Just wanted you to know what desperation you've driven me to. Ten-o'clock mass—I'm going to pray that you get back to town in time to do the work on Milton. I'm taking communion, Ira. I'll be on my knees eating God's flesh and drinking His blood in about an hour and a half. I hope you're satisfied. I'm going to confession while I'm there, too. I haven't gone to confession since I was sixteen. By the time the priest gets done hearing me out, I'll be saying Hail Marys the rest of my life. Call me, will you? Let me know you're still alive."

Then Ruthie. "You're not back yet," she began. "I knew you wouldn't be. I'm calling at noon on Sunday. It's raining here, what else is new. Well, look . . . I hope everything went okay for you back home. You're a good son, Ira. You're a good brother. I haven't told you that in a while, but it's true. You take pains. You're a Boy Scout—you really are. You're crazy, but that's okay. You're still a Boy Scout. Josh and I are going to the San Juans for a couple of days—his brother lent us his cabin 'til Wednesday. I'm not going to do anything but read mysteries and drink wine and watch the storms come in. I'll call you the minute we get back. Love you."

And finally, Pauline. "Ira?" she began, then stopped. Her voice was thick and wet, and Ira held his breath, leaning in closer to the answering machine to hear her over the pounding of his heart. "Ira, it's Pauline. If you're there, pick up the phone, will you? Please?" She waited, and he could hear her breath, ragged and moist and expectant. "I'm calling Sunday night. I don't know what time it is. Seven-thirty. I don't know. I'm not wearing my watch. Ira, I need to talk to you." Again her voice faltered. "So, uhm, call me, okay? Please. I'll be waiting." He heard another breath, and then the click at the end of the tape.

Quickly, not giving himself time to think about what he was doing, he dialed her number. When she answered, he said, "Pauline? Am I calling too late? Were you asleep?"

"Oh, Ira. Where were you?"

"I was out of town. I just got back. I know it's late."

"Listen," she said after a long moment of silence. "I was wondering. About this Friday night." Another pause. "I was wondering if you'd like to have dinner."

In the time it took for air to flood into Ira's lungs, he considered the possibilities: maybe she'd had second thoughts; in the message she'd left on his answering machine, he'd heard tears in her voice; perhaps she'd realized that she loved him, after all—that these past two years had meant to her what they'd meant to him. But what if that wasn't it at all? Perhaps something had occurred to her, something she'd forgotten to tell him at dinner on Friday night? She wanted the key to her apartment back; she needed his signature on something, some final legal document left over from their divorce; but no, Pauline wouldn't do that. She was better than that. But she was human, too; maybe poor confused Kenny had arrived at her door on Saturday night wearing the kimono again, his hands flapping away madly, his voice a shrill falsetto, all his pledges to her forgotten.

"Of course I'd like to have dinner," Ira told her.

"Cacciatore di Spello?" she asked. "Our usual table?"

"Oh, no. No, I don't think so. Let's try someplace new. There's a place on 24th Street I'd like to take you. Thessaloniki—their speciality is Greek fish on the grill, and they make their own pita bread. Everybody in Noe Valley's raving about it." Ira was making some of this up, of course—he'd walked past the place dozens of times but had never gone beyond reading the menus and glowing reviews taped to the window. But it was pretty inside, light and airy, all done up in blue and white, with small tables and old-fashioned bentwood chairs. And anyway, it was time for a change.

"I'll meet you there," Pauline said. "Our usual time—six-thirty?"

"Let's make it seven."

"Oh, Ira. I'm so glad you called."

That night before he slipped into the cool sheets of his bed, Ira promised himself that he'd never ask her what had changed her mind. Never, never, ever. He could ask her anything he liked, but not that—not if they had dinner together every Friday night for the rest of their lives. And if she ever brought up the subject, he'd clamp his hands over his ears until the danger had passed. There were many things Ira Mittelman wanted to know about the world, many things he'd wanted to know all his life—but this was not one of them.

The next morning he awoke refreshed, as if he'd spent two days at an expensive Napa Valley spa, covered in herbal mud wraps and massaged by Swedish experts. Even before his first cup of coffee he was energized, even slightly giddy. He flicked on the lights in his work room, and turned his cautious, skillful gaze toward Henry Cruikshank's first edition of *Paradise Regained.* He worked steadily through the morning hours, stopping only for coffee and juice breaks: he cut and glued new hemp cords to the spine; he sewed new headbands in muted blue and gray, suitably dignified, given the nature of Milton's subject; he picked carefully through all the rolls of leather in the oaken barrel before selecting a piece of tawny brown calfskin for the new binding. Then he scraped the calfskin out on the litho stone, working away at it until mid-afternoon, by which time he'd thinned it to the delicate consistency of butter. Finally he glued it painstakingly it to new boards, then glued these to the spine. While the glue was drying, he brushed and cleaned the book's pages, one by one, with his good boar's head brush.

He stopped in the early evening to eat a sandwich of lettuce and cucumber and cream cheese with chives on wheat bread. He stood at his work table as he ate, pushing the sandwich into his mouth without thinking much about it. He was totally consumed with the task at hand, a state of mind he often entered when he was deep in the middle of a restoration project. Henry Cruikshank would be happy with this once it was finished. He'd been right, of course, all along: it was a gorgeous book, a masterpiece worth saving. He'd make his profit, he'd stay afloat a little longer, and the world would have this book to cherish for another three hundred and fifty years. Ira leaned over the book, inhaling the aroma of calfskin and glue, the smell of history. It smelled more delicious than anything he'd ever eaten in his life.

He retrieved the box of gold leaf from the cabinet and set it beside *Paradise Regained* on the work table, then turned on the hotplate and mixed a *glaire* in the battered saucepan. When bubbles just broke the surface of the liquid, he painted a light coating of *glaire* onto the upper-most section of the new spine. Using his tweezers, he lifted a stamp-sized piece of gold leaf, so light it might have been weightless, from the box. Ira held his hand steady as he transferred the gold leaf onto the spine, where it lay bunched up over the newly *glaired* surface. Then he leaned down, spreading his legs slightly to brace himself. He pursed his lips, then popped them, a soft "ppp," like a kiss—like a baby's first try at "Papa."

And as if it knew exactly what to do—as if it were coming home to rest in its own bed at last—the tissue of gold leaf fanned out perfectly over the calfskin.

bernard, the mummy

Bernard and Marilyn won the iron in a raffle at the Home Show. The grand prize, a Cuisinart, would have been even better, but Marilyn was very happy with the iron. She already owned an iron, of course, but not one with a telephone in the handle. "Look at this," she said excitedly several days later, when the iron arrived in the mail. "You can talk on the phone while you're ironing your shirt in the morning."

"No kidding," said Bernard.

"You just talk in a normal tone of voice while you're ironing. Isn't that something?"

"What'll they think of next," he asked, and turned back to the television. The Cubs were behind 9–7, in the bottom of the ninth, but they'd loaded the bases with two outs, and Sammy Sosa was at the plate.

"A lot of people entered that raffle and didn't win anything," Marilyn told him.

"That's very true."

"I think this is amazing," she insisted. "Remember that TV show where the guy was always talking on the phone in his shoe?"

"That was a comedy, Marilyn." Bernard said this over his shoulder without taking his eyes off the television. Sosa took a called strike at the knees.

"All I'm saying is, here it is thirty years later and we have a telephone in our iron, of all things. I'm going to call you at the office tomorrow while I'm ironing my pleated skirt."

Sammy Sosa hit an infield pop-up and the game was over. Bernard stared at the screen silently for a long moment. The phone rang in the kitchen, and Marilyn went to pick it up. Bernard could hear her end of the conversation. "Oh, but," she said tentatively after a moment's pause. "We already have a—and anyway, we don't even own this place. Yes. We're renting. It's not a condo, it's an apartment. Yes, all right. I understand. Of course. I see. Well, if you have to, you have to." She hung up, walked back into the living room, sighed, and turned to Bernard. "Don't laugh. In order to get the iron with the telephone in it, we have to let a salesman come over and demonstrate a vacuum cleaner," she said. "He's coming over tonight."

Bernard stared at her. "Don't we already have a vacuum cleaner?"

"Of course we do. I told him that. Or I tried to. He said he didn't care, it doesn't matter if we buy it or not, he just has to come over and demonstrate the thing so we can keep the iron with the telephone in it."

"But why couldn't we just say no? Is 'NO' not an option?" he asked, his voice rising with each word. He snatched the remote control and brusquely turned off the television

"Bern, the guy sounded desperate." Marilyn approached him from behind and curled her hands around his head, gently teasing his thinning hair with her fingers until his shoulders relaxed.

Moments later their doorbell rang, and when Bernard opened the door, a husky, sweating man burst through, carrying the largest vacuum cleaner Bernard had ever seen. "This won't take but a few minutes of your time, folks," the salesman said, and began to unpack a variety of tools and attachments. The vacuum cleaner, which resembled a small off-road vehicle, had a tubular chassis made of thick silverplated metal, and oversized tires capped by polished chrome hubcaps that shone in the dim light of the entry hall. "Let's see," the salesman said, whipping out a thick electric cord. "Let's plug this puppy in and see what she can do."

"How much is that thing?" Bernard asked. "It looks like it'd cost a mint."

"Let's not talk money just yet," the salesman replied.

"You know, we already have a vacuum cleaner," Bernard told the man. "It's in the closet. You want to take a look at it?"

The salesman put down the electric cord and gave him a pained look. "Sure," he said. "Let's see what you've got."

Bernard led him to the living room closet and showed him the vacuum cleaner. "See?" he said. "It's a Hoover. I bought it myself, new, at Marshall Field's. It cost two hundred bucks. It was the first time in my whole life I spent that much money on something that wasn't any fun." He hated the thing—had always hated it—but he wasn't going to say anything like that to this vacuum cleaner salesman.

The salesman examined the Hoover for a moment, then gave Bernard and Marilyn a moist, amused smile. "Hey," he said, "I'm not going to knock the other guy's merchandise. It's not my style. But let me say, just for the record, just because I like you people, I can tell you're good folks, you have a certain quality to you that I really like, let me just say that this thing"—he pointed briefly to the Hoover in the closet—"is not a vacuum cleaner. Not really. Not the kind of vacuum cleaner that people like you deserve."

"We like it," Marilyn said.

"Of course you do," the salesman told her. "Because you haven't seen what my little buddy can do."

"How much is the one you're trying to sell us?" Bernard asked again.

"I don't want to talk money yet," the salesman said. He led them back to the entry hall, where the chrome-plated off-road vacuum cleaner stood at the ready. He took a paper bag from his coat pocket and upended it on the carpet. A fragrant cascade of dirt rained down, and the salesman quickly ground it into the carpet beneath his heel.

"Oh, gosh," Bernard said. "I wish you hadn't done that." The ground-in dirt had formed a large bulbous stain the size and shape of an eggplant on the pale beige carpet.

The salesman chuckled. "Relax, pal," he said. "Don't get your bowels in an uproar." He ground the stain into the carpet again, rocking back and forth on it, putting all his weight into it this time. Then he plugged in the vacuum cleaner, adjusted a couple of dials on the control panel of the chassis, flipped a switch, and the machine roared to life. Bernard watched in mute, horrified fascination as the salesman put the machine's gearshift into DRIVE and ran the vacuum cleaner over the ground-in dirt. Within seconds, amazingly enough, the stain had disappeared with a vicious sucking sound and now, as the salesman continued passing the vacuum cleaner back and forth over the once-begrimed area, the carpet rose up into the jaws of the machine, puffing up from the floor like the skin of a balloon. Bernard had never seen a carpet do that before, and in a moment of wild, irrational fear he imagined this monstrous vacuum cleaner sucking the wall-to-wall carpet right up into its belly. What were he and Marilyn going to say to their landlord? How were they going to explain what had happened to the carpet?

At last the salesman put the gearshift into PARK and turned off the machine, which gave out a long, plaintive wheeze and then fell silent. "Was I right?" he asked, "or was I right?"

"So how much is it?" Bernard asked.

"Three thousand dollars," the salesman said. When Bernard began laughing, the man quickly added, "That's the manufacturer's suggested retail price. Because of this special deal with the Home Show and the iron, we're cutting the price to two thousand, and that's just this month. This machine will last a lifetime. You buy this thing, you'll put it in your will, give it to your kids. You can't buy this kind of quality in a store."

"We don't have any money," Marilyn said. "We're young, we're just starting out."

"You know, I like you folks. I said that before, people say stuff like that a lot, but I really mean it," the salesman said, and moved closer to them. Bernard could smell the man's sweat. "I'm going to give you a deal on this machine, because I've taken up your time and the fact is, I'd hate to have to lug this baby back out to the van. It weighs a ton. That's all-metal construction for you—no plastic parts, no nylon, nothing but steel and chrome, inside and out. So listen: what would you say to . . . a thousand bucks! What did I just say? Well, okay, I said it, I can't take it back, so I'm going to give this thing to you for a thousand bucks, to hell with my commission, I'm going to regret this, but what the hell, I said it, it came out of my mouth, and now I'm going to stand by it."

"Get out of here," Bernard said, and motioned toward the door with his head.

"Can we keep the iron with the telephone in it?" Marilyn asked.

"Okay, look, I can tell you folks are sensible, you know a bargain when you see one, I'm not really authorized to do this, but I'm going to toss out the company's mark-up, too, even though it's going to get me in dutch with my supervisor, and I'm going to give this thing away for seven hundred dollars. What am I talking about? That's ridiculous! Seven hundred dollars! That's an amazing price. The metal alone is worth seven hundred bucks. You'll never have to buy another vacuum cleaner as long as you live. Think about it! This is it! Your last vacuum cleaner! If somebody offered you a car that'd last the rest of your life, you'd jump at the chance, wouldn't you?"

Bernard went to the door and opened it. "In about one minute I'm going to pick up our iron and call the police," he said, and stood there stiffly until the salesman had unhooked all the attachments, stowed them with elaborate care in the appropriate slots of the vacuum cleaner's complicated storage compartment, and wheeled the entire contraption out into the hallway.

"You'll regret this," the salesman said just before Bernard shut the door in his face.

■ ■ ■

Now, six months later, Bernard found himself suddenly regretting everything. This had been the worst week of his life. First, there was the small matter of his job at Bradley-Beach, which just this Monday morning had gone suddenly into the toilet, the result of some sort of leveraged buy-out of the parent company, a ruthless maneuver that had taken place in a boardroom halfway around the world, leaving Bernard jobless, cut loose without so much as a severance package after three years with the company. He had his savings, of course, but they wouldn't last forever.

Then on Tuesday Marilyn broke up with him. They'd been planning a winter trip to Cancun, and now he couldn't go. How could he go away for an entire week, he asked her—how could he throw money around like an idiot, when he'd just lost his job? "Hey," he said, "it's crisis time. This is when we have to stick together—when we find out what we're made of."

"What are you talking about," Marilyn told him, and lit a cigarette. In recent months she had become one of the world's leading experts on Cancun she owned more brochures on the place than most Mexican Tourist Bureaus. She'd been practicing her Spanish, she'd lost fifteen pounds so she'd look her best on the beach, she'd planned their trip down to the last detail, selecting each and every restaurant already. One night, Camarones a la Plancha at El Pescador, the next night dancing up a storm at Mirabel, the private club atop the Cancun Ritz Carlton.

And now they couldn't go. "Well, I'm going by myself, then," Marilyn said. She looked at him in wide-eyed alarm above the smoke of her cigarette, as if seeing him for the first time. "And when I get back, I'm moving my stuff out of the apartment. I don't like you anymore."

The irony of all of this wasn't lost on Bernard. Two years ago, when he and Marilyn were still just dating, his star at Bradley-Beach had been rising and he'd just been given a generous raise in salary, and so he'd taken her to Cancun, planning to break up with her over drinks while they were down there. He'd grown tired of Marilyn—although she was only twenty-five, she'd begun to put on weight in her thighs; she sneered at his taste in movies and clothes; she mocked his adolescent preoccupation with televised sports; her widowed mother was loud and overbearing and lived only a mile away and besides, there was a long-haired girl who roamed through Bernard's office selling sandwiches from a cart every morning, and her nipples showed through her T-shirt in a way that caused his heart to stop. Some mornings he had to punch himself in the chest with both fists when he caught sight of her. He knew he'd never speak to her, he couldn't even bring himself to smile in her direction, but the thought of her unlaced something deep inside him that had been tied in knots his whole life, and he knew he'd never be happy until he was single and free and available to her.

So he took Marilyn to Cancun, and oddly enough, given the purpose of the trip, they had a great time. They swam every day, made love at night on the lumpy mattress in their hotel room, and drank beer and margaritas in the swimming pool, at the swim-up bar. As the days passed, he kept on meaning to tell her that this trip was their goodbye vacation, a kind of going-away gift, but he never quite got around to it. Every time he thought that the moment had come, precisely the right moment when he should just tell her and be done with it, something would happen—a waiter would interrupt them and ask if they wanted another beer, another margarita, some more tortilla chips and salsa; a guy would walk by who looked exactly like Nick Nolte; birdshit would land on the table next to theirs with a wet splat—and the moment would be gone. On the flight back to Chicago, Marilyn told him she wanted to move in with him. "I mean it," she said, snuggling into his shoulder under the thin airline blanket. "I wasn't sure if you really loved me before this trip, but now I know."

Bernard went to the office the morning after he got back from Cancun and found that the sandwich girl with the nipples wasn't there. She never showed up again, and even two years later, Bernard still harbored a secret wistful hope that she'd killed herself out of loneliness because he'd been out of in the office for a week. Oddly enough, now that he had the time to think about it, he could see that his star had begun to sink at Bradley-Beach at just about the time of his Mexican vacation. They'd given him the big raise, he and Marilyn had gone to Cancun, then he got back, and things weren't the same. That was the order of events as he remembered them. Maybe something had happened while he was gone for that week. What could it have been?

Then there was the vacuum cleaner salesman's dire warning: "You'll regret this." That was six months ago, and things had certainly tumbled into the toilet since then. Bernard picked up the iron with the telephone in the handle, and pondered the possibility that the salesman had inflicted some sort of slow-acting hex on him, like a time-release capsule full of misery. He entertained this idea all morning as he idly catalogued the dimensions of his wretchedness. But Bernard wasn't much of a believer in hexes, especially when they were issued by someone as sweaty as the vacuum cleaner salesman.

On Wednesday, the day after Marilyn had broken up with him, two days after he'd lost his job, Bernard had some time on his hands. First he watered the plants on the patio outside his living room. That took five minutes. The day stretched out before him, bleak and empty. He decided he would iron his entire wardrobe. This would take a while, because he had lots of clothes, but he had plenty of time. He'd even iron his underwear, he decided. Why not? His clothes were worth it. He could depend on them. His clothes weren't going to fire him without warning. His clothes weren't going to take off for Mexico without him in his hour of need. They deserved the very best. He opened his closet and surveyed the contents with wan satisfaction. Everything he owned was taupe, which was not only his favorite color, it was actually the only color he liked at all. Taupe was neutral, an attitude Bernard fervently wished the entire world would adopt. As a child his mother had dressed him in garish bright colors, reds and yellows and greens, which drew a steady barrage of taunts from his schoolmates, year after year. When he left home for college he bought a pair of used khakis at an Army surplus store, and for the first time in his life, the taunts stopped. That was ten years ago, and this past decade Bernard had put together one of the largest all-taupe wardrobes in Chicago. Now he stood at his closet and stared at his array of taupe apparel: slacks, jackets, shirts, and sweaters hung in neat, sophisticated rows, an ocean of taupe as far as the eye could see.

As he ironed, he pondered the downward spiral of his fortunes. How had things turned so sour for him? Forget about the vacuum cleaner salesman's muttered warning; the roots of Bernard's undoing might extend back to his early childhood, for all he knew. The littlest thing could set you off on a path to ruin. Like the day of school he'd missed in the second grade, for instance the crucial day when they explained everything you'd ever need to know about arithmetic. Since he'd been out that day, home sick with a cold, he'd missed it, and they never repeated that vital information, the secret that would have unlocked geometry, algebra, trigonometry, even calculus for him later in life. Everybody else was there in class that day—everybody but Bernard. This explained why he'd done so poorly in math his whole life—a failing that had walled him off from many employment opportunities, leaving him stuck in the career path from which he'd just been ejected. All because he'd had a cold one day when he was seven. Probably while he was in Cancun, eating barbequed shrimp with rice and beans and washing it all down with beer, executives at Bradley-Beach were going cubicle to cubicle, explaining to everyone else—everyone but Bernard—how to keep their jobs in the coming global crisis.

Or maybe it was all the sandwich girl's fault. Maybe she'd been his strongest ally at the place. His *only* ally. Maybe once she'd departed, there'd been no one left in his corner. What a fool he was. He should have known! The T-shirt, the nipples, the sandwiches—they were all just a front. She probably owned the company! He remembered stories he'd read as a child, about a king who put on peasant's clothing and walked among his people. Bernard couldn't remember whether the king had sold sandwiches as he walked, but that detail didn't really matter.

Wednesday afternoon, as he was still making his way through his wardrobe, the phone in the kitchen rang: Dellinger and Barkus, a rival firm down the street from his former employer, calling to see if he'd be interested in interviewing for a job similar to one he'd just lost. "We can't make any promises," the woman on the phone said. "But if you're interested in us, we're interested in you."

This rival firm had been the butt of constant jokes at Bernard's old office. "Dickwad and Bullshit," people called it. Whenever anything went wrong at Bradley-Beach—a presentation got lost on the way to the client, sales figures didn't add up, invoices were mislaid—the usual response was, "Who's in charge here—Dickwad and Bullshit?" One night not long after he'd been hired at Bradley-Beach, Bernard got roped into an after-work pub-crawl with a crowd of senior executives—the only time he'd ever been invited out with any of his co-workers during the three years he'd been there. After several hours of steady drinking, the group found themselves in front of the building that housed the offices of Dellinger and Barkus. Someone in the crowd shouted up at the sky, "Hey Dickwad! Hey Bullshit! Hey! Wake up!" And then, despite the bright glow of streetlights illuminating the scene, everyone unzipped and urinated on the office building, laughing so hard that one fellow, a senior manager in Bernard's department, fell over on his back and kicked his heels on the sidewalk like a baby.

Bernard had always gone along with these jokes—after all, he was trying to fit in around the office—but secretly he felt guilty about it. What had Dellinger and Barkus ever done to anyone to deserve such bullying and teasing? He'd briefly known a guy who worked at Dellinger and Barkus—they'd played racquetball together a couple of times at a place downtown that was running a special introductory offer for young executives and the guy seemed nice enough, smart, affable, stylish. Bernard wanted to ask him, "Say, how did your company and my company ever get—" But then he realized he didn't know what it was he wanted to find out.

On Thursday morning, the day after the phone call from Dellinger and Barkus, Bernard stood barefoot, ironing a pair of slacks, the slacks he was going to wear to his interview the next afternoon. He was lost in thought. What would it be like to go to work for Dickwad and Bullshit, after spending the past three years snickering at the place? Maybe at Dellinger and Barkus they spent a lot of time telling Bradley-Beach jokes. But there was only so much you could do with Bradley-Beach, which simply wasn't a very funny name. He was thinking about all of this —thinking about what you could do with Bradley-Beach to make a joke out of it, then against his will, thinking of his former co-workers, imagining their mirthful reaction when they heard he'd been taken on at Dickwad—when he ironed over his left index finger.

Bernard's hand flew up reflexively and hit him the face, knocking his glasses off. He ran to the kitchen and held the finger under a stream of cold running water. Oh, my God, that hurt. He'd never done anything like this to himself before. He'd always been a careful person. He looked both ways, even when he was crossing a one-way street. He maintained a long list of things he had no intention of ever doing: skiing (cross-country *or* downhill), skydiving, bungee-jumping, hang gliding, windsurfing, rollerblading, and so on. He shaved with an electric razor. He wore sunblock even on the cloudiest of days. And now this: he couldn't even iron a goddamned pair of slacks without maiming himself! He felt himself grow faint, and leaned forward, resting his elbows on the kitchen counter, holding the finger very still under the spray of cold water. He could see it through the water. His finger looked like a miniature bratwurst, hot off the grill.

Anger welled in him, deep and hot, rising like lava. If it hadn't been for Bradley-Beach he wouldn't have had to iron the goddamned pair of slacks. He'd have been at work today, processing forms, which was what he *should* have been doing, and would have been glad to do. But no. No, just because he'd been in Cancun that week two years ago, the week when they went around explaining to everyone else how to keep their jobs, the week when the sandwich girl disappeared, now he'd ironed over his left index finger, turning it into something you'd want to stuff into a bun with mustard. Goddamn them. They were probably at the office right now, chuckling about him. If he could have transported himself magically just that second, that instant, back to his old office, he would have punched somebody in Senior Management right in the nose.

But there was no way to magically transport himself anywhere, and there was nobody in Bernard's apartment to punch. He put his burned finger in his mouth and stalked into the living room, planning to beat the life out of a sofa pillow—but then he spied the iron, sitting smugly on the ironing board, just as he'd left it only moments before, and before he could stop himself he did the only thing left to do, which was to punch the iron as hard as he could with his right fist. He hit it so hard that it flew against the wall and bounced, oddly enough, as if it had been made of rubber. First it hit his glasses, which he'd failed to retrieve from the floor. Then it bounced and landed, flat side down, on his bare left foot. Bernard heard the brief sizzle of the iron and sniffed the odor of burnt flesh in the instant before he leapt straight up in the air, knocking the iron off his foot —and then something must have gone completely haywire inside his head, because all he could think of in that instant was that he had to call 911—he had to call an ambulance for himself—he had to do it right now. And so without thinking about it any further, he reached down and snatched the iron off the floor, punched 911 on the telephone in the handle, and confidently pressed the iron to his ear.

■ ■ ■

So that was Thursday. Now it was Friday, and at the appointed hour Bernard made a dramatic entrance at Dellinger and Barkus. One lens of his glasses was cracked, and his head was cocked to one side so that he could see out of the good lens. Various part of him were wrapped in gauze—his left arm and the lower half of his left leg, as well as most of his face. The right half of his head was buried beneath an inch-thick bandage. He lurched like the Mummy, dragging himself toward the receptionist's desk.

"Have a seat," she said, waving toward a row of Barcelona chairs, and looked at him with a pitying smile. "I'll buzz Mr. Leffingwell and let him know you're here."

Bernard stared at her, his head still cocked. Before he could stop himself he said, "You look familiar." But that was ridiculous—she didn't look like anything at all. Without being able to see her out of both eyes, he couldn't stop her image from swimming around his field of vision like a tadpole.

"Oh, I don't think so," the receptionist said. Bernard watched her fluff her hair out around her head with a nervous hand. "Mr. Leffingwell will be right with you."

Bernard couldn't help himself. "Are you sure?" he asked. "We've never met before?"

"I think I'd remember," the woman said, smothering a chuckle.

"Oh, I don't usually look like this." He wagged his head to get her into focus, then motioned toward the gauze wrapped around his head, his left hand, peeking out of his shoe. "Actually this has been the worst week of my life," he added, and chuckled ruefully.

"Is that right?"

"Yep." The throbbing in his left instep had come back now—the pain medication was wearing off—and he hoisted the foot up on the edge of a sleek glass coffee table.

"You'll want to take your shoe off that table," the receptionist advised him.

"Yes, of course," Bernard said, and lowered the foot gingerly to the floor. "Sorry. Well, anyway, it's been a tough week, and I normally don't look like this, I'm really not accident prone or anything like that. One thing after another like this—you know."

"Let me ring Mr. Leffingwell again," the receptionist said. She punched the buttons of her telephone with what seemed to Bernard an unnecessary amount of force. After a pause, she hissed into the phone, "He's *here.*" She fell silent for a few seconds, then said, "Well, fine, then. Just fine." She slammed the receiver back into its cradle as if trying to break the machine. "He'll be right with you," she said to Bernard. "He's been caught in a meeting."

Presently Mr. Leffingwell strode through a pair of swinging glass doors into the reception area, and swept Bernard back with him down a dizzying maze of narrow, dimly-lit hallways. He'd always marveled at the sheer noise level at Bradley-Beach—the place had always been in an uproar, a constant Babel of office clamor. These hallways, by contrast, were as quiet as a tomb. Bernard couldn't even hear the sounds of his own footsteps, which were muffled by the thick carpet. Finally they reached Leffingwell's office, a large walnut-paneled room with a broad view of the Chicago River, its brackish water glinting like polished bronze in the cool afternoon light. If it hadn't been for a tugboat slowly churning upriver, the entire scene might have been an oversized photograph. Bernard was seized by the uncanny feeling, the sudden certainty, that he and Leffingwell and the receptionist were the only three people in the building.

Mr. Leffingwell leaned back in his chair and laced his hands together behind his head. "So," he said, smiling at the ceiling, "you put in three years over at Buttfuck-Bitch, eh?"

"Excuse me?"

"Buttfuck-Bitch. That's what we call it." Leffingwell turned his head and shot Bernard a knowing smile.

Bernard straightened in his chair. His foot was throbbing again, and now his left index finger felt like it was on fire again. "You mean Bradley-Beach?" he asked.

"Oh, give it a rest. You guys aren't the only ones who can come up with a nickname. And don't give me that innocent look. We know what everybody over there calls us. We have ears. We're not deaf."

"Not everybody over at Bradley-Beach went in for that kind of thing," said Bernard. "Some of the folks over there are as nice as anyone you'd want to meet. Decent, caring people."

"Oh, yeah. That's why they dumped you like a sack of potatoes," Mr. Leffingwell said, and rolled his eyes. He took a pencil out of the top drawer of his desk and snapped it in two.

"I'm telling you the truth," Bernard protested. "There are people at Bradley-Beach who'd walk through fire for a friend. They'd give you their last nickel if they thought you really needed it." He didn't mean any of this, but it seemed like the thing to say.

"I'm touched," Leffingwell sniffed. "I think I might start to cry in a second."

Bernard struggled to get to his feet. "And you wonder why people call this place Dickwad?" he muttered.

"Buttfuck!" Mr. Leffingwell cried, and lunged across the desk. He clawed Bernard's shirt into a bunch and held him suspended on tiptoes for a moment before relaxing his grip.

▪ ▪ ▪

Oddly enough, a senior partner at Dellinger and Barkus called the following Monday to offer Bernard a position with the firm. "Are you sure?" he asked. "My interview went badly."

"Oh, not by our standards," the senior partner said in a jovial tone. "We like your grit."

The next morning Bernard reported for work, still lurching from the pain in his foot, his head still cocked to one side as he tried to focus on the world through the good lens of his glasses. His head still throbbed, of course, but the doctors' initial reports had been optimistic about his chances of avoiding plastic surgery on his ear. Mr. Leffingwell showed him to his new office, which was small but brightly lit, and much more centrally located than the office he'd occupied at Bradley-Beach. Here he was right in the thick of things. It would be difficult to get fired with an office like this, Bernard told himself. At Bradley-Beach he'd been stuck back by the copy machines, at the end of a dead-end corridor, a location that should have told him something about his long-term prospects with the firm. All morning long, co-workers at Dellinger and Barkus came by to welcome Bernard to the company, cooing and chuckling over his many wounds and cuffing him gently on the chin, adding quiet words of encouragement to get him through the tough healing process that lay ahead of him.

This was a far cry from his first day at Bradley-Beach, which he remembered even now with a shudder. The firm had been in a frenzy of hiring at the time, and there were several new employees who started their careers with the company that same day. All of them were herded into a small, airless room that first morning, and forced to watch slide shows of the senior partners' recent family vacations. The slide shows, narrated by someone who sounded a lot like Harry Caray, the Cubs' announcer, depicted trips to Hawaii, Alaska, the Great Barrier Reef, Washington, D.C. and other destinations. The group of new employees sat in stunned silence through the first round of slides, but then, as the morning dragged on and the slides continued, grumbling began to surface in the darkened room. "What are they doing to us?" one newcomer asked. "I'm supposed to be in the Accounting Department. What does any of this have to do with accounting?"

"It's hazing," another suggested. "We're being hazed. There's a law against this sort of thing, isn't there?"

"Keep it down," Bernard hissed. "How do you know they're not listening to us?" At that, everyone fell silent and slumped lower in their chairs.

But of course it was hazing, and sure enough, by lunchtime two of the new arrivals had broken down and bolted from the room. Bernard thought of them now, in his new office, and realized that he'd never seen them again. He wondered where they'd gone, what had become of them. How awful: you work your way through school, keep your grades up, apply for jobs, get an offer from one of the city's most prestigious firms

—and then on your first day of work, you wash out, you can't hack it, you can't make the grade! Oh, the inequity of life. Bernard pondered this matter for quite a while, asking himself why he had stayed in the room watching the slide shows, while others, no less talented, no less committed to their career than he'd been to his, had fled. Perhaps the senior partner at Dellinger and Barkus had been right in commenting on Bernard's grit. He'd never thought of himself as someone with grit. Quite the opposite. The schoolyard taunts of his youth had not toughened him—in fact they'd made him frail in his own eyes. Only in the past decade, his "taupe period," had he come to feel any true self-esteem at all. He found it difficult, just now, to hold himself in high regard, considering the business just a few days ago with the iron. What a fool he'd been.

But it was hard to maintain a low mood for very long here at Dellinger and Barkus. He had to make a routine presentation to a committee of senior partners that afternoon at three-thirty—just a few introductory remarks, nothing to worry about—and so he spent the morning unpacking a box of personal mementoes—his framed college diploma, an autographed photo of Lana Cantrell, and his collection of swizzle sticks, which he'd inherited from his mother. At eleven-thirty a boisterous crowd of co-workers elbowed their way into his office. "We're taking to you lunch!" they cried, and lifted him from his office chair, pooh-poohing his groans and mild protestations. At the Horse and Plow, the dimly-lit bar and grill across the street, the bartender, a large, bearded man named George, shook Bernard's hand and gave him a business card that read, "Thank you for sharing your sorrow with me. I have never heard a story as sad as yours. Believe me, you have my deepest sympathy. Now go fuck yourself."

"I only hand those out to guys from Dellinger and Barkus," George said. "You can run a monthly tab here if you like. Just pay up the first of the month and we'll be acey-deucey. Today's your first day with that outfit, right? I never seen you in here before, have I?"

"No," Bernard said, which was a lie. Actually, he'd been here once before, several years ago, with Marilyn, shortly after they'd started going out, back when they were still in the first bloom of romance, before her thighs had begun to expand. They'd occupied a dark table near the back for most of an evening, groping each other under the table in that state of perpetual, unquenchable sexual frenzy that had marked the first year of their relationship. Bernard cringed inwardly when he remembered that time in his life now. What a dope he'd been! Once, just around that time, he and Marilyn had been invited to a mutual friend's house for Thanksgiving and had excused themselves halfway through the dinner to go upstairs and fuck on the host's bed. Someone had walked in them, humping like monkeys atop a pile of guests' overcoats.

"So what's your story? You messed yourself up pretty good, eh?" George said, eyeing Bernard's various bandages. He polished a shot glass with a stained towel as he stared.

"I certainly did," said Bernard, and managed what he hoped was a self-deprecating smile.

"I bet the other guy looks even worse, though—am I right?" George asked, and raised his eyebrows expectantly.

"Oh . . . well, there really wasn't another guy. It's kind of a long story."

"Well, I tell you what: new guy comes in the door the first time, I always buy him a drink. Your money's no good here," George said. He slid the shot glass he'd been polishing along with a fifth of rye whiskey down the bar to Bernard, and said, "Drink up. On the house."

"Oh, gosh, it's a little early in the day for me," said Bernard. "But thanks."

Mr. Leffingwell suddenly appeared to Bernard's left, and clapped an arm around his shoulder. "Did I hear you say you're not going to take a drink? Let me get this straight: here we are at the Horse and Plow, George is telling you your money's no good, and you're playing like you're too much of a pussy to put one down the hatch?"

"I didn't say that," Bernard protested.

"Did George show you that business card?" Leffingwell asked.

"Yeah—yes, he did." Bernard pulled the card out of his shirt pocket with his good hand.

"He doesn't give one of those cards to everyone who walks through the door."

"No, I'm sure he doesn't."

Mr. Leffingwell uncorked the bottle of whiskey and filled the shot glass with a steady hand. "Here's how," he said, and downed the rye in one gulp. Then he slammed the glass down on the bar, filled it again, shoved it toward Bernard, and said, "And one for my Mummy."

George pulled an ancient car horn from beneath the bar and squeezed the rubber bulb, letting out a loud, raucous "KA-DOO-KAH!" that cut through the clamor of the crowded bar. "Oh, yeah. That's a good one," he said to Leffingwell, and punched him in the arm. Then he turned to Bernard. "Go ahead," he said. "Show him who's a Mummy and who's not."

The doctors had told Bernard to go easy on himself while he was on the pain medication. He hadn't had so much as a beer for three days now. But George looked like he meant business, and Leffingwell's grip on his shoulders was tightening, so Bernard took a sip of the whiskey, holding it in his mouth until he couldn't keep from swallowing it any longer. It burned all the way down. Good God, what was this stuff? Lighter fluid? He managed a grimacing smile. "Okay, then," he said. "Well, that's probably my limit."

"Not a chance," Mr. Leffingwell said. "Not even close."

"I've got a presentation to make at three-thirty," said Bernard.

Leffingwell screwed his face into a mask of concern. "Oh, my goodness," he said in a falsetto voice, "Mummy's all worried that he's going to get in trouble with the big bad senior partners his first day on the job! Mummy's all upset and thinks he'd better stick to milk for the rest of his life!" He pounded Bernard on the back. "C'mon, little fella! You get in any kind of trouble, you just tell them you were with me and George! Nobody wants to get on George's bad side. Now get that stick out of your butt and live a little!"

"All right, fine, then," Bernard muttered. He gulped the rest of the whisky, slammed the glass down, then pounded on the bar for a moment as the liquid set his gullet on fire.

"That's more like it," George said. He poured another shot. "Go on. The second one tastes a helluva lot better than the first one."

Bernard didn't hesitate this time. "Down the hatch," he said. One of them, Leffingwell or George, filled the shot glass again, and this time Bernard didn't bother to say anything; he simply raised the glass to his lips and drained it in one gulp.

"And one more for my baby," George sang, filling the glass again and sliding it under Bernard's nose.

"You're going to cover my ass about this three-thirty presentation, aren't you?" Bernard asked Mr. Leffingwell. He squinted at Leffingwell through the good lens of his glasses.

"Hey, would I leave you in the lurch? We don't do things like that at Dellinger and Barkus, my friend. We're all for one and one for all. Just remember that. It's our motto."

"That's just what I wanted to hear," said Bernard, and dumped the whiskey down his throat. After a moment, when he could speak again, he added hoarsely, "Well, I think that's my limit, now, wouldn't you say? I mean, how many is that?"

"I don't know. Two," Leffingwell said. "Two, maybe three. My grandmother can drink more than that, and she's ninety-six."

"Your grandmother's dead," George said.

"Well, if she was still alive she could out-drink anybody in this bar." Leffingwell filled Bernard's shot glass again and shoved it toward him. Bernard looked at it for a long, dreadful, collapsing moment. He hadn't eaten any lunch, and he'd skipped breakfast, too, because it had taken him so long to arrange himself with all his bandages that he'd been afraid he'd miss his bus if he took time to grab so much as a bagel. His stomach was empty—empty, that is, except for the pint of rye whiskey now sloshing around inside him. "Oh, what the hell," he murmured, and emptied the shot glass into his mouth.

At eleven o'clock that night, Bernard awoke in a cold sweat. He was lying curled on a couch somewhere, but he had no idea of where he was. His head was pounding, and his mouth felt full of dust. Something had happened, something was terribly wrong—oh, yes, now he remembered, the three-thirty presentation, the shots of whiskey, Mr. Leffingwell and George, it all came back to him in an instant, the horror of it, the sick stupidity. He'd stumbled blindly into the senior partners' conference room half an hour late, interrupting another presentation. He'd come in swinging his good arm in front of him like a white cane, and something incoherent had come unbidden out of his mouth, a kind of ranting monologue about how terrible a week he'd been having, the tragedy of Marilyn's betrayal in his hour of need, the iron with the telephone in the handle, the vacuum cleaner salesman and all the rest of it. He'd used the word "fuck" and the word "motherfucker" several times. Remembering it all now, even vaguely, at once he felt he might vomit, and in a panic he fumbled in the dark, swinging his arms wildly, found a lamp, switched it on, and let out a gasp.

He was in someone's living room—and then he saw her, the receptionist from Dellinger and Barkus, the woman who'd advised him to take his foot off the coffee table the day of his interview with Mr. Leffingwell sitting across the room from him in a comfortable club chair, dressed in a white terrycloth robe, her dark hair still wet and glistening from the bath. She stared at him, her eyes suffused with pity. Without her business suit, her heavy white silk blouse, her paisley scarf tied in a bow at her throat, she looked quite different, and even more hauntingly familiar to him than she had the day he'd first seen her as he waited in the reception area.

"Would you care for a sandwich?" she asked. "You must be hungry."

With a sudden cry, Bernard arose from the couch and lurched toward her. "Is it you?" he asked. "Can it really be you?"

She opened her robe and met him in the middle of the room. Those nipples! He'd have known them anywhere. "Take me," she said in a throaty whisper. "Take me, you mad boy. Do things to me—naughty things."

As he nuzzled the fragrant hollow at the base of her neck, he murmured, "I have to ask you something. Do you by any chance know anything at all about math?"

"Mathematics?" she asked, pulling away to give him a sidelong, ironic glance.

"Yes. Square roots, algorithms, probability—set theory, trigonometry, basic differential equations, anything at all."

She shrugged. "Sure, I know some of that stuff. I had to learn it all in school."

"Let's start with long division, can we?" asked Bernard.

She pulled him close to her and gently placed his good hand, the one without the gauze, on her breast. "We'll start with long division if that's what you'd like," she said, her voice a soft moan. She dropped her hand to his groin and massaged his erection through the taupe fabric of his slacks.

"I need to learn everything," Bernard warned her in a breathy voice. "I missed school the day they explained all of this stuff. I was only seven, but it was the most important day of my life. Oh, hey, watch out for my foot, will you?" he said as she maneuvered him back to the couch. "And my ear—don't do anything to my ear. The ear is off-limits."

"Whatever you say," the sandwich girl replied, and lowered him gently onto his back.

the naming of parts

When Joan Winkler was a sophomore in college she had a roommate named Rita, a big-chested brunette who referred to her clitoris as "Little Nell," and made a habit of bringing it up in casual conversation. "I'm taking Little Nell to the movies," Rita told her one night soon after they started rooming together, and it took Joan a minute to remember what Rita was talking about. Occasionally, on Sunday mornings over coffee, Rita would lean across the table and sing, "Little Nell had herself some fun last night! Oh, yezz—oh, yezz." Or, arriving home early after a frustrating date, she was apt to mutter, "That yutz couldn't have found Little Nell with a road map, a flashlight, and a pack of police dogs." At first Joan found this kind of talk dimly amusing, but after a few months the charm of it wore off, and one evening she took a deep breath and said, "Look, I'm sorry, but I really don't like hearing about your clitoris all the time."

"You mean Little Nell," Rita said.

"I don't care what you call it, I don't want to know how it's doing, who found it, who lost it, what it wants to do after dinner. I don't need updates. It's none of my business."

After that, Rita shut up about her clitoris—in fact she shut up about everything, and when the semester ended, she moved out without notice, and Joan had to scramble to find a replacement. She picked Wanda, a drab little woman she'd met in the laundry room of the dorm. Wanda had hair the color of dust, and never spoke unless spoken to. She and Joan lived together for the next two years, and as far as Joan could tell, Wanda had no clitoris—at least not one worth talking about.

Joan graduated from college and moved to San Francisco, where she soon met her future husband, Bill, at a crowded, noisy singles bar on Union Street. Bill pushed aside a palm frond, stuck his head through the foliage, and handed Joan a beer, then before she could take more than a sip of it, he asked her if she wanted to go someplace and get some fresh air. This sounded like a good idea; there was a lot of smoke in the bar, and Joan was feeling a little drunk (she'd had several beers before Bill appeared). She felt strangely free in his presence, like a balloon floating above a crowd. They left the singles bar and took a cab through rainy streets to Bill's ratty-but-very-sexy basement apartment, where they smacked into each other abruptly, like two bumper cars, and began kissing passionately, just like that, without a single awkward, fumbling preliminary gesture. This had never happened to Joan before in her life. *Wow,* she thought—*I'm in San Francisco.*

Bill's apartment smelled like old socks and cat pee, and there were signs of water damage everywhere—brown bladder-shaped stains cascading down the walls, bulging wallboard, warped and bloated books piled high in tottering pyramids—but Joan was willing to ignore all of that, because she'd decided that she liked Bill. She liked him so much, in fact, that without so much as a deep breath or a moment of contemplation she slipped out of the little black dress she'd worn to the singles bar, and threw it back over her shoulder like a wedding corsage. She was reaching back to unhook her bra when Bill leaned toward her and whispered wetly in her ear, informing her that he liked to call his penis "Mr. Bill," after the hapless clay figurine who died a thousand deaths on *Saturday Night Live.*

Joan blanched and dropped her hands from her bra. "Oh, no. Really?" she asked. "Do you have to?"

"Absolutely. I've always called him that," Bill told her. "Ever since high school." He winked, so she'd know that he was just a wacky guy, then he flipped his boxer shorts down to his ankles. There was Mr. Bill, all right.

"Whatever," Joan sighed under her breath, shook her head and bit her lip, thinking of Rita and her clitoris. She knew all about Mr. Bill and *Saturday Night Live.* She'd watched the reruns. She thought the whole thing was stupid. She took off her bra and panties grimly and slid under the greasy, damp sheets of Bill's bed. As long as he didn't decide to name her breasts anything, everything would be fine. A boy she'd come within inches of having sex with during her sophomore year in high school had referred to her breasts as "Itsy and Bitsy, the Boobsey Twins." He'd come out with this witticism suddenly, just as Joan was wriggling out of her jeans while trying to keep her panties on. She'd never tried this maneuver before, alone or in company, and it was difficult, because her jeans were snug and her panties were small and slippery, made of something that felt like silk but wasn't. She didn't know why she was trying so hard to keep her panties on, considering that she'd be taking them off in a minute or two anyway, but it seemed like the thing to do—one layer of clothing at a time—so she kept at it. But in the midst of her efforts, the boy blurted out the business about Itsy and Bitsy, and suddenly Joan, who hadn't been entirely sure that she wanted to do this in the first place, heard the grating sound of metal gears grinding to a halt inside her head. She sighed and yanked her jeans right back up her thighs, snapped them closed, then shrugged on her bra and T-shirt, and that was the end of that.

What was it about her, she wondered now, tracing water stains down the walls of Bill's ratty apartment—what quality attracted these body-part-naming oddballs to her? Was it that she was so normal? She gazed at Bill, trying not to look at his penis, afraid it might have a frantic little face painted on its tip. She'd seen pictures of penises, plenty of them, in art history and biology textbooks, and she'd even seen one briefly in the flesh (the Itsy-Bitsy fellow), but—well, there wasn't anything especially appetizing about looking at a penis, at least not that Joan had ever noticed. Besides, it was rude. It was like looking at somebody's goiter.

Above all, she didn't want to think of anybody's penis as "Mr. Bill." She didn't really want to think of it at all. She just wanted to *do it,* please, and not make a big production out of it—because the plain fact was that she was twenty-one by this time and hadn't ever gotten around to having sex. That was the way she talked to herself about it: *I've just never gotten around to it,* that's all. She'd shrug breezily to herself as she tossed off this thought—as if having sex were the same kind of thing as alphabetizing your CDs, or cleaning out your garage, top to bottom, once and for all. *Let's just do it, already,* she told herself, *and not turn it into World War Three.*

Fat chance. Just as he was about to enter her, Bill began to murmur into her ear, in a falsetto voice so high and thin it pushed the hair up on the back of her neck: "Oh, nooohh! Mr. Bill's scared of the dark! It's dark in here! Don't make me go inside! It's a tunnel, and it's dark, and I can't see where I'm going! Oh, nooohh!"

■ ■ ■

But there were good things to be said for Bill, Joan decided over the next few weeks. Lots of good things. Bill was tall and thin and had a high-domed, distinguished, beaky-looking face. His eyes were brown and mournful, and he had a diffident, guilty cast to his mouth, like a British cabinet minister who's been caught sleeping with whores. Joan especially liked his hands, which were long-fingered and graceful, a violinist's hands. Bill knew what he was doing with those fingers. If he could have shut up about "Mr. Bill," that would have a definite plus—but as long as he kept his hands fluttering about her, performing Paganini-like virtuoso vibrato riffs in all the right places, she could put up for the time being with the nicknamed penis and that blood-curdling falsetto. She was sure that he'd outgrow the "Mr. Bill" business. Give it a month, she told herself, he'd can the falsetto and settle down. She just had to be patient. And she was willing to be.

Because the thing was, not only was Bill tall, thin, long-fingered and diffident—he was rich. Joan was careful not to use the word "rich" when she thought of him, and it certainly wasn't a word that Bill threw around, either. ("I prefer the expression 'well-to-do,'" he told her.) He had a trust fund (dead parents) that gave him enough money to live on comfortably, he told her. Joan wasn't sure she really understood Bill's definition of "comfortably," given the state of his apartment, but she was willing to withhold judgment. After all, she was new in town. And besides, what did she know about the lives of the rich? Maybe they had a different ideas about everything. Joan came from humble Midwestern stock and before this had never known anyone who had two nickels to rub together. Her wealthiest relative was an uncle in Ontario, Canada who'd collected a bundle from an insurance company after being hit by a cab. But the uncle was in a wheelchair now, a vegetable, and needed round-the-clock care, so that didn't really count.

Joan tried to imagine herself with a trust fund. It was hard. She concentrated, and came up with an image of herself waking up at ten in the morning and ringing a bell so that someone (this part was hazy—all she saw was hands holding a tray) could bring her a pot of coffee, a croissant, and a copy of the *Wall Street Journal.* Beyond that, nothing—she couldn't think of anything. She'd never read the *Wall Street Journal* before, and had no idea what was in it. What would she do if she was rich? What would she worry about? What would she wear, how would she spend her days? It was unfathomable—like trying to imagine the end of the universe, or what happened before time began.

Bill didn't act like he had a trust fund. He didn't sleep until ten. In fact he hardly slept at all. He worked sixty hours a week, sometimes more. Bill was only twenty-two, but he was already heavily involved in the stock market, in ways Joan only dimly understood. (He'd skipped college entirely, he told Joan, having been thrown out of three very expensive prep schools and then spending some time in a corrupt, sadistic military academy in Pennsylvania—"the same one J.D. Salinger went to," he said, and Joan had to think a minute before she remembered who J.D. Salinger was.) Joan had spent her undergraduate years back in Wisconsin waiting tables at a pancake house part-time, and most months barely had enough money to pay her share of the rent. Now that she was in San Francisco with Bill and having the kind of adventures she'd hoped for and dreamed of, she was still poor. To keep herself occupied while Bill was at work, after a couple of weeks she got a job as a nurse's aide in an old-age home. Her salary was a joke, but Joan wasn't in the mood to laugh. If it hadn't been for Bill, who paid the rent on the miserable water-damaged apartment and bought all the food for the gourmet meals he made for her, Joan would have been reduced to begging for scraps in Union Square.

She didn't know the first thing about the stock market, and Bill wasn't very forthcoming about what he did. Whatever it was, he loved it, though, and spoke of it in grand, sweeping, romantic gestures while he made dinner for the two of them in his apartment. He'd wax poetic over various merger deals, selling short, selling long, leveraged buy-outs, and hostile takeovers while he tossed squid in its own ink or put the finishing flambé to a coq au vin spiked with wild mushrooms. Sometimes he even brought up his financial dealings while they were having sex, at moments when Joan would have rather he simply shut up and concentrate on the task at hand. "Oh, my God, Joan darling," he'd whisper as he thrust into her, "if you only knew—if you could only see what it's like! The deal's coming through! *WHAMMO!* Something happens! I'm telling you!"

"Uhmm-hmm," Joan would breathe, and gaze at the water stains on the ceiling as though they were clouds. One moment they looked like sheep grazing, the next like boulders tumbling out of the sky. She thought of Rita and her clitoris, Little Nell; then she thought of Wanda, poor dust-haired Wanda who had nothing where her clitoris ought to have been. Joan counted herself lucky. How far she'd come since the old days back in the Midwest. She was in San Francisco now, and she was in love. The water stains on the ceiling looked like two rhinos fucking.

Joan catalogued Bill's good points for herself at odd moments, while she helped old people to the bathroom at the nursing home, or on the bus to and from work. She started with Bill's trust fund, the exact dimensions of which she did not really know, then let her thoughts wander to his hands, his long, elegant hands. He was going to get over this "Mr. Bill" business, and once he did, she was going to make sure he never came up with any names for any parts of his anatomy, ever again. No names, no falsetto screaming, no nothing. Just point and say "it," if the occasion arose. The occasion might arise. She knew that. Sex was strange. She'd known that all along, without really knowing that she knew it. But now she was sure.

■ ■ ■

After a decent interval, they got married. It was a small ceremony, tasteful and short. Joan wore a light blue linen dress she'd bought at I. Magnin's—she would have insisted on white, but who was she kidding? Anyway, her parents couldn't come; they were trapped in a small town in Alaska, where her father, a failure in many previous enterprises, had gone in desperation to work for an oil company. Bill's folks were dead, of course (hence the trust fund). Bill had picked out the church—the Swedenborgian chapel in Pacific Heights. It was a beautiful building, a landmark, with handcrafted timbers arching overhead in the sanctuary and massively handsome stained glass windows spilling bands of brilliant light across the pews. The sanctuary smelled of eucalyptus—not the scent you might find in a bed-and-bath store, but real eucalyptus, the genuine article. Joan wasn't sure what Swedenborgians believed in (she'd been raised a half-hearted Methodist, and she wasn't sure what Methodists believed in, either), but Bill told her it didn't matter what the Swedenborgians believed in, because he'd chosen the church primarily because of the windows. That made sense to Joan. She would have picked it just for the smell.

Joan hadn't lived in San Francisco all that long, and the only people she knew were the patients she nursed at the old age home, none of whom had the wherewithal to go to the toilet unaided, let alone come to a wedding. For his part, Bill said he really didn't like most of the people he knew, so they ended up inviting just two guests: Bill's boss, a man named Mayes, and his wife. Mr. Mayes was dapper and tiny, a fiftyish, thickset man just a shade over five feet tall, with thinning hair that had once been blond, and a veiny, bulbous nose that looked like it had been smashed up at the bridge by a baseball bat. His wife Eleanor, a nail-biter with big blue eyes, was much taller than Mr. Mayes—younger, button-nosed and wan.

The service was short and serene. Pastor Ambrose Cannon presided, offering a few pithy, Swedenborgian words of wisdom *sotto voce* to Joan and Bill before settling down to the vows. They'd made it clear beforehand that they wanted the ceremony to be brief and to the point, so Pastor Cannon, a tall, sunburned man with dyed red hair swept up in a bouffant, barged through the service breathlessly, pausing for nothing, and pronounced them man and wife so quickly that Joan, whose attention had wandered for just a moment as she watched a beautiful shaft of colored light dance across the polished wooden pews, was surprised when Bill lifted her chin to his face and kissed her. "Is it over already?" she asked him. Pastor Cannon hugged her to himself then, for a long moment, and Joan could have sworn that he rubbed himself against her inappropriately, grinding his pelvis delicately but determinedly into hers before letting her go.

At the reception after the wedding, Bill's boss Mr. Mayes offered to sing a toast to them, and when Joan and Bill agreed, he sang the jingle from old Lowenbrau commercials ("Tonight, tonight . . . let it be Lowenbrau") in a voice just like Arthur Prysock's.

"Gee, thanks. You sound just like Arthur Prysock," Bill said in a voice full of wonder.

"Who's Arthur Prysock?" Joan asked.

"Get a load of her," Bill said, and punched Joan in the arm so hard she spilled some of her champagne. She looked at him sternly. "Arthur fucking Prysock!" he shouted at her, as if that answered her question. Bill had been drinking before the ceremony.

"I don't sound like Arthur Prysock," Mr. Mayes said. "Arthur Prysock sounds like me."

"Oh, give it a rest," Eleanor said bitterly, and rolled her eyes.

Mr. Mayes retrieved a bottle of champagne from a nearby tray, and poured drinks for all four of them. "I'm simply making a point, my dear," he said, and drank his champagne in one gulp. Joan noticed the network of veins swarming over the tip of his nose, which appeared to be lit from within. "The beer you pour . . . should say something more . . . somehow," Mr. Mayes crooned in a mellow baritone, and pulled Joan toward him. "So tonight . . . tonight. . . ." He stood on tiptoes and breathed the last line wetly into her ear: "Let it be Lowenbrau."

Joan leaned down and kissed Mr. Mayes on the cheek, inhaling his odor, a combination of cigarettes, champagne and sweat. She knew Mr. Mayes was supposed to be sexy—Bill had told her about him repeatedly, regaling her with epic sagas involving Mr. Mayes's great prowess, his worldly success on many fronts, his combination of continental je ne sais quoi and American brashness—but Joan wasn't entirely convinced. He was so short, for one thing. Joan didn't have a problem with height, per se—she'd had a crush on a French professor her junior year of college, and he couldn't have stood more than five-seven—but Mr. Mayes was different. He went beyond short, all the way down to tiny. He was like a person, only smaller. Besides, there was his nose to consider.

Still, it was hard to ignore all those anecdotes Bill had told her. "Once he got thrown out of the Plaza Hotel in New York for breaking a desk clerk's index finger," Bill said, his voice breathless. "The desk clerk was wagging it at him, so Norton—Mr. Mayes—just broke it. They threw him down a flight of steps to get him out of the hotel. A whole flight of steps. He was pretty drunk, I guess. Another time he was thrown off a Pan Am flight from L.A. to Hong Kong—they put the plane down in Hawaii, emergency landing, just to get him off. He was smoking dope in the lavatory, and the smoke alarm went off, then he punched somebody—one of the stewardesses, actually. They said he did, anyway. I just heard about it. He's some kind of guy. He's banned at the Beverly Wilshire—banned for life. Something involving cocaine, I don't know. He was staying in one of the cabanas by the swimming pool. He can't set foot in the Chateau Marmont, either. And forget about the Ritz in Paris, too. Not a chance. He walks in there, they call the gendarmes in two seconds flat."

"Say, how's about you two lovebirds coming back to our place for a little post-wedding celebration?" Mr. Mayes said now. He grinned at Joan and waggled his eyebrows suggestively.

"Oh, I don't know," Bill said. He gripped Joan's shoulder and pulled her to his side.

"Norton, they just got married," Eleanor said. She knocked back another glass of champagne, leaned toward Joan unsteadily, and stage-whispered, "He's just trying to be friendly. Don't take it personally. This is just the way he is."

Joan peered at Eleanor. They were probably about the same age—but Eleanor was married to a man old enough to be her father! What was it like to have sex with a guy only slightly taller than a midget? Was that some kind of turn-on that Joan had never thought about? She tried to imagine her father, the poor guy, in bed—and immediately felt herself getting woozy. And if Mr. Mayes's nose looked like that, what would the rest of him look like? Joan wasn't sure whether she should feel sorry for Eleanor or envious of her. After all, Mr. Mayes might be five feet tall and have an unsightly nose and a checkered past, but he was richer than God, according to Bill—and Joan, having gone through her share of deprivation over the years, had a healthy respect for the transitory, shallow sort of happiness that money could buy.

Eleanor was very pretty—prettier than Joan, in fact. This was not a happy fact but it was a fact, and Joan lingered on it, just to prove to herself that even on her wedding day, she could face the truth about the world. Eleanor had high cheekbones—the kind of cheekbones Joan had always wanted. Not that Joan didn't have cheekbones of her own, of course; she did—but they weren't high. In fact, they were fairly low, and she had to poke herself in the face to feel them. She did this once or twice a day, just to make sure they were still there. Eleanor's chin was nice, too.

It wasn't prominent or mannish, but it wasn't weak, either, and when she pouted—which she was doing right now—her chin crunched up in a way that made it look like there was a dimple right in the middle of it. But then there were her nails—bitten down to the quick. Joan, on the other hand, had nice nails. No one ever complimented her on them, but she knew.

"I know they just got married," said Mr. Mayes. "You don't have to tell me that. I was there. I was a witness."

"Well, then. You ought to realize," Eleanor said, lengthening the word "realize" into a moan, "that they don't want to be coming over to our place on their wedding night. It's their wedding night, Norton. You know. Wink, wink. Their wedding night."

"Oh, well, no," Bill said. "It's not like that, really. We've been living together a while." He looked at Joan and must have seen something in the expression on her face, because he added, "That came out wrong. What I meant to say—"

"I know what people do on their wedding night," Mr. Mayes said. "I know perfectly well what people do on their wedding night. I've been married three times, you think I don't know what people do? In some cultures—listen to this—in some cultures, the whole town camps out around the house where the newlyweds are sleeping, and they bang on pots all night and throw bottles at the windows and get totally shit-faced, then in the morning the husband comes out holding the sheet, see, and if there isn't blood on it, the whole town goes inside and kills the bride. Isn't that something?"

"Oh, really," Eleanor said drily. "Where'd you read that, Norton?"

"I didn't read it," said Mr. Mayes. "I lived it. My first marriage. Island of Corfu. I was very young. I was a goddamned child. Believe me, you don't want to know about it. Bet you've never been to Corfu," he said, turning to Bill. "I bet you don't even know where Corfu is."

"I—you're right. I don't," Bill said. Joan stroked his shoulder, as if to tell him that it was okay not to know where Corfu was. What expression had crossed her face just a moment ago? She had no idea.

"So, you two coming over or not?" Mayes demanded. "It's a simple invitation. Just a friendly gesture, a boss inviting his employee over for a drink." He stared at Bill sternly.

Bill squeezed Joan closer to him. "Sure," he said in an unsteady voice.

"We'll drop by for a drink. Just for a little while." He gave Joan a sidelong glance. "We won't stay long," he added.

■ ■ ■

Joan took one look at the interior of the Mayes's apartment and gasped. She put a hand to her mouth and bit it gently. Wherever she looked, she saw money. The very air smelled rich—as if they had a filtering machine hidden somewhere pumping the atmosphere full of gold dust. Brightly colored Persian rugs lay in dazzling layered heaps upon the dark, gleaming hardwood floors; the walls were crowded with museum-quality works of art by the Old Masters—oils and watercolors, acquatints, drypoints framed in curlicued gilt. Music came floating softly toward her in the entry hall—something tasteful but jazzy, with a bossa nova beat. Facing her, a wall of picture windows afforded a panoramic view of the bay, the Golden Gate, the first tendrils of fog just starting to slither in from the Pacific.

This apartment—it was in an old pre-war building atop Pacific Heights—was enormous. Perhaps it was endless, Joan mused silently. Maybe it curved around on itself, like the universe. Then she shook her head, suddenly aware that she was thinking in gibberish. She'd had a glass of champagne after the ceremony, and it had obviously gone to her head. Now Norton Mayes handed her a flute of champagne. "Here, my dear," he said in his deep, throaty Arthur Prysock voice. Joan drank it down, hoping it would shock her back into sanity, then she sank into an overstuffed sofa upholstered in a beige fabric so rich to the touch that she had to suppress a moan of pleasure. What was this? Linen, raw silk? Perhaps a combination of the two. Oh, it felt so good just to sit here. So good—as good as anything she'd ever felt in her life. God, if He existed, probably took naps on a sofa just like this one. But Joan doubted He had a view this magnificent to go along with it. She could see sailboats dancing on the bay, little white triangles moving back and forth gaily, as if doing the foxtrot—and beyond, the green hills of Tiburon and Belvedere and Sausalito, places so posh and privileged that Joan had never even allowed herself to visit. Joan knew perfectly well that ferries took passengers to Tiburon and Sausalito every day, and she'd been tempted to hop aboard one several times, during her first weeks in San

Francisco, before she'd met Bill—but each time she'd thought of taking the ferry across the bay to one of these heavenly destinations, the thought of visiting someplace so lovely—just visiting without being able to stay—depressed her so much she couldn't bring herself to pay the fare. Now here they were, and here she was, ensconced in this drop-dead gorgeous apartment, nestled deep in the cushions of a couch so fabulous it brought tears to her eyes—and she could, she knew, stay here as long as she wanted to. She'd heard the offer in Mr. Mayes's throaty voice: she could stay put, right where she was, until the day she died.

"Hey, how about watching some home movies?" Mr. Mayes asked. He rubbed his hands in a show of glee.

"Oh, shit. I knew it. I knew this was what you had in mind, you sonuvabitch," said Eleanor. "This was what you had in mind all along. Norton, I'm telling you, if you do this, I'm calling Marty tomorrow morning, nine o'clock sharp." Her eyes were slits, and her cheekbones seemed to have little fists inside them, ready to spring out and start throwing punches.

"How about it, Bill? Joan?" Mayes asked. "You kids up for some video pleasure?"

"Norton, I'm serious. Nine o'clock sharp tomorrow, I'm calling Marty, you sick fuck," Eleanor warned.

"So call him. Call Marty. Nine o'clock sharp. He'll call you back at eleven, when he gets to the office. Tell him I said hello. And have him read you paragraph six of our pre-nup. Go ahead."

"Oh, gee, listen," said Bill. "Home movies! Holy smoke. That sounds like a hassle, doesn't it? Maybe some other time, hey?"

"No way! I've got it all set up," Mr. Mayes said, and rubbed his hands together again. "I've got every high-tech gadget in the world. Stuff you've never even heard of yet—I get it imported from Japan, they sneak it through customs for me down at the docks, the stuff's not even on sale yet in this country. I'm five years ahead of the market here. It's my hobby."

"Your hobby! Christ! Your hobby!" cried Eleanor in a voice choked with irony. She put a hand over her eyes, and wrapped her other arm around her waist like a seatbelt. "You're only doing this to humiliate me," she said. "You're a sick human being, Norton."

"My dear, that's absurd. It's so silly I won't even dignify it with a response." Mr. Mayes drained another flute of champagne.

"Oh, but now, wait a minute. If Eleanor really doesn't want to," Joan said, then fell silent. She didn't know what the rest of the sentence ought to be. Sisterly solidarity was great, but this was Bill's boss, after all, and it was Bill's turn to say something. She turned to him, but he was staring straight ahead into space, a little half-smile pasted on his lips.

"Okay, then! Let's roll 'em!" Norton Mayes cried in his Arthur Prysock voice, and thrust a remote control device toward the wall of windows. Blinds came down silently, and in seconds the apartment was plunged into darkness. A big-screen TV appeared (where had it been hiding?) and a moment later, the movie began. At first Joan couldn't tell what was going on. Everything was pink and fuzzy.

Soon it became apparent that the pink wasn't pink at all, but flesh—the flaccid, quivering flesh of someone's buttocks, moving in and out of focus. The camera eventually pulled away to show a man and woman having sex, the man on top, the woman's long and graceful calves wrapped around his thick waist. As the camera moved slowly upward, it revealed that the man was wearing a rubber full-head mask topped by a Nazi officer's cap. He looked very small.

"Who's that supposed to be?" Bill asked. "Oh, hell. Is it—oh, dammit, I should know this—what's his name? The guy with the moustache?"

"It's Heinrich Himmler, Bill. Available at a novelty store near you. You've heard of Himmler, haven't you?" asked Mr. Mayes. "The Gestapo? The Third Reich? I hate to say this, kiddo, but you sure missed a lot by not going to college."

The man wearing the Himmler mask was thrusting hard into the woman beneath him—smack, smack, smack. His buttocks and love handles jiggled on every downstroke. Joan was glad Bill didn't have love handles, because it would have been disconcerting, it would have taken away some of the thrill of having sex with him. Bill was very thin. You were never far from the bone when you touched Bill. She thought about that for a moment—anything to take her mind off what she was watching on television. Then her curiosity got the better of her, and she found herself cocking her head to one side to try to get a better view of the woman's face, which was hidden, for the most part, by the man's sturdy right arm. Was this Eleanor? It had to be. Certainly it had to be. Who else would it have been? The little man wearing the Himmler mask must have been Mr. Mayes—but no, she couldn't imagine Eleanor allowing a video camera into the bedroom. Not Eleanor. Not for something like this. And not just a camera, mind you—a camera man! Or woman, it wouldn't have made a difference. Who cared whether it was a man or a woman standing over the bed, moving around, zooming in and out, probably giving them directions! "Let's have a little more thrusting now, folks! Give me some emotion, will you? Shake it, baby! Open those thighs a little wider! Give me some torque! I want to feel the earth move!"

The camera zoomed in on the woman's breasts, which were small and long-nippled, then moved down to her lean, pearlescent belly, rippling in the shadows under the man's thick gut. Joan kept her head cocked. Gee, it did sort of look like Eleanor, though, the longer she looked. Poor Eleanor—married to a five-foot-tall sex maniac. The video ground on, the rhythmic smack of the man's pounding like the ticking of a metronome. Watching people have sex wasn't as interesting as Joan had once imagined it might be. In fact there was something hypnotic about it, and Joan felt her eyes growing heavy. It was like watching ocean waves pound the shore. Still she held her head cocked. If this went on much longer, she was going to throw her neck out.

Then finally there was a break in the action, the man reared up on his haunches and got his arm out of the way, and Joan got a good look at the woman's face at last. It wasn't Eleanor, after all. The woman was sharp-featured, a brunette, attractive in a dark, feral sort of way, but not as pretty as Eleanor. Joan felt so relieved that before she could stop herself, she blurted out, "Oh, thank God." Her eyes had adjusted to the dark by now. She cast a furtive glance toward Eleanor, who had retreated to a sofa at the far end of the room, where she sat with her legs drawn up tight against her chest.

"You bastard," Eleanor moaned, not to anyone in particular. "How could you? You're a sick, sick fuck." She balled a fist into her mouth.

On the television, the man in the Heinrich Himmler mask beat his chest with his fists and then, withdrawing abruptly from the woman he'd been smacking into, he wagged his penis at the camera. The penis was short but thick, its oversized head glistening, throbbing with dew. "Holy shit, look at the plumbing on that guy!" Mr. Mayes crowed. "That thing means business! Whoa, Nellie!"

"Well, hey," Bill said. He glanced at his watch and pushed the button to illuminate the dial. "We probably ought to be heading on down the road," he said, and patted Joan's knee.

"Oh, gee," Joan said. "Really? Already?"

"Wait a second! You gotta see this!" cried Mr. Mayes. The man in the Himmler mask jerked his penis brusquely toward the camera, and after a few strokes, a gob of cum spurted onto the camera lens, where it hung in a viscous mass for a long moment before dribbling down and out of frame. "The end," Mr. Mayes announced theatrically. "Wow, that last part always gets to me. I find it very moving. But that's just me—I'm a soft touch for romance."

"Let's get going, honey," Bill said to Joan in a tense, urgent whisper. "Let's go home."

"Every party needs a pooper, that's why we invited you—party-pooper!" Mr. Mayes sang to Bill, and rubbed his hands in delight.

"Joan," said Bill insistently, and tugged at her sleeve.

"We just got here, dear," Joan told him. "It'd be rude to leave now."

"Nine o'clock tomorrow morning, you prick," Eleanor muttered. "Nine o'clock sharp."

It was very dark in the apartment, but Joan could see quite clearly now. She pulled her sleeve away from Bill's touch and rested her hand in her lap, where if she held her index finger just so, she could feel her clitoris throbbing through the silk of her panties and the thin linen of her wedding dress. *Oh, my goodness,* Joan thought. She leaned back further into the soft, enveloping cushions of the sofa. Her clitoris was named Dominique. Joan had never realized that until now, but suddenly it was as clear and undeniable as her own name. Dominique might be calling the shots for a little while, Joan now realized. She flicked her finger lightly across the linen material of her dress. Oh, yezz, oh yezz. Dominique was feeling mighty fine just now.

"Joan?" said Bill. "Honey?"

teeth

After he'd gotten his elderly mother settled securely in a nursing home in Cleveland, not far from her old apartment, Arthur Kornfeld drove through the night and most of the next day to reach Parkersburg, Iowa, the town where he'd just been hired to teach World History at the high school. He drove like something was chasing him. His car was old and unreliable, and he told himself that if he stopped for very long, it might not start again. School would be starting in just a few days, and since this was his first full-time teaching job, he felt terribly anxious about the burdens of his new position. Arthur was shy. Throughout graduate school his weakest marks had come in courses that demanded a great deal of classroom participation. Now, thanks to his job, it would be his turn to lead class discussion every single day, five times a day. The thought of this made his heart bang against his breastbone as if trying to break it, and he tapped out syncopated rhythms on the steering wheel to keep his hands from shaking.

His first morning in Parkersburg, Arthur made the bed in his motel room, even though he knew the maids would be by eventually. Then he used toilet paper to wipe out the bathroom sink, and considered scrubbing the tub with a washcloth, but decided that he was being foolish. Finally he sat on the edge of the bed and drank the coffee he'd brewed in the miniature Mr. Coffee machine in the bathroom. A copy of last week's edition of the Parkersburg *Clarion* had been left on the television set, and Arthur fanned through it idly, noting the club news, the lists of honor students at the elementary school, the recipes, the school lunch menus and the rest of it. On page seven he saw an advertisement that carried the headline, "I Got My Teeth Straightened In Only Nine Months!" A before-and-after black and white photo was positioned below the headline, and the transformation was truly amazing. The left side of the photo looked like Arthur's teeth. The right side looked like a movie star's. The ad didn't mention how much this transformation might cost, but as he stared at the side-by-side photos, Arthur told himself that the cost didn't matter. He'd always hated going to the dentist and had avoided it for years, but he'd left all that behind him now. He was a teacher now—a professional man. This was the beginning of a new life for him, and a new life meant making some changes. And so before he could talk himself out of it, Arthur called the number listed at the bottom of the ad, and made an appointment.

Two weeks later, he sat fidgeting in the waiting room at Dr. Pratt's office, thumbing through a tattered copy of *People* magazine dated August of three years ago, not really reading any of the stories. Naturally enough, he was brooding about the state of his teeth, which constituted one of the saddest aspects of his not-very-cheery life. He'd been poor for many years, and during college he'd had three of his molars pulled, simply because that was cheaper than more elaborate dental procedures such as root canals. Even routine fillings had stretched his meager budget past the breaking point. The result of these many years of neglect was that now, as he sat pretending to look at *People*, he was preoccupied with worry over how he was going to pay for what was surely going to be a major overhaul of all the teeth left in his head, and how he was going to look in front of five classes full of students while he was on the mend. He'd be rambling on about the Battle of Hastings or the Papal Schism, and they'd be staring at the mess in his mouth. He could see it already, could hear the back-row snickering, the whispered comments.

No one in Parkersburg seemed anxious to call him Arthur—which was fine with him, because he'd always detested the name—and so he'd begun to introduce himself in social situations as Mr. Kornfeld, the name his students used when they spoke to him. He realized that this sounded formal, but he'd come to the conclusion that formality was not a thing to be avoided in life. He bore himself with what he assumed looked like dignity, his head thrown back, shoulders straight (the residue of a two-year hitch in the Army), and he'd kept a watchful eye on his waistline, having seen his father balloon out of control as he plummeted through late middle age toward death. Because he kept his head so erect, Arthur ended up looking down his nose at people, but even so, there was something sad and defeated in his demeanor. He looked like a man who'd lost everything—lost it so long ago that he no longer remembered what it was he'd had to start with. His hair, what was left of it, had faded over the past two years from a dull brown to a transparent shade of gray, so that from a distance, a woman he'd known in graduate school had told him not long ago, it appeared that he was bald.

The ragged issue of *People* he was thumbing through was devoted almost entirely to the death of Princess Diana. Arthur looked at picture after picture of her, but couldn't tell if she'd been attractive or not. She was tall. He'd read that about her more than once. It was hard to beat height in a woman, he told himself—and then he added, *Oh, yeah, as if you know anything about women,* which was a little jab to remind himself of the lonely wasteland he'd made of his life so far, and the likelihood that things weren't going to look up for him in the foreseeable future. He kept flipping through the memorial issue of *People,* trying to come to some conclusion about Diana's appearance. This was important to him—as if he'd been hired to evaluate her beauty for a contest of some kind. In some pictures Diana's nose appeared to be so long that it almost touched her upper lip—but in others she looked positively gorgeous. A lot of it must have had to do with the camera angle. She had a radiant smile—that much was clear. Her teeth were as white as the underbelly of a shark. They were huge, too—though not out of proportion to her face. Her teeth made her nose look smaller, actually. And they were perfect, as straight and proper as a row of chiclets. With teeth that impressive, there wasn't much you couldn't do in this life, Arthur told himself.

A year after Diana's fatal accident, when Arthur was still in graduate school, he'd seen a British fellow, someone close to the Royal Family, a former friend of Diana's, being interviewed on Ted Koppel. This former friend came out with the information that despite the fact that she was so popular with the common folk of England, Diana was one of the dumbest, most vacuous people he'd ever met. "Not a thought in her head," he'd told Ted Koppel. "Dense as a stone." That struck Arthur as a nasty thing to say about someone who'd died so horribly, even if it was true. He put down the magazine now and picked at a loose thread coming from a button on his brown cardigan sweater, and sure enough, the button popped off and landed in his lap. He sighed: something else he'd have to do this evening, sew on this button. As if grading five sets of quizzes wouldn't be enough. It was already clear to him that some of his students were very likely among the dumbest, most vacuous people he'd ever met, but he'd never say something like that about them on television, especially if one of them had died in a terrible car crash.

"Mr. Kornfeld?" the dental assistant called out. She was a tall, thin young woman with narrow shoulders and curly brown hair that tumbled out like mattress stuffing from under her nurse's cap. She held his chart in front of her chest like a schoolgirl would hold a notebook. "We're ready for you now."

He followed her to the examination room, which was paneled in something that might have looked like wood to anyone who'd never actually seen the real thing. Arthur settled into the reclining chair, gripped the armrests, and stared up at the bright overhead light. Dr. Pratt strode into the examining room a moment later, snapping on latex gloves. He was thin, with a pink complexion and a bright, gleaming smile. "Hello there, fella," he said. "Let's see what's going on here." Without any further conversation he opened Arthur's mouth and peered inside, then quickly jerked his head away, as if he'd seen something dead in there. "Oh, brother," Dr. Pratt said with a cluck. "Oh, boy." He stepped away from the chair and frowned at Arthur.

"It's that bad?"

"I wish you'd come to see me a year ago."

"A year ago I was still in graduate school," Arthur said. "I was selling my plasma to pay the rent. I only just got hired at the high school here last month." Normally he wouldn't have said anything like this to a perfect stranger, but there was something accusatory in Dr. Pratt's tone that stung him into confession.

"Is that right. What's your subject, if you don't mind my asking."

"World History. I called for an appointment the minute I got to town. I hadn't even rented an apartment yet. Honest."

"World History. Isn't that something. All those dates! Well, anyway, I'm glad you came in when you did. Not a minute too soon," said Dr. Pratt. "We'll take some x-rays, for starters. Lily here will take care of that for you." He nodded toward the dental assistant.

Lily smiled. "Don't worry, Mr. Kornfeld. It'll be over in a minute or two," she told him.

"All the pain comes later," Dr. Pratt said with a chuckle, and cracked his knuckles. "That's a joke, of course. Well, okay then," he added on his way out the door.

Lily bent a small piece of cardboard and stuck it into Arthur's mouth. "Bite down on that, will you?" It hurt, the cardboard felt like it was cutting into his gums, but he continued biting down while she stepped out of the room. He heard a mechanical click, and then Lily was back at his side. "You can open up now," she told him. She lifted the bent cardboard out, put another piece in on the opposite side of his mouth, and told him to bite down again. Another click, and they were finished. "All righty. I'll just put these in to be processed, and I'll be back in two shakes," Lily said.

While she was gone, Arthur practiced his deep breathing, an exercise he'd been working on to overcome his stage fright before teaching. He imagined himself in a warm, fragrant, dimly-lit room. Soft music played somewhere nearby. He breathed in deeply, held the breath, exhaled slowly and completely. He felt himself relax into the chair. Everything was going to be all right, he told himself. He didn't believe a word of this, but it was nice to hear himself say it.

Several minutes later, when Arthur had stopped trying to reassure himself and had slipped into a peaceful, dreamy state approaching sleep, Lily returned with Dr. Pratt in tow. "Let's see what we've got cooking," Dr. Pratt said, and snapped a small sheet of x-ray film into position on the screen of a light-box. Arthur looked at the images on the screen. Good grief, these were his teeth, jutting this way and that, gaps between them. They reminded Arthur of Stonehenge. Dr. Pratt put on a pair of reading glasses and studied the x-rays at close range for several minutes. Finally he turned to Arthur. "Does it hurt when you put something cold in your mouth?" he asked. "Iced drinks?"

"Yes," Arthur confessed.

"How about hot? Coffee? Soup?"

"Yes. That hurts, too."

"I'm not surprised." Dr. Pratt took a metal pointer the length of a conductor's baton out of his breast pocket and pointed it at various spots on the x-rays. "Look at what we have here . . . here . . . here . . . and probably here, too." He turned to face Arthur squarely. "Cracked teeth, cavities—some real beauts—and see right here, and here—you've got some bite problems because of the teeth you've lost."

Arthur nodded. "My gosh, this is terrible," he said. "Isn't it?" He looked up hopefully.

"Oh, it's not so bad. Want to hear the good news? We can fix you right up," Dr. Pratt told him. "What do you say to that? Thanks to our patented 'Accelerated Straightening Program,' in nine months we'll have you looking like a movie star."

Lily patted Arthur's arm. "Isn't this exciting?" she asked in a hushed voice, and Arthur felt a sudden wobble in his heart, as if someone had reached inside his chest and adjusted something slightly.

▪ ▪ ▪

The health plan that came with Arthur's teaching job was fairly good for dental work: after he'd used up his two hundred dollar deductible, the school system would pay ninety percent of his bills. His teacher's salary wasn't grand, but compared to the poverty of his early life and his school years, he was doing rather well. His room at Mrs. Arnold's rooming house was spacious, well-lit, and cheap; and since it came fully equipped with both a comfortable bed and a desk large enough for him to spread out his work each night, he hadn't had to spend a penny on furniture. The wallpaper in his room was ivory, dotted with a small beige pattern of fleur-de-lys that conjured up memories of *The Three Musketeers,* one of the set of handsomely illustrated books Arthur's parents had kept in a cabinet in the living room when he was a boy. His parents hadn't had much time to spend with him—they'd both worked long hours in order to keep the family afloat—and so Arthur spent a great deal of his childhood alone, thumbing through these volumes, staring at them for hours. He'd read the first two chapters of *The Three Musketeers* about a dozen times. Now, at night, just before he turned out his bedside lamp and went to sleep, he stared at the fleur-de-lys wallpaper in his room, and recalled the lonely boy he'd once been. He thought about his parents, his father long dead, his mother in the Cleveland nursing home where he'd left her. Of course he was saddened by these memories—he lingered on them as if probing a sore tooth with his tongue—but hidden within the sadness, Arthur sensed a kind of pleasure, as well.

He ate his breakfast and dinner alone most days at Merle's Eagle Cafe down the street, where the food was decent and cheap. For lunch he normally grabbed a salad from the cafeteria at school, eating it quietly in the faculty lounge while his colleagues played raucous games of cribbage at the table nearby. If he watched his pennies, he might be able to put aside a little bit each month, and by the time he turned forty, he could have enough for a down payment on a little house near Parkersburg's high school, somewhere within walking distance, so that he wouldn't have to wait on the bus in cold weather. And in the meantime, he'd be having his teeth fixed. If he'd been a different sort of person, Arthur might have felt a new sense of hope for his future. But he wasn't a different sort of person, and so he didn't feel much of anything at all.

He went back to the dentist's office for his second appointment several days later. Dr. Pratt was out of the office for the day, playing golf. Lily took plaster molds of the inside of his mouth, top and bottom, which came out looking like a pale version of the wind-up chattering teeth Arthur had seen once in the window of a novelty shop, when he was just a boy. He'd been mesmerized by them then, though now that he was no longer a boy, the memory of them sickened him. His teeth looked even worse in plaster than they did when he looked at them in the mirror each morning. They looked like they belonged to a dead person—somebody who'd been shot in the teeth, in fact.

"Oh, no, everybody says that," Lily told him when he remarked on the appearance of the teeth. "Yours aren't so bad." She touched his arm again, just as she'd done during his last visit, and again he felt his heart seize up for a moment, as if it had lost its sense of balance. Arthur nestled back in the reclining chair and thought about Lily, and what her hair might look like without the little white nurse's cap perched on her head. He knew almost no one in Parkersburg aside from the friends he'd made among the teachers at the high school. A month wasn't very much time to make friends, after all, and besides, Arthur was shy, and didn't speak to strangers unless they spoke to him first.

Most of the other teachers at his school were quite a bit older, married with children, and so even though they were friendly enough to him during the course of a school day, none of them had shown any real interest in seeing him outside of work. Mrs. Arnold, his landlady, a widow in her seventies, seemed genuinely pleased to have him as a roomer in her house. She'd tried to engage him in polite conversation on the day he moved in. "Do you have family nearby?" she asked. She was standing in the doorway of his room, watching him put away his clothes.

"No," he answered, and continued unpacking.

"No one?" Mrs. Arnold asked. "No parents, no sisters or brothers?"

"I'm an only child. My father is dead. My mother's in a nursing home back in Cleveland."

"My, my, and you, such a young man. You poor thing."

"My parents were quite old when I was born. I think I was a surprise," Arthur told her. He hadn't meant to say this—it was out of his mouth before he had a chance to stop himself. He'd emptied his suitcase now, and so he shut it and slid it under the bed.

Mrs. Arnold went on for a few more minutes about the sadness of life, but he'd stopped listening, and when she noticed this, she apologized for taking his time when he was trying to get settled, and went away. In the days that followed, however, Mrs. Arnold found several more opportunities to bend Arthur's ear. Her voice was loud and tinny, and as it turned out, she had the unpleasant habit of punctuating her remarks with bursts of nervous laughter, unconnected to anything amusing—laughter pitched in a register so high that dogs in the neighborhood howled when they heard it. This laugh drove Arthur to thoughts of violence, and so despite his loneliness, which as the weeks went by felt like a weight pressing down on him from the ceiling, he began to avoid her company.

That left Merle at Merle's Eagle Cafe—and here again, there were problems. Merle knew how to poach eggs so that the whites were set firm and the yolks were still runny, which was just the way Arthur liked them. He had a way with grilled onions, too—they were sweet, limp and glistening, but never oily. But the Eagle Cafe was a dusty, dismal place, and since Merle was gregarious by nature, he listened to crackpot right-wing talk-radio shows all day long, and talked back to the radio constantly, as if butting in on conversations. Once he'd learned that Arthur taught history, it became Merle's sole purpose in life to goad him into arguments over international politics. One evening just a few days after Arthur had arrived in Parkersburg, Merle leaned across the counter and said, "What would you say if I told you that Franklin Roosevelt is actually still alive? He's a wreck, of course—he's being fed through a tube in his stomach—but he's still at work, handing this country over to the Commies piece by piece, operating from a hospital bed in an undisclosed location." This was absurd, of course. Franklin Roosevelt would have been about a hundred and twenty years old by now, Arthur knew, and anyway, he just wanted to eat his supper, he just wanted to sit and eat his roast chicken and buttered noodles and brussels sprouts, was that asking too much? He raised his eyebrows as if seriously contemplating this fascinating information about Roosevelt's ongoing perfidy, then he offered Merle a noncommital nod and turn his attention back to his food.

▪ ▪ ▪

The following Wednesday afternoon, Dr. Pratt began to work on Arthur's teeth. The ordeal went on for two hours, with much drilling and wiring and gluing, and when it was over, Arthur stumbled out of the office into the fading light of early evening, unable to feel anything between his nose and his neck. He kept poking himself in the jaw with his thumb, just to test the lingering aftereffects of the novocaine. The numbness lasted until bedtime, when his mouth began to throb. He swallowed two of the pain pills Dr. Pratt had given him, and awoke the next morning feeling like he'd been dropped into his bed from a great height. He taught all his classes that day, and everything seemed to go smoothly, though he realized after supper that evening that he'd forgotten to administer a quiz on the Treaty of Ghent.

That began his nine-month course of treatment. Each Wednesday thereafter, he arrived at Dr. Pratt's office after school, where as the weeks went by he underwent a staggering array of dental work. First Dr. Pratt would tighten the wires that ran along the inside surface of Arthur's teeth, and then he turned his attention to fillings, crowns, and the rest. Lily was always at Dr. Pratt's side during these sessions, handing him various instruments as he required them, squirting water into Arthur's mouth and suctioning away his saliva and blood. She patted him on the arm reassuringly from time to time. Arthur imagined that she did this whenever Dr. Pratt turned away for a moment. He lived for these secret pats, anticipated them with the breathless excitement of someone in love. Indeed, he thought he might be in love with her, because he'd begun to think about her at night, just before he turned out his reading lamp and went to sleep. In his thoughts, he envisioned her taking off her nurse's cap and letting her curly mop of brown hair tumble down over her face. This was as far as he'd allow his imagination to travel. One night he dreamed that he and Lily were on vacation somewhere exotic, walking together through a jungle so lush that it blotted out the sunlight. They held hands as they made their way through endless leafy darkness.

Was this love? Arthur wasn't sure. But it was something, and he wanted very much to speak to Lily, to ask her to accompany him to a movie, a recital, a play, or perhaps just a walk around Parkersburg's town square, which was beautiful in the fall, with the leaves on the elm and maple trees in full color. This desire was like an ache in his heart, a physical pain that felt both sharp and tender.

Each Wednesday he would arrive at the dentist's office convinced that this would be the day he'd speak to Lily. He would watch her in silence as she arranged the dentist's tools across the white napkin that covered the tray by the chair. Occasionally they exchanged small talk: hello, how are you, how was your week, it might rain, and so on. Then, after Arthur's wires had been tightened, Dr. Pratt would sweep into the room with an outsized hypodermic needle, moments later the novocaine would take effect, and by the time they were finished and Arthur finally had Lily's undivided attention, he'd be incapable of saying anything at all.

The general appearance of his teeth was undoubtedly improving, with remarkable results. A slender blonde in his 10:30 European History class, Kristy Ferguson, lingered fidgeting at his desk at the end of the class period one Monday morning, and after much hesitation finally asked him if he'd consider sponsoring the Future Astronauts' Club. She picked at a mole on her arm as she spoke to him, and in her eyes he saw infatuation. "Wouldn't you rather get one of the science teachers for that?" he asked her.

"Oh, no. We'd rather have you, Mr. Kornfeld," Kristy said in a breathy whisper. "Really." Her eyes were large and pale blue, and her skin was remarkably clear for someone her age. There was one small pimple in the middle of her forehead, like a third eye, and this tiny flaw was endearing.

"Well, Kristy, if you're sure I'm your first choice . . ."

"Oh, you are. You are, Mr. Kornfeld. Honest."

"All right, then," he said, and smiled. Smiling somehow felt different now that his teeth were on the mend; his jaws ached, for one thing, but it was a good ache, because he knew it meant his teeth were rearranging themselves along straighter, more aesthetically pleasing lines. He patted Kristy's shoulder as she beamed up at him. This was something he wouldn't have tried before he'd begun to have his teeth worked on; it was a casual, avuncular, asexual gesture—but if it was so asexual, why did he feel a tremor of excitement rushing down his arm?

That night before bed, he tried to think of Lily taking off her nurse's cap, but a vision of Kristy Ferguson elbowed its way into his imagination instead. She took off an astronaut's glass bubble helmet, lifted her long blonde hair, then let it drop around her bare shoulders, then repeated this lifting and dropping several more times. Her hair rose in a blonde cloud around her head, then dropped like a curtain, hiding her features. Arthur was transfixed by this scene, and it so disturbed him that he hardly slept at all. In graduate school he'd known quite a few professors who'd had affairs with their students. Men in their fifties carried on with students young enough to be their daughters, and occasionally even married them. But that was graduate school, where the students were in their twenties, and everything was between consenting adults. This was different—Kristy Ferguson was probably around sixteen. Arthur wasn't naive; he knew that these days, young people were having sex in Junior High, and it was very possible that Kristy Ferguson was already familiar with sexual positions he'd only seen sketched on bathroom walls. A recent article in the Parkersburg *Clarion* had trumpeted the terrible news of declining morals among the town's youth—teenaged pregnancies, abortions, sexually transmitted diseases—and Arthur had read it with a grim but undeniably excited appetite. None of that made any difference, though. There were laws about things like this. This would be considered Statutory Rape, and the penalties for it were severe. It had taken him a lifetime of scrambling and sacrifice to attain his current position. He'd be hounded from his job if he so much as laid a hand on Kristy Ferguson—publicly shamed, denounced from every pulpit in Parkersburg, perhaps strung up from a lamp post.

The next Wednesday at Dr. Pratt's office, Arthur took the plunge. "Excuse me," he said as Lily arranged the dentist's tools on the white napkin. "Before Dr. Pratt comes in to adjust my wires and give me my shot—I was wondering if I might ask you something."

"Of course," Lily said. "Go right ahead." She smiled at him, holding a dental tool, something that resembled a snub-nosed set of pliers, beneath her chin.

"Okay, here goes," Arthur began. He was very nervous, but he knew he had to lunge ahead with this. He simply had to. After so many nights spent envisioning Lily, watching her hair tumble down over her face, he'd come to believe that he was getting to know her. At some level, he knew that this was untrue—but still, the feeling wouldn't go away. "Would you care to have dinner with me some night?" he asked her. "A night when I can chew, that is? Tomorrow night, maybe? Or Friday?"

"Oh, my. Mr. Kornfeld, that's certainly a very kind offer," Lily began—but there was an apologetic falling-away in the timbre of her voice, a sad, regretful quality that was unmistakable to him. Arthur had heard this tone of voice before. Suddenly he could see that he'd been kidding himself, something he tried never to do.

"That's all right. Forgive me for asking," he said, interrupting her. "Let's pretend I never said anything. Please."

Lily put down the pliers and smoothed her starched white frock. "It's not that I wouldn't love to have dinner with you. I'd consider it a pleasure. It's just that—"

"No, please. It's all right. Consider the matter closed," Arthur said. He sat back in the reclining chair, shut his eyes, and blew out a sigh.

That night Mrs. Arnold stopped him in the foyer, where he was picking up his mail, and asked him if he'd like to come to her singing recital the following Tuesday. "I can't remember if I told you about my musical ability," she added, and then broke into peals of laughter.

He gathered his mail into a small pile and backed away from her. "No, I don't think you mentioned it," he told her. His mouth was still completely numb, and he wasn't sure if the words had come out the way he'd meant them to; what was worse, he was afraid that he was drooling without realizing it. He wiped his free hand clumsily across his lips: nothing there, thank God.

"You know the Methodist Church on Garfield?" asked Mrs. Arnold.

"I've seen it," said Arthur, nodding his head like a ventriloquist's dummy. "It's a very pretty building."

"Seven-thirty. You can't be late, now, Arthur—we're hoping for a very large crowd," she warned, and then was overcome with another sudden surge of laughter, which burst from her like water from a hydrant.

When she'd regained control of herself, she said, "Do you know the Schubert song, 'A Little Yellow Bird'? That's my signature tune. I perform it every year at my recital." She clasped her hands together at her throat and looked toward the ceiling. "'A Little Yellow Bird.' I truly doubt that you could find a more beautiful song in the world."

"I'm not familiar with it," he told her.

"It's quite lovely. It sings of the joy and perfection of a little yellow bird in springtime." Then Mrs. Arnold's face suddenly crumpled. "A shot rings out," she said, her voice breaking, "and the little yellow bird is dead. It falls lifeless to the forest floor, never to fly again."

"That's very sad."

"Oh, yes. It's so sad I can hardly bear it," said Mrs. Arnold, and laughed so hard that the pearls in her necklace danced across her bosom like a conga line.

That night at Merle's, Arthur gummed his way through his tossed salad, his meat loaf, his mashed potatoes and gravy, and his green beans in peace. It was only when he moved on to his dessert, a wedge of apple crisp, that Merle emerged from behind the counter and approached Arthur's table carrying a dishtowel. He pulled out a chair and sat in it backwards. "You being a teacher and all, I guess you've heard about the subliminal thought experiments—laymen call this 'brain-washing'—being conducted by Communists on television, many of them earning six figures a year in the employ of the KGB?" he said in a casual tone.

Arthur swallowed a bit of apple crisp and pushed the plate away. "No, as a matter of fact I haven't heard anything about that," he said, and suddenly he couldn't contain himself any longer. "To tell you the truth, it sounds crazy. Whoever told you that is some kind of lunatic. There aren't any Communists anymore. There's no Soviet Union. The Cold War's over. We won! Jesus Christ." Having made this dramatic pronouncement, he wiped his mouth with his napkin, then wadded it up and placed it lightly atop the debris of his dinner.

Merle frowned. "Say now, what the heck's got your underwear so snug, young fella?"

"I had a hard day."

"That's no reason to bite a man's head off." Merle stood up and pushed the chair back to its original position. "What do you teach, again?"

"World History."

"Oh, well, that explains it. You told me that. History was my worst subject. All those dates! I ever tell you about my teacher, Mr. Kloefkorn? Taught Algebra?"

"No."

"I hated him," said Merle. "Everybody hated him. I bet his wife even hated him. He had a metal plate in his head from World War Two, but that's no excuse. He had this rule, see. Anybody who did anything wrong in his class had to stand up at the front of the room and say, 'I'm a little stinker,' real loud. You couldn't just whisper it, he'd make you do it over if you did. It didn't take much, either—you could do just about anything, some tiny mistake, and he'd make you stand up there and say that. And if you didn't do it, he'd send you to the principal's office and they'd tan your hide."

"Is that right. When was this?"

"Thirty-seven years ago, and here I am still beefing about it. Come to class five minutes late, 'I'm a little stinker.' Show up without your homework done, 'I'm a little stinker.' Pass a note in class, 'I'm a little stinker.' I mean, what's the point."

"You've got me," said Arthur. "I've certainly never tried anything like that."

"Thirty-seven years ago," Merle said, "and I still think about that little white-haired prick."

That night Arthur couldn't get Mr. Kloefkorn out of his thoughts. He flailed about in his sleep, imagining the white-haired, metal-plated Algebra teacher strutting back and forth in front of a classroom like a drill sergeant, hands behind his back, barking orders. He awoke the next morning exhausted but full of resolve, and when he saw two boys scuffling in the back row during his 10:30 European History class, Arthur called their names and asked them to approach his desk. He thought he heard the sound of blood rushing around inside his head—like waves pounding a seashore—as he waited for the boys to come forward. He should have done something like this long ago. He'd been waiting for this moment for a very long time. "I want you to turn around to the class and say, 'I'm a little stinker,'" he told the boys. "Say it right in front of the whole class."

"What?" they asked, more or less in unison.

"You heard me. Turn around, face the class, and say, 'I'm a little stinker.' Matt, you go first. Then you, Andy. From now on, by gosh, there's going to be some discipline in this classroom." Arthur flashed a thin smile at them and folded his fingers together under his chin like a tent.

The boys stared at him in disbelief. He sat still, listening to the waves crashing inside his head—listening to his blood swirling tirelessly through his veins and arteries, pushing itself into every nook and cranny of his body. Seconds ticked by. The boys stood gaping at him, wide-eyed, until finally he made a whirling motion with his hands, urging them to turn around. "Class," he announced. "Let me have your attention. Let's have it quiet, please. Andy and Matt have something they'd like to say." He shooed them away, toward the front row of seats.

After a long moment, Matt stepped forward and bit his lip, staring intently at the linoleum tile floor. Then he pointed to Arthur and said in a choked, reluctant voice, "He's a little stinker." The class erupted into laughter.

"All right, wise guy," Arthur snapped. The rushing sound inside his head grew to a roar, and though he gasped for air, his lungs felt empty, deflated, as if he'd been run over by a piece of heavy machinery. He grabbed Matt's shirt and held him by the sleeve. "That's twenty demerits and five hours of detention for you," he muttered. "Plus you can forget about the field trip to the state capitol next month." He could see Kristy Ferguson at the back of the room, staring at him, her face a pale mask of disappointment.

■ ■ ■

It came as no surprise to Arthur when his contract was not renewed by the Parkersburg school district, shortly before the end of the spring semester. He'd be able to stay through the end of the school year, and then in May he'd be done. No one gave him a definitive reason, but he figured it was the "I'm a little stinker" episode that had done him in. Word of it had reached the local newspaper, and an angry editorial denouncing Arthur's "outdated and childish mistreatment of students" had caused quite a vigorous response around town. There were indignant letters to the editor. He even received a few pieces of hate mail, though they were worded so politely that he had to read them several times to figure out their intent.

"Would it be possible for you to make other living arrangements?" Mrs. Arnold asked him three weeks after the editorial appeared. "You can take as long as you like, of course, Mr. Kornfeld, but I'll be needing the room sooner or later. My niece might be coming to stay with me. She's thinking about leaving her husband now that she's had her miscarriage and he's lost his job, and she says she has nowhere else to go." Arthur flinched instinctively, waiting for a cascade of Mrs. Arnold's laughter to accompany this dreadful news, but none came. She'd been cool toward him ever since he'd missed her recital at the Methodist Church. She was still polite, but she hardly laughed at all when she spoke to him—in fact, she didn't even smile very often.

Oddly enough, in the immediate aftermath of the "I'm a little stinker" scandal, Merle greeted Arthur like a hero every time he entered the Eagle Cafe. "There's the man!" he'd cry from behind the counter, and Arthur's food would come flying out of the kitchen only minutes after he'd ordered it. "Well, the scientists have done it, finally," Merle said one evening as Arthur ate his spaghetti and meatballs. "They've proven once and for all, beyond a shadow of a doubt, that Eleanor Roosevelt was a man." Merle scooted his chair closer to Arthur's table. "A lot of people knew that already, of course—there's never been a woman that ugly in the whole history of the world, and you know that as well as I do—but the historians, well, you couldn't get a straight answer out of one of them if you held a gun to his head. Which, by the way, wouldn't be the worst idea in the world." He paused. "Did you ever see the *teeth* on Eleanor Roosevelt?"

"No," said Arthur, though that wasn't entirely true. He'd seen some pictures. Her teeth were very big. He kept his eyes on his plate.

"Eat up. Seconds are on the house," Merle told him, and clapped him on the back. "Little guy like you, dealing with these goddamned punks every day, you need to keep your strength up."

"All right, that's it, that's just about enough," Arthur said, and abruptly stood up. The words came tumbling out of his mouth before he could stop himself, but now that he'd said them, he felt he had to do something dramatic to accompany them. He was still holding his napkin, so he wiped his mouth with it and tossed it on the table along with ten dollars, which was considerably more than he owed for his dinner.

"What? Did I say something wrong?" Merle asked.

"Yes," said Arthur, then his resolve weakened, and he added, "I don't know. Not really." He let the cafe door slam behind him. On the way home he stopped at the Rexall Drugstore and bought a one-burner hotplate for his room. Then he stopped at the Jiffy-Quick Market and bought six cans of chicken noodle soup and a can opener.

He was reaching the end of his nine-month course of dental work—luckily for him, because without a job, soon he'd have been unable to pay for the treatments, anyway. He'd had visions of growing old in this town, becoming white and hunched-over and beloved, like Mr. Chips—*"There's old Mr. Kornfeld, son—he was my history teacher back when I was your age, and I hated him at the time, but now I've come to see how much I learned from him, and I love him like a second father, the way all his students do, and you will, too, my boy"*—but all that was gone now. Lily still greeted him cheerily enough on Wednesdays at the dentist's office, as if she hadn't heard anything at all about the incident at school—and for his part, Arthur always tried to put on a smile for her, no matter how blue he might be feeling that day. Dr. Pratt had stopped making small talk with him, and Arthur, who'd gotten used to a certain steady level of discomfort associated with his dental appointments, could swear that the pain from the wire adjustments and the other procedures was getting worse now, week by week. He thought of saying something, issuing a complaint of some kind, but couldn't bring himself to.

Finally, on the last Wednesday of the school year, he arrived at Dr. Pratt's office for his final appointment. Lily had made a second plaster set of teeth for him the week before, and now she presented them to him, along with the old set, so he could see the difference all the dental work had made. "Look at you," she told him, her face beaming. "You're a new man."

"Oh, I don't think so." He stared at her for a long moment. Her smile was radiant and blissful, as if they were at the very beginning of something, rather than at the end. "I might have been a new man, if you'd been willing to go to dinner with me that night," he whispered in a voice so soft it might have been simply a breath—and he felt a great release inside his chest, as if he'd taken off a corset he'd been wearing for many years. He could say this to her now, since he was sure that they would never see each other again. For a moment Lily was silent, and Arthur wondered if he'd actually said anything to her, or just wished he'd said it.

But then she said, "Oh, but I was willing—" and then stopped short, and put a hand to her mouth as Dr. Pratt walked into the examination room.

"Well, let's see how we've done, shall we?" he said, and opened Arthur's mouth. He turned Arthur's head this way and that, saying, "Aha. Aha. Ahum. Yes, indeedy," as he continued his examination. Lily handed him the pliers, and Dr. Pratt set about pulling the wires off the inside surfaces of Arthur's teeth. Then Lily sprayed water into his mouth, and when Arthur spit it out into the white porcelain bowl, there were yellow bits of dental cement and tiny, unidentifiable pieces of this and that. After another quick inspection, Dr. Pratt finally pushed the overhead light back on its retractable arm, slipped the latex gloves off his hands, and announced, "That's not the mouth you walked in here with a few months ago, my friend."

▪ ▪ ▪

Several years later, after he'd moved to a town in Vermont and established himself successfully in a teaching position at a second-rate prep school, Arthur's mother died, so he took a short leave of absence and went home to Cleveland to collect her personal effects. She'd been in the nursing home for nearly five years by this time, and didn't have much left in the way of personal property. The supervising nurse in the hospice wing showed Arthur a cardboard box full of the tattered detritus of his mother's life: cheap floral-print nightgowns, faded underwear that had turned gray with time, worn terrycloth slippers and a few pieces of costume jewelry. Not surprisingly, his mother's will named him as her sole heir. At the bottom of the cardboard box, underneath the nightgowns, he found a black and white photograph of his smiling parents standing side by side in front of an automobile. Had he ever seen this picture before? He couldn't remember. They were already in their forties in this photograph—his father was nearly fifty, in fact—and they must have thought, incorrectly, that their luck was about to change at last. His mother was obviously pregnant, so Arthur told himself that he was in the picture, too, in a manner of speaking.

He thrust his hand deep into the box and rooted around beneath the clothing until he came upon the thing he'd dreaded finding: his mother's dentures, which rested in a pale blue plastic container hidden under the pile of her underwear. When he was a child he hadn't known that his mother wore false teeth. He'd lived in her home for eighteen years and had never noticed. He hadn't known her at all. He must have been distracted all those years, or simply not paying attention to her.

At some point in his twenties, after his father had died and Arthur had left home for college, he'd become aware of the fact that she wore dentures. He couldn't remember how he'd come by this knowledge; perhaps she'd mentioned it to him casually in conversation, when the subject of his own dental woes had come up—but he'd never actually seen his mother without her teeth until the day he'd moved her out of her apartment and settled her at the Cleveland nursing home, just before he'd driven to Parkersburg, Iowa to start his first teaching job. He'd never gone back to see her at the nursing home—had never seen her again at all. Even now, now that she was dead, he hadn't seen her. They'd asked him if he wanted to view the body before cremation, and he'd told them no.

His memories of the day he'd moved her into the nursing home were very clear. Once she seemed comfortable in her room and the staff doctor had come around to welcome her, Arthur told his mother he'd be back at four-thirty, then he returned to her apartment to vacuum and dust the place once more before turning in the keys. He did a hurried job of it. He knew he'd have to be on the road soon in order to drive through the night and part of the next day to reach Parkersburg—his new job, his new life—and besides, what was the point of cleaning his mother's mildewy apartment on his hands and knees, scrubbing the floors, mopping and waxing? In all his years of renting apartments he'd never gotten a cleaning deposit returned to him, and he didn't imagine that his mother's landlord would be any different. He did what needed to be done, turned in the keys, and when he returned to the nursing home earlier than he'd expected, the nurses in the hospice wing nodded to him to go on back to his mother's room. He walked in on her without knocking, hoping to surprise her as he'd done from time to time when he was a little boy.

There she lay, an old woman who couldn't have been his mother, though she must have been. Her dust-colored hair was in disarray on the pillow, like a cloud of lint around her head. Until this moment he hadn't known that this would be the last time he'd ever see her, but as he approached her bed he suddenly realized that that was his intent. At the sound of his footsteps his mother turned to him—this wretched stranger he'd never seen before—and her horrible mouth opened up toward him beseechingly, all tongue and helpless pink gums.

spivak in babylon

President Reagan began to make brief guest appearances in Leo Spivak's dreams during the summer of 1982, about six months after Leo had come to work at Bowles and Humphries, one of Chicago's largest advertising agencies. Previously he'd spent several years at Dunne, Crowell and Gold, a sweet-natured little Mom and Pop agency where everyone went bowling together twice a month and secretaries routinely brought homemade delicacies like chocolate-sauerkraut cake and mock apple pie made with Ritz crackers to the office. It hadn't taken Leo very long to realize that Bowles and Humphries wasn't the kind of place where anyone brought desserts from home. The secretaries here wore fishnet stockings, push-up bras and short leather skirts, and they didn't look like they could cook anything worth eating. Nobody went bowling, either—or if they did, they had the good sense not to talk about it at the water cooler. In fact there wasn't a water cooler at Bowles and Humphries—and if there'd been one, Leo told himself, it would have been full of gin.

He'd just turned thirty-two, and since he'd come to work at Bowles and Humphries, he'd begun to worry about everything. His wife, Rachel, was four months pregnant with their first child, and though all the doctors' tests had come back perfectly normal, Leo was terrified that something would go wrong. His supervisor, Ward LaPlante, was a cocaine addict, and had let Leo know in no uncertain terms that things would go more smoothly for him around the office if he kicked in a hundred bucks for a gram of coke now and then. Mary-Louise Whitaker, a smoldering, heavy-breasted young art director whose cubicle was just next door to Leo's, hadn't managed to return a simple hello as of yet, even though he'd gone out of his way to greet her cheerily every morning in the hallway. He was pretty sure that the woman who ran the supply room hated him, too, though he had no idea why.

Worse than all of these, though, was Harriet Rubin, Bowles and Humphries' Creative Director, who positively scared the shit out of him. Every time Leo caught a glimpse of her, his heart flapped desperately against his ribcage like a dying fish. He was too ashamed to admit this to anyone but his therapist, Dr. Findlay. He couldn't mention it to Rachel. She'd laugh right in his face. *Scared of a fifty-year-old woman! Don't be ridiculous!* He tried to remember anyone else who'd ever frightened him this much, but except for a schoolyard bully named Chapellow who'd terrorized him as a child, there was no one. He wasn't sure what it was about Harriet Rubin that frightened him so much, though he assumed the fact that she was his boss must have something to do with it. He'd never really worked for a woman before, but until now, he'd been under the impression that he wouldn't mind the experience. After all, when he and Rachel had sex, he liked it just fine when she got on top. In fact he considered it a particular turn-on. That had to say something about him, Leo was sure of it, though he couldn't have said exactly what.

He couldn't imagine Harriet Rubin making love to anyone. He tried to form a mental image of what her body might look like under the no-nonsense business ensembles she wore to the office, but he saw only another layer of gray pinstriped material. Peel that layer back, there'd be another layer just like it underneath. With Harriet Rubin, it was gray pinstripes all the way down. Her eyes were deep brown, almost black, wide-set and penetrating, and when she looked at Leo, he got the unsettling feeling that she could see inside him, like an x-ray machine. Harriet was tall and dignified, small-bosomed, slender. She wore her salt-and-pepper hair in a Mary Tyler Moore bouffant. Her blouses were demure, with high necklines and big, flouncy sleeves. She had a beaky nose and a long chin, a face that reminded Leo vaguely of Mrs. Monardo, his saintly kindergarten teacher back at Hartley Elementary School in Kansas City—except that Harriet Rubin didn't have whiskers growing on her chin and a wart the size of a marble on the side of her nose. She didn't wear black support hose and big, clunky orthopedic shoes, either. No, the more Leo thought about it, Harriet didn't look much like sweet old Mrs. Monardo. Mrs. Monardo hadn't been able to see inside him at all—and besides, he'd been in kindergarten at the time. At the age of five, what could there have been inside of him to see?

It wasn't just his co-workers at Bowles and Humphries that frightened Leo these days—there were imponderables, too, like failure, fatherhood, disgrace and death. In fact, he couldn't even bring himself to catalogue all the things that he was scared of; it was a list too long and too frightening for him to contemplate. In the midst of all this terror President Reagan's willingness to make an appearance, if only briefly, in his dreams brought Leo something akin to comfort. President Reagan was busy, after all—he was the leader of the free world, and so on. And he was no spring chicken. He couldn't appear in everybody's dreams. Just the previous year, Reagan had been shot and nearly killed by a crazy guy who was in love with Jodie Foster, but he'd already made what the newspapers called a miraculous full recovery, and at least in Leo's dreams, he did, indeed, appear to be in great shape, indestructible, in fact—a big lug of a guy. President Reagan seemed younger, less wrinkled than he did on the nightly news—more the way he'd looked back in the 1960's, before his entry into politics, when he was still just a has-been movie star hosting *Death Valley Days* on TV. In Leo's dreams, *Death Valley Days* was just about all that President Reagan really wanted to talk about. One night in mid-June he asked Leo, "You remember Rosemary DeCamp, the woman who did those commercials for Twenty Mule Team Borax?"

"Sure, I remember her, Mr. President," Leo replied.

"Oh, was she a hottie. Never wore a stitch of underwear." President Reagan licked his finger, then touched it to his hip and made a sizzling sound through his teeth.

"That's hard to believe," Leo said.

"You can take it from me," said the President, then he leaned forward and dropped his voice to a whisper. "Don't let a word of this get to Nancy! Rosemary DeCamp, she had flesh where a woman's supposed to, and she could move it, too. Oh, mama. Ha-tcha-tcha."

Leo pondered the meaning of this dream, but he couldn't come up with anything. He had no idea why he remembered "Death Valley Days," surely one of the most forgettable television shows he'd watched as a boy—or what possible significance it might have for him now. He hadn't voted for Reagan, and was, in truth, appalled that he was occupying the White House—but to hell with that. President Reagan happened to have one of the most soothing voices Leo had ever heard in his life. That was all that mattered. You could have bottled that voice and sold it as a sedative.

The morning after Leo dreamed of President Reagan dishing the dirt about Rosemary DeCamp, he was sitting in his cubicle trying to write a commercial for Dazzle liquid laundry detergent, the account he'd been stuck on for months, when Herb Pinsker, a sad-eyed, paunchy fellow with white wavy hair and a tremor in his right hand, knocked on his cubicle's doorjamb. Leo had heard rumors of an old geezer named Pinsker, an art director who'd been at the agency since the dawn of time, but he'd never even seen him until now. "When I came to work here, television hadn't been invented," Pinsker said by way of introduction. The tremor in his right hand made his fingers drum the doorjamb. "Back when I was in your age, Harriet Rubin was just a girl typing scripts in the steno pool. Now everybody in the Creative Department works for her, including me. A lot of people in my position would be pretty upset about this, but I'm not that way. Everybody here is young enough to be my kids. They all make more money than me. You probably do, too." Pinsker's voice was high and clear, held aloft on a jet stream of indignation, and he spoke quickly, as if he feared the arrival of building security guards who might whisk him away at any moment for a behind-closed-doors session with a leather sap. "I've got stock in this company. Used to be, if you worked here five years, they gave you stock. They don't do that anymore, though. They can't fire me, because they'd have to buy back my stock, and I'm not selling. Everybody thinks I'm washed up—I know that. They snicker right in my face. Soon enough you'll start snickering right in my face, too."

"Oh, no. I don't do much snickering," Leo said.

Pinsker dismissed this with a trembling wave. "The time will come," he said. "You'll go along with the flow, I don't blame you. You know what they've got me working on now? Happy-Time Incontinence Shields. That's right. Forty years in this business, I worked on all the big accounts, now I'm drawing storyboards for adult diapers. One day, this was years ago, I'll never forget it, all the bigshots walked into my cubicle and asked me what I thought of the idea of a cowboy as the symbol for Marlboro. They had it narrowed down to either a cowboy or a matador, and I was the one they asked to make the final decision. I said, 'Go with the matador.' Spain sounded better than Wyoming—and I still feel that would've been the right choice. Think about it: the red cape, the bull charging across the arena, trumpets, cheering crowds, this guy stands there, ice-water running in his veins, smoking a Marlboro and risking his life, armed with nothing more than a little sword the size of a letter opener. Now *that's* macho!"

"I see your point," Leo said.

"I was in the room when they came up with the Hathaway Shirt man, too," Pinsker continued. "The guy with the eyepatch, you remember that?"

"Sure."

"I told them, 'Why an eyepatch? It's been done. What about a hearing aid?' Well, I was off-base on that one. It takes a man to admit it when he's wrong."

"I guess that's true."

"Well, I'd like to stay and chat, but I'm busy. I've got to get back to my office and draw another storyboard. If they ever put you on the Happy-Time account, believe me, it's time to pack your bags." Pinsker's voice dropped to a stage whisper. "Mr. Bowles, God rest his soul, wouldn't have let them put me on this account. He hired me himself. There was a gentleman. That man was a saint. When my first boy was born, Mr. Bowles came into my cubicle and handed me two twenty-dollar bills, peeled them off a roll he carried in his front pocket, just like that. Forty dollars! That was something I'll never forget. Every year at Thanksgiving, what do you think? We all got turkeys! Then at Christmas we got a ham. Biggest ham you ever saw." Pinsker ran his tongue over his lips and looked away, his eyes hooded with disappointment. "Then Mr. Bowles died in that snowblower accident, and Mr. Humphries took over the operation, and like the saying goes, that's a horse of a different color." He sighed, "Water under the bridge. Or over the dam, I can't remember which."

Which one was it? Under the bridge, or over the dam? The important part, Leo knew, was that it was water, and it was gone now, and you couldn't retrieve it. He turned back to his electric typewriter and tried to think of something snappy to say about Dazzle liquid laundry detergent, but no words came. He thought he might never write another sentence, in fact. The English language had fled his brain. Leo had always harbored vague, amorphous fears about his future—what he'd end up looking like when he got old, who he'd be, what he'd sound like to young people. Now that formless angst had congealed into something all too vivid. What if he ended up like Herb Pinsker?

Leo took all the paper clips out of his top drawer and made them into a necklace, which he whirled around on his index finger until it flew off and hit the wall with a soft metallic clack. Now he'd have to go to the supply room and ask for a new box of paper-clips. No, wait a second: he was scared of the woman who ran the supply room. Maybe he could unhook all the paperclips and put them back in his drawer. That sounded like a plan. If he worked at it slowly, that would take the rest of the morning. Then he could spend his lunch hour at his weekly therapy session with Dr. Findlay, where he could talk about how scared he was of the woman in the supply room, and everyone else he knew.

At ten-thirty, Mary-Louise Whitaker knocked on Leo's doorjamb. She was short, small-boned but not at all thin, with large green eyes and thick, luxuriant auburn hair piled on top of her head in a messy bun. "I've been meaning to stop by and say hello ever since they hired you," she told him. "But I figured I'd wait to gauge the cut of your jib."

"Oh. I guess I didn't realize I had a jib," Leo said, and waited for her to laugh. But she seemed not to have heard him.

"You've probably already heard that I'm the office sex object," she said. "Everybody around here wants in my pants. *You* probably want in my pants, and you just met me."

"Whoa—wait a second," Leo began, but Mary-Louise waved him off.

"Oh, come on," she said. "Let's not kid ourselves. I'm young and pretty good-looking, and I bet you can tell from the way I bounce around and giggle that I'd be hot in bed." She opened a manila envelope and withdrew a short stack of glossy 8" x 10" black and white photos of herself. "A friend of mine took these a few weeks ago," she said, sliding the pictures across Leo's desk to him. "They're artistic, don't you think? I believe nudity can be extremely tasteful if it's done the right way." She licked her lips and patted her hair while Leo stared at the photos.

In the top photograph, Mary-Louise was staring insouciantly at the camera, thrusting her nipples toward the camera. Her breasts were snow-white, and her nipples were very dark. In the light of the camera's flash, they shone like polished hubcaps. "Well, this is certainly nice," Leo said, then cleared his throat.

"Oh, you think so?"

What the hell was he supposed to say? He couldn't think of anything. "Yessirree Bob," he sighed, then swallowed deeply and drummed his fingers on his desk, gingerly casting his eyes around the room, avoiding both the stack of photos and Mary-Louise herself. This was turning out to be a pretty unsettling morning.

"I think my hips have started to go—just a little tiny bit. Right here," she said, pointing to one of the pictures. She leaned over the desk and pulled a couple of the photos around, staring at them with frowning concentration. "My breasts are *very* good, though, I have to admit. Very good. Verging on perfect. And I love my stomach." She raised her head and gazed at him critically. "You look like you could lose a couple of pounds," she told him.

"I guess so." He patted his stomach and felt the shimmy of his flab beneath his fingers.

She shrugged. "Well, who am I to say? We hardly know each other, we just met, we haven't gone to bed yet or anything." She got up to go. "I could leave these with you for a while," she said, pointing to the photos.

"Oh, thanks, but I don't think so. I probably ought to be getting back to work," Leo said. "I'm married," he added. "My wife's pregnant, in fact. I just thought I should throw that in."

"Lucky you," she said, and thrust the photos back into the manila envelope. "I knew that already, by the way. Words gets around. Anyway, don't tell anybody I showed you these," she warned him. "There are people in this office who would kill to get a chance to drool over naked pictures of me."

"I won't mention a thing. Honest."

"If Ward found out I showed you these, he'd have us both out of here like that," Mary-Louise said, and snapped her fingers. "Ward LaPlante wants inside my pants so bad it isn't even funny. He's always undressing me with his eyes. Not that I mind."

Ward LaPlante had hired Leo, and Leo felt he owed the man some loyalty, so instead of clucking something sympathetic to Mary-Louise, he just shrugged his shoulders and smiled at her blandly. After a moment of silent staring, she turned on her heel and was gone. Well, what did Leo know about it, anyway? Maybe she was right—maybe Ward LaPlante undressed her with his eyes every day of the week. What was Leo supposed to do about it? Tell him to knock it off? He was the new guy in the office—what right did he have to tell Ward to knock anything off? And besides, he had his own problems with Ward LaPlante.

Ward, Leo's supervisor, was a thin, big-nosed, nail-bitten guy with a goofy blond hairdo that flopped down over his eyes and made him look like an Afghan hound. His wife, Sylvia, made her living as a professional shopper—she bought household furnishings, clothing, groceries, even real estate and automobiles for wealthy clients too busy to shop for themselves. Leo had only met her once, when she stopped by the offices of Bowles and Humphries during a shopping expedition on Michigan Avenue. Sylvia, a tall, broad, buxom brunette, must have outweighed Ward by eighty pounds, and the instant Leo met her, he found himself trying to imagine Ward's pale, puny thighs wrapped ineffectually around her exploding flesh. Still, as far as Leo could tell, Ward and Sylvia seemed happy enough. Maybe the difference in their size was some kind of kinky turn-on. They could be *shtupping* like bunnies every night for all Leo knew. But that didn't mean Mary-Louise Whitaker's eye-undressing comment was out of line. Who could say? If there was one thing Leo knew about the world, it was that you could never tell for sure what was going on inside somebody's head.

For that matter, at first glance Ward didn't look like a cocaine addict, either. Leo wasn't sure what coke addicts were supposed to look like, but he was willing to bet most of them didn't look as goofy as Ward LaPlante. So much for appearances! Fridays were payday at Bowles and Humphries, and the very first Friday of Leo's career there, just after Vinnie the mail boy, a badly damaged fellow who wore a Chicago Bears football helmet (to protect what rumor had it was an open bullet hole in his head) had delivered Leo's paycheck, Ward knocked on the doorjamb of his cubicle and invited him out for lunch. "It's a tradition around here, Leo," Ward said. "Your first payday, your supervisor takes you to lunch. At Bowles and Humphries, we're very big on tradition." Downstairs, they hailed a cab, and Ward gave the driver the address of his apartment. The LaPlantes owned a pre-war condominium on Lake Shore Drive, a vast, shambling expanse of white walls, elaborate moldings, and dark, polished hardwood floors, crammed to the ceiling with exotic rejects, stuff that Sylvia had originally bought for her exclusive—and apparently very picky—clientele. "C'mon, I've got something to show you," Ward said, "Just a little token of my appreciation." He led Leo down a hallway to a small den furnished in leather and walnut. Though they were alone in the apartment, Ward shut the door to the den and locked it once Leo was seated. "Got a little Welcome Wagon present here for you," he said with a crafty smile, and presented a small mirror which he slid across the coffee table toward Leo. Six fat white lines of powder crawled across the mirror like little slugs. Ward held out a rolled up dollar bill, and said, "Don't be shy, now, fella. I've got plenty."

Leo scooted his chair away from the coffee table so fast he almost toppled over. "What's that?" he asked. "That isn't cocaine, is it?"

"No, it's corn starch." Ward winked and flashed Leo a moist half-smile. "We had stir-fry last night. It's left over."

"Oh, no," Leo said. He glanced nervously around the den. "No, thanks." Was this a test? Were Bowles and Humphries' Managing Partners watching this transaction on closed-circuit television? "It's awfully nice of you to offer," he said, "but I try not to put anything up my nose except my finger."

Ward stared at him, his smile fading.

"Don't get me wrong. I really appreciate your asking. But I don't really think I want to start up with anything," Leo went on. "I've never tried this stuff, but I've heard it's pretty addictive. I smoked dope in college, but that's about it. Ditchweed, fifteen bucks an ounce. You could smoke two joints and maybe you'd get a little high. It'd take all night sometimes, just to feel a buzz. I've heard some people are just born addicts, and I think I might be one of them. You know? It's like some genetic thing, a time bomb inside of you just waiting to go off—you don't even know it's there until you're hooked. Just the thought of it gives me the willies. And besides, there's the money and all that. We're trying to start a family. You know how that is. And our house needs a new roof." He stopped. Did the house need a new roof? Well, it might. What if Ward drove up to Winnetka to check? "I don't know," Leo said. "Maybe it needs a new roof. It's an old house. We're not sure. It's basically a fixer-upper. I think it probably does."

Ward continued staring at Leo for a long moment. "Right. Hey, that's cool," he said at last. He slid the mirror back across the coffee table and put away the dollar bill. Then he got out a pair of nail clippers and started in on what was left of his fingernails. The silence built for thirty seconds, forty-five—Leo watched the second hand moving in its path around the wall clock, unable to take his eyes off its progress—while Ward clipped away, staring fixedly at his nails as if they might contain the secrets of the universe. Finally Leo looked at his watch and muttered something about needing to get back to the office to work on a script. Ward shrugged and said, "Yeah. I guess we'd better get back," and they rode downstairs in the elevator, hailed a taxi, and were back at the office in fifteen minutes.

That had happened months ago, and things hadn't been the same between them since then. Ward was still affable around the office, but he'd never invited Leo out to lunch again, and often days went by without a word exchanged between them. Sometimes at night Leo kicked himself—literally kicked himself—for having refused Ward's attempt to bond with him. Why couldn't he have snorted a line or two, just for the heck of it? Would it have killed him? How many of these chances did he think he was going to get? He ran the loop of film over and over again in his mind, the hushed, darkened atmosphere of the den, Ward scooting the mirror toward him, saying, "Don't be shy now, fella. I've got plenty."

Promptly at noon Leo put aside the task of unhooking all the paper clips and went to his therapist's office, where he sat twiddling his thumbs, waiting for Dr. Findlay to fall asleep. It happened every week, sooner or later. He'd been meaning to say something to Dr. Findlay about this, but hadn't worked up the nerve yet. To postpone Dr. Findlay's nap as long as possible, Leo launched into a rousing account of his morning, starting with Herb Pinsker's dispiriting visit to his cubicle and quickly segueing to a fairly graphic description of Mary-Louise Whitaker's perfect breasts. Sure enough, when he got to the part about hubcaps, Findlay's eyes, which had begun their usual fluttering slide into slumber, blinked open. "Well, that's certainly something," Dr. Findlay said.

"Yes. I thought so, too."

"Speaking of your work situation, have you followed through on my advice?"

A couple of weeks earlier, Dr. Findlay had suggested that Leo simply lay his cards on the table and tell Harriet Rubin that she scared the shit out of him. Once he'd made this confession, Dr. Findlay told him, Leo could move on, get past his fear of her, and live a richer, fuller life.

"Well, not exactly," Leo said. "Although I really appreciate the suggestion. But—look, are you sure that'd be a good idea?"

"What could it hurt?" Dr. Findlay asked. "After all, what can she do? Fire you?"

Well, yes—of course she could fire him—that was precisely what she could do. Any idiot would know that. Harriet Rubin wasn't just Leo's boss—she was his boss's boss. She could fire him with one phone call, and Dr. Findlay knew that perfectly well. Leo had told him repeatedly about the turnover rate at Bowles and Humphries. People were getting shit-canned right and left—it was common knowledge around the office. Rumor had it there was a list of those about to be fired, locked away in a file cabinet somewhere in the hushed, deeply-carpeted, walnut-paneled privacy of the Managing Partners' offices on the Sixteenth Floor. At least once a week, Mel Kleinfelder from down in Personnel, the company's designated "hatchet man," would sweep into some poor yutz's office, shut the door, and unceremoniously chop the guy off at the knees. Leo saw Mel Kleinfelder now and then in the elevator, and it was like seeing the Angel of Death; just the sight of him made Leo's bowels clench into a complicated, painful knot. In fact, it was almost as bad as catching a glimpse of Harriet Rubin.

So despite Dr. Findlay's urging, Leo wasn't in any hurry to come clean with her. And besides, he wasn't really sure he trusted Dr. Findlay's counsel all that much. First of all, the man was non-Jewish—perhaps the only non-Jewish therapist in Chicago. Leo didn't know much about psychotherapy, but his general impression was that it was essentially a Jewish invention, and while he felt that non-Jews certainly had every right to try their hand at the profession, he saw no reason to believe they'd be any good at it. He'd signed on with Dr. Findlay in the first place simply out of convenience: his office was in the Huber Building, the same skyscraper that Bowles and Humphries called home. Why spend money on taxi cabs, get caught in traffic, soaked by rain, pelted by hail, frozen to the bone by icy winds, Leo reasoned, when he could stay right there in the cozy confines of the Huber Building? And besides, the Huber Building was going through a slump of late (once it had been the tallest building on this stretch of Michigan Avenue, but recently a gigantic chrome-plated monstrosity with an atrium lobby had been erected directly to the east of it, blocking the Huber's view of the lake, and fickle tenants had been jumping ship like mad), so Leo felt a certain amount of loyalty to the building and its occupants. But what was that about, anyway? This was his therapy, for crying out loud—his psychological health was at stake. Was it worth it to stick with Dr. Findlay out of building loyalty? What had the Huber Building ever done for him? It was a *building,* for crying out loud! *It didn't have any feelings!*

Leo was turning all of this over and over in his mind because in addition to the question of Findlay's non-Jewish background, there was the nagging issue of his tie. Every time Leo had seen him, Dr. Findlay had been wearing the same necktie, a tartan plaid which Leo assumed belonged to the Findlay clan. *The same tie.* What kind of a message was that supposed to send? Admittedly, stability was nice, especially given the turbulence of life at Bowles and Humphries, and the tartan tie was colorful and attractive, sure—but couldn't Dr. Findlay have gotten another one, some other tartan, or just a simple stripe? Why not try the tie-less look now and then? Just a nice cashmere turtleneck would have done the trick. And while Leo was on the subject of attire, he couldn't understand why Dr. Findlay always wore a white shirt—probably not the same white shirt, but still, it was the principle of the thing. Couldn't he afford a blue one once in a while?

All right: Leo had to admit it, the shirt and tie issue was basically small potatoes, and unless he was going to be a jerk about it, he'd have to ignore the non-Jewish part, as well—but no matter how much he thought about it, he still couldn't get past the fact that Dr. Findlay fell asleep every time he came in for his session. This was too much. At the beginning of his appointment every week, after a moment of pleasantries, Leo would start in on a summary of how things were going with him—a little of this, a little of that—and a couple of minutes into his recitation, he could see Dr. Findlay's eyes begin to flutter. A moment later the therapist's head would start to jerk forward and snap back, and in no time the man would be sound asleep, sitting up in his chair. At times he even snored. His mouth would fall open—Leo could see right down his throat, count his fillings.

The first couple of times this happened, Leo kept right on talking until his fifty minutes were up, though he politely lowered his voice to a whisper once it had become obvious that Findlay was asleep. After a few of these strange sessions, though, he began to feel foolish sitting there talking about himself to someone who was dead to the world, and so instead he fell silent and sat there studying his nails and checking his watch until his time was up. The chair he sat in was very comfortable, upholstered in a soft, buttery leather that gave off the rich perfume of age. Once or twice Leo considered dropping off to sleep himself. Why not? Take a nap, just let go a little. But no, that would have been inappropriate. Dr. Findlay had the uncanny ability to wake up just as it was time for their session to be over. What if he caught Leo napping? What would he think?

If Leo was going to start confessing his true feelings to anyone, shouldn't he start with Dr. Findlay himself? That seemed logical. After all, if he told Dr. Findlay how disheartening it was to sit there watching him snore for fifty minutes once a week (not to mention the fact that his health insurance was paying a hundred dollars a pop for these sessions), what was Findlay going to do? Fire him? Not likely. Would Dr. Findlay ever willingly terminate Leo's course of therapy? It was out of the question. Leo could tell him exactly how he felt about him, down to the small stuff, the necktie, the white shirts, even the whole non-Jewish thing, and there'd be no reprisals. Dr. Findlay was very likely the only person in Leo's life who came without any strings attached.

Rachel, on the other hand, came with many strings—so many of them, so complexly arranged, that at times Leo felt them tightening around his neck like a noose. She was small and slender, with an explosive turban of thick, luxurious black hair that seemed at times to be ready to take over the entire house. Her eyes were a deep shade of gray, large and luminous. At night, when Leo lay sleepless beside her in bed, staring up at the ceiling in the dark for hours on end, he watched her gentle breathing and told himself that her condition was no doubt the root of all his current anxieties. A large flashing neon sign hung over his head in the dark, visible only to him, reading PREGNANT!!! It wasn't that anything had gone wrong with her pregnancy so far. In fact, in her fourth month Rachel looked radiant, glowing, more beautiful than ever. So far everything had gone smoothly—nothing at all out of the ordinary for a first pregnancy, according to her obstetrician, not even the tiniest deviation from the norm in any of her vital statistics.

Leo had been reading books on the subject of pregnancy ever since she'd broken the big news to him. He pored over these books compulsively at the kitchen table most nights after she'd gone to bed, searching for warning signs—anything, however small, that might be an omen of impending doom. Nothing had cropped up so far, but still he couldn't shake the feeling that something was terribly wrong. It was the thought that something was growing inside of her—something that might turn out to resemble him, in fact—that made him so nervous. Leo knew he was supposed to be thrilled, and there were, in fact, isolated, fleeting moments when he found himself floating off the ground with delight at the thought of becoming a father. Mostly, though, he was scared out of his wits. What if he turned out to be as bad a parent as his own father had been? For that matter, what made him think he'd be any better? He wasn't any smarter than his father, and he probably wasn't any nicer, either, when it came right down to it. That was a sobering thought. Not any nicer than his own father.

That was why Leo felt so blessed when President Reagan began to visit him in his dreams. Talk about *genial!* President Reagan would sit down by Leo, cross his long legs, and start spinning out some stale yarn full of Hollywood gossip from the old days, as though he might be talking to one of his cronies over cocktails at Chasen's or the Brown Derby. Where did Leo come up with all of this crap? He had no idea. He must have dredged it up from some forgotten magazine article or late-night television documentary; these were his dreams, after all, and if he didn't have this collection of B-grade Hollywood bullshit stored someplace in his memory banks, how could President Reagan come out with it?

All Leo knew for sure was that seeing President Reagan's lopsided grin in his dreams gave him hope. Unlike nearly everyone else in Leo's life, the President never said anything that sounded cynical—in fact it seemed to Leo that cynicism simply wasn't in President Reagan's vocabulary. The first time he'd appeared in one of Leo's dreams, Leo had cut to the chase, asking him, "Is everything going to be all right, Mr. President? I hate to ask you this. But I have to know. All this stuff, it's really got me worried." Just a moment before, he'd been alone in an empty landscape, a void, but now he and the President were on a boat, a yacht, rocking gently on sun-sparkled water.

"How do you mean?" President Reagan answered.

This wasn't President Reagan's boat, and it sure as hell wasn't Leo's. They were invited guests, though Leo was afraid that he'd somehow mislaid his invitation, and he was going to be asked to leave any minute now. In fact that seemed like a distinct possibility. He tried patting his pockets to search for the invitation, but his hands couldn't find his pockets. He knew he had pockets, but they kept shifting around on him, eluding his grasp. "You know," Leo said. "With everything. I've all this stuff on my mind."

"Oh, that. Well, now. Freedom is not a delicate flower. It will grow wherever it's planted, unless you do your digging with a bayonet."

"Yes, Mr. President?"

"You know, that reminds me of a story."

"But sir? Can you just tell me? Can you just answer the question?"

President Reagan stood up. Leo noticed for the first time that the President was wearing swimming trunks. His torso was hairless as a child's, impressively muscled, a thick, white slab of meat. "Look, Leo," the President chided, "Watch this. I'm the Leader of the Free World." Then he gracefully dove over the side of the boat and was gone.

▪ ▪ ▪

When he got back to his cubicle after his lunchtime appointment with Dr. Findlay, Leo got a call from Harriet Rubin's secretary, asking him to come up to her office for a chat. He muttered a quick, "Of course, I'll be right there," then hung up the phone and fell headlong into a state of despair. Sonuvabitch. This was it: his career was over. Rachel was four months pregnant, swelling up like a tender, sweet-natured balloon—in a few more months he'd be a father, with another little Spivak to feed, doctor's bills, toys, car-seats, a five-figure college fund to start, the whole paraphernalia of child-rearing to pay for—and now, with the worry of all of that keeping him up at night, here he was, about to be thrown out of Bowles and Humphries on his ear. Herb Pinsker had been sent around that morning to sniff him out, like one of those cats they keep around a nursing home to comfort the terminally ill. Then Mary-Louise Whitaker and her nude photos—he could see now that it had all been just a clever ploy designed to give them a reason to throw him out the door. UNEMPLOYED! Just the thought of the word, the sound of it echoing softly inside Leo's head, was enough to make him consider throwing up into the metal wastebasket by his desk.

At the age of ten, Leo had seen his father fired. It was what Dr. Findlay would have called a "primal memory," if he'd ever stayed awake long enough to make such observations. Leo's dad had been in the hospital, laid low by a vicious bout of shingles, and his boss, a brutal, box-shaped man named Dworkin, had come to the hospital during evening visiting hours just to tell him he was out of a job. Leo wandered into the room just after Dworkin had departed, hoping to beg a quarter from his mom for candy down in the hospital canteen, and he saw his father hunched over, crying uncontrollably in his bed. The image had made an indelible impression on him; even now he could summon it up—his father's face, contorted by tears, half in shadow, half lit up by the glare of the lamp on the night stand. His father's thin shoulders heaved as he cried. At first Leo hadn't known what was going on—he'd never seen his father cry before. He thought it might have been a fit of hiccups, or some strange, silent kind of laughter. Then he saw what it was, and his knees went to jelly.

After the call from Harriet Rubin's secretary, Leo called Rachel at work—she was a junior accountant at one of the large firms on LaSalle Street—but she was away from her desk and her secretary didn't seem anxious to fetch her. "Give her a message for me, then, will you?" he asked in a grim voice. "Tell her the shit has hit the fan."

"Oh, I couldn't write that," the secretary said.

"Then don't," Leo said, and threw the receiver back into its cradle.

Forty thousand a year. That was his salary at Bowles and Humphries. He saw the figure written in the air above his head, then watched it transformed into a bird that promptly flapped away into nothingness. Gone. Forty thousand a year. This was major league money—half again as much as his father was making, still grinding himself to death, on the road three weeks a month, selling a line of wholesale children's clothing at the age of sixty-eight. Leo had casually dropped the figure into a phone conversation with his parents just after he'd been hired as a copywriter at Bowles and Humphries, and his father had abruptly hung up the extension, leaving Leo listening to the whistle of dead air until his mother came on the line, short of breath, to apologize.

Leo needed that forty thousand a year. With Rachel's parents as in-laws, he needed all the loot he could get his hands on. Her family took baths in money—her father, Chub Sperling, was in corporate law, and cleared an easy quarter-of-a-million a year, not counting bonuses and stock options. Over the four years of his marriage, Leo had noticed his mother-in-law, Bernice, staring at his crotch on several occasions, as if trying to assess the size of his penis, measuring it against the undoubtedly impressive heft of her husband's *shvantz.* Thank God the Sperlings lived one time zone away, in the suburbs north of New York City. It wasn't far enough, as far as Leo was concerned, but it would have to do. He saw them twice a year, at Chanukah and Passover, which was plenty. The Sperlings weren't just rich—they were devout, too. Who wouldn't be, with all that money? Their conversation was crammed full of references to the synagogue building fund, the Sisterhood used-book sale, the rabbi's contract negotiations, Hadassah fund-raiser luncheons, B'Nai Brith charity balls. The Sperlings had a *bruchah* for everything: Blessed art Thou, O Lord our God, King of the Universe, who hath given us this bottomless bucket of cash.

Well, screw their piety, Leo told himself. For all the davening, the chanting, the breast-beating talk of *Adonai* and *Elohainu* and *Shema Yisroel,* when it came right down to it the only thing that mattered to them was the contents of your wallet. Rachel's older sister, Stephanie, was married to a urologist, a sandy-haired little prick who was a corporation unto himself—he had his own clinic in a wealthy suburb of Philadelphia, he was written up in medical journals all the time, he was one of the world's leading experts on bladder infections. Bladder infections! Leo needed forty thousand a year just to be able to sit down at the same table with this guy. Thank God for Randy, Rachel's little brother, who lived in an obscenely expensive Greenwich Village studio apartment, sponging mercilessly off his parents and hanging out with a succession of suspiciously good-looking Italian boys, all of them named Guido. Had it not been for Randy, Leo Spivak would have been the most significant bad news of the entire family. Against his will, he imagined himself around the dining room table at the Sperlings' next family get-together. *So, Leo, tell us, what is it you do, again? Oh, that's right, you were fired. Isn't that a shame.* Forty thousand a year. And now it was gone.

On the way up to Harriet's office in the elevator, Leo tried to talk himself into the idea that this was actually good news. The salary had been sweet, sure—but there was no use denying it: working as a copywriter at Bowles and Humphries was about two steps up from giving blow jobs to bums in the men's room of the Greyhound bus station. He'd never given anybody a blow job, at the Greyhound bus station or anywhere else, but having worked at Bowles and Humphries for six months, Leo was pretty sure he knew what it felt like. He spent his days like everyone else in the Creative Department at Bowles and Humphries, coming up with marketing strategies for consumer goods, pandering to the worst fears and insecurities of an unsuspecting public. "If you *really* love your family, you'll be sure to give 'em Wagner's Ol' Fashioned canned peas, because the good folks at Wagner's pack a little love into every can," or "Now you can *forget* about embarrassing clogged pores! With Skin-so-Smooth facial cleanser, let him get as close as he wants to." Leo wasn't a purist—he wouldn't have insisted that tending lepers or finding a cure for cancer was the only decent way to make a buck. But it would have nice to have a job that let him look at himself in the mirror without wincing.

This was his living. How depressing. This was how he put bread on their table. He tried to recall what it was that he'd actually wanted to do with his life, once upon a time, when he was a boy and dreamed boyish dreams of his future—when his life stretched out before him like an empty landscape waiting for someone to fill it in. He must have wanted *something*—not this, certainly—but *what?* Some sort of noble career, an honorable means of earning his passage through the world. He couldn't remember anything—couldn't conjure up a moment when he'd dreamed of being a cowboy, a doctor, a fireman. Maybe he'd wanted to be a matador.

But dammit, Bowles and Humphries was paying him forty thousand dollars a year. And there'd been the promise of more to come! In fact Ward LaPlante had recently hinted that Leo was due for a raise pretty soon. For months now Leo had been laboring away at Dazzle, one of the agency's smaller, less attractive accounts. The good news, though, was that the latest Dazzle television commercial to hit the air, "It Doesn't

Matter What The Dirt Is!" contained several lines that had Leo had come up with in various drafts. Lines he'd written—and now they were on national television! Millions of people were watching professional actors saying his lines! The script had gone through a number of versions, and at this point it was hard to remember which lines were actually his and which were Ward's—but Leo was pretty sure he recognized a couple of his own in there somewhere.

The Dazzle campaign used a format known around the office as the "2-C-K"—shorthand for "two cunts in a kitchen." Harvey Bowles, the agency's founder, had devised the "2-C-K" commercial back in television's infancy, and it was generally acknowledged as the most influential advance in advertising since the invention of the sandwich board. The basic format of "2-C-K" was simple: two women discussing a matter of some importance (laundry detergent, for instance) over coffee or tea in a kitchen setting. At its best, a "2-C-K" commercial was a miniature drama, a realistic, gritty slice of everyday life which just happened to revolve around a consumer product. For instance:

As Arlene and her old friend Louise sip coffee in Arlene's kitchen one afternoon, Arlene's ten-year-old son Timmy runs in from the playground, wearing his school uniform, which is covered head to foot in some unidentifiable gunk. It's an awkward moment. Arlene looks at him lovingly.

ARLENE
And where've you been, young man?

Timmy, an endearingly uncommunicative child, just shrugs and flees to his bedroom.

LOUISE
(Clucking with sympathy)
Oh, you poor thing. How're you ever going to get Timmy's school outfit clean? If you knew where he'd been, you might be able to get those stains out. But you don't even know what kind of dirt that is!

ARLENE
(Not a care in the world)

Oh, don't worry—I've got a new detergent! It'll take care of it.

LOUISE
(She's shocked)
New detergent? I thought you used Dazzle! You're the one who told *me* about it!

ARLENE
Well, goodbye, Dazzle. I've moved on to something *better.*

LOUISE
(She's having none of this)
Better than Dazzle? No way!
Arlene pours them both another cup of coffee.

ARLENE
(With a knowing wink)
Oh, I *used* to use Dazzle. But now I've switched to . . . new *improved* Dazzle.

She puts down the coffee pot and holds up the jug of Dazzle.

Because with new improved Dazzle, it doesn't *matter* what the dirt is!

Cut to animated insert showing new improved Dazzle at work lifting stains and dirt off fabric.

ARLENE
(Voice-over)
See? With a specially formulated, patented blend of anionic and nonionic surfactants, new improved Dazzle's got cleaning power unmatched by any other laundry detergent.

Cut back to kitchen scene. Louise is impressed.

LOUISE
Wow. I never thought I'd see a better detergent than Dazzle!

ARLENE
Neither did I! But that's all changed—'cause with new improved Dazzle . . .

ARLENE and LOUISE
(They laugh insanely as they say the line in unison)
It doesn't *matter* what the dirt is!

Leo tried to remember which of those lines might be his. He was almost sure he'd come up with "Well, goodbye, Dazzle." He had to admit it: he was proud of that line. It had some moxie to it—some real dramatic oomph. It was a line that took no prisoners. And he thought he might very well have written "Better than Dazzle?" as well. It sounded like him; it had the sort of high-pitched, manic quality he identified as his "voice." Arlene, the serene true believer, was a mystery to him—her faith in the power of Dazzle to solve her problems struck him as sweet but fundamentally stupid. Leo identified completely with Louise, the skeptic, the existentialist; he'd invented a whole life for her, imagining her as a hardbitten divorcée, a bit of a lush, perhaps involved in a shameful affair with a manipulative married man at her office—a cad who took her to cheap motel rooms and forced her to perform degrading sex acts while wearing see-through lingerie. He imagined that Arlene, on the other hand, had never slept with anyone but her husband, Bob; she was pure of spirit, with a conscience as spotless as her kitchen counter.

Well, Louise and Arlene would have to get somebody else to write their sequel, Leo told himself. This was curtains. He wasn't going to be a baby about it. They'd never see him cry.

▪ ▪ ▪

That resolve vanished when Leo arrived in the anteroom outside Harriet Rubin's office, and saw that Ward LaPlante, dressed as always in tight jeans and a herringbone tweed blazer, was waiting for him. "Ward," Leo said, and grabbed him by the sleeve. "Do something. Get me out of this, will you? I'll do anything. I need this job."

"What?"

"Help me out here. You gotta put in a word for me. No kidding, anything. Name it."

"Leo, what the hell are you talking about?" Ward put a hand on Leo's shoulder. "Get a hold of yourself." He ushered Leo into Harriet's office and closed the door behind them.

Leo hadn't been inside Harriet's office since the day he'd been hired at Bowles and Humphries, but he remembered the place very well. Her office was large and bright, flooded with light from a bank of tall windows, and would have overlooked Lake Michigan if it hadn't been for the mountain of chrome and glass that had recently gone up next door. As it was, you could see right into the offices in the new building. Leo stared across, wondering if anyone over there might be getting fired right now.

Harriet's office was awash in the detritus of her success: a row of framed CLIO awards; a little forest of plexiglass ADDY statuettes atop a polished mahogany credenza; souvenir props from photo shoots; a signed thank-you note from Burt Lancaster. Sleek black leather Barcelona chairs flanked a Noguchi coffee table. The Afghani tribal rugs on the floor appeared to be antiques. "Leo," Harriet said in a rich contralto, and swept an elegant hand toward the chairs, inviting him and Ward LaPlante to sit. Leo perched at the front edge of his chair and gripped his knees. "You haven't been here very long, have you?" Harriet asked him.

"Here at Bowles and Humphries? No. No, I haven't. Six months. I'm just getting started, really."

"Well, you're off to a good start. Ward tells me you're doing very well on Dazzle."

Leo flashed Ward a desperate grin. "Oh! Well, thanks! I've been trying hard, Harriet."

"I know Dazzle's not a lot of fun," Harriet said. "But it pays the bills." She opened a file drawer in her desk and lifted out a bottle of single malt scotch and three crystal tumblers. "So tell me, Leo—how'd you like to work on something a little more . . . high profile?" she asked. She poured a finger of scotch into each glass.

"Oh, sure. I'd be glad to," Leo said. "I'll work on anything." His voice sounded tinny in his ears, like it was being played back to him through a bad transistor radio.

"We have an assignment for you. You don't have to take it. You can stay on Dazzle if you'd like." She paused.

"Oh, no. I think I'm ready for something new."

"Good for you. Ever heard of Lambert Touchet?"

"No, I don't think I have," Leo said. She handed him a glass, then gave one to Ward, and beckoned to them both to drink. Leo looked nervously at the scotch in his glass. He wasn't much of a drinker, and found it hard to swallow anything alcoholic before dark—but this was no time to be a prig. Down the hatch.

"Lambert Touchet invented the idea of body odor," Harriet said. "Invented it out of thin air. He's responsible for an entire industry. You can't say that about many people, but with Lambert Touchet, it's not an exaggeration. Everybody always knew they smelled bad if they didn't take a shower, but before he came along, nobody'd realized B.O. was actually a problem."

"The man's a visionary," Ward LaPlante said, and knocked back his scotch in one gulp.

"Lambert has a new product coming out in test markets in three months," Harriet said. Then she stopped and sipped her drink slowly. "He's given Bowles and Humphries the chance to handle the introduction," she said. "I gave the project to Ward, and he's written the first commercial. It's all approved, ready to go. Now Leo, I need to emphasize that this project is top secret—very hush-hush. It's not just a new product. It's . . . breaking new ground. Nobody's gone this direction before. "

"Wow, this is exciting," said Leo.

"Yes," Harriet said tonelessly. "Exciting. It certainly is." She paused. "You've heard of feminine hygiene spray?"

"Yeah. I think so." Leo sank back in his Barcelona chair and assumed what he hoped was a thoughtful expression. Heard of feminine hygiene spray? During his college days he'd spent countless evenings drinking beer, listening to frat boys tell each other raunchy jokes about feminine hygiene spray, and he'd laughed himself silly over some of them, too—but somehow that didn't seem like anything to throw into the conversation just now.

"Traditionally feminine hygiene sprays have been targeted at sexually active women over eighteen. That makes sense, it's the target audience you'd expect. But this new product—we're calling it Diana—this is different." Harriet went to the bank of windows now, and looked out in the direction of Lake Michigan as she spoke. "It's aimed at girls. Not even teenagers, really," she said. "Girls, ten to twelve—that's our target audience."

Leo took this in for a moment. "Gee, that's kind of young," he said at last.

"Yes," Harriet said. "You might say that. It's a bit young." She stared out the windows.

"Do girls that age need feminine hygiene spray?" asked Leo.

"They will if we make them think they do," Ward announced.

"That's what we do, Leo," Harriet said. "That's our business. It's why we come to work every day." She turned to Ward. "Why don't you run Leo through the first script."

"You bet," Ward said. "Listen to this." He got up and paced for a moment, his eyes half-shut. "A young girl alone on a windy, mysterious landscape. She's wearing a teddy, but there isn't enough meat on her bones to get you thinking things you shouldn't be thinking—not unless you're an absolute pedophile. Don't get me wrong. She's sexy—but what does she know about 'sexy' at her age? Okay, get the mood: think *Wuthering Heights* meets *Young Miss,* with a little *Lolita* thrown in, just enough to make things interesting. You with me?"

"Sure. I guess so," Leo said.

"Camera pans across this windswept landscape, and ever so slowly pulls in on her face," Ward said, using his hands to frame the shot. "The music is building. Something French—well, not *French* French. Think of Edith Piaf. Okay, now take out Edith Piaf and put in Julie London, only Julie London's still got Edith Piaf's accordianist, plus about half of her heartbreak. Sexy—it's got the soft pulse of femininity—but with a little backbeat. Anyway, at last this young waif's face fills the screen. She turns to the camera. It's surprised her—what's it doing here, she thought she was alone, this camera's disturbing her privacy, her most intimate moment, here she is wearing nothing but a teddy! But she's not ashamed. What's she got to be ashamed about, anyway? She's a virgin! She's such a virgin, she doesn't even *know* she's a virgin. It's not her fault she's gorgeous and wearing a teddy. Okay, so we're in our close-up now. And she says: 'Diana. Goddess of the Hunt,'" Ward intoned, his voice high, girlish, but sultry. "'The scent of nature on a spring-soft morning. Diana.'"

He paused. "'For those days when you know you're becoming a woman.'"

Harriet sat silently for a moment, letting the drama of Ward's performance sink in. "Ward, that was lovely. Really." Was she being serious? Leo had no idea. With Harriet, he never had a clue as to what she was really thinking. "So what do you think, Leo?" she asked at last. "Are you interested?"

"You mean . . . ?"

"The account. We'd like you to help out," Harriet told him. "We're moving quickly on this one. Zip-zip-zip. We're shooting our first spot for Diana next week. The director's already on board, and we'll be starting pre-production in just a few days. We want you there."

"Where's there?"

"Los Angeles. We're shooting in Hollywood."

"Oh, look. That's great . . . but I'm new. I don't know anything about shooting film."

"Don't worry, Leo. You don't have to know anything," Ward told him. "You're a copywriter. Nobody expects copywriters to know anything. You're just supposed to stand around and look intelligent. The director's the one that knows about shooting film. That's why we'll be paying him so much money. That's why there's a crew—a cinematographer, a casting director, lighting, make-up, all the rest."

"Oh, I don't know. Couldn't I take a little time, read up on the process first?"

"You don't read a book to learn how to shoot film. You go do it. And anyway, we don't have the time, amigo," Ward said. "The product's about ready to be shipped. This thing's going to be airing in test markets just as soon we can put some film in a can."

"It's more like a fashion shoot than anything else," said Harriet. "Atmospheric, very moody. You'll simply be there to help with the casting—you'll watch, you'll listen, you'll learn the ropes. This is a big opportunity for you, Leo."

That much was true, of course. Leo had never been anywhere near a shoot before. Back at Dunne, Crowell and Gold he'd spent his time writing copy for direct-mail brochures, end-of-aisle displays in supermarkets, the occasional print ad for magazines and newspapers. Even here at Bowles and Humphries, where they generally recommended television as the most effective medium for any product, the nearest he'd come to a shoot so far was a post-production session for Dazzle at a sound studio in Chicago, where he spent most of his time on the phone, arranging for lunch to be brought in. He'd never seen such an impressive array of deli sandwiches.

Hollywood! He'd never been west of Denver in his life. All Leo knew of Los Angeles was what he remembered from *77 Sunset Strip,* his favorite detective show from the 1950s. He wondered if Sunset Strip was still there. It had to be—what were they going to do, after all, shut down the street just because the show was canceled? That would be something—walking up Sunset Strip, running into Efrem Zimbalist Jr. and Ed "Kookie" Burns having a nostalgic cup of coffee together. But forget about Kookie Burns. This wasn't the time to be going out of town. Absolutely out of the question. Leo rubbed his palms together now, and felt them sliding in their own sweat. "You know, the thing is, my wife, Rachel—she's pregnant," he said. "She's scheduled to go in for an ultrasound in a few days. I was going to go with her."

"Can't she put it off a week?" Ward asked him. "This is important, Leo."

"Is she having problems?" asked Harriet. "Complications?"

Again Leo saw himself strolling along the sidewalk in Los Angeles, wearing sunglasses, snapping his fingers in time to the theme music from "77 Sunset Strip." That would really be something. "No, no, she's fine," he told Harriet. Oh, what the hell. "Everything's going along smoothly. The doctor says she's doing great. I guess she could go in by herself. It's just that we were going to go together. It's our first time."

"Call her up. Ask her what she wants you to do," Ward suggested.

"Oh, no. That's okay. It's just an ultrasound. She can do it by herself, I guess."

"That's my boy," said Ward.

"Well, okay, then," Leo said, and managed a weak smile. "When do I leave?"

"Good for you, Leo," Harriet said, her tone spiced with dry amusement. "You could have a future in this business." Again, Leo couldn't tell if she was being serious or sarcastic. He studied her face intently, but the mask of her features gave away nothing, and so after a moment's hesitation he shrugged and decided to take her comment at face value. After all, he reasoned, he wasn't being fired. That fact alone flooded him so thoroughly with a sense of well-being that he felt himself rising off the floor, held aloft by pure joy.

Besides, nobody had ever told him he had a future at anything before—not once in his life—-and Leo wasn't going to ruin this moment by second-guessing it to death. Throughout his childhood, his parents had made anguished remarks about his apparent lack of potential, and in high school his guidance counselors hadn't been very encouraging, either. One of them, a lizard-like creep named Mr. Langford, had even suggested that Leo switch from college-prep to a vocational program. "Do you like to . . . clean things, Leo? Make 'em all nice and shiny?" the bastard had asked him. "Hmm? Does that sound nice?" Well, they could all go screw themselves. Here he was at the age of thirty-two, a head full of hair, about to become a father—and suddenly he had a future in advertising.

"And don't worry," Harriet added. "You won't be all by yourself. Ward will be there with you, just to make sure everything's going smoothly. And I'll fly out for a day while you're there. We'll all have dinner together."

"You'll see—this is going to be a piece of cake," said Ward. He massaged Leo's neck. "This is the fun part. You ever flown anywhere first class?"

"Oh, no. God, no. I peeked into first class once, when I was about ten. We were flying to New York to stay with relatives, and I just stuck my head through the curtain to see what was going on up there. The stewardess threw me out on my ear." Leo could still recall her face; she was wearing pink lipstick, the most garish shade he'd ever seen in his life. Ever since then, he'd imagined first class as an exotic, pink-lipsticked place where someone of his ilk would never be allowed to set foot.

"Well, kiddo," Ward told him, "at Bowles and Humphries, we fly first class, or we don't fly. Come on," he said. "We've got some talking to do." Ward stood up, and Leo followed suit. "Harriet," Ward said, "don't worry about a thing. We'll take care of everything."

"Oh, I know you will," Harriet said. She turned slightly away from them and fingered the beads in her necklace.

Leo could see her profile, the long lines of her nose and jaw, silhouetted against the light from the windows. He stared at her for a long moment. It was the longest look he'd ever allowed himself to take. She carried herself with elegant self-confidence, as if she owned every square inch of the world she walked through, but now he could see the network of lines around her eyes, not just at the corners but underneath them, too, a concentric ring of wrinkles he'd never noticed before. What price had she paid to move from the steno pool to this grand office? "Thanks for giving me this chance, Harriet," he said. "I can tell this is going to be an exciting account to work on."

"Oh, yes. It's exciting, all right. Telling ten-year-old girls they stink," Harriet said. "How could anything be more fun?" Then she turned back toward Ward and Leo and flashed a bright smile. "Oh, well. Never mind. What's important is that Diana's going to bring us five million a year in billings—and that's just for starters. Have fun. I'll see you out in Lotus Land."

Ward put his arm around Leo's shoulder as they left Harriet's office and steered him down the hall, away from the elevators and toward the other side of the building. "Just take a minute—I have to stop by my office, pick something up," Ward told him.

"Oh. Okay." Leo let Ward herd him along. As they walked, Leo mulled over what Harriet had said just as they were leaving. Had he just made the worst mistake of his life? Was this a test of some kind? Was he supposed to have refused to work on the account? What had he gotten himself into? After all, what did he know about feminine hygiene spray? What did he want to know, for that matter?

When they were inside Ward's office, Ward shut the door and locked it. He sat down behind his desk, got out his nail clippers, and started to do his nails. A long moment of silence went by. Finally, not looking up from the clippers, he asked, "So, you excited?"

"Are you kidding? Sure I am. This is a huge break. And I owe it all to you and Harriet."

"Harriet didn't have anything to do with it, Leo." Ward fixed him with a steady gaze.

"She didn't?"

"C'mon, don't be silly. Harriet's way too busy running the world to take the time for something like this. She listens to me, she takes my advice. I told her you'd be perfect for this shoot. I talked you up, amigo—your talent, your drive, all of that. You're my boy."

"Wow. You know, when I got that call from Harriet's secretary, I thought—I know this sounds silly—I thought I was going to get canned. I really did. You really went to bat for me, and I'm not going to forget it. No kidding. I'm going to work my butt off, Ward. I can't tell you what this means to me."

"Oh, I know all of that. What I want to know is, are you a team player?"

"A what? A team player?"

"Yeah. You know what I'm talking about."

"I do?" Leo bit his lip. "Oh. Yeah. I guess I do." He thought he could hear his watch ticking. He recalled the day that Ward had brought him to his Lake Shore Drive condominium and offered him coke. What kind of a weenie was he, anyway? Did he want this job, this career, or not? Well, what the hell; he wouldn't tell Rachel, of course, and there was no way for Harriet Rubin or any of the Managing Partners to see any of this. There weren't any hidden cameras in Ward's office. And anyway, the Managing Partners were probably locked in their suites on the sixteenth floor, smoking opium right now. They were probably up there wearing leather underwear and Halloween masks, flogging each other with a bullwhip. "I tell you what," Leo said. "I've changed my mind. Let me give that stuff a try, will you? Just a sniff?"

"Oh, you don't have to do that," Ward said. He looked up from his nails now, smiling.

"Let me just try one line, so I can see how it works. What the hell. I'm curious."

"Only if you're sure. I don't want to twist anybody's arm here."

"You're not twisting my arm. I want to give it a whack. Really."

So Ward opened his desk drawer, got out a mirror, and quickly used a razor blade to lay out some lines of coke. He slid the mirror back toward Leo's side of the desk, and handed him a rolled-up dollar bill. "Just sniff, right?" Leo asked.

"Blow out a breath first, before you lean down to the mirror," Ward advised him. "Blow out off the side—like this." He demonstrated the maneuver. "Then just sniff—like you've got a runny nose. It's simple."

Leo blew out a long breath, then leaned down and inserted the dollar bill in his right nostril. "Just sniff," Ward repeated. And Leo did. "Do another line," Ward told him, and Leo leaned his head down, put the rolled up bill in his other nostril, and snorted again.

"I don't feel anything," he said.

"Give it a minute," Ward told him. "This stuff doesn't clobber you over the head.Coke is something you can reason with—it's not trying to overthrow your government, like LSD, hash oil, mescaline—you know what I'm talking about."

"Oh, yeah," Leo said, though in fact, of course, he didn't. He sniffed gently and rubbed his nose. "Are you sure I did it right?"

"You did it just fine." Ward leaned over and neatly snorted two lines. "Relax," he said after a moment. "Just kick back, buddy boy, and think about Hollywood. Go ahead. Settle in and have another toot. These are on the house."

▪ ▪ ▪

There were linen napkins and crystal salt and pepper shakers in first-class—not to mention cracked dungeness crab with sauce remoulade for an appetizer, followed by freshly carved slices of leg of lamb, medium rare, served over minted garlic couscous, accompanied by vintage claret poured from the bottle by a flight attendant wearing the starched white uniform of a sommelier. Amazing. At the front of the 747, at the top of a spiral staircase, there was an intimate cocktail lounge reserved for first-class passengers, with piped-in Frank Sinatra tunes and a cute, snub-nosed blonde flight attendant hovering, just waiting for someone to snap their fingers and ask for more champagne.

Unfortunately for Leo, first class also contained Hector Benevento, the senior producer who'd been sent along by Bowles and Humphries to babysit him and handle the pre-production details for the shoot. At the last minute, Ward had to stay behind in Chicago—a sudden flare-up on the Dazzle account that had to be put out—so it was just Leo and Hector flying west together. Leo had never met him before they got on the plane at O'Hare. In fact almost no one knew Hector, because he spent most of his time on the road, living out of a suitcase, shuttling back and forth between production trips to New York and Los Angeles, stopping in at the Chicago office of Bowles and Humphries just to turn in his expense reports, screen the latest rough cuts of new commercials for various agency bigwigs, and get a fresh batch of shirts from the cleaners. Now, since he had Leo's undivided attention throughout the four-and-a-half-hour flight from Chicago to Los Angeles, Hector took the opportunity to tell him in detail, through a snack, a movie, several rounds of drinks and a three-course dinner, just what a putz he thought he was. He seemed driven to do this, unable to stop himself even for a bathroom break.

"What's an F-stop?" he asked Leo in the upstairs cocktail lounge not long after they'd reached their cruising altitude.

"I don't know, " Leo said for what already seemed to be the fifth time. "I don't know anything about production, Hector. I'm new. I haven't even been at the agency a year. I'm just a copywriter. Copywriters don't know anything. Ward told me that. He and Harriet sent me out so I could learn something—this is my first production trip." He knocked a fistful of cashews—cashews!—into his mouth. Unbelievable. Back in coach, Leo knew very well, you were lucky to get a pouch of stale pretzels.

"Tell me about film speeds. We'll be shooting in a few days—tell me about film speeds."

"I don't know a thing about it. I told you that already."

"Give me a comment or two about camera angles," Hector demanded.

"No-can-doosky."

"Come on! You've been to the movies! Wide-angle, close-up—what're your thoughts?"

"It's all Greek to me," said Leo with a bashful smile. "I'm a complete idiot about all of this. Don't ask me anything about lighting, either. I'm not sure I could tell the front of a camera from the back. What's a 'gaffer'? What's a 'key grip'? What's a 'best boy'? Why're they called that? I've always wondered. Is someone the 'next-to-best boy'? And how do you tell one from guy from another? Do gaffers wear a sign on their back that says 'gaffer'?"

Some hecklers might have wilted in the face of such ingenuousness, but not Hector Benevento. Hector, as he reminded Leo every few minutes, was no sucker. In fifteen years at Bowles and Humphries, he'd seen it all—copywriters who could barely spell their own name, color-blind art directors who'd never drawn anything fancier than a stick figure, senior account executives with the I.Q. of a gerbil. Anybody tried to put something over on Hector Benevento, they'd end up sleeping with the fishes. He was in his fifties, a small, sallow man with a five o'clock shadow, thinning hair and a quivering, delicate nose—the kind of guy, Leo guessed, who probably couldn't summon the strength to start a lawnmower, though his demeanor suggested that he was on temporary leave from his job as an enforcer for the Gambino Family. Hector's verbal style was lifted from shopworn mafia movies—long riffs of invective, sprays of insults like buckshot, all of it couched in a side-of-the-mouth wiseguy accent. If only he'd had someone else to harass—anyone but Leo, in fact—Leo might have found all of this mildly amusing.

But even Hector Benevento couldn't spoil the effect of the weather that greeted them when the plane landed in Los Angeles. When they'd left Chicago, the city seemed locked inside a pressure cooker, one of those protracted spells of stagnant, humid misery that served as a reminder that summer in the upper Midwest could be, if anything, worse than winter. But here in Los Angeles, everything was different. When they arrived at LAX at seven o'clock that evening, the sky was a perfect blue, a darker, richer hue than Leo had ever seen before, and the temperature hovered at a dry, mild eighty degrees. As Hector drove up the San Diego Freeway toward the city, Leo rolled down his passenger-side window and smelled the tang of something sweetly exotic drifting in the air. Everywhere he looked, the world was in bloom—honeysuckles, rhododendrons, swaying palm trees, lemon trees and jacarandas, their graceful foliage floating like blue clouds. Could this really be the same continent, the same country, he'd left just that afternoon? Who could keep a coherent line of thought in his head amidst all this beauty? No wonder the movies they made out here were so witless, Leo told himself—the whole place was like a gorgeous, golden child who'd been held back a grade in elementary school.

He missed Rachel. He'd been planning all along to be there with her, to hold her hand at the doctor's office as the ultrasound technician mapped the outline of the child growing in her belly. Now she'd have to do it all without him. If he were back home, they'd be together right now, sitting in front of the air conditioner in the den, sweating to death, side by side. He checked his watch: if it was seven o'clock here in Los Angeles, it'd be nine now in Chicago, they'd be done washing the dishes, and maybe they'd be watching TV, eating popcorn, necking between bites like a couple of school kids.

Rachel had been understanding about this trip, even enthusiastic about it—at least until he told her about Diana. "*How* old?" she asked, wide-eyed.

"Ten to twelve. That's the target audience."

"Leo, that's ridiculous. Ten-year-old girls? Feminine hygiene spray?"

"I guess that's a little young." He put down his fork—they were in the middle of dinner—and gave Rachel what he hoped was an imploring look. "Look, I need this," he told her. "This is a big break for me. I didn't pick the product—it picked *me.* I'm not kidding."

"Selling feminine hygiene spray to pre-adolescent girls?"

"You don't know that. Girls are starting puberty earlier every year."

"Oh, please."

"No, it's the truth. I read about it in *Newsweek.* They think it has to do with all the sex on television. Nobody knows. It could be something in the water. Everybody's got a theory. Anyway, the bottom line is, they're starting their periods at the age of nine these days."

"I wish you were still working on those end-of-aisle displays for Pepsi."

"See, that's just what I'm talking about. First of all, that stuff rots your teeth right out of your head. Did you know that? There's a boatload of toothless children out there gumming their food now because of the stuff I wrote for that job."

"You're telling me there's nothing else you could be working on?" Rachel asked him. "It's either this . . . this feminine hygiene thing, or nothing? It's the only account they could put you on?"

"I have news for you," Leo said. "All the noble accounts are already taken. There aren't any warm, fuzzy consumer products out there waiting for me to write commercials for them. Mother Teresa doesn't have any openings for copywriters right now." He paused. "Do you remember what I was making at Dunne, Crowell and Gold? Remember when we had to ask your parents for a loan so we could scrape together a down payment?"

"They were glad to give it to us, Leo."

"Well I wasn't glad to take it, let me tell you. I'm pulling in forty grand a year now—and Ward's already talking about giving me a raise. We need that money."

"You need that money," said Rachel.

Okay, Leo told himself—fine, he needed the money. He wouldn't argue the point. But did he need it this much? Yes, the cracked crab in first class was an eye-opening change from the squalor of flying coach—but how much cracked crab could you eat, after all? And if he kept buying grams of coke from Ward LaPlante, what was the point of making forty thousand a year, anyway? The first few lines had been free, sure—but everything after that was cash on delivery. If his salary went up his nose, how was he supposed to start a college fund for little Whosit? And what if the roof on their house really did need to be replaced? If he'd snorted up his raise already, where would they find the money for new shingles? He imagined rain pouring into the attic, and there he was, snorting coke all night long, rubbing his gums and sniffling, feeling like an idiot, moving buckets around to catch the drips.

It seemed only fitting that Ward had reserved a room for Leo at the Chateau Marmont on Sunset Boulevard—the place where John Belushi had overdosed on cocaine and heroin just a few months before. Leo had never heard of the Chateau Marmont before John Belushi died there, and from what he'd read about the place in the newspaper, it sounded pretty seedy. "Don't worry, it's one of the world's great hotels, Leo," Ward had told him. "Very funky. Rock stars stay there. Actors, writers, jazz musicians. The weather's always snowy at the old Chateau." He touched his nose and gave Leo a knowing wink.

"Oh, right," Leo said after a moment. "I get it."

Hector Benevento had reserved a suite for himself at the Westwood Marquis, his usual spot in Los Angeles. "The Chateau Marmont's a dump. Only freaks and winos hang out there," he told Leo as they sped north on the freeway. "I wouldn't stay there if you paid me. But hey, that's just me." The sky deepened into twilight as they drove, and as they wheeled into the curved driveway of the Chateau Marmont, night fell suddenly, as if someone had turned off a gigantic lamp. Hector screeched to a stop beneath the vine-covered cave of the hotel's entryway. It was dark and leafy and mysterious here, and Leo lingered nervously for a moment in the passenger seat. "This is where you get off," Hector told him. "Get unpacked, get settled in, relax a while, kid. I'll pick you up in an hour and a half, we'll go meet the director." Leo got out with his bags, and Hector sped away into the night. Leo wasn't sure he liked being called "kid," but compared to the barrage of insults that Hector had lobbed in his direction during the flight, this sounded like pillow talk. He stood at the curb for a moment with his luggage, feeling much like he'd felt as a forlorn, homesick little boy going off to Camp Shalom for the first time.

The lobby of the Chateau Marmont struck Leo as something out of a Spanish vampire movie—just as dark and foreboding as Dracula's castle, but prettier, somehow, with Moorish arches and a terra cotta tile floor that echoed cool and hollow beneath his feet. At first no one at the reception desk seemed to notice him standing there, but finally a young man with slicked-back yellow hair looked up from his reading and greeted Leo with a distinct lack of enthusiasm. He rang a bell on the desk and a dark, slender bellboy wearing a skintight black turtleneck appeared to deliver Leo to his room. They rode up in the tiny elevator along with an actor Leo recognized—a tall, thin, pockmarked fellow with lank black hair, who was burdened with what looked like three weeks' worth of dry cleaning. Wow, this was something, Leo told himself. Ward was right! Here he was in Hollywood, he hadn't even gotten to his room yet, and he'd spotted his first actor.

Before he could stop himself, Leo said, "Hey, I can't believe I'm standing here next to you. You were in *In the Heat of the Night,* weren't you. I never forget a face. I loved that movie. You were the guy who swatted the fly at the diner, right at the beginning, right?"

Without looking at him, the man cleared his throat and replied, "Yeah." He shifted the mass of dry cleaning on his shoulder and swallowed. The guy had the biggest Adam's apple Leo had ever seen.

"Then at the end you turned out to be the real killer, didn't you?" Leo said. He knew he was stepping over the line here, but he couldn't help himself.

"Uh-huh. My big break," the man murmured, still staring at the elevator's peeling faux wood veneer. The elevator stopped at the fourth floor and he got off without saying goodbye.

The bellboy with the skintight turtleneck rolled his eyes and smiled, but he didn't say anything. When they got to Leo's floor he led the way to the suite, unlocked the door with a flourish, and said, "Greta Garbo occupied these very rooms for a year, back in the 1930s."

"Wow. Garbo. That's amazing," said Leo, and on the spur of the moment he whipped out three one-dollar bills for the man, mostly as payment for the tidbit about Garbo. As soon as the bellboy had pocketed the bills and slipped out the door, Leo began to regret the handsome tip. What if he got a reputation around the hotel as a big tipper? He was going to be here for several days. How could he keep that up? Three bucks here, three bucks there, pretty soon you were talking about real money.

He explored the suite, opening doors and peeking into cabinets, and in a few moments he realized it didn't matter much that Garbo had stayed here fifty years ago. If she'd left some underwear behind, admittedly, that would have been pretty impressive. But there didn't seem to be any lingering evidence of her anywhere. In fact, the place was a mess. He tried out the mattress: sleep where Garbo slept! Forget about it—this lumpy piece of crap couldn't have been Garbo's bed. And surely the pervasive odor trapped in the brown wall-to-wall shag carpeting hadn't been there back in her day. He was pretty sure it was cat pee. God, he hated the smell of cat pee. When he parted the thin curtains to gaze out on the traffic and bright lights of Sunset Boulevard, choking clouds of dust exploded into the room. When had this place been cleaned last? The bathroom smelled of mildew, the kitchenette was overrun by cockroaches. Garbo stayed here? Who were they kidding? Garbo probably *died* here, and they hadn't come to pick up the body yet.

Looming over the back of the hotel was an enormous billboard advertising Marlboro cigarettes, with a fifty-foot picture of the Marlboro Man, his hands cupped to his face as he lit a cigarette. Leo opened the window and craned his head out to gaze at the squinting cowboy, and thought of Herb Pinsker, the poor bastard. Maybe a matador would have been a better way to go. Pinsker had probably never gone on a shoot in his life. How many commercials would the Happy-Time Incontinence Shield account need, after all? And anyway, what kind of actor would be willing to appear in a commercial for adult diapers? Talk about flushing your career down the toilet. You could get typecast so easily: *Oh, sure, I've seen you on TV! You're the woman with the bladder control problem.* Poor Pinsker. Laboring away at his drawing board, year in, year out—for what?

What was he talking about? Poor Pinsker? Why feel sorry for Pinsker–the man owned stock in the company! Mel Kleinfelder wasn't about to sweep into Pinsker's office and tell him to put his shit in a box. Not a chance. Pinsker might have had a miserable job, but at least it was secure lifetime employment. And he didn't have to spend any nights half a continent away from home, trapped in a hotel room that reeked of cat piss and death. Pinsker was no doubt asleep in his own bed right now, dreaming untroubled dreams in which President Reagan played no part whatsoever.

Leo sat down on the threadbare sofa, took out the small plastic vial of coke that Ward had sold him, unscrewed the cap, and gave himself a couple of toots. At a hundred bucks a gram, coke was an expensive hobby, but right now Leo needed a lift, and this stuff was without a doubt the fastest, most reliable mood elevator he'd ever encountered in his life. A hundred dollars for a gram of coke, or a hundred dollars to watch Dr. Findlay snore for fifty minutes. Was there any question as to which one gave him more bang for his buck?

He got up and closed the curtains, then tried out one of the easy chairs, which turned out to have a broken leg. He gave himself one more tiny snort, then put the vial back in his pocket. He needed this, he told himself. He needed it. Here he was, all by himself. Poor little Leo. Oh, all right, just one more toot, and that would do it for the evening. He could hear Hector Benevento's constant patter of insults fading into the distance. And soon, sure enough, the only sound left inside Leo's head was the peaceful sibilance of white noise.

■ ■ ■

As soon as Leo climbed into Hector's rented Porsche a little before nine that night, it began all over again. "When we get there, don't say anything," Hector warned him as they pulled out onto Sunset Boulevard. "You're new, you don't know anything, so don't open your mouth. And for the record, let me tell you something: we're goddamned lucky to get a director like Don Beacham," he added in an aggrieved voice, as if Leo had just been badmouthing the fellow. "This guy could be shmoozing with Jack Lemmon, he could be banging Faye Dunaway, the big studios could be all over him, the man's a genius, he shoots film like an angel."

"I don't get it, then. Why's he making commercials?" asked Leo.

"Are you kidding? Five grand a day, that's why. That's his day rate. He shoots seventy days a year, figure it out—he takes his money and plays golf the rest of the time. Feature films are just so much aggravation. Everybody's an artist! An auteur! Don't call it a movie, call it a *film*." Hector's lip curled. "And the *deal*-making . . . you want backing from a big studio, suck *this* dick. You want a good distribution deal, suck *that* dick. Who needs it!"

Hector steered the Porsche through tortuous curves, higher and higher into the hills, and finally whipped the car into a driveway nearly hidden from the road. Don Beacham's house was set back behind a tall fence, a sprawling cedar shingle bungalow lost amidst a stand of sequoias. "Take a look. See what good taste plus a boatload of cash can buy?" Hector muttered out the side of his mouth. "Oh, mama mia, get a load of this. This is what a five-grand day rate will get you. Oh, I'm jizzing. I'm coming in my pants."

Don Beacham met them at the door and ushered them in, and Hector muttered a barely audible introduction for Leo. Beacham, small, handsome, and as thin as the breadsticks at Villa d'Este, Leo's favorite Italian place back in Chicago, handed them each a glass of wine and led them through the living room toward the back of the house. He was probably the best looking man Leo had ever seen—better looking even than Brad Pettybone, the only guy at Leo's high school who'd had a noticeable cleft in his chin. Leo had heard the expression "lit from within" before, but until he saw Don Beacham he'd never known what the hell it meant. Beacham really did glow, as if a miniature track-lighting system had been installed somewhere inside him, not far beneath his skin. The man looked like he lived on sunlight and rose petals. A lock of his hair, an indeterminate shade of brownish gray, fell carefully over his forehead. Only the network of tiny lines around his eyes gave a hint at his age, which must have been around fifty. He probably starved himself mercilessly, Leo told himself. Nobody could be that thin on a normal diet. Wheat grass water for breakfast, gluten tablets for lunch, a protein shake and a glass of oaky Chardonnay for supper. Maybe he'd had his stomach stapled—Leo had read of such things in tabloids. For some reason Leo's waist had recently turned to pudding, a change that Rachel claimed not to have noticed, though how she could have missed it was beyond him. Just a year ago he'd still had some vestige of muscle tone left in his abdomen, but now it was all gone—he could stick his finger in there up to the knuckle without encountering any resistance whatsoever. Maybe he should have his stomach stapled. It probably hurt, but what the hell, when there was a chance you could end up looking like Don Beacham?

The interior of the house was dimly lit, furnished sparsely, the dark floors set off by white upholstered pieces. In the deep twilight of the back yard—the night air seemed a bit lighter here than it had down on Sunset Boulevard—Leo could make out a rectangular swimming pool which seemed to have been carved out of a ledge of solid rock, surrounded by a dense thicket of foliage. He stood staring on the patio, lost in a tidal wave of envy, and nearly dropped his wine when a barefoot young woman with skin the color of burnished copper cookware suddenly emerged from the leafy shadows, dressed in a shimmering blue silk sarong, and glided toward him smiling, a smile so wide and bright it seemed like moonlight. Jesus Christ, where had she come from? She was so beautiful she barely looked human. She tilted her head back and shook her dark hair behind her, as if standing under a shower. Her collarbones were the most delicate he'd ever seen.

"I'm Lesley," she said. "I'm Don's new assistant."

Leo stared at the hollow at the base of her taut, lovely throat—he couldn't help himself, there it was, what was he supposed to do, just ignore it, pretend it didn't exist?—then he coughed out something desperate that sounded like a greeting, and turned to Hector for help.

"Leo's new—he's never met a director before," Hector said to Don Beacham and the girl. "Why they sent him on this production trip is beyond me. He's an ignoramus. He gets a load of this place, he looks around, he sees your friend here…" he fanned the air as if cooling off a sudden hot flash. "Oh, mama mia, he's jizzing in his pants." He turned to Leo. "You know who this is?" he demanded. "You know whose goddamn house you're in?"

"Don Beacham?" whispered Leo.

"Don Beacham! You see the film this guy shot last year for Buick? The thing with the car up on top of one of those—whaddatheycallit—those rocks."

"Oh, the Grand Canyon? That one?"

"Thing won every award there is. The man is a *genius*," Hector said. He lit a cigarette and flipped his Zippo shut with a metallic clack. "I'm telling you you're standing here with your dick in your hand, talking to a genius," he repeated in an insistent tone, as if Leo had argued the point, then he took several deep drags off the cigarette and let the silence build. "Well, okay, then," Hector announced at last. "We came, we saw, we conquered. Thanks for the wine, now let's get out of here, get some sleep. Tomorrow we get down to business."

"Casting at ten?" Beacham asked.

"Yeah," Hector said, and puffed again on his cigarette. "I hope to Christ somebody with some acting talent shows up. Child actors ought to be rounded up and shot. No, wait, I take that back. That's too harsh. It's the parents who should be shot. The kids ought to be herded into pens someplace and left to die. Out in the middle of nowhere, maybe in Utah. I swear to God. I don't want a repeat of last time." He gazed at the girl at Beacham's side. "You look fantastic, by the way. How old are you, anyway?"

"Twenty-four," she said.

"Lesley just started working for me a couple of months ago," Beacham offered. "She's a dream. Takes care of everything. The best assistant I've ever had."

"Oh, yeah," Hector said, "I bet she assists you plenty." He fanned the air again as he led Leo back to the car, tugging at his sleeve. On the drive back to the Chateau Marmont, Hector gripped the wheel and took the curves at ten miles above the speed limit. A fresh cigarette was clenched in his teeth. "Pussy, pussy, pussy," he said at last in a philosophical tone, as if he was summarizing a conversation they'd been having. "Hey, listen, here's a tidbit you might find interesting. You know who Don Beacham used to be, before he became a director?"

"No, Hector. Am I supposed to guess?"

"You ever see *Surfin' Safari? Tammy and the Dentist?"*

"I don't think so."

"Don Beacham had third billing in both of those. Yeah—the guy you just met—*that* Don Beacham. He made a dozen movies back in the fifties, maybe more. Redondo Beach, that was the name the studio gave him. He says he hated it. Surfer movies, that was all they'd let him do. He wanted to break out, but they told him forget about it, he was under contract. The tan on that guy! He had his own fan club. Girls used to send him their underwear. He could have been big—I shit you not. He could have been another Tab Hunter."

When they got back to the Chateau Marmont, Hector whipped the Porsche into the driveway and barely came to a stop before Leo had vaulted out. "I'll pick you up at nine-thirty tomorrow morning," Hector told him. "Get yourself some sleep."

Leo leaned into the car through open passenger window. "Where you off to?" he asked.

"There's a strip club up on Alta Loma where all the girls are U.C.L.A. coeds—they have the registration papers to prove it, recent report cards and everything," Hector said. "Look out, girls, Hector Benevento's back in town!" he cried as he sped away into the night.

In the Chateau Marmont's darkened lobby, Leo checked at the desk for messages—there weren't any—and then, he rode upstairs in the hotel's tiny, decrepit elevator, hoping to see the actor from *In The Heat of the Night* again. No one else got on, and he rode up alone. It was nearly ten now, too late to call Chicago. Rachel would love to hear about the actor in the elevator—it was the kind of thing she'd squeal over—but it would just have to wait. Leo poured himself a glass of rusty water from the sink in the kitchenette, and stood at the window for a long while, watching the lighted ribbons of traffic zooming up and down Sunset Boulevard. Then he spooned himself a little pick-me-up from the vial in his pocket. He held the vial up to the light. Still plenty left. Oh well, what the hell: one more tiny toot for mankind.

There was no way Leo was going to sleep anytime soon—a blow from a sledge hammer couldn't have put him under in his present state of mind—so he took the elevator down to the lobby and woke the yellow-haired fellow at the front desk to ask for directions to the swimming pool. The desk clerk looked at his watch dubiously, then pointed vaguely toward a darkened hallway and went back to sleep.

Okay, so it was late, Leo told himself. Big deal. A place like the Chateau Marmont, there was likely always somebody out at the pool. And anyway, he was feeling so damned smart right now, so charming and verbal and witty, he hoped like hell there'd be somebody out there, so that he could knock their socks off. He didn't care who it was—he was ready, able and willing to charm the pants off anybody. It could be Warren Beatty and Julie Christie kicking back in adjacent lounge chairs, pouring martinis down each other's throat, and Leo wouldn't bat an eye.

Outside, in the walled confines of the pool area, Leo felt that he'd arrived in Hollywood at last. He was disappointed to find that he had the place all to himself. The noise of traffic from Sunset Boulevard was drowned out by the rhythmic rise and fall of crickets' croaking; there must have been thousands of them, from the sound of it, hidden in the thick blanket of ivy and privet that covered the walls around the deck. Moonlight danced on the dark surface of the pool. The hotel's bungalows lay beyond the wall, just east of the swimming pool. He wondered which one of them was John Belushi's. Leo sat down near the pool and listened to the crickets, trying to hear his own voice above them. But after a few minutes he realized he didn't have anything to say to himself, so after he'd taken a final turn around the deck, looking at the foliage and smelling the perfume of gardenias, he went back upstairs and got into bed.

At one-thirty in the morning, after the noise coming from the party in the suite on the fifth floor had finally died down, he settled into the kind of fitful, disheveled sleep he'd grown accustomed to in recent months. He dreamed that he was out on the deck by the swimming pool, only now it was daytime, and the sunlight was bright on the water. President Reagan was there, too, dressed in a conservative navy blue suit, despite the heat. His forehead shone with sweat, and he smiled affably in the sunshine. As always, Leo felt grateful for his presence.

Lesley, Don Beacham's beautiful copper-colored assistant, suddenly glided into view, dressed in the same sarong she'd been wearing earlier that evening. "Oh, golly," President Reagan said, "back when I was a young fella, we'd have called you a dish!" As if in response to this, Lesley quickly disrobed, flicking the sarong to the ground with a jerk of her thumbs. But underneath it was another sarong, this one flecked with sparkles of gold. "Could you try that again?" President Reagan asked, and Lesley, her face impassive, complied. The gold-flecked sarong slid to her ankles, but again there was another one underneath it. Leo felt the terrible sinking weight of disappointment at this. Lesley was nothing but sarongs, layer after layer of them—she could keep peeling them off at this rate for the rest of her life and she'd never get down to flesh. He turned to President Reagan, hoping the President might say something authoritative, something that would get to the bottom of all those sarongs, but Reagan merely chuckled and bobbed his head to the left the way Leo had seen him do so often on television, smiling reluctantly, as if shaking off an errant thought. His hair shone brilliantly in the sun, a rich orange-brown. He looked like he might live forever.

Then Rachel entered the dream, hugely pregnant—much bigger than she'd been when Leo had last seen her, just a day ago. She seemed confused, perhaps even disappointed to be here at the Chateau Marmont. "Rachel!" Leo said. "Aren't you're supposed to be in Chicago?" But Rachel merely shook her head at him sadly. She was wearing a blue one-piece bathing suit, its material so thin that he could plainly see the bump of her navel at the center of her enormous belly. As he stared at her, she delicately dropped the straps of her suit and peeled it down her torso, then leaned on a chair and stepped out of it. She stood in the sunshine by the side of the pool, profoundly naked. Wait a second: were those her breasts? They looked suspiciously like Mary-Louise Whitaker's, but Leo was unable to tell for sure—a fact that disturbed him greatly. After several years of marriage, shouldn't he have been able to identity his own wife's breasts?

And anyway, why was everybody taking off their clothes? Leo looked down and noticed now that he, too, was naked. Oh, shit. He tried to cover himself but his arms were glued to the lounge chair, and all he could hope for was that Rachel wouldn't observe the fact that he wasn't wearing any clothes. This was terrible. If she noticed that he was naked, she'd immediately understand that he'd been snorting coke—that much was certain. In order to avoid looking at Rachel's breasts, which might not have been hers at all, he stared at her legs, which were so white and shiny that they might have been made of polished ivory. "Mr. President, this is Rachel, my wife," Leo said, hoping that if he simply adhered to the basic rules of polite society, he could get out of this awkward situation with his marriage intact. And besides, President Reagan's presence would no doubt make his own nakedness more acceptable.

But when he turned to see the President's reaction, Reagan wasn't there anymore. Neither was Lesley; perhaps they'd gone somewhere together, one of the secluded bungalows, where Lesley could continue to unwrap herself, one sarong at a time. Rachel turned to Leo and shook her head. "Leo?" she asked—and though she didn't complete the question, he immediately understood what she was asking.

He reached toward her, horrified—his arms were free now—and cried, "It isn't what you think! You have to believe me!"

Not very much later that same night—it might have been three in the morning, though Leo couldn't find his watch—the phone rang by his bedside. "How's everything in Tinseltown, amigo?" a deep voice asked.

"Ward? Is that you? My God. What time is it?" Leo croaked. "Are you in Chicago?" He was still mired in the world of his dreams, in which everyone seemed drawn to the pool at the Chateau Marmont.

"Of course I'm in Chicago. I'll be there tomorrow. Okay, so tell me: how's the forecast for snow out there?"

"The what?"

"Come on, Leo, don't be stupid."

It took Leo a minute to shake the cobwebs loose. "Oh. Oh, yeah. Right," he said, then lowered his voice to a whisper, as though the phone might be tapped. "Right. Uhm . . . I don't know. The forecast is—I'm sorry, I haven't asked around yet. We just got here this evening, and we went out to Don Beacham's house, and that's really all we've done so far. We've been kind of busy."

Ward sighed into the phone. "You're not on the ball, are you, Leo?"

"I was just trying to get some sleep, Ward. You and Harriet sent me out to learn how commercials are shot, but so far I haven't learned anything. I'm worried that she's going to be pissed."

"Harriet?"

"She scares the shit out of me. Is it okay for me to tell you that? I don't know who to talk to about it. I tried telling my therapist, Dr. Findlay, and he fell asleep on me."

"What the fuck are you talking about?" Ward said. "Do you know what time it is?"

"Hector's been ragging on me pretty hard. My God, that guy's got some mouth. I'm tired. In fact I'm exhausted."

"I'm crying, pal."

"I have insomnia. I don't really even know what I'm doing here."

"You're out there in La-La Land, where everything's beautiful. Do you know how hot it is back here? People are dropping like flies—an old woman died today on State Street, just dropped dead on the sidewalk. And you're exhausted. Hector's been ragging on you. Oh, I'm weeping, Leo. Pardon me while I dab at my eyes."

"I'm just saying when you get out here we'll take care of it, that's all," said Leo.

"You made any contacts yet?"

"Ward, I just got here this evening. How'm I supposed to—"

"You're staying at the Chateau Marmont, for crissake. There's so much coke around there, you could go *skiing* in it."

"Ward, that's why John Belushi *died* here."

"Don't bring that up."

"I went out to the pool tonight and thought about him in one of those bungalows."

"Oh, forget about it, will you? The man had a death wish."

"Speaking of which, I think that something died in my room. The smell—I don't know what it was, but it used to be alive and now it's dead." Leo paused. "Anyway, I thought you still had some. I asked you a couple of days ago, you said you were fine, you didn't need any more."

"Well, I was wrong, wasn't I? I miscalculated. So shoot me."

"Okay, so when you get out here tomorrow—you'll be here in no time, just sleep on the plane, you'll wake up in Los Angeles."

"You've still got some, haven't you," Ward said in an accusatory tone. "I can tell by the smug tone in your voice. You've been hoarding it, haven't you."

"I have a little left. Yes. I'm just doing a little now and then."

"You've got to get with the program, buddy—learn to binge once in a while."

"I don't have the money for that, Ward. Give me a raise, I'll start to binge." Leo sighed. "Listen, let me get back to sleep, will you? Tomorrow you'll get here, we'll make a call, we'll get you set up in no time," he said in what he hoped was a reassuring tone, and then he hung up before Ward could say anything else, and rolled back into the troubled world of his dreams.

■ ■ ■

The next morning Leo awoke to a yellow haze of sunshine which floated into his room through the dusty, billowing curtains. Somehow the stench of cat urine was a bit less pervasive now. As he showered in the crumbling bathroom, he listened to the pipes banging and thought of Garbo. Once upon a time she'd stood here, stark naked, dripping wet, right where he was standing now. Well, on second thought, she probably took baths, not showers—but still, it was pretty damned exciting to be this close to her. The bathroom had probably looked nicer back in her day. The building was newer back then, and stuff hadn't started to fall off the walls yet. How could the present owners have let the place go to hell like this? Okay, he could certainly understand why they didn't want to replace the original ceramic tiles from the 1920s, and yes, it was true that the old, mottled plumbing fixtures had an undeniable patina of faded luxury—but would it have killed them to scrub the grout once in a while, to mop the floor, get the rust stains out of the sink? Whatever happened to basic housecleaning techniques?

Downstairs he picked up a newspaper in the lobby and walked out into the bright morning air of Sunset Boulevard. Greenblatt's Deli across the street offered a place to sit and read the headlines, and besides, Leo was hungry (the stomach stapling, he'd decided, would have to wait), so he ordered a platter of scrambled eggs with lox and onions and a poppy seed bagel along with his coffee.

He couldn't get over it. Why did everybody out here look so much healthier than he did? While he was buying his newspaper he'd noticed a guy cleaning the ashtrays in the lobby of the Chateau Marmont—sleek and tan, the fellow had a chin that looked like it was sculpted out of bronze. He was cleaning ashtrays! The girl pouring his coffee here at Greenblatt's could have been snapped up by one of New York's top modeling agencies if she'd only been willing to take that gum out of her mouth. Even the bums he'd passed on Sunset Boulevard, stinking of stale Colt 45 and piss as they drifted aimlessly along the street in the bright morning sunshine—all of them looked like they'd jogged five miles in their rags before stopping to beg for breakfast scraps. Was Leo the only human being in Los Angeles who didn't have a suntan?

To calm himself after he'd paid his bill, he slipped into the men's room at Greenblatt's, bolted the door on one of the stalls, got his vial out of his pocket and quickly spooned two petite toots up his nose. Oh, yes, that was better. Fuck these people. Yes, indeed. He rubbed his gums with the residue, checked himself out discreetly in the mirror to make sure nothing white and powdery was sticking to his nostrils, and made his way out into the sunshine again, a new man. How the hell did anybody make it through the day without an occasional bit of coke? How had he managed to live for thirty-two years without giving this stuff a try?

He walked back across the street with his newspaper and was reading it in the Chateau Marmont living room when Hector honked for him at 9:45. "Just sit there," Hector advised him once Leo had gotten in the car. "When we're looking at talent, don't open your mouth."

"Are you ever in another kind of mood?" Leo asked him. "Is there anything else you do besides this? Ever?"

"Don't crack wise with me," said Hector. "I've got your number."

The casting session took place in a suite on the top floor of a seedy apartment hotel on Hollywood Boulevard. Leo and Hector slouched on a sofa in the living room of a shabbily-furnished apartment, sipping cold soft drinks and eating mixed nuts, while twenty-five attractive young girls, most of whom appeared to be at the cusp of puberty, marched out from the bedroom one by one, wearing lace teddys. The casting director, a squat, gray-haired woman named Dorianne Wachtel, paced back and forth across the room, eyeing the girls critically. "Remember, " she told each of them, "you're Diana—goddess of the hunt. That's lovely, sweetheart. Simply ravishing." For nearly every girl, Dorianne whispered an aside in Hector's direction. "She has a very believable look, don't you think so?" or "Great personality. A hard worker. A new face." One or two of the girls got no whispered boost from her at all, and a few others got panned: "A bitch to work with. She says she's been clean for three months, but take it from me, she's lying." For the most part, Dorianne ignored Leo, which was fine with him. What did he know about casting, anyway? He stared at the girls, some of whom were so beautiful that they stopped his heart. Was it time for a tune-up in the bathroom? Just a quick toot? He could wait a bit longer. For now it was enough just to pat the vial in his pocket, to rub his finger over the little bump it made against his thigh.

Dorianne had sent home all but five of the girls by the time Don Beacham arrived at the casting session. Leo scooted aside on the sofa to make room for Beacham to sit down. "We've got some lovely girls for you," Dorianne told him. She called out to the bedroom, "Girls? Mr. Beacham is ready for you now." She lit a cigarette and stumped around the room like an animal stalking its prey. One by one, the five girls came out of the bedroom, turned, stood impassively before them, then went back into the bedroom.

"Do you want to hear them speak?" Dorianne asked *sotto voce*. Hector nodded curtly as he lit a cigarette, and she called out, "Girls? Can we hear you speak? Say the lines, please."

So one at a time, they entered the room and delivered the lines: "Diana. Goddess of the Hunt. The scent of nature on a spring-soft morning. Diana. For those days when you *know* you're becoming a woman." Each girl retreated into the bedroom after she'd had her turn, and when they'd all gone, Dorianne tapped her ash onto the carpet and asked, "So what's your pleasure, gentlemen? Do we have our Diana?"

Hector said, "I liked the blonde. The tall one. I gotta have those long legs."

"Tamora's very nice, a sweet girl," said Dorianne. "If you want to go with an upscale look, she's perfect. She's twelve, but she has a lot of presence. She's a hard worker. She did two covers for *Seventeen* last year, and she's up for a good part in a new George Lucas film."

"What about the one with the dark hair?" Beacham asked. "The third one. She had an exotic quality, something special."

"I think it's called a moustache," said Hector.

"You know? It's funny. But I liked the shorter one, with the brown bangs," Leo said. He knew he was supposed to keep his mouth shut, but he couldn't help himself. "She looked . . . vulnerable," he went on. "Sort of normal—you know, not so much like a model."

"Chloe's a sweetheart," Dorianne told them. "She's new. Lovely voice. She was Maria in *Sound of Music* last year at her school. But I know what you mean—she's not the model type."

Emboldened by Dorianne's comment, Leo continued. "It's exactly what I liked about her," he said. "She looks like the girl next door, sort of—not like a model at all. You know—like she might be a real person?"

"Would you listen to this? The fucking Oracle at Delphi has spoken," Hector said, his eyes lifted to the ceiling. "Why would we want a girl-next-door type selling this stuff?"

"You better hope the girl next door's going to be buying it," Don Beacham said. "Why don't we bring out both of them, Tamora and Chloe, and let me see them again."

The girls came out, Tamora walking ahead, Chloe lagging behind. They stopped in the middle of the living room. Leo stared at them for a moment and then had to look away. It was late morning, warm and sunny outside, but in this shabby hotel room the air-conditioning was blowing full blast, and he could see that the girls were cold in their teddys. He didn't want to think about it, because if he thought about it he'd start feeling bad all over again—but he couldn't stop himself. There they were, right in front of him, not five feet away, and they had goose bumps all over their arms and legs, their skin so pale he could see the faint blue network of their veins just beneath the surface. Dorianne waved them away, and they retreated into the bedroom.

"I think Leo's right," Don Beacham announced. "Chloe's perfect. I like that girl-next-door look." He turned to Hector. "Unless you've got a serious problem with her."

Hector shrugged and gazed at the ceiling. "What do I know, anyway? I'm just the producer. It's just my fucking living, that's all. I've only been doing this fifteen years."

"Oh, look, c'mon, we're on the same team here."

"No! It's fine! I'm serious!" Hector said. "Let it be on your head." He abruptly stood up. "You want the girl next door—okay by me," he said. "You and the film genius here—if this thing turns to shit, you're the jerks taking the rap, not me."

"Trust me, Hector, it's gonna be fine," Beacham said.

Hector glanced at his watch. "My doctor tells me I have to stop giving myself grief. I'm fifty-five—he tells me I've got the heart of a seventy-five-year-old. I'm serious. I'm supposed to sit back and take things as they come. 'Go with the flow,' he says. So I tell you what. You say it's gonna be fine. That's nice. That's beautiful. You're the director, you're making the five gees a day. So you'll make sure everything turns out fine. Let it be on your head," he said, pronouncing the phrase as if it were a curse. "In the meantime, I'm hungry. The boy genius and me are gonna go have lunch."

▪ ▪ ▪

Le Dome was crowded by one o'clock, and Hector Benevento had to stop several times to shake hands and pinch cheeks on his way to the sunny corner booth at the back of the restaurant. He apparently knew everyone here—it was old home week. Meanwhile the maitre d' led Leo to the booth, where he sat down and waited, tapping the tablecloth idly and trying not to stare at the celebrities he recognized. When Hector finally arrived at the booth, Leo cleared his throat to get his attention, then pointed furtively to a nearby table and whispered, "Look over there—is that Barbara Eden?"

"Yeah, that's her," Hector muttered. "For the love of God, look at her. Most people, by the time they're that thin, they're dead already."

"Oh, hey, guess what. I saw an actor last night in the elevator at the Marmont," Leo said. "He was in *In the Heat of the Night.* He played the guy who swatted the fly on the counter? In the diner? At the very start?"

Hector lit a cigarette, snapped his Zippo shut, and leaned back against the leather upholstery. "Is that right?" he said.

Leo knew he should stop, but he couldn't. "He turned out to be the real killer in the end," he added, then flinched, waiting for Hector's reply.

Hector didn't say anything at first; he sighed and shook his head gently, an expression of world-weariness cascading down his face. Then he said, "You want me to have a heart attack, don't you. I've got you pegged—you've been hired by my enemies. You want me to collapse and die right here at the table. Well, I'm not going to do it. I'm gonna go with the flow."

The waiter, a sallow little man whose eyebrows met over the bridge of his nose, brought a bottle of Pellegrino to the table, uncapped it, and poured their glasses full. "Good afternoon, gentlemen, how are we today?" he asked. His accent and manner were vaguely European, but Leo couldn't identify the country. French, perhaps? No, not French. Maybe he was from one of those tiny countries the size of a casino. "Will we be needing menus?" he asked, and before Leo could say anything, Hector shook his head and waved the man away.

"No menus?" asked Leo.

"Only manicurists from Des Moines order off the menu here. At Le Dome, you tell the waiter what you want, they make it."

"But I've never been here before. I don't even know what they have."

"They've got everything. It's Le Dome."

"You're kidding. Anything I want, I just tell them. And it's all on my per diem?"

Hector blew smoke across the booth. "That's the general idea," he said. "I always order the same thing here. It's my own salad. I invented it—salad à la Benevento!"

Leo sat back and grinned. Anything he wanted. Amazing. No menus! Just tell the man what you want, and they make it! He could definitely get used to this. The next time he and Rachel went to Villa d'Este back in Chicago, he was going to pull this. Throw away the menu, forget the Chicken Vesuvio he'd been ordering faithfully for the past three years—make that Chicken à la Spivak! When the waiter returned a moment later to take their order, Leo said confidently, "Okay. I'd like a shrimp cocktail. Make it a double—lots of shrimp, the biggest ones you've got, and here's the most important part: make sure there's extra horseradish in the cocktail sauce." He leaned back and basked in the glow of this new experience. Hector was right—this was wonderful.

"I'm sorry—I'm afraid that's impossible," said the waiter. He smiled faintly, without showing any teeth, then licked his lips. "Would you like to see a menu?"

"Wait a minute. Let me get this straight, Leo," Hector said. "We're at Le Dome, one of the greatest restaurants in Los Angeles—a goddamn temple of haute cuisine—and you're ordering a shrimp cocktail?"

"It's what I want. I love shrimp cocktails. You told me to ask for what I want, so I did."

"Would you get a load of this schmuck?" Hector asked, addressing the ceiling.

"We don't do a shrimp cocktail," the waiter said. His eyes roamed briefly around the restaurant, as if scanning the neighborhood for celebrities. "We've never done shrimp cocktail."

"Which part don't you do?" asked Leo.

"Any of it," the waiter said rapidly. His accent was getting thicker now.

"You mean you don't have any shrimp back there?"

"We have shrimp. We have tiny bay shrimp, we have scampi, we have several kinds of shrimp, yes."

"Do you have ketchup?"

"Of course. We make our own ketchup. It's delicious. Dustin Hoffman comes here for the ketchup."

"And how about horseradish?"

"Yes, sir, we have horseradish."

"And lemons, you have lemons."

"Yes, we do. We have many lemons. Many, many lemons."

"There you go—that's my shrimp cocktail!" said Leo, smiling as if he'd just fanned out a royal flush. "Shrimp cocktail à la Spivak!"

"I'm sure it is. But as I told you, we don't do shrimp cocktails," the waiter said.

"He told you that already," said Hector. "Get over it, will you? Move on."

Leo turned to him, defeated. "Okay, so what are you having?"

"I told you. My special Le Dome salad," Hector said. "Le Dome salad ala Benevento. It's what I always have here."

"Well, can I have one, too? Or are you the only one allowed to have your special salad?"

Hector sniffed and turned his eyes up to meet the waiter's gaze. "Two salads à la Benevento," he said. He sounded disappointed, as if now that Leo was ordering the special salad, it wasn't so special anymore. "Just tell Marcel it's Hector Benevento, he'll know what to do. Just tell him to make two Le Dome salads à la Benevento, he'll take it from there."

"Marcel is no longer with us," the waiter said, and flashed the same brief smile he'd given Leo just a moment before.

Hector hesitated a moment. "When did that happen? For God's sake . . . okay, so tell Umberto—he's made them before, too. Just say it's Hector Benevento, he'll know what to do."

"Umberto is on vacation."

Hector flipped his cigarette lighter open and shut several times rapidly. "Is anybody back there?" he asked. "You're open for business, aren't you?"

"Yes, we are, sir."

"You got somebody working in the kitchen?"

"We have Felix," the waiter said. "We have Sophie. We have Alain. The kitchen is very busy today. Just tell me what you want and they will make it for you, Mr. Benevento."

"Just tell them it's a cobb salad with shredded radicchio and a diced fresh roma tomato on top. Heavy on the radicchio. Blue cheese dressing. If Marcel was here, he'd know what to do. Umberto, he'd have it done in two seconds."

"Two cobb salads, shredded radicchio, diced roma tomato, blue cheese dressing," the waiter murmured through pursed lips, and skipped briskly away.

"That's my special salad," Hector said, and put his cigarette out in the ashtray. "Only this time it's not going to be so special, I'll tell you that right now. Don't get your hopes up."

"They've got shrimp cocktails back there," said Leo. He pounded the table with one fist. "It's ridiculous. Don't tell me they don't have any shrimp cocktails back there."

"Would you get off that?" Hector blew out a long sigh. "I don't know what the hell's happening to this place. Marcel was a genius. I can't believe he left. The guy was here forever. Who the hell is Felix? And who's this Alain? I've been coming to Le Dome for fifteen years, I've never heard of Alain." He lit a new cigarette and blew smoke rings into the air, one-two-three of them, watching their flight with rapt attention. "This is all your fault," he told Leo. "Marcel probably saw me walk in here with you, he said, 'What the fuck's Hector doing coming in here with that putz?' then he threw his apron on the floor and quit on the spot. You've single-handedly ruined one of the greatest restaurants in America. I hope you're happy."

Leo felt his face flush with heat. He was going to say something this time, he really was. This was hitting below the belt. It was too goddamned much to tolerate, and he wasn't about take this sitting down. Dr. Findlay had told him he needed to be a bit more assertive, more up front in his dealings with co-workers, right? Well, okay, then—here was one of those moments. Of course, just the thought of Dr. Findlay made Leo feel worse than he was already feeling about Hector. At least Hector stayed awake in Leo's presence, if only to insult him.

Leo might have said something, he really might have, he was working up a reply, and he would have come out with it, too, if only to fill in the desperate silence building at the table—but just as the awful moment seemed to be stretching out before his eyes like pulled taffy, he saw Ward LaPlante and Mary-Louise Whitaker sweep into Le Dome's sunny dining room, and he leapt to his feat to welcome them. He was so glad to see them, he almost wept.

"Compadres," Ward said, "We just got into town. Hopped a cab to the Marmont, called Don Beacham, and he told us we'd find you here." He gave Hector and Leo a hug, and what had seemed just a moment ago to be an ordeal now suddenly turned into something festive. Mary-Louise sat down on Leo's right and squeezed his thigh under the table. Ward, to Leo's left, caught the waiter's eye, and seemingly out of nowhere, two bottles of wine appeared at the table, one a Côtes du Rhone, the other a Sancerre. Now Ward took charge, pouring everyone's glasses full. A small terrine of satiny duck liver paté arrived, surrounded by a generous ring of toasted croutons, then a moment later a busboy delivered a enormous platter of oysters on ice. Another waiter brought an oval platter of asparagus napped in vinaigrette.

"Ooh, oysters," Mary-Louise said. "Yummy. You know what they say about oysters."

"I do?" Leo asked.

She squeezed Leo's thigh again, and leaned closer to whisper in his ear. "You're really unbelievable. You do something to me."

"I do?"

Mary-Louise squeezed lemon juice over an oyster and slid it down her throat. "Mmmm," she said, and sipped her Sancerre. "It's so nice to get out of the office once in a while."

Leo felt her hand working its way up his thigh toward his groin. "Mary-Louise?" he said after a moment.

She gazed at him, her face a blank, guileless mask. "Yes?"

"Your hand's on my leg."

Mary-Louise smiled at him. "I begged Ward to bring me along for this trip. I got down on my knees and begged," she whispered. "I would have done anything. I would have shown him my pictures if that's what it took. You know why?"

"No. No, I really don't."

"You're an idiot, Leo." She squeezed his knee. "That's why I find you so alluring."

"I know I'm an idiot. Hector's been telling me all about it ever since we got on the plane." Leo gulped his wine. "You remember the part about I'm married, right? I mean, you haven't forgotten?" He wagged his ring finger in her face. "My wife's pregnant—our first baby."

"What's that got to do with anything?"

"I don't know," he said. "I just thought I'd throw that out there, just in case."

She inched her hand closer to his groin. 'I'll keep it at the front of my mind," she said. Her hand beat out a happy rhythm on his thigh, and Leo's heart sank. He heard a faint but distinct ringing in his ears—the sound of distant alarms going off.

Ward took small bites of paté and asparagus as he talked, and Mary-Louise kept on slurping oysters, but even when the two salads à la Benevento appeared, and Hector and Leo began to eat in earnest, Ward and Mary-Louise never bothered to order anything more for lunch. They kept drinking, though—several glasses of wine apiece, going back and forth between the Côtes du Rhone and the Sancerre. Meanwhile they maintained a lighthearted rush of banter, and Leo tried to keep up with them, chomping on his salad (which was actually very tasty) and drinking wine as fast as he could pour it down his throat. He never drank alcohol before dinner if he could help it, and now, after downing several glasses, he sank back in his chair with a sodden sigh, unable to hold up his end of the conversation, content to simply listen to them talk. More wine came to the table. Ward's voice blended with the clinking of glasses and the burble of conversation that floated to Leo from other tables, all of it sounding to him like the ringing of cash registers.

In the midst of Leo's stupor it dawned on him: Ward and Mary-Louise were coked to the gills. Of course; he should have been able to tell from Ward's ebullient demeanor that he'd scored some already. Leo had come to recognize that particular Ward LaPlante smile—confident, boyish, the grin of a man in possession of a gram or two, maybe more, wrapped neatly in his pocket. When the bottles of wine were empty and the platter of oysters had been reduced to a pile of shells and crushed ice, Ward tapped Leo's shoulder and whispered to him, "Listen, I hate to be a party-pooper, but if you think you can get Mary-Louise's hand off your thigh for just a minute, there's a matter of some importance I'd like to discuss with you in the men's room."

The rest of that afternoon was a blur of trips to the men's room at Le Dome, blended with yet another bottle of Sancerre. The restaurant gradually emptied. Even Hector finally left, muttering that unlike some people, he actually had work to do. At some point the location shifted to the Chateau Marmont, though Leo couldn't recall how they got there. They wouldn't have walked, and none of them was in any shape to drive, which meant they must have hailed a cab—but were there cabs in Los Angeles? He hadn't noticed any, but he hadn't been looking.

He and Mary-Louise and Ward ended up late that afternoon sitting out by the swimming pool, in the shade of a striped umbrella, drinking gin and tonics. The sunlight was very bright on the brick deck, so dazzling as it sparkled on the water that it hurt Leo just to look at it. Near them a young woman lay baking in the sun, face down on a beach towel, the top of her white bikini undone. Leo gazed at her shapely back, which was slowly turning the delicate pink of steamed shrimp. What would it be like to go over to her and strike up a conversation? Just a simple "Hi, how are you, that's some back you've got there" would be a good opener. He sat there contemplating this scenario for several minutes. Then a tall, thin man with a deep orange tan walked out into the pool area. He was older, with a full head of wavy white hair. He wore outsized sunglasses, a thick gold necklace and a tight black thong swimsuit that bulged impressively in front, as if he had a dildo the size of a brick wedged into it. In a continental accent he called to the woman on the beach towel: "Arielle?"

The woman on the beach towel raised herself onto her elbows and squinted up at him. Her breasts seemed to go on forever. "Oh, it's only you," she said.

"They'll be by at six," he told her. "We should get ready."

The woman reluctantly sat up and closed the back of her bikini top. She grabbed the beach towel and followed the white-haired man into the hotel lobby. She wasn't as pretty as Leo had hoped she'd be—her face was a bit puffy, and her mouth seemed weak and childish. Perhaps she'd been napping, and the fellow with the brick in his swimsuit had woken her. Leo watched the couple walk into the hotel, his eyes glued to the smooth, fluid movement of the woman's hips. He observed her silently, so rapt that when she'd disappeared, he realized that he was staring into space and his mouth had fallen open. "Well, okay then. I guess I'd better go take a nap," he announced. "I'm exhausted."

"You need to rest up," Mary-Louise said. She pulled her sunglasses down on her nose and fluttered her eyelashes at him.

"Yes," Leo said. "All righty. Yes, I do." And then he fled to his room, locking the door behind him and making sure the deadbolt was securely fastened.

■ ■ ■

Two hours later Leo woke up on the couch without any memory of how he'd gotten back to his room. He stared around him at the tattered furniture, the cheaply framed reproductions of French Impressionist paintings which adorned the walls, the dusty, gently billowing curtains, the shit-brown shag carpet. As awful as it all was, this place was starting to feel like home. He was disturbed by this realization, but he couldn't deny it.

He called home and listened to Rachel weeping over the phone. "Oh, Leo, I'm so big," she moaned. "I feel like I swallowed a whale. I ate an entire pizza tonight for dinner—the whole thing. Pepperoni and mushroom, from Jimmy's. I was so embarrassed when the delivery guy came—he could tell I was all by myself, I just know it, and he must have thought I was some kind of . . . I don't know what. There was a story on the news tonight about a guy in Berwyn who was so fat that when they came to take him to the hospital they had to tear down the front wall of his house to get him out. He weighed seven hundred pounds." She blew out a long, ragged breath. "How could anybody eat an entire pizza?"

"I think you're beautiful," Leo told her. This was the truth. He could have stopped there, still on solid pavement, but instead he went on, wandering off into dense underbrush. "We did the casting session today, and there were a lot of actresses there, and you know what? Not one of them could hold a candle to you. You're more beautiful than the day I met you. You walk in a room, the lights go on." He wasn't lying to her, exactly, and at the moment the words left his mouth he almost believed them—but still, he knew he was playing footsie with the facts. Plenty of the girls he'd seen that morning would have knocked Rachel out of the running, pregnant or not. But why would he tell her that? What possible purpose would it serve to divulge that at this moment? "We picked a nice girl, a kid named Chloe—you'd like her. She's sweet." He left out the part about the lace teddy, of course—the goose bumps, everyone wedged together on the sofa, staring at her—because there wasn't any point in mentioning any of that, not when Rachel had just eaten an entire pizza and was already feeling a little vulnerable.

Rachel sighed, a sound that flew from Chicago to Los Angeles like a dry wind. "Are you at least having a little fun?" she asked.

"Not a bit."

"You're just saying that to make me feel better."

"This guy I was telling you about—Hector? He won't let up. He calls me every name in the book. He's an asshole."

"I wish you were here with me."

"I do, too, honey." Oh, if she only knew. He hadn't been able to bring himself to tell her anything about the expensive lines of coke disappearing up his nose over the past few days, and Rachel would never guess. He could come home with coke sprinkled over him like dandruff, and she'd assume he'd been sampling brands of baby powder at the drug store. Anyway, Rachel wouldn't have understood what was at stake with Leo and Ward LaPlante and Bowles and Humphries—not in a million years. In fact, if Leo had tried to explain the situation to her, she would have told him he was being an idiot. *Oh, please! Your job's on the line? Over cocaine? You've got to be kidding!* How could she possibly understand? At the LaSalle Street accounting firm where she worked, the strongest drug allowed on the premises was probably caffeine.

And Rachel's family! Forget about it! To the Sperlings, snorting coke would be considered off the map of acceptable behavior—perhaps the most completely unkosher behavior imaginable—not just because it was illegal, but because it was both fun and expensive. They'd never liked him all that much anyway—and if he'd already been clinging precariously to the very bottom rung of acceptability in their eyes, what would they make of this latest wrinkle? He cringed just to imagine the mournful gossip around their dinner table. *Oh, yes, our son-in-law, Leo, he's putting drugs up his nose. A hopeless addict. We said Kaddish for him last week. He's as good as dead to us now.* Compared to this, Randy and the good-looking Italian boys were just a bunch of guys having some good, clean fun.

"Leo? Are you okay?" Rachel said.

A knock sounded at the door. "I—I think that's room service, honey," he said. "I ordered up some dinner." He heard what he thought might be giggling outside in the hallway. Who was out there? Ward and Mary-Louise? Oh, Christ—maybe it was Mary-Louise, all by herself. She might have a whole new batch of pictures to show him. Shit, she might even have a camera with her. The knock sounded again, louder this time.

"Oh, okay. Well, I love you," Rachel said.

"Love you too. I'll call you tomorrow," he told her and hung up to face his fate.

It was, indeed, Ward and Mary-Louise at the door. Mary-Louise was cradling two bottles of wine in her arms, and Ward was hefting a foot-long subway sandwich from Greenblatt's delicatessen. "Compadre," Ward said as Leo let them into the room, "we've come to rescue you from yourself."

"I was just talking to Rachel," Leo said. "She ate a whole pizza." Why had he added that? It felt like a betrayal, somehow. "She doesn't usually do that kind of thing," he went on.

"Oh, puh-*lease,*" Mary-Louise groaned, and set the wine bottles down on the coffee table. "Don't you ever talk about anything but that wife of yours?"

"She's pregnant," Leo said. "I should be back there with her. I don't even know what I'm doing here."

"You're helping us eat this sandwich," Ward said. "That's your job. You've got to eat, buddy boy. Have to keep your strength up." He unwrapped the sandwich and handed Leo and Mary-Louise each a section. "We start shooting tomorrow. Think about it! Making movies! Lights, camera, action!" He bit a big chunk off his portion of the sandwich, then he turned to Leo, his head cocked at a bizarre angle, his eyes wide and crazy. "Mr. DeMille," Ward said, the words muffled by his mouthful of sandwich, "I'm ready for my close-up now."

▪ ▪ ▪

By nine o'clock the next morning Leo had showered and shaved, was sipping a cup of coffee while reading a newspaper in his room when Ward called. "Are you alive?" Ward asked him in a hoarse, phlegmy voice.

"That depends on what you mean by 'alive.' What happened last night?"

"Don't ask."

"I remember the sandwich and the two bottles of wine. Everything else is a blur."

"Good. You're a lucky man. You ready to go? We're due at the studio in half an hour. Harriet's flying in today."

"Oh, no. Harriet Rubin? She's coming here? You're kidding."

"Don't worry so much, Leo. You knew she was coming. Anyway, she's not going to bite your head off. Harriet gets to leave the office now and then, just like the rest of us."

"Yeah, right. Oh, shit. Shit, shit, shit. I'll be down in the lobby in five minutes."

"When you see me, whatever you do, don't make any loud noises," Ward warned him.

Mary-Louise was sitting in the lobby, stirring the sand in an oversized ashtray with her fingers, when Leo came out of the elevator. Her face was blotchy, and she gazed at him with bloodshot eyes. "Hi there,

Tiger," she said. She got up unsteadily, as if she were a little girl wearing her mother's high heels. "Ward's waiting out in the car. He said he needed some fresh air."

The drive to the studio was long and tedious, made longer by the fact that Ward LaPlante didn't seem to know where he was going. For the better part of an hour they toured the San Fernando Valley, meandering in a loopy circle, before Ward threw up his hands, pulled into an Exxon station, and made a desperate phone call for directions. But when they finally got to the studio, no one seemed to notice that they were late. In fact, it seemed to Leo as if no one cared that they'd arrived at all. Harriet hadn't shown up yet, thank God. The crew had been at work since six-thirty that morning, setting up the sound stage and the lighting; Chloe, the young actress they'd cast as the spokesperson for Diana, had come at eight, and was now secluded in a nearby trailer studying algebra with her tutor, a requirement in order to skirt child labor laws. The studio resembled a construction zone—the floor was covered by a tangle of thick, snaking electrical cords, and a cacophony of hammering and sawing filled the air, punctuated by the percussive beat of nail guns and an occasional chorus of shouts and grunts. In sharp contrast to the grimy jeans and T-shirts of the crew, Don Beacham was dressed in immaculate khakis, woven leather huaraches, and a multi-colored Hawaiian shirt that set off his tan exquisitely. He issued calm, measured instructions to the crew, and at his command, flood-lights were turned on, then off, repositioned, turned on again. His ethereally beautiful assistant, Lesley, served as a laconic stand-in for Chloe, posing first here, then there on the sound stage, managing to look both bored and luminous. Those collar bones! Meanwhile the camera operator, using a light meter, assessed the lighting in each pose, adjusting filters to achieve the proper shadows under Lesley's cheekbones. The crew moved a giant fan from one side of the studio to the other, checking the best wind angle for the breeze that lifted Lesley's lustrous hair.

Leo found all of this impressive, in the way that organized chaos can be impressive—but he was puzzled; where was the windswept, mysterious landscape that Ward had described in such vivid detail in Harriet Rubin's office? Whatever happened to Wuthering Heights? All he saw here in Studio 3-B was a sheet of bright blue material stretched across the back of a thirty-foot stage.

"Ward?" he asked. "Where's the landscape?"

"Oh. I thought I told you. Didn't I mention that? We're doing blue screen," Ward muttered. "Where's the coffee?"

"What's blue screen?"

"It's all done with mirrors. You think we're going to be shooting that landscape on location? Forget about it. Too many things can go wrong with location shoots. It starts raining on you, you're shit out of luck. We've got some stock landscape photography we'll edit in later. You can buy it from a photo bank. Post-production, amigo. That's where the magic happens." Ward looked around. "Can somebody please get me some coffee?"

"I don't know what you're talking about," Leo said.

"Coffee, Leo. It's black, it's bitter . . ."

"What's 'blue screen'? I told you, I don't know anything about this stuff."

Ward looked at him. "Blue screen. It's how Superman flies." He put an arm around Leo's shoulder, and waved Mary-Louise closer. "C'mon. We'll have something to eat, I'll tell you all about it. Professor LaPlante's handy-dandy seminar on film production is now in session. First of all, though, I want you to meet the caterer. This guy'll knock your socks off."

The caterer, Buck Wanamaker, was tall and beefy, with a waxed handlebar moustache and the largest incisors Leo had ever seen. He wore a toque and a white smock with "Buckaroo Catering" stitched over the left nipple, and as he leaned closer to shake hands, Leo could smell his cologne: English Leather. The scent brought back unsettling vivid memories of high school, so visceral, in fact, that Leo blinked and was transported back to the polished halls of DeLesseps High in Kansas City. Buck turned to Mary-Louise, shook her hand, and took time to gaze appreciatively at her chest. "Ward here gave me instructions," Buck said in a confidential tone. "He told me I'm supposed to take extra special care of you good folks."

Leo looked at the spread of food displayed on the catering table: a glistening array of smoked sable, whitefish, sturgeon and salmon, two dozen bagels, three tubs of cream cheese, a platter of thinly-sliced Spanish onions and beefsteak tomatoes, butter lettuce, a generous fan of sliced imported cheeses, a bowl of melon balls, a neatly sectioned pineapple, jugs of freshly-squeezed orange juice. "Wow," he said. "This is pretty special, all right. You really did it up."

"Oh, no," Buck told him. "That's not what I'm talking about. This here's nothing much. Ward asked me to go the extra mile." He patted Leo on the shoulder with one hand, and with the other he slipped a small, plump packet of folded paper into Leo's shirt pocket. "Buckaroo Catering says thanks," he said.

"Is this what I think it is?" Leo softly asked.

"I guess that depends on what you think it is," Buck replied with a smile, then he slipped another packet into the front pocket of Mary-Louise's pants. "There you go, honey," he told her.

"Oh, gee, I don't know about this," Leo said. "Is this covered in the catering bill?"

"Can I tell you something, Leo?" Ward asked. "For a person of normal intelligence you can be awfully dumb at times." He put an arm around Leo's shoulder. "Listen, if you don't want it, just give it to me. I'll make sure it goes to a worthy charity."

"I didn't say I didn't want it."

"You're sure? I don't want to corrupt you."

"You're not corrupting me," Leo said. "I'm corrupting myself. That's the story of my life. What the hell is blue screen, anyway? Teach me something." And so for the next half-hour, as the three of them stood by the catering table, munching on smoked fish and bagels and cream cheese, nibbling fruit and sipping coffee and orange juice, Ward did just that, explaining the basic workings of the blue screen method. First, Chloe would be photographed against the bright blue background. Then in post-production, back in Chicago, when the film was processed and run through a red filter, the blue would turn black, and the stock footage of a windswept, moody landscape would be superimposed. Presto: she'd appear to have been transported, as if by magic, to the English countryside. Leo listened to all of this, nodding occasionally, trying to follow the thread of Ward's explanation, hoping to seem interested—but for all the sense it made, Ward might as well have been speaking to him in Esperanto. Leo's head hurt, his eyes felt sticky and swollen behind his sunglasses. He hoped no one from the crew approached him, because he knew he couldn't think of anything to say to anyone, not even hello. Thank God

Harriet wasn't here yet, and Hector wasn't around to yell at him. Where was Hector, anyway?

Leo tried to remember what he'd done the night before, because he needed to know how rotten he should feel this morning. This was a matter of some importance. He could live with himself if all he'd done was drink too much, laugh at Ward's dumb jokes, and put a hundred dollars up his nose. That was stupid—but stupidity, he'd come to realize, was more or less acceptable as a way of going through life. After all, Ward LaPlante was his boss, and Ward was basically forcing him to do all of this stuff. Leo was just trying to be a team player. But if there'd been any hanky-panky with Mary-Louise Whitaker—well, that was something else again. Rachel was pregnant, and there were rules about what you could and could not do when your wife was pregnant. The thing was, his lips felt strange—sore and puffy, as if he'd been blowing into a tuba all night. This was what he couldn't stop thinking about: was it some sort of unusual side-effect of all the coke he'd been doing, or had there been some kissing going on last night? For the life of him, he couldn't remember. He clearly recalled the phone call home, Rachel's tears, the entire pizza; after that, he had a vague memory of watching Ward and Mary-Louise dance around the room, and he was pretty sure there'd been some singing, too. "Oh, Suzanna" was stuck in his mind, and "She'll Be Comin' Around the Mountain," too. He must have been singing them last night. Why else would he be unable to stop humming them now?

Ward droned on and on about various aspects of the blue screen method, and Leo listened, or tried to listen, nodding when he thought a nod was in order, but he felt increasingly distracted by the slight but noticeable bulge of the folded packet in his shirt pocket, the delicate heft of its contents. Oh, his head felt awful. Thanks to Hector's stream of insults, he'd felt ignorant and useless ever since he'd boarded the plane to fly to Los Angeles, but now that he was here in the studio, the camera was in place, the lighting was being checked and the shoot itself was about to begin, Leo realized the full extent of his ignorance and uselessness. A crowbar could fall from a scaffold and brain him right now, and the shoot could continue without so much as a moment of silence in memory of him. Other than the few tidbits he'd managed to glean from Ward about the blue screen method, he hadn't learned a thing about film production so far, and no wonder: in the midst of all this racket, the pounding and shouting and sawing and drilling, with a packet of coke worth a couple of hundred dollars in his shirt pocket, Leo realized he couldn't hold a coherent thought in his head. A few more minutes of this clamor and he'd forget his own name.

At last Ward finished his explanation and flashed Leo a wide grin. "See?" he said. "It's simple. Ain't show business fun?"

"Uhm-huhm," Leo said. "Okay, well, thanks. That was really something. What'll they think of next. Listen, you don't need me for the next few minutes, do you?"

"No. You . . . ah . . . need to stop in the men's room for a little pick-me-up?" Ward asked.

"Oh, no. I don't think so. No pick-me-ups right now. I need to get some air, okay? I think I'll take a little stroll outside. It's kind of loud in here." Without waiting to hear whatever Ward might have to say in response, Leo aimed himself toward the hazy light that seeped into Studio 3-B through a gap in a wall of enormous sliding doors. Outside, he wandered down the crowded alleyway, which was lined with corrugated metal buildings on both sides. It took him a moment to realize that these were all sound stages. How else to explain the raucous throng of actors in costume, makeup artists, stage hands, electricians and carpenters pawing and goosing each other in front of him? Leo joined the parade, blending in and trying to pretend that he belonged here. He passed a dingy green mobile home parked in the alley, where twenty dogs on leashes awaited their talent call. He peeked into the next sound stage and saw a woman who looked a lot like Gloria Vanderbilt under the lights. He leaned in to listen and get a closer look for a moment—hey, it was Gloria Vanderbilt! She was rehearsing a commercial for her women's blouse line. This was really something. He'd have to tell Rachel the next time he called home. Across the alley, Tommy Lasorda was signing autographs while he waited for the lighting to be corrected for a Dodgers commercial. This alley was like a warehouse full of minor celebrities.

There must have been an elaborate shoot going on in one of the studios that day, Leo figured, because there were crowds of extras milling in the alley, all dressed in costumes from the eighteenth century, plumed hats and tights, velvet capes, swords, low cut, lacy bodices for the women, and high-domed, powdered wigs. They strolled around the alley punching each other and laughing, smoking cigarettes, sipping coffee through straws to prevent damage to their makeup and costumes. Suddenly, George Plimpton appeared among them, tall and graceful, sad-eyed despite his toothy grin, striding out of a studio across the alley, leaning down now and then to sign an autograph or answer a question, his gray hair flopping down over his forehead like a schoolboy's as he bowed his head.

Leo remembered seeing George Plimpton recently in a series of television commercials hawking video games, but he'd never really stopped to think of him actually being forced to spend time on a set. On television Plimpton had an ironic, self-deprecatory wit and an elegant prep school drawl that sounded more British than American. How could anybody with an accent that aristocratic make his living selling video games? Maybe he was broke—maybe he'd blown his inheritance on ill-advised New Jersey real estate ventures, and now he was stuck with his aristocratic accent, a wardrobe of good tweed sportcoats, a palate for fine wine, and no money in the bank. Or maybe his in-laws were a pack of money-grubbing hyenas like the Sperlings, and George needed to take in a little bit of extra income just to keep his good standing at family get-togethers. But wait a second: wasn't Plimpton a literary figure, a writer and editor—someone of substance? Back in high school, Leo had read one of his books, in fact—something about playing football. George Plimpton was a goddamn man of letters! This was no place for him. What the hell was he doing here?

Suddenly George Plimpton's presence in the alley struck Leo as a tragic mistake, an embodiment of everything that was wrong with the business of advertising. Forget about Herb Pinsker and his stupid incontinence shields; George Plimpton was worth ten Herb Pinskers—ten Leo Spivaks, for that matter—and yet here he was, selling junk on television, just like Rosemary DeCamp did on "Death Valley Days" back in the sixties. Jesus, this was depressing. Who were they going to get to next? The Pope? *Hi, Pope John-Paul the Second here. Say, have you ever thought about . . . life insurance?*

Leo walked back into the murk and construction clamor of studio 3-B, shaking his head. Chloe stood clutching a terrycloth robe around her, looking forlorn. And twenty feet away, in a corner by the catering table, Ward and Mary-Louise were huddled in what appeared to be tense conversation with Don Beacham, Hector Benevento and Harriet Rubin.

■ ■ ■

Harriet Rubin! Leo's stomach coiled into a knot, as it did whenever he spotted Harriet in the hall at Bowles and Humphries—only this time it was worse. He happened to have a gram of coke in his pocket at the moment, for one thing—and besides, even though he tried not to notice the expression on Harriet's face, it was obvious that she was pissed off about something. What had he done? He hadn't been gone more than ten minutes. He'd just taken a walk! Of all the rotten luck: he just happened to have stepped outside for a breath of fresh air at the moment of her arrival. Could she fire him for taking a walk in the alley? Should he have been on the set, standing at attention, maybe peering through the camera lens when she walked through the door? Or wait a second: maybe Buck Wanamaker, assuming that everyone from the agency was on the take, offered her a neatly packaged gram, pure pharmaceutical grade, to go along with her bagel and cream cheese. Oh, that would have gone over beautifully with Harriet. Or Hector might have let slip something about yesterday's shrimp cocktail fiasco at Le Dome. Leo swiftly catalogued all his recent mistakes, and found that he could hardly stand up under the weight of them. He bit his lip, hesitant to approach the group, but even more reluctant to return to the alley, where he'd have to ponder the tragic extent of George Plimpton's debasement all over again.

Ward was wagging a finger at Harriet. Leo approached the catering table, and as he came within earshot he heard Ward say, "You can't do that, Harriet. That's ridiculous."

"Just listen to me for a minute," Harriet replied. Her voice was softer than Ward's, but it cut through the continuing tumult of construction noise.

"You can't just come out here and shut us down," Ward said. "You can't do it. It's—it's unprofessional. It's unacceptable. I can't let you do that."

"Ward, if you'd just let me explain myself," said Harriet.

"Can I say something here?" Mary-Louise asked, and when both Harriet and Ward stared at her silently for a brief moment, she backed away and said, "Oh, well, never mind."

Ward said, "You're telling me you . . ."

"Look at her, Ward. She's a child." Harriet pointed an elegant finger at Chloe.

"Of course she's a child! That's our target audience!"

"And that's what I'm getting at. That's what's wrong. We shouldn't even be working on this. We should resign the account. Just let it go."

"We let this go, you better believe somebody else is gonna pick it up," said Ward. "Lambert Touchet's got five million bucks to spend, and somebody's gonna let him spend it."

"So let them. We don't need it. Bowles and Humphries doesn't need it. Lambert Touchet's a marketing genius, I'm not saying he isn't, Ward—but this thing, this . . . Diana. It's . . . look, I'm no prude. You know that."

"Are you kidding?" Ward said. He took out his nail clippers. "I've worked for you for ten years, Harriet. You'd drive over your own grandmother to get a five-million-dollar account into the agency. I've seen you do it."

"I know," she said. "That's very true." Her voice sounded tired.

"So what are you saying? That's all in the past now?" Ward asked. "You found God?"

"No, no, no. I don't know. All I'm saying is, I'm not going to sit still and watch us make this—thing. It'll have my name on it—and I won't have that."

"It won't have your name on it!" Ward said. "How's it going to have your name on it?"

"I'm the Creative Director at Bowles and Humphries. I'm responsible for the creative work that gets produced at the agency."

"So go back to Chicago and be responsible!" said Hector Benevento. "You wanna be responsible, think about this a minute. We're out here, we've got tens of thousands of dollars spent on this thing already—we're gonna start shooting film in a little while. This guy," he said, pointing to Don Beacham, "makes five grand a day, and counting pre-production phone calls he's into us for four days already. We booked this guy and reserved him, we're taking up his time, he's making a living here. You can't just cancel on this guy. You want to change your mind, you should have changed it two weeks ago." He lit a cigarette and snapped his lighter shut with a crack. It sounded to Leo like the blade of a miniature guillotine coming down.

"We can still stop it," Harriet said. "We've done that before—canceled a shoot at the last minute if something wasn't going well. It doesn't happen very often, but we've done it before."

"But that's my point!" Ward cried. "There's nothing going wrong here! We've got it under control. The client loves the copy! Don's here, he and his assistant have been framing shots with the camera crew all morning. Our talent's on the ball, she knows her lines, she's been here a couple hours already, over in the trailer with her tutor," he said, gesturing with a half-eaten bagel he'd picked up from the table. Chloe had wandered a bit closer, still clutching the robe close to her body. She looked so small, and a little frightened, lost amidst the construction chaos, stumbling over the snaking electrical cords which lay in tangled heaps across the floor.

"Look at her," Harriet said. "Look at her. She's a little girl. She's a child."

"*Hello?* Of *course* she's a child! What's wrong with that? That's what this product is all *about!*" Ward cried. "The lighting crew's been here since six-thirty. They've been working all morning long to get the filters right, and they've finally got it set up, everything's ready to go. Like Hector says, we're gonna start shooting in a few minutes. You can't stop this now."

"I'll tell you something. We break this set now, the agency's gonna eat the entire cost," Hector told her. "You can bet on it." His tone was ominous, and the words came out in a staccato burst, like a succession of little fists. "You think Lambert Touchet's gonna pay for a nickel's worth of this? Not on your life. And I'm not just talking about the five million in lost billing. Let me tell you what the budget is here: thirty-second spot plus a twenty-second lift, we're talking a hundred and twenty grand plus change, and that's not counting prints. We're in the soup for all of that—Don's kill fee alone runs probably twenty grand, then there's studio time, crew costs. We're contracted for the music already, too, so we'll be paying a kill fee there, too—I don't know how much, I don't have the contract in front of me, but ten grand wouldn't surprise me. You wanna go back and tell the boys on the sixteenth floor you just threw that money down the toilet, be my guest—but you better make damn sure you leave me out of it. You tell them I had anything to do with it, I'll sue you for slander, and I'll win big. I've never seen a stunt like this in fifteen years. I'm a sick man. I've got a bad heart. Are you trying to *kill* me?"

"What's got into you, anyway?" Ward asked her. "You were the one who brought this account to the agency. You came to me with it. You *gave* me this thing."

"I know," Harriet said. "I didn't know then how I'd come to feel about it. I should have. But I didn't. I hadn't seen her yet," she added, and gestured again toward Chloe.

"Well that's just great," Ward said. "Harriet, you can't do this to me. I won't let you."

"Okay. Listen. Here's the thing. I should have told you this. I have a daughter," said Harriet. She sat up straighter in her chair and held her head erect. Her eyes were glistening. "I don't know how else to explain what I'm saying. Her name's Maggie. She's thirteen."

"You have a daughter?" Mary-Louise said in a tone of wonder. "I didn't even know you were married."

"I'm not," Harriet said. She gazed at Mary-Louise steadily. "I'm raising her by myself."

Leo stared at her, pondering over all the things about Harriet Rubin that he didn't know, had never thought of. He tried now to imagine her with her daughter, tried to construct a scene with the two of them together—eating ice cream cones, walking along Oak Street beach, buying back-to-school outfits. He tried to envision her walking her daughter to school, making her breakfast on a Sunday morning, laying out her clothes at night—all the things a parent would do for their child. Nothing came into focus. Harriet Rubin, a mother. He couldn't get over the strangeness of it all.

Ward shook his head. "Wait a second. So what you're telling me is . . . "

"How old is Chloe?" Harriet asked. "Did anybody ask her how old she is?"

"Oh, sweet Jesus. *That's* what this is all about?" Hector asked. He rolled his eyes toward heaven and gestured lazily with his cigarette, as if to say, *Would you listen to this?* "She's *twelve,"* he said. "We got signatures on everything—releases, permissions, the whole nine yards. Her parents are absolutely thrilled. Biggest break of her career, getting this part. She's dying to do it."

"I can't help that. I just can't do this," Harriet said. She wasn't speaking to Ward, or to Hector—in fact she seemed to be talking to no one in particular. "I looked at that girl . . . "

"She *wants* this job," Hector said. "Don't you get it? She wants to be a movie star. The residuals from this thing are gonna send her to Yale, for crissake."

"I can't be a part of this." Harriet shook her head primly, like a schoolgirl being offered a dissected frog.

"But that's just it," Ward said in an insistent voice. "You're *not* a part of it. I wrote the script. Blame *me.* I did all the *work*—it's *my* account, *I'm* supervising the shoot, *I'll* be handling the day-to-day maintenance, dealing with the client, the account execs, the media department—it'll all be *my* responsibility, not yours."

"If you had children, you'd understand, Ward," Harriet told him. She turned to Leo now, and looked at him as if she'd forgotten he was there until this moment. "Oh, Leo—I'm sorry," she said to him with a sigh. "There you are. I almost forgot about you. You thought this was going to be your big break, didn't you. Well, there'll be other shoots up the road."

"Leo, stay out of this. It doesn't have anything to do with you," Ward said, waving him away. "Harriet, listen to me. This is ridiculous." He put down the half-eaten bagel now and leaned toward her, his hands clenched into fists on his knees. "I'm gonna call the agency and talk to Mr. Humphries. We can't just—"

"Fine. That's a good idea. We'll call him together," Harriet said. "You talk to him first, then I'll get on the line. We'll see what he says." She stood up.

Ward bit his lip and got to his feet. He looked a little shaky, as if he might be about to fall over. "You're serious? You're really ready to talk to Humphries about this?" he asked her.

"Absolutely," Harriet replied. "Mr. Humphries and I respect each other. We have an understanding. She looked at Leo again. "I'm sorry," she told him. "Your very first production trip, Leo—and here I am, making a mess of it for you."

"Where's a phone around here?" Hector yelled, and a member of the crew motioned toward a hallway.

"Tell me, Leo—just for the sake of curiosity—what do you think of all of this?" Harriet asked. She cocked her head and stared at him. "What would you do?"

"You don't have to answer that," Ward told him.

"No, I'd like to know," she insisted, and kept her gaze focused on Leo's eyes. "You're a part of the group. You're here. Before we make our phone call. I'm curious."

Leo stared at her. What was he supposed to say? He could feel the folded packet in the breast pocket of his shirt; it seemed to be growing heavier by the minute, and any second now it might rip through the material of his shirt and spill onto the floor of studio 3-B like a snowdrift. He thought of all the months he'd spent terrified of this woman, the nights he'd spent nursing his fear of her, the lengths he'd gone to in order to avoid running into her in the hall, frightened most fundamentally that if she spied him outside the confines of his cubicle, she'd fire him on the spot—but afraid more profoundly that Harriet, equipped with that special kind of shit-detector only women could possess, might see through him completely, see him for what he really was. Her eyes, cool and brown, gave away nothing now; she gazed back at him with an expression of mild amusement, awaiting his answer.

"I don't know what to say," he told her. "I'm new here. I'm just starting out. I've got my whole career ahead of me. At least I hope I do. I haven't really thought too much about the product." That was a lie, of course—he'd thought about it, all right. Rachel had given him no end of grief about it. He'd lost sleep over it. But this didn't seem like the time to bring any of that up. "It's just an account," he said. "It's five million dollars—and that's a lot of money."

"There, you hear that? That's the voice of reason," Ward said.

Harriet looked at Leo for a long moment before she spoke. "You've got a future in this business. Did I tell you that already?" she asked.

"Uh . . . yes. Yes, you did. You said something like that in your office last week."

"Good," Harriet said. "That's good. I always prided myself on having an eye for talent." Then she turned and walked toward the phone. Ward and Hector followed her, but when Mary-Louise and Leo started to come along, Ward brusquely waved them away.

Don Beacham sipped his coffee and carefully rearranged the lock of hair falling over his forehead. Lesley sat down next to him—or rather, she seemed to float down slowly, like a leaf in autumn—and dreamily ran a hand over his arm. They seemed so insulated, so locked into their private world, that Leo wouldn't have dared to speak to either of them. He turned to Mary-Louise and gave her what he hoped was a smile. Suddenly the chaotic clamor of construction died down, and the studio fell silent, as if the building itself might be holding its breath, waiting.

Leo excused himself, went to the men's room, locked himself in a stall, and gave himself a quick spoonful of coke—and in a matter of moments, things began to look a bit brighter. What the hell, anyway. So Harriet Rubin had a daughter who looked like Chloe. Okay. That was kind of strange, thinking of Harriet as a mother—a single mother, even—but he could handle that. Anyway, she was his boss's boss, and she had to know what she was doing; if she wanted to stop the shoot and resign the account, what business was it of his? He snorted another petite line, just a dab for that extra tingle of contentment he craved. This was something between Harriet and Ward, some sort of power struggle that had nothing to do with him, and as far as Leo was concerned, they could duke it out—he'd just watch from the bleachers. Either way, he still had his job, his forty grand a year, his pregnant wife, his dysfunctional relationship with his therapist. None of that was going to change. And besides, here he was in Hollywood, staying in Greta Garbo's suite at the Chateau Marmont. Eating lunch at Le Dome. He'd flown first class, and nobody'd tried to throw him out, not even once! Not long ago he'd been standing in the alley, ten feet away from George Plimpton! When he got back to Chicago, he was going to tell Dr. Findlay this stuff—he was going to give him the entire story—and if that tartan-tied sonovabitch so much as blinked, Leo would leap across the desk and shout, "Hey, wake up, you Presbyterian dickhead!" right in his face.

The best news about this trip to the coast was that as far as Leo could tell, he hadn't irredeemably disgraced himself so far. Admittedly, he hadn't learned anything about film production, and yeah, okay, he'd pulled a boner at Le Dome with that shrimp cocktail business—but that was basically nothing to worry about. So far, he'd kept his nose clean. Well, not literally, of course. In a literal sense, he had to admit, his nose had recently been transformed into Depravity Central. Figuratively, though—metaphorically speaking—he was still more or less clean as a whistle. He carefully refolded the paper packet and stuffed it back in his pocket, then glanced at his nostrils in the mirror, a quick once-over, checking for powdery debris. Then he walked out of the bathroom.

The entire crew was on break, most of them smoking cigarettes in the alley, huddling in groups of twos and threes, drinking coffee and muttering to each other about the Lakers. They looked just like the construction workers Leo walked past on Michigan Avenue most mornings, on his way to the office—the same squat, muscular builds, the boots and jeans and rowdy good humor of men at work. This shoot was just a job to them, another day spent hooking up electrical circuits, nailing two-by-fours together, rigging floodlights, adjusting filters, telling jokes, smoking cigarettes and drinking coffee. What did they care whether the shoot went on or not? They'd get their standard union wage, plus time-and-a-half for anything past five-thirty, no matter what.

Meanwhile, Chloe was playing checkers with her tutor at the back of the studio, near the catering table. Lesley and Don Beacham were giving each other neck massages, staring into each other's eyes as if hypnotized. Mary-Louise sat next to them in a zen state, seemingly oblivious, staring straight ahead. As Leo approached the coffee urn, none of them looked at him. The crew ignored him, too. He felt suddenly invisible—like Claude Rains in *The Invisible Man*—and while this was undeniably unsettling, there was something powerfully liberating about the sensation, too. He was free to do anything he wanted to, he realized—he could balance a bagel on his head and start singing "Stayin' Alive," and nobody would notice.

This feeling of invisibility lasted for several more minutes, until Harriet, Ward, Don and Hector returned from their telephone call. Harriet led the parade. She walked slowly, her head still held high. When she saw Leo, she looked at him for a moment as if she didn't recognize him, then she smiled faintly.

"Harriet, listen to me," said Ward. "You're not making any sense about this."

"No, I don't suppose I am," she replied.

"I think you ought to take a few days and think this over, don't you?" he asked.

"Not really. No." Harriet looked at her watch. "I need to get back to the airport, there's an afternoon flight I can catch. Could somebody call me a cab?"

Hector looked at Don Beacham, who whispered something in Lesley's ear. She got up slowly, floating to her feet as if pulled by invisible strings. How did she do that? Leo wondered. How could a human being move so gracefully?

"Forget the cab. Don't do this," Hector told her. "You think you're making some big statement, well, let me tell you something."

"Anybody want to go back with me?" Harriet asked. She looked at Mary-Louise, who shook her head silently, her mouth open in wonder. Then Harriet turned to Leo. He held her gaze for a moment, then looked away. What was he supposed to say?

"You're not making a statement," said Hector. "You're blowing your career. And you're giving me a coronary. You're cutting a year off my life. Call him back, for crissake. Get on the phone and call Humphries, tell him you were kidding."

"But I'm not kidding," Harriet said. "We can swing by your hotel, Leo—you can get your things." Was there a hopeful tone in her voice?

"This shoot's happening today," Ward said. "We're putting film in the can, and Leo's staying right here, where he belongs. He's a part of my team. He's learning."

"Yes," she said. "I suppose he is."

Leo didn't know what to say. Who was he supposed to listen to here? He felt like a rag doll being pulled apart by two willful children. He shrugged and said, "Look, Harriet . . ."

"You should have stayed in Chicago," Hector told her. "You should have stayed away, let us handle the shoot, and none of this would have happened. You should have known better."

"Hector's right, Harriet," said Ward. "Call him back, just tell him you've been working too hard, you're under a lot of stress. Take a couple days off."

"Don't," she said. "Don't you dare talk to me like that. I hired you."

Lesley returned to announce, "They said they'd be here in five minutes."

"Fine. I'll wait outside," Harriet said. She managed a fragile smile that quavered across her lips for a brief moment.

"We'll talk this out when we get back to Chicago," Ward told her. "This is gonna be okay. Humphries says stuff like that sometimes. I got off on the wrong foot with him the first year I was here, he called me into his office and told me to put my shit in a box, remember?"

"I don't know," Harriet said. "That was a long time ago."

"You saved my butt, you remember that? You went in and talked him out of it."

"Oh, I don't think so," she said. "Anyway, that was years ago."

"The minute we get back to Chicago, I'm going into see him."

Harriet slung her purse over her shoulder. "Ward, why would you do that?" she asked. In the silence that followed, the rhythmic clicking of her heels along the polished concrete floor sounded like the clack of castanets. Then she was gone.

Ward waited for the door to shut behind her. Then he whirled around, cracked his knuckles, and announced, "All right! We're in Hollywood! Let's make a movie, ladies and gentlemen! Lights, camera, action! Fame and glory are waiting!" Suddenly the studio was noisy again, alive with the buzz of a dozen conversations. "Chloe!" Ward shouted. "Where's our talent?" He looked around and spotted her near the catering table, where she'd been huddled with her tutor during all the commotion. "There you are," he said. "You ready to be a movie star?"

"I guess so," she said, and flashed a thin, wan smile.

"Let's get cracking, everybody," Don Beacham said. He clapped his hands. "It's showtime! Let's get those lights on. And let's have a little quiet in the studio, please."

Buck Wanamaker, who'd somehow disappeared during the fireworks, sidled up to Leo and tapped him on the shoulder. "Hey there—how's things going?" he whispered.

"You mean . . . ?"

"How'd you like that little present from your Uncle Buck?"

"Oh! It was great," Leo said. "Thanks."

"You ready for a refill? There's plenty more where that came from."

"Oh, no. No, really. I've still got some." Leo patted his shirt pocket—but then he reconsidered. What the hell. When was he going to get a chance like this again? Free coke? Besides, he needed to get his energy level up; this could turn out to be a long day. "Wait a second," he said. "I guess I could use a little more. Now that you mention it."

"That's just what I was hoping you'd say," Buck told him.

■ ■ ■

By five o'clock that night, when Don Beacham called a fifteen-minute crew break and Leo stepped next door to phone Rachel, he'd gradually consumed the contents of the first packet, having slipped into the men's room for a quick toot every half hour throughout the afternoon. He was humming with the giddy bonhomie of coke, and he had to talk to somebody or he was going to explode. Best of all, the second packet was still safely tucked away in his shirt pocket, just waiting. Was there any sensation on earth more comforting than the heft of a backup gram of coke in your pocket? None that Leo could think of.

"Oh, honey, I'm so glad you called," Rachel gushed when she got on the phone. "I've got some news."

"So do I. You ready? Listen to this: Harriet Rubin tried to shut down the shoot. My boss's boss, Harriet Rubin—Capo di Tutti Capi. Can you believe that? She flew out here this morning and just went nuts. She ended up getting fired over it. I mean, she's out, boom, end of sentence. No more Harriet Rubin. Goodbye! I watched the whole thing. This all happened this morning. It was unbelievable."

"Honey?"

"She got the early flight out here, came right to the set, took one look at the actress we'd cast, and just went bananas. She told us we had to resign the account. Then they called Mr. Humphries—he's the Senior Managing Partner—they called him back in Chicago and he fired her over the phone. I've never met Mr. Humphries. I've never even seen him. He's about ninety now and he still comes into the office every day. Somebody told me he keeps a loaded revolver in his office, and if we ever lose the Ordway account he says he's going to blow his brains out in the Managing Partners' lunch room. Anyway, Harriet's been there forever, she started out in the steno pool and worked her way up, and now she's unemployed. She had this great career, and she just threw the whole thing away. I've been thinking about it all day long."

"That's really sad, honey."

"Yeah. I guess so. I don't know."

"Well, listen: let me tell you my news. I went in for the ultrasound today."

"Oh! Yeah, that was today! Shit. I'm sorry. I forgot." Leo smacked himself in the forehead. God, what an asshole he was. How could he have forgotten Rachel's appointment for her ultrasound? Well, with all the tumult over Harriet Rubin—but no, that wasn't it. Who did he think he was kidding? He'd forgotten because of all the shit he'd been putting up his nose. Shit, shit, shit. "So how was it? How'd it go?" he asked.

"It went fine. I'm healthy, everything's normal, no problems at all."

"That's wonderful. I knew it. I knew everything was gonna be okay."

"But wait, there's more. Are you ready for this?"

"Sure."

"It's a girl, Leo," she crooned. "We're going to have a daughter. Isn't that something?"

Leo leaned back against the wall and shut his eyes. If the wall hadn't been there, he'd have fallen over on his back. It took all his strength to hold the phone to his ear. A daughter. Why had he left that part out a moment ago—the part about Harriet Rubin's daughter? Why hadn't he included that? He couldn't very well mention her now, could he? How could he do that? He'd tell Rachel about her some other time. "That's wonderful, honey," he said at last.

"Isn't that amazing?" she asked. "We're going to have a daughter, Leo. All day long, I've been in a trance. I mean, I would've been happy either way—it didn't matter, really—but I'm just, I don't know. So . . . happy." Her voice was soft and suddenly full of tears.

"I'm happy, too," Leo told her. "I love you."

"When'll you be home? I miss you, honey. I can't wait to see you."

"Tomorrow evening. We'll catch the noon flight tomorrow afternoon. I think it gets us into O'Hare about six o'clock. I'll cab it home. We'll celebrate, how's that?"

"Okay. Tell me you love me one more time."

"I love you. Hey, I gotta go. The crew's probably back already. It's been a long day, and they're not done yet. They just go on and on. God, what a boring process. It's pathetic. It's like watching a sidewalk start to crack. Seriously. One take after another, the same thing over and over again. I'm not kidding, they've probably had this poor girl say her lines a hundred times already. She's about to puke. I swear, I think I'll be listening to this stupid commercial in my sleep for the rest of my life. Diana, goddess of the hunt," he recited, "the scent of nature on a spring-soft morning, blah blah blah, vomit upchuck barf."

"Oh, Leo. Oh, honey. This is what you wanted, isn't it?" Rachel asked him. "And anyway, nobody said show business was going to be all fun and games, honey. Hey, I hear the timer going off in the kitchen—

gotta go. I'm having Stouffer's. Swedish meatballs. My fave." Then she hung up, and Leo reluctantly went back into the tense, snappish atmosphere of studio 3-B, where he stood by the camera monitor, watching on the small television screen as Chloe, a bit bedraggled now, suffered through another twenty takes.

In between each one, a middle-aged woman jumped into view with a brush and comb and a compact, and adjusted Chloe's hair and makeup. Don Beacham, still calm and seemingly tireless, kept up a steady stream of praise: "You're beautiful, Chloe. You're just great. That was fantastic, darling. Let me have just that same tone one more time. That was perfect. Absolutely on the money. Yes. That one was a keeper. The camera loves you, baby." But he kept asking for one more take, just one—and then another.

Finally Ward broke the spell. "Don, if we don't have it by now, we're not going to get it," he said. "I think we had it about two hours ago." Beacham looked at him, and at Hector, who'd smoked two packs of cigarettes since the shoot had begun, and had taken on the greenish pallor of someone about to lose his lunch. Hector gave Beacham a furtive nod—and at last there was nothing left to do but call it a day. "Okay, thanks, everybody—it's a wrap!" Beacham announced. Leo thought he could hear everyone in studio 3-B sighing in unison.

After a few goodbyes and some scribbled signatures on the required paperwork, Chloe was bundled off by her mother, a big platinum blonde with a drinker's nose who'd been hanging around in the alley all afternoon. The crew went to work breaking down the set, making even more noise than they had when they'd put it together that morning. Did they have to be that loud—was it something stipulated in their union contract? Didn't anybody know how to set something down instead of dropping it? How could they think in the midst of all that racket? Leo shook his head and ducked into the men's room, which was both a nice refuge from the bedlam, and a perfect place for a last little tootsky-wootsky before the drive back to the hotel.

He and Rachel were going to have a little girl. A daughter. He thought of her as he stared at himself in the men's room mirror. He peered up his nose, checking for telltale dregs. Not a speck. In the yellow light of the bathroom his skin looked green. What would she look like? he wondered. Who would she resemble? He hoped she'd look like

Rachel, of course—her small-boned elegance, her dark, curly hair, her eyes. Her heart.

Her heart. He shut his eyes. A daughter. He felt the weight of it, the responsibility of it, pressing down on him like an anvil, threatening to drive him straight through the floor. How could he possibly be anyone's father? It was hard enough simply to be himself—to be Leo Spivak. If he could just take a break, be someone else for a few days—was that asking so much, just a little vacation?—he might be able to get back to the grinding work of being himself. Goddamn that Harriet Rubin anyway. And goddamn her daughter, too. He stared in the mirror again. There were a few leftover grains of coke on the tip of his finger, so he rubbed his gums to get the added zap. This was it. No kidding around, there'd be no more coke binges for him. This was the last of it. When he got back to Chicago from this stinking trip, he was done with coke for good. He'd had his flirtation with disaster. From now on he was going to be a different kind of guy. If Ward LaPlante didn't like it, he'd have to get himself another boy. There were other advertising agencies in Chicago. Leo could go back to Dunne, Crowell and Gold, rejoin the bowling team. He could do that. He'd give them a call when he got back to town. He was going to buy a cardigan sweater and sit in the living room after dinner and read the newspaper, and make ironic comments to Rachel about world events. He was going to slow down, mow the lawn, tend the shrubbery around the house. If the roof needed fixing, they'd get it fixed. He breathed out slowly, then took in a deep chest full of air. This was going to be okay.

Goddamn that Harriet Rubin. Another deep breath. Goddamn her, anyway. What right did she have, getting on her high horse? Was he supposed to believe she was some sort of superior being—she'd never worked on any morally questionable products in her entire goddamn career? If she'd been that picky, she'd have never made it out of the steno pool. Fuck Harriet Rubin. He opened the second packet of coke and gave himself one more toot.

That night Leo ate dinner with Ward and Mary-Louise at a Thai seafood restaurant overlooking the water at Marina Del Rey. They watched the sunset over the ocean, a dramatic flood of red and orange and purple that flamed out, spanning the western sky. None of them had any appetite—they'd each snorted several fat lines of Ward's coke in his room at the Chateau Marmont before heading out to dinner—but just on general principle (they were on expense accounts, after all), they ordered everything on the menu that looked promising. They started with a bottle of crisp dry Sauvignon Blanc, an order of Thai crabcakes with ginger-chili sauce, and a platter of delicate Ahi tuna "tartare," minced with chili paste, soy sauce and garlic, served in lettuce leaves. The wine came first, and Leo drank a glass of it as if putting out a fire in his throat. The crabcakes and tuna arrived soon after, artfully arranged, surrounded by miniature vegetables sculpted into animals and flowers and geometric shapes, looking so pristine that it seemed positively criminal to disturb their beauty. Ward, Mary-Louise and Leo just stared at the platters open-mouthed, as if the crab cakes, the tuna, the sculpted vegetables might be about to speak.

Several minutes later, their waiter came by to ask if something was wrong with the food. He held his hands clasped at his breastbone in an attitude of prayer. "If there's been a mistake," he began, then paused.

"Oh, no, don't worry," Ward told him. "We're just admiring it. The food, I mean."

"Oh," the waiter said.

"Somebody back in that kitchen's a real artist. You should be proud to work here."

"I'll pass along your compliments to the chef."

"In fact, I tell you what," Ward said. "Let's just go for it. Shoot the moon. Let's get—let's see—let's get the grilled whole red snapper stuffed with scallions and lemongrass. Yeah. That's the ticket. Bring it on! And give us the pad thai with prawns and scallops, too. Heavy on the peanuts! And you might as well bring us another bottle of wine while you're at it."

"Very good choices, sir. Would you like me to take away these appetizers?" the waiter asked. "I could wrap them up for you."

"Oh, no. You can leave them. We'll get around to them in a minute here."

After the waiter left, Leo dutifully tried to eat a crab cake. It was delicious, there was no doubt about that—in fact it was probably the best crabcake he'd ever had in his life, spiced with ginger and garlic, lifted by the tang of lime—but he gave up after a bite. He had enough coke in his system now to keep an infantry division up and marching for a week. His nose was probably close to falling off into his plate. That was a comforting thought. He'd probably end up having to wear a plastic nose, like one of those attachments that used to come with Mr. Potato Head. He'd have to tie it in place with a piece of string. His in-laws would have a field day with that one. He imagined himself sitting around the dinner table with them, trying to eat his mother-in-law's chicken soup while he fended off polite questions about how he'd managed to disfigure himself in such a disgusting manner.

When the red snapper and pad thai arrived, once again the presentation was breathtaking—the snapper was so big that its head and tail flopped over the edges of its plate, and the bowl of steaming pad thai was covered with a delicate pattern of cilantro leaves and chopped peanuts. The table was gridlocked with platters of food. Leo stared at all of it. This was ridiculous. Why had they ordered all of this food? Who did they think they were kidding?

"Ward, what's going to happen to Harriet?" he asked.

Ward stared at him. "Excuse me?"

"When she gets back to the office, I mean. Is she cooked? I mean, is her goose cooked?"

Ward took out his nail clippers and inspected his left thumbnail critically. "Where'd this come from?" he asked. "You thinking of joining the Peace Corps or something?"

"I was just wondering. I've been thinking about it all day."

Mary-Louise drank the rest of her wine, and poured herself another glass. "Harriet was asking for it," she said. "Maybe her goose was asking for it. Her goose wanted to be cooked."

"Well, what do you think Mr. Humphries ought to do about it?" Ward said.

"I don't know. I was just asking," said Leo.

"She goes apeshit over nothing, she tries to resign an account that's going to bring in five million bucks a year, just for starters, she tries to shit-can a production trip that's already costing an arm and a leg. She basically calls Lambert Touchet, one of the only true geniuses American marketing has ever produced, a pervert," Ward said, ticking off Harriet's sins one by one on his fingers. "You tell me. What would you do?"

"She didn't call Lambert Touchet a pervert, did she?" Leo asked.

"You've got to get with the program, kiddo," Ward told him. "The train's about to pull out of the station. You're either onboard or you're not. You get my drift here?"

Before Leo could answer, their waiter appeared again to hover by their table, his hands still clasped anxiously at his breast-bone. "Are you sure everything's all right?" he asked.

"Oh, absolutely," Ward said. "We're just a little slow out of the gate, that's all."

"I could take the food back to the kitchen and reheat it if you'd like," the waiter offered.

"Not necessary. Absolutely not required," Ward said. He sniffed and massaged his nose gently. "Hey, here's an idea: I think we'll just take it with us," he told the waiter, and watched him trot off obediently in search of carry-out boxes. "How'd that be, boys and girls? Let's do take-out, whaddya say?" Ward asked. "It's our last night in town. What's the point in hanging out in this dump, when we could be back at the Chateau? Eh? Do I have a point?" He sniffed again. "Uh-oh. Oh, boy. Your Uncle Ward thinks he feels the need for a little tootsky-wootsky coming on. Oh, yeah. How's that sound?"

"Thanks, Uncle Ward," Mary-Louise said in a dreamy voice. "You're about the nicest uncle in the whole wide world." She reached for Leo's thigh under the table. "Isn't he about the nicest uncle in the whole wide world?" she asked. As her hand spider-walked up to his groin, Leo groaned aloud and spilled half his wine.

▪ ▪ ▪

Late that night, when there was nothing left in his second packet of coke, Mary-Louise got dressed and left his room. Leo watched her shut the door, and when he was alone he began to weep. He hadn't cried in ages—he couldn't even remember the last time he'd shed a tear. He wept for several minutes, then he grew tired of it and stopped abruptly, blowing out a long, ragged sigh. He'd forgotten how exhausting crying could be. He got out of bed and took a shower, scrubbing himself raw, trying to get the scent of Mary-Louise off his body. He stayed in the shower a long time. Then he went back to bed and fell asleep, and dreamed of his secluded backyard in Winnetka.

He knew it was his yard, but oddly enough, the Chateau Marmont's oval pool had been moved there. It fit perfectly, and Leo thought, Gee, why'd we never think of putting a pool in before? Or maybe it wasn't the Chateau Marmont's swimming pool, but a pool that looked just like it, one that Leo and Rachel had somehow recently acquired. They hadn't taken very good care of it, though, and the water was stagnant, choked with algae and other crud. The ivy and privet hedges surrounding the pool were just as lush as the ones at the Chateau Marmont, and Leo even had the sense that beyond them stood a row of bungalows just like the one in which John Belushi had died. He was vaguely unsettled by the similarity, but figured that all this added luxury, even with the stagnant, algae-choked water, had to be good for the property value of his house. This was a smart move. His in-laws were going to be impressed by this when they came for their next visit.

It was nighttime. Chloe was there with him, stretched out in a lounge chair, wearing a teddy even skimpier than the one she'd worn all day long in studio 3-B. He was glad to see her, but worried that she was staying up too late; wasn't tomorrow a school day? She was just a girl, after all, just a school girl, and she'd worked so hard that day, saying those ridiculous lines again and again. In fact, she was still saying the lines now—she seemed unable to stop herself—the words poured out in a stream, all run together in a sad, soft murmur that she couldn't control. Leo told her, "You can stop that any time you want to," and Chloe simply looked at him in mid-recitation, shook her head, and went on with it.

He turned his head and saw that President Reagan was there. Oh, thank God. "Sir, it's so good to see you," Leo began. "I've been hoping to see you, but things have been so crazy."

President Reagan responded with a long, powerful sniff, then rubbed his nose vigorously. "Oh, I know what you mean. This darn summer cold," he muttered at last. He gave Leo a broad, bashful, lopsided smile and a quick duck of the head, that special what the heck grin that had won the hearts of so many of his fellow Americans. He gazed up at the nighttime sky then, and suddenly, for the first time, his face was illuminated by something, a streetlight, or the moon. In that instant Leo could see a small corona of white powder around each of President Reagan's nostrils.

"Mr. President?" he said. "Oh, no. No. No. Mr. President." This was awful. He turned to Chloe, wanting suddenly to protect her from President Reagan, who was, it was now clear, not who Leo had thought he was. He hadn't voted for him, but what did that have to do with anything? This was different, it had nothing to do with the sentimental bullshit of political parties, with the left or the right or the middle. This was something else, something much worse. Chloe seemed to be sleeping on her lounge chair. The night breeze ruffled her hair, and in the pale gray light he could see the meager outline of her body through her teddy. Her breathing was regular. Her chest rose and fell, rose and fell.

"Oh, come on, now, fella," President Reagan said in a chiding voice. "You know how it is. Get with the program, will ya? The train's leaving the station. You're either onboard. . . "

"No!" Leo cried. "No, I'm not going to . . . " Then he stopped. Not going to what? He didn't know. He only knew that he had to get away from there, had to get out of there—and so he leapt to his feet and began to run. In a panic he pumped his legs, his shoes slapping desperately at the ground with every lunging stride—but in the midst of his panting, frantic efforts, even though he was still deeply asleep, in the dark, moonless night of his heart, Leo knew he wasn't going anywhere.

CPSIA information can be obtained
at www.ICGtesting.com
Printed in the USA
LVHW090157250221
679869LV00002B/2

9 780814 257524